THE LOVES OF MRS MCALLISTER

THE LOVES OF MRS MCALLISTER

HANNAH McNIVEN

POOLBEG

Published 2020
by Poolbeg Press Ltd.
123 Grange Hill, Baldoyle,
Dublin 13, Ireland
Email: poolbeg@poolbeg.com

A catalogue record for this book is available from the British Library.

ISBN 978178199-395-8

www.poolbeg.com

About the Author

Hannah McNiven is an Irish-born writer of Scottish and Irish descent. She has been longlisted (2017) and shortlisted (2018) for the Colm Tóibín International Short Story Award. This is her first novel.

Acknowledgements

Firstly, thanks to the Wexford Literary Festival for their 'Meet the Publisher' opportunity.

Thanks to Paula and all the team at Poolbeg. To Gaye for editing.

Debbie and Úna, your positivity and faith in me have been heartening – thank you.

Thank you to my sister Dee for being the first person to read everything and ask me for more. It made me keep going. Dee again, Dale (another sister), Mam and Dad for your notes and editing. And Mam and Dad especially for all your stories that continue to fuel my imagination.

Finally, to all my (somewhat bemused) family. You have so generously allowed me to sit and write. That allowance is a debt I can never repay. From the bottom of my heart, thank you.

Dedication

This book is for two Ruths.

To my mother, Ruth. I hope you know why.

And to the memory of Ruth Deacon. The teacher who first asked me to write her a story. I wish she knew what a gift that was to me.

Prologue

1943

The boy to his left was keening noisily. It had started several hours before when their ventral gunner had been shot. The gunner's body still lay in position beneath them, though they tried not to look. Rocking back and forth in his seat, the youth strained against the creaking harness that pinned him down. Lately, his breath began to catch as he whined the words "*God in Heaven*" and "*Mother*" along with the names of various saints in between sobs. Sometimes, he cursed fluently then apologised to no one in particular, adding, "*Help me! Please, help me!*" Was he talking to the other men in the cockpit? Or was he simply appealing to whatever or whoever was prepared to listen?

The boy. *The boy*. It was all he could think to call him. He hadn't the faintest idea what the teenager was called. When they met for the first time, he didn't get a chance to speak to him. Albert had jumped in to gruffly introduce himself to the boy as the pilot and Peter as their forward gunner, bombardier and co-pilot. The name of their now deceased ventral gunner followed. Then Albert added, "And this here is our dorsal gunner and radio man. He has another name but we all just call him Tommy," giving Tommy a playful shove, "since he's so terribly fond of dear old England." Albert wheezed out a nicotine-stained giggle, eying Tommy, daring him to disown the nickname given to him by his fellow airmen.

He never did.

Observing the boy, he tried to make out his features. In the darkness of the hulking metal shell the light was so poor that all he could see was the sharp nose but otherwise soft features of the newly minted gunner. He remembered being shocked by how child-like the boy was – his severe haircut at odds with the soft, pink, unshaven face. God, it made him feel old. But all the replacements they were getting these days were young. They were running out of men so were sending boys instead. Next thing they'd be sending women, he thought. Soon, they'd have one of them flying the plane rather than foul-mouthed Albert whose oaths were heard even above the deafening throb of the engine.

Many of the men were losing their hearing, having flown so often and so long in the company of the thundering, unmuffled exhausts that screamed their protests from the moment the propellers began to turn. They complained constantly about their deafness but – strangely – he found the sound comforting, soothing even. It meant they were still airborne, still flying, still alive. When the engine cut out – now *that* would give him cause for complaint.

It was only a matter of time before it happened – before their engine sputtered and coughed itself into silence.

He wondered how they were still travelling at all. He glanced at the holes peppering the skin of their bomber but couldn't hear the wind whistling through them above the sound of the engine. They had taken enemy fire on previous bomb runs but nothing as bad as this. So much for the protection of cloud cover.

When the bullets ripped through the fuselage and cockpit, the boy had screamed like a little girl, his voice breaking as his hand clenched on the trigger of his machine gun, spraying bullets in every direction. It wasn't until Albert yelled a string of commands at him to stop – followed swiftly by curses – that he ceased. It was a wonder he hadn't shot the wings or tail off their own aircraft. Who knew, maybe the boy had. But given the damage the smaller enemy fighter aircraft had done, it was hard to tell.

The boy's snivelling was really starting to irk him. Instead, he focused on the co-pilot and forward gunner which did little to calm him. Peter had been hit in the arm by one of the dozens of streaking bullets that whizzed through the plane, ricocheting off whatever they couldn't pass through. Though the bleeding had stopped, Peter's arm hung limply across his lap. He had hissed through his teeth when Tommy went up to help stem the dark-red blood oozing from the hole in his arm. It was the only sound he made. The co-pilot's face had been a grim, grey mask. But that was nothing new. Peter always looked bloody miserable.

For the umpteenth time, Tommy fingered a hole in his trousers. It was a through-and-through that had seared perfect round holes in the fabric before zipping straight past his right cheek. Again, he felt his leg to make sure there was nothing other than a slight burn. No blood. But he could still feel the bullet speeding past. He shivered and glanced at the depression in the floor of the aircraft – the bathtub – where the other gunner lay dead at their feet. He was the first crewmate who had been hit. The first to die.

He dragged his eyes away from the body of his friend. It was too close – too strong a reminder that they had all cheated death for too long. Prior to this, he seemed to possess a cat-like ability to survive what was thrown at him. He was held as some kind of lucky charm among the other men, who saw him live through flight after flight while others never returned home. Men who experienced death as often as they did were inclined to cling to whatever they could. They hoped it would give them one more day, even if it was just one more day of war.

Initially, he was amazed by his own will to survive. It took him by surprise. Since joining the Air Force, he realised that nothing urged a non-violent man to fire a gun like being shot at. Before the war, nothing would have induced him to take up arms against another human being. But he realised very quickly that he could disassociate the two conflicting parts of his brain. He could override his conscience, squeeze the trigger and so prolong his life just enough to do the same thing all over again. It was a routine he got into – one that he had become so familiar with over the past four years, he now barely felt anything at all. The days went by without incident or exception. He did not laugh, he did not cry, he did not fear. He simply survived at the lowest possible human ebb.

But now he felt a flicker. A whisper of unease ruffled the hair at the back of his neck. Fear was beginning to gnaw at his bones. It was quite disconcerting to feel these emotions stir once more after lying so long dormant. His carefully honed self-control was slipping, sliding off his body like the sweat that beaded on his brow and ran into his frantically blinking eyes.

So *this* was what it felt like to know you were going to die.

Well, he supposed, his luck had to run out some time. He felt a twinge of remorse for the others in the crew who had put their faith in him. They believed in his invincibility and he did nothing to dissuade them of the notion. Was he, therefore, partly responsible for their deaths?

No. It was the fault of the small craters scattered across their instrument panel like dropped coins. The bullets had ripped through the gauges and wiring that were their lifeline. They were flying blind. Their fuel gauge had resolutely continued to show nothing other than empty for well over an hour. Their navigation equipment had fared little better. Besides, Peter probably wouldn't have been much use at reading it since he was listing precariously to the left last time he checked on him.

They had been flying for what seemed like hours in the fog and darkness, still none the wiser as to where they were. They just about knew they were over land and heading north. Albert had made the grim decision to attempt a landing on actual land instead of risking a flight back across the Channel. If they ran out of fuel and ditched in the sea, they had virtually no chance. If they ran out of fuel and ditched in some disgruntled farmer's field, their odds were probably not much better. Either way, they all knew they weren't going home.

"*Dawn.*" Albert's voice was tinny and cracked in their ears. "*Might see somewhere to land.*"

He said it as the pitch of the engine changed. The plane shook and the boy squealed, the volume of his sobbing increasing.

What was his name? It was something for Tommy to focus on outside of their immediate danger. He tried to visualise their walk to the aircraft again where the boy had introduced himself but that only brought to mind the size of the plane they were walking towards and the knowledge that said plane – which they were all strapped into – was currently falling out of the sky.

Suddenly, all the noise ceased. For a fraction of a moment he thought he had gone temporarily deaf. Yet there was a tinnitus whistle in his ears. Then several things happened at once.

Just as he realised the reedy sound was the wind whistling through the holes in the fuselage, the plane dropped several feet and left their stomachs somewhere above their heads.

Albert began to curse fluently, and the boy shrieked like a child.

"Fucking shut up!" Tommy hissed across at the boy, taking his fear out on the nearest target. He was usually such a mild-mannered person too. Nothing like war to change a man, he thought. Like changing him from living to dead.

"There!" Albert shouted, managing to gun the engine once more as they broke through the bottom of the clouds. *"Fields! Fuck! Trees too!"*

The engine died again and they continued to glide downwards as Albert fought to maintain control. Looking out beside his machine gun, Tommy could see the ink-blue farmland below them beginning to turn grey in the light of the dawning sun. It was much too close and, despite having no power, they were still moving far too fast. Albert was a good pilot but a landing on uneven ground at this speed was probably beyond him.

Tommy wondered if the plane would catch fire once it crash-landed. It carried several hundred rounds of ammunition which would very likely explode if they were exposed to high temperatures. And he was sitting in close proximity to them. He tried not to think about which would be the quickest death: fire or a stray bullet. But then they had so little fuel left, a fire was unlikely. Perhaps the plane would break up. He might get thrown from the cockpit or crushed by a collapsing fuselage.

Albert was still swearing. The boy was still crying.

I don't want to die, Tommy thought suddenly. The conviction came to him so abruptly, so strongly, it was as if someone screamed it in his face. But what could he do? It was out of his hands. He had to trust his pilot. A thrill of nervous energy coursed through him like an electric shock. His body twitched in annoyance at his inactivity. He wanted to move. Yet he knew he couldn't. He checked his harness, making sure he was securely strapped to his seat. It was all he could do.

Still they sank lower. The engine briefly sputtered into life then cut out again. It was like listening to someone fall asleep then wake up with a start only for them to doze off once again. Now he could pick out trees, ditches, houses, farmyards and fields – lots of fields. He pondered what part of the country they might be over. They could have been over lakes, mountains, dense forest, but instead they had a chance to land in open space. A small glimmer of hope fluttered in his chest. But then the engine died again and, no matter how loudly Albert swore, he couldn't get it to restart.

For the first time since sitting in a bomber several years ago, Tommy heard the hydraulics of the landing gear as they slid from hatches in the wings. Usually he only saw it happen to the roar of the engine. Either Albert had spotted somewhere to land or he was simply hoping that by exposing his wheels, a suitable patch of ground might present itself. They were, after all, surrounded by promising-looking fields.

It was something of a shock, therefore, when the tip of an evergreen tree took a swipe at the right wing. Then another. And another.

Thump. Thump-thump. Crack!

They were gliding over an area of tall pines that seemed to be reaching up to bat them out of the sky. The sound as the trees scraped along the bottom of the fuselage turned his blood cold. In a fit of terror, the boy scrabbled at his harness, trying to rip it off with ineffectual fingers. Tommy tried shouting at him to stop but his voice caught in his throat, coming out in nothing more than a gasp.

Suddenly, the noise stopped. He glanced out his window and saw there was open ground no more than forty feet below them. This was it.

The trees had done little to slow them down. And they still had no engine to control the landing.

Thirty feet.

The boy had stopped whimpering and was now sitting bolt upright, pale in the dawn light with a kind of silent scream holding his mouth open.

Twenty feet.

"Here we go!" Albert shouted.

They hit the ground hard. Tommy's head snapped back against his seat and he felt a searing pain down the left side of his neck and into his shoulder. For a moment the pain was so excruciating he blacked out. Coming to a few seconds later, he was brought back to reality by the pain in his chest as he tried to breathe against the constriction of his harness.

The boy fared much worse. As Tommy was thrown forward then back, he saw the boy's torso burst through his restraints. His rag-doll body was hurled forward by the impact when they hit the ground. Despite the fact he had wailed for several hours prior to their landing, his death was so quick he never managed to utter a sound. The last Tommy saw of him was as he slid past along the floor, banging off the seats but continuing backwards as the plane bumped and swung from side to side. First one then the other wheel was ripped from the underside of the wings. The bottom of the plane ground itself into the earth before keeling to the right. The wingtip dug in, kicking up soil and grass, turning the bomber around it before the whole thing sheared off, making the body of the plane spin faster. There was an almighty crunch as the left side collided with something, followed by an ominous creak from the protesting metal outer shell of the plane. It rocked for a moment before there was a dull thud, a soft hiss and then … nothing.

He sat very still. He hardly had a choice since he was strapped to his seat so tightly. He waited for another boom, another crash, for the plane to move again, for the tell-tale whoosh of fuel catching fire. But there was nothing other than a dull hiss coming from somewhere outside. Vaguely, he wondered what they might have hit. But that did not seem to be the most pressing issue at hand. Carefully, he began to test his limbs one by one. They all seemed functional if bruised. His right knee smarted when he stretched out. But the more he moved it, the more the pain eased. His biggest issue was the back of his neck which burned as if it had been scalded.

It took him a while to unfasten his harness since he struggled to look down and see what he was doing. It felt like someone had hooked a finger under the base of his skull and was trying to pull his head back. Eventually, however, he managed to free himself and drunkenly stagger through the plane to look for a way out. As he searched, he checked all his crewmates and found that Albert was the only one who still had a pulse. Otherwise the pilot looked completely lifeless, an egg-sized lump forming on the side of his head. Part of the Perspex nosecone had been ripped open beside him and there was just enough room to squeeze out through it. What waited for them once they were outside was something he didn't yet want to think about.

As he attempted to manhandle the pilot into a position where he could be pulled free from the wreckage, he kept expecting to hear a commotion outside – someone telling him to come out with his hands up. But there was nothing, aside from the sighs of the damaged engine which continued to fizzle and groan.

Gritting his teeth, he lowered himself out of the hole, his neck screaming in protest. He felt his coat snag on the twisted metal ribbing that had recently held sheets of Perspex but was now sticking out at strange angles. As his feet hit solid ground, his legs buckled and he collapsed onto the grass only a few feet below. The morning dew was still on the land and immediately soaked into the knees of his trousers and wet his hands. Even though the grass was damp, he really wanted to just lie down. The mental strain of the past few hours was fogging his brain, clouding his judgement. Plus, every movement he made hurt.

Instead, however, he turned and stood again, cautiously straightening on shaky legs while also being careful not to hit his head on the plane which was sitting much closer to the ground than it usually did. Reaching into the hole he had just come out of, he grabbed the shoulders of Albert's jacket and pulled. He swore as pain shot through his neck and shoulder, making his vision hazy. Grinding his back teeth and breathing hard through his nose, he tugged the pilot once more, moving him inch by sluggish inch closer to the gap in the nosecone.

It was a slow process. Albert was dead weight and the angle was awkward. Tommy also had to keep stopping to allow his vision to clear. He began to sweat though the morning was chilly and had to take off his jacket before rolling up his sleeves. Finally, the pilot's head was out and resting on Tommy's shoulder, but the rest of his body just didn't seem to want to follow. No matter how hard he pulled, Albert wouldn't budge. Desperately, he reached in and grabbed a large fistful of his crewmate's clothing, took one slow, steadying breath then gave the pilot's limp form an almighty heave.

Without warning, Albert suddenly came free and dropped like a stone through the hole in the Perspex. As the pilot fell, he trapped Tommy's left arm against the side of the hole where a piece of the edging had sheared off. The remaining jagged metal point sank into the soft underside of his forearm before he was propelled backwards by Albert falling on top of him.

Roaring in pain, he momentarily forgot about his neck as his arm was sliced from elbow to hand by the exposed metal. Blood welled from the wound and spattered across the grass while Albert lay prostrate on top of him. Furious and in agony, he unceremoniously shoved the pilot off him and sat up, cradling his arm. Tearing at his shirt, he popped the buttons as he stripped to his vest and did his best to wrap the garment around the wound with one hand. He rocked and keened, willing the pain to go away. He was just like the boy sitting beside him in the plane.

Robert! How could he have forgotten the look of affront on the boy's face when Albert insisted on calling him Bobby? And why was he remembering it now when it no longer mattered? The boy was dead. So was Peter. But he and Albert were still alive. Just.

His eyes watered as he tightened his makeshift bandage. He tried to slow his breathing and heartrate down since he knew that the faster his heartbeat, the more blood he would lose. He toyed with the idea of getting back into the plane for the medical kit but was still worried it might burst into flames. Now that he thought about it, they should probably move away in case it did.

Still sitting on the ground, he tapped Albert on the cheek. The pilot groaned. It was the first sound he had made since their expletive-filled landing. Tommy almost toppled over, his relief made him so light-headed. If Albert stayed alive, it just about made the damage to his arm worthwhile. Absent-mindedly, he noted that his neck didn't feel quite as bad as it had. That did not, however, make the prospect of hauling several kilogrammes' worth of live human flesh any more appealing. Yet it still had to be done.

Resigning himself to the job at hand, he stood on unsteady feet with only his right arm wrapped around Albert's ankles and began dragging the pilot away from the crash site. He got what he thought was a reasonable distance away then fell to his knees and got violently sick. Was it concussion, he worried? Or was it just shock? Whatever it

11

was, it did his sore neck no favours. He began to shiver as he tried to give Al a more thorough examination.

Perhaps there was more colour in the pilot's face. Or maybe it was just that the sunlight was much brighter now. Other than the lump on his head, he seemed fine. But then there was no way of knowing how bad the bang to his head had been. Either way, both of them needed help and it looked as if he was the one who would have to get it.

Taking in their surroundings for the first time, he saw that they were sitting in an empty field that looked as if it had been recently grazed or, at least, what grass was left looked short and well chewed. A large swathe of ground running along the centre of the paddock was ripped to shreds as if some gigantic monster had dragged its claws across the earth's surface. There was also a scatter of debris from the plane, both sets of landing gear and the right wing. The progress of the main body had been halted by a wood of evergreens which edged two sides of the field. One of the trees had been felled by the impact and was lying over the rear of the fuselage as if to pin it down.

Tommy felt a pang of guilt for the damage they had done but then winced at the thought of the damage their bombs must have done to the cities they dropped them on. The benefit of night-time bombing runs was that you didn't see the damage, unlike the field that spread out in front of him.

Getting to his feet once more, he threw a final glance at the pilot. With a senseless giggle, he told Al to stay put and headed off towards a gate further along the edge of the woodland.

The woods seemed to ring with an eerie peace after the aural assault he experienced in the previous hours. Had he been more aware, the animal and avian sounds would have set his nerves on edge. As it was, he simply kept his head down and placed one foot in front of the other, cradling his injured arm while the blood seeped through his fingers, steps muffled by the thick detritus of pine needles. He spotted human and animal footprints moulded in patches of soft mud as he walked through the pools of sunlight that found their way through the boughs above. But mostly he was in the shade until the trees thinned and he saw he was approaching a smallholding.

It was an idyllic-looking little place with rows and rows of vegetables growing around a tiny two-up-two-down house with rough stone walls and a slate roof. Off to the side was a leafy green orchard with a fat, squat pony grazing under the trees. On the other side were whitewashed outbuildings. That was obviously the farmyard. Between the chatter of the rooks in the trees above his head, he made out the soft sound of chickens clucking from behind the white walls. He made a beeline for the yard since he thought it would be rude to dribble blood across such a beautiful garden. However, when he saw the cleanliness of the yard, he almost couldn't bring himself to cross it either. Almost.

Opening the gate, he carefully slid inside. He had to fight the urge to tiptoe for fear of leaving his large footprints on the perfectly brushed cobblestones. He considered calling out a greeting but didn't want to disturb the peace. But he needn't have worried. There was someone there already who was perfectly capable of disturbing the peace herself.

"Norman! The pig's got scabs on her tits again!"

The shout and several rotund, red-feathered hens preceded a short, hefty, grey-haired woman out of one of the buildings at the far end of the yard.

"Shoo! Shoo!" she admonished the chickens, a basket of eggs clutched to her chest.

He froze. He hadn't planned what he might say to whomever he met. And he didn't want the woman to drop her eggs by suddenly introducing himself to her. However, he had apparently underestimated his conspicuousness.

Once the woman's glance rose from the chickens at her feet, she spotted him standing awkwardly by the gate. He was white as a sheet and drenched in his own blood. But, of course, she didn't know it was his blood. Her whole body stiffened and she reeled backwards, colliding with the door of the barn she had just vacated.

Sensing she was on the verge of total panic, he held out his hands, palms facing her.

"Please don't drop your eggs," he begged her in English.

He was surprised how easily the words came to him after four years speaking nothing but his native tongue. It was something of a relief to realise he hadn't lost them. He was so relieved, he smiled at the woman who stared back, dumbfounded.

He needn't have troubled himself about the eggs. Their eyes locked over the basket. She clutched it protectively to her bosom, as if she thought he was there to steal it. They observed each other in silence for several moments.

He was about to speak, to beg help for his pilot when, without warning, the lady expanded her chest and screeched: "*Norman! There's a Jerry in the farmyard!*"

Chapter One

1946

Esther sat in the window seat, watching the sun rise over the brow of the distant hills. She had been ensconced between the bedroom curtains and cold glass since before dawn, waiting for the pink-orange rim of light to pick out the dark peaks in sharp relief. Sometimes, she saw nothing at all through thick mists that often shrouded the house and low-lying fields. Other times, she would see the estate's deer walking along the ridge at the top – elegant black shapes in the dawn light. They were her favourite mornings. Yet, come rain, shine or heavy fog, Esther was always at her window.

Insomnia had stolen her restful nights almost six years before and, since then, the only peace she found while others lay happily abed was watching through her window as the dark world slowly came alive. She always sat facing east, wrapped in the blanket her mother had woven for her when she was a child. Even though she longed for sleep, those quiet hours she spent with something her mother had put so much effort and love into made her feel calm. It allowed her to forget her cares and responsibilities, of which there were many.

As light spilled over the edge of the hill and flowed towards the house, she searched the slopes for the small movements of animals. If she was lucky, she spotted pheasant and grouse or the odd fox but, more often than not, she saw only the larger creatures like the sheep and cows. In her youth, she also learnt to distinguish the muddy brown coats of the McAllister estate's deer from the burnt-sienna foliage of various bushes, gorse, heather and dead ferns. This morning, she saw the herd off to the left meandering up one of the many paths that crisscrossed the hill. On other occasions, she saw the half-wild ponies pottering about. They were much easier to spot since there were always a few elderly greys among their number.

If the air was still, occasionally she could hear the chuckle of the pheasants as they sifted through the undergrowth. But usually it was the birds in the garden below her room that were heard above everything else. In the silence of such vast emptiness, the dawn chorus was quite spectacular. The fact that such tiny birds could produce songs of such sweetness and volume never ceased to amaze Esther. As she listened, the profusion of natural life eased her out of her solitude and prepared her for the tasks of the day ahead. Yet still she stayed where she was, drawing out the last vestiges of rest her mind allowed her. She waited to see the cows trundle up the lane to the dairy, their back legs swinging out around their milk-swollen udders, on their way to be milked by some of the local women and the few remaining Land Girls. She remembered a time when she was one of the people who occasionally sat on a stool at the back-end of a cow at the crack of dawn. She could remember the feeling of her own childishly soft cheek against the coarse hair of a cow's flank, the soft warmth of the cow's teats in her hands when her mother taught her how to milk. Once again, she heard the tinkle of milk hitting the bottom of an empty bucket, the grinding of cows' back teeth as they chewed their hay. She saw the wisps pulled from the manger floating through the air like feathers drifting down to rest on the backs of the cattle as well as in the hair and clothing of the milkers. She hadn't milked a cow in years, though that didn't mean she had forgotten how to do it. But she couldn't.

Instead, she sat on high and observed.

A few minutes later, Ivor Beattie, the old gardener, entered through the door in the garden wall. In all the time she sat, Esther couldn't think of a single day when the old man wasn't up with the birds to tend his garden. Though his hands were now stiff with arthritis, he was never late for the beginning of his workday. She watched as he bent to observe the vegetable patch, fingering the leaves, testing the moisture of the soil, picking off snails which he crushed under the heel of his boot. He was fiercely protective of his garden. But before he disappeared through the hedge, he would always glance up at Esther's window and give a single nod, acknowledging his mistress.

She always waited for his nod. She was so used to seeing him do it, she thought it might put the old man out if she were not there to receive his solemn greeting. Older folk were funny like that. She worried that the gardener might feel obliged to come up to the house to ask if the mistress was quite well. And if there was one thing old Ivor couldn't abide it was coming into the house.

Wrapped in her blanket with her knees up and her back resting against the white window shutter, she watched Ivor's morning routine, saw his nod and, sighing, slid off the window seat. Her cold bare feet hit the patterned carpet without making a sound before she shuffled into the bathroom. There was no need for her to keep quiet since she was the only person who slept on this side of the house. But she still moved noiselessly for her own sake rather than anyone else's. She appreciated the calmness of silence before the rush of the day.

Once she had performed her ablutions, plaited her blonde hair and dressed in her breeches and a light tweed coat, she headed out along the landing, bypassing the main stairs to the far end of the corridor. Reaching the end, she turned right and sneaked along to peek through the open doors of the children's bedrooms. She stood watching them, heard their soft, snuffling breath and smiled. Without a sound, she retraced her steps to the servant's stone staircase back along the landing which brought her to the bowels of the house. Though the lower floor was as spotlessly clean as the ones above, there was a lingering smell of damp along the whitewashed corridor. The only illumination in the passageway came from the kitchen. Light streamed out of the archway but only managed to stretch a few feet before it was swallowed by the shadows. As Esther ambled along towards the light source, she heard voices.

The three women sitting at the worktable were some of the few the war had not taken. Most of the men had enlisted while many of the younger women had gone off to build aeroplanes in East Lothian. A few travelled further south to become lumberjills. The only women to remain below stairs were the cook, the housekeeper and one housemaid, Ada Bryant, who struggled with loud noises. The other two were much too old and set in their ways to contemplate leaving.

With easy familiarity, Esther perched on the one remaining seat and joined their conversation as the cook, Mrs Colman, handed her a mug of hot milk. It was the way all four women had started many mornings since the war began, the distinction between mistress and servants all but forgotten. They asked after one another's family, shared local gossip and what titbits they had picked up from the radio or the papers. Mrs Morris, the housekeeper, often complained about her bad knees. Ada said very little at all. To an outsider, their little coven would have seemed completely inappropriate. Esther's own husband probably wouldn't have approved. But he wasn't there so the women had free rein to do as they pleased.

Once she drained her cup, Esther stood to leave. "I should be back in an hour and a half. I'll have breakfast then. And Caroline said she might call up, so I suppose we'll have to feed her too."

Caroline was one of only three close friends Esther possessed. When she wasn't braving London or Edinburgh, Caroline lived in the estate's gate lodge and was married to Esther's stepson. At thirty-two, she was older than her husband and Esther, but there was such a childish vivacity to her everyone couldn't help mothering her. Yet it was a boyish rather than feminine youthfulness. She was buoyantly energetic and generally tended to make life better for everyone even if she was exasperating at times. Esther, like everyone else, loved her dearly.

Guided by the sounds of excited whimpering, Esther collected the two English Pointers from the gunroom where they sometimes slept and headed out into the chilly morning air. Sadie and Jasper gambolled about, sniffing their way across the courtyard to the stables where Alfie the stable lad was pushing a wheelbarrow full of freshly collected dung. He stopped midway down the passage to give the dogs a pat before tipping his cap to the mistress. Though broad-shouldered and strong as an ox, Alfie was hampered by a deformed right leg which was slightly shorter than the left. It meant he walked with a limp, but it was that limp that kept him out of the army. Sometimes, it seemed the only people left behind were the ones that were already broken. Yet, despite his physical difficulties, Alfie worked hard and, as far as Esther was concerned, was unsurpassed as a horseman.

"I've tacked up the big lady for you, mistress," he murmured before picking up his barrow and carrying on. He was never very talkative.

If the weather was any way decent, Esther rode first thing in the morning. She felt that being outside in the fresh air was a good way to start the day – like a good, brisk walk. However, riding a horse was a good deal faster. She loved the creak of the leather, the clip-clop of a trot and the deeper rhythmical thump of the horse's hooves as they cantered along lanes and around headlands. There was a freedom to it.

Pulling the mare out of her stable, Esther checked the girth, tightened it then mounted out in the courtyard. Gathering her reins, she clicked the mare on into a brisk trot along the lane towards the local village of Kirkmore. Every once in a while, she collected and delivered letters for the local postmaster who was seventy if he was a day. It gave her the opportunity to pick up news but also to check on some of the locals. Though most people in the area were quite self-sufficient, some elderly residents as well as the young women with small children struggled with their plots of land and unsatisfactory ration cards. Esther thought it her duty as the largest landowner in the area to help wherever she could, whether that was bringing the odd pheasant to someone who wasn't getting enough meat or supplying some of the weaned local children with fresh cows' milk. It was her way of giving back to the community that raised her. And it was also a means of assuaging the guilt she felt for ascending to a position far beyond what she could have imagined, while they continued to toil and suffer below.

Chapter Two

Esther Muncie was a beautiful child. Born not long after the end of the hay harvest, she was a good size with healthy lungs and a shock of pure white hair. With her lively blue eyes and pale colouring, some thought she might be an albino. But her mother wouldn't hear of it. Fair hair ran in her family so Lizzie Muncie simply put the child's striking appearance down to her own respectable lineage. She also made sure to focus on what she saw of herself in her little girl: the eyes, the nose, the simple fact that she was female. Had Lizzie given birth to a boy, she wasn't sure she could have coped. A male child would have reminded her too much of her husband.

Oliver Muncie was the best of sorts. Tall and lean with a thick wave of brown hair and strong cheekbones. Aside from his handsomeness, everyone knew he was a good boy who cared for his widowed mother from the age of thirteen, worked hard, swore little and didn't drink too much. A few years younger than Oliver, from afar Lizzie always admired the handsome 'Muncie Boy'. It was something of a shock to Lizzie, therefore, when Oliver picked her to be his bride. She was the envy of every woman around for having snatched up such an eligible bachelor. Yet their wedded bliss did not last very long. When Kitchener called the men of the country to join his army against the Third Reich, the men of Kirkmore answered in their droves, Oliver Muncie included. In fact, so many local men joined at once, they formed their own company under the command of Major Fraser McAllister.

McAllister was of an age with many of his men, including Oliver Muncie. However, he was a man who, despite his youth, could command respect since he was the son of the laird of Kirkmore estate. Most of the men in his company were already employed by his father so when they joined the Kirkmore company, they simply exchanged the authority of one McAllister for another.

After receiving their basic training, the Kirkmore men shipped out to France where they had a brief period of rest before being thrown headlong into the fray. Their company became legendary among others in their battalion since, no matter how much action they saw, the Kirkmore boys were always the ones that came out of it with the fewest casualties. This was partly down to their commanding officer who, despite his youth, was fiercely devoted to his men and determined to keep them alive. McAllister had grown up with many of the men, knew their mothers, their wives, their children and, therefore, felt a deep-seated responsibility to bring them home alive. It was with an almost lightheaded sense of relief that he would send the men back to their families after their fifteen months on the Western Front. And it was with sickening regret and worry he would recall them once their stay in Blighty came to an end. But that wasn't before the men of the company had had their fill of mothers fussing over their underfed sons, children showing off newly acquired gap-toothed smiles and wives making sure there was another new baby ready to greet them the next time they came back.

Esther was conceived on one such occasion. But rather than presenting Oliver with his first child when he returned

22

to her, Lizzie Muncie showed off her new-born to twenty-six-year-old Major McAllister when he came to offer his congratulations following the birth of her daughter as well as his sympathies following the death of her husband.

Fraser McAllister had seen too many men die. Yet, it was the death of Oliver Muncie that haunted him long after the war was over. Or rather, it was the image of a forlorn young mother cradling her child in the knowledge that the little girl would never see her father that haunted him. She would never get to hold her father's hand or show him her missing teeth.

Guilt made Fraser continue to visit the now all-female Muncie household even after the birth of his own son in 1919 and the death of his wife and father from Spanish Flu shortly afterwards. Suddenly, Fraser found himself the proprietor of three thousand acres of Scottish farmland while also grieving the loss of two family members.

The estate was never supposed to be his. Fraser had set his mind on climbing through the ranks of the army and making his way in the world through distinguished military service rather than serving the estate and the land belonging to his family. His brother Stuart was destined to take over when their father died but when he was killed in the Great War the responsibility fell to Fraser.

Soon after he inherited the estate, rumours began to circulate that Lizzie Muncie had caught the eye of their new laird but as the years progressed nothing came of it. The relationship between widow and widower remained strictly that of master and subordinate. However, that did not mean Lizzie didn't benefit from their friendship. Fraser made sure Lizzie had a good, permanent job on the Kirkmore estate and that her daughter was well educated. Esther was, therefore, the only girl among her acquaintances who continued with her schooling after the age of fourteen, attending a boarding school for young ladies in Edinburgh away from her mother.

At first, separation was hard for Esther who had never experienced a single day in her life without her mother. She did not know who she was without her mother's constant presence. As the offspring of two labourers, she was the odd one out among the daughters of the moderately wealthy. Initially, she was picked on by both teachers and pupils. Yet, as they came to know her, they saw how hard she worked, how deserving she was of the education she was afforded. Her origins were overshadowed by her efforts to fit in – something she did admirably.

When she finally came home for the summer of her eighteenth birthday, the friends she had once played with, shared a childhood schoolroom with, were strangers to her. The strong brogue she previously shared with them had been replaced by the softer Edinburgh Scots accent of her peers at boarding school. She was more worldly than the simple people she came from, more refined. No matter how hard she tried to slip back into the easy familiarity she once had with them it was gone for good. The Kirkmore set were more cautious of what they said around her, afraid to show themselves up or seem like the poor relations.

There were only two people she found she could talk to. One was a boy a few years older than her by the name of Freddie Robertson. Freddie's father had been another one of the Kirkmore company who perished in the war and, as in case of Oliver Muncie's family, Fraser McAllister made sure the remaining Robertsons were well cared for and that the boy received a good education.

The other person she could talk to was Andrew McAllister. Drew was Fraser McAllister's only son and a year younger than Esther. They spent their childhood running around with Freddie and the other children on the estate. They climbed trees, built dams in the river, swam in the lake and generally got in the way of their parents and other labourers.

But, like Esther and Freddie, once Drew was old enough he was packed off to boarding school. While she was off learning how to be a lady, they became gentlemen. However, Freddie – instead of returning to Kirkmore at the end of his final year – was joined in Edinburgh by his mother who decided there were too many ghosts of the boy's father to remain on the estate alone. But Esther and Drew still had many others they called their friends at Kirkmore. Yet, when they returned every summer, they each felt the disconnect from their former playmates no matter how hard they tried to fit in once again.

Part of this divide was due to the fact that all the people left behind now had occupations to entertain them. Their days were spent in the fields or the big house whereas Esther and Drew had nothing to entertain them other than the odd jobs they were given by their respective parents. They began to spend more time together, riding on the estate's horses, walking in the woods and hills. Drew taught her to shoot. When it rained, Esther would run up to the big house and they would spend all day poring over books in the library. She loved books and, though her education had been thorough, when Drew introduced her to the likes of Plato and Homer, Esther felt she learnt more from those texts and the way he spoke about them than she had in a whole year of schooling.

Drew, for his part, enjoyed her company. She was lively, quick-witted, very pretty and he was flattered by her interest in the knowledge he could share with her. There was no doubt that he was attracted to her. She was fair-haired, athletic and possessed a beautifully feminine face with arched eyebrows and full lips. He liked to brush against her as they walked, sit close when they were reading together. Had he been sure they wouldn't be interrupted, Drew probably would have pushed their relationship further but, being young, he was afraid of what others might say if they discovered the laird's son having a flirtation with a girl who was, in almost every respect, the laird's ward.

It was, therefore, with great anticipation and excitement that he waited for the Midsummer dance which, for some reason, was held near the end of August. If he asked her to dance, he would have an excuse to hold her hands, to press up against her. But when the evening came, he could hardy get near her. Wearing a beautifully simple cream dress with her hair loose and flowing, she was swamped by the boys and men of Kirkmore. Everyone danced with her, including Drew's father who whirled her around the floor like a man half his age.

It was less than a week later that Esther's life took a turn no one would have predicted. Thinking that her final summer at home was over and that she now had to look for work, a melancholy swept over her, keeping her away from everyone except her mother. She haunted the family home and generally got in the way, despite her mother's gentle chastisement.

The morning of her eighteenth birthday found her at the kitchen table poring over one of the books she had borrowed from the McAllisters' library. It was something of a shock to her when the laird himself walked into their kitchen after a short rap on the door. So much so that she immediately whipped the book out of sight under the table. However, she needn't have worried since Mr McAllister didn't even look at her. Instead, he kept his eyes firmly on Lizzie Muncie and asked her for a private conversation. Perplexed, Lizzie had followed him outside and shut the door.

Esther sat gaping at the space where her mother had stood moments before. There was such an agitated, wild look on Mr McAllister's face that she wasn't sure her mother should be left alone with him. But then a memory stirred in her mind. On occasion, she had overheard neighbours saying that the laird had a soft spot for Mrs Muncie and that, as soon as her daughter was old enough to leave, Mr McAllister would surely propose to her. A thrill went through Esther as she remembered. She wondered what Mr McAllister would be like as a stepfather but then felt a pang of sadness when she realised Drew would become her stepbrother. She wasn't sure why that upset her.

Yet, when Lizzie walked back into the kitchen there was no happy, girlish glow, no bubbling excitement, no smile. She simply looked stunned.

"Mr McAllister wants to speak with you, Essie," she said, her voice completely flat. "Go out to him, there's a good girl."

He didn't propose to Lizzie. He proposed to Esther.

For a birthday gift, he brought her an engagement ring which he offered to her standing in the garden of her mother's cottage. As he stood waiting for her reply, Esther looked anywhere but at him. She studied the ground, the sky, the roses in the flowerbeds until finally her gaze rested on her mother who was peering through the kitchen window. Lizzie did not speak or move her mouth. She did not wave her hands. She simply gave one barely perceptible nod and disappeared from view.

Turning to look at the sweaty, pained face as it scrutinized hers, Esther saw the fear in Mr McAllister's eyes. It made him look younger. Smiling shyly up into his waiting face, she gave him the answer she thought he wanted.

However, what Esther could not have known was that Fraser did not want her to accept his proposal. As he had stumbled over his offer of marriage to her, he felt his desire diminish. The infatuation of the recent evening was doused by the cold reality of the sweet, young creature before him. She was not for him. She could not cure him of the aversion to intimacy he had harboured since the Great War. Yes, there were times when he needed a woman but they were few and far between. Those moments were not to be shared with a girl barely beyond childhood no matter how attractive she was.

Yet, Fraser had asked for her hand and she had accepted. He had her mother's consent and she had given it. Being laird, he could have called the whole thing off. He even considered not going to the church on his wedding day. But Fraser was an honourable man. He couldn't do that to Esther when her name was suddenly on everyone's lips as the future mistress of Kirkmore. He couldn't do it to good, honest, hardworking Lizzie. And he most certainly could not do it to Oliver Muncie's widow or daughter.

Chapter Three

Returning from her postal round, Esther didn't bother to change out of her riding clothes. She never did. Though she tried to be the lady of the house, there were some traditions she struggled to adopt and dressing appropriately for different parts of her day was one of them. She did not have the patience or the time to waste on visits to her dressing room, instead choosing to spend much of her time in outdoor clothing. After all, half of the business she attended to was conducted out of doors.

As she approached the breakfast room, she heard the raucous laugh of a woman joined by high-pitched giggles. Esther smiled to herself. She always loved the moments when she saw or heard people who did not know she was there. There was something wonderfully candid about their laughter and their speech when they did not think they were being watched or listened to.

When she entered, all three of the room's occupants looked up. They all sat on one side of the table. In the centre was Caroline, short-haired, kohl-eyed, cheeks naturally bright and pink. To her left was a boy of eight-nearly-nine, his jaw working furiously on a piece of toast. Archie was tall for his age and had the look of Oliver Muncie about him. On Caroline's right was an individual who was a good deal smaller. Florence was an elfin creature with the same white-blonde hair Esther had at the tender age of five and three-quarters. There was a mischievous smile on her face as she squirmed on her seat.

Esther didn't even bother saying hello. "What?" she asked, half exasperated, half amused.

Florence began to giggle furiously while the others sat po-faced.

"Nothing, nothing," Caro said airily. "Just telling them about some of the high jinks I used to get up to at their age."

"And no doubt they were telling you about what they put in Muldoon's boot?"

Two days before, the children sent the estate's gamekeeper into an apoplectic rage when they secreted a dead mouse in one of the muddy boots he had left at the back door while he was in the laird's study with Esther. Since Muldoon carried a thinly veiled dislike for both Esther and her children, her sympathies were limited. When he came storming back in with steam coming out of his ears, Esther had to fight hard to maintain passivity. However, her urge to laugh was quickly quelled when the gamekeeper asked permission to punish the children for the prank they had played. Esther refused and he left in even more of a fury than when he had entered. Though she couldn't really admit it, she was quite proud of the children for their mischief even if it had further soured what little relationship was left between her and Muldoon. If Esther had her way, the old man would have been dismissed years ago but he had worked for old Mr McAllister and was unswervingly loyal to Fraser. That, however, didn't mean he was going to respect the laird's young wife and children.

"I was just saying that I hoped they washed their hands after touching a dead mouse," Caroline said with a shiver of revulsion. "And gave them a few tips for next time."

"I don't think my two need advice from you to come up with their next scheme," Esther said with a smile. "Besides, if they do anything else to Muldoon, he's likely to string them up by the ankles."

"You'll protect them," Caro said confidently.

Esther laughed without humour. "Only if I haven't been strung up with them," she muttered.

"Can we go out to Beattie and see if he has any strawberries in the greenhouse?" Archie asked, finishing his toast.

Esther nodded. "Off you go then. Don't annoy the poor man too much though."

They didn't need telling twice. They were up and out the door with squeals of excitement. Esther heard them clatter down the corridor to the garden and then there was silence.

"Aren't they sweet?" Caroline murmured. "So carefree." She paused. "What's going to happen when your *guests* arrive?"

Esther sighed heavily. She was fed up with all the questions she was being asked about their *guests*. When the idea initially came to her to invite them, she thought it was the simplest solution to all her problems. But then everyone else started to take issue with her plan, questioning her and disapproving at every turn. Yet she still managed to get her way in the end.

"It shouldn't be that different. I suppose we'll find out, won't we?"

During the war Esther had taken over the responsibility of Kirkmore while Fraser moved permanently to London to work for the army.

When his first wife Annabel and his father died, rather than focus on running the estate, Fraser had thrown himself back into his life in the military. He had always enjoyed life in the army: the camaraderie, the discipline, the feeling of actually doing something worthwhile. Though an excellent field soldier, he was also an excellent strategist and, therefore, indispensable in a war. He also – thanks to a childhood tutor

– had a good grasp of German which gave him an advantage over many of the other soldiers with similar experience.

Though initially wary of a job so far from any real action, Fraser came to love his work. It challenged him in a way that was unfamiliar to him while also occupying his mind just enough to block out the memories of war that he always carried. And it took him away from Kirkmore which, though important to him, held too many memories of the dead.

For many years, he split his time evenly between Scotland and London. But once war was declared, Fraser was almost permanently in the capital. Yet even now – when the war had been over for more than a year – he remained down south. He told Esther that he was still helping the army while also taking his place in the government as the local MP. She suspected he was simply trying to get away from another wife – this one, very much alive.

Esther didn't bother herself about what her husband might be doing with his time. What she did wonder at was how he ever managed to work for the army and maintain several thousand acres of Scottish country estate. However, when she took over, she did so with the distinct disadvantage of a skeletal workforce. Many of the men and women who laboured on the estate followed in the footsteps of their forebears in the Great War and joined the army or went to work in the factories. Though a large posse of the Women's Land Army descended on Kirkmore, there was still need of many more capable men and women to run it since virtually all the suitable land on the estate had been turned over to food and flax production.

Admittedly, she was given some respite when the Italians finally surrendered to the Allies. It followed that the large number of Italian prisoners of war captured in previous years were let loose on the fields of Britain to shore up the worrisome shortage of labourers in the countryside. However, to say the Italian POWs *laboured* on the land was a stretch.

From the off, Esther disliked them. There was something louche about the way they carried themselves, hands in their pockets, feet scuffing the ground as they slowly shuffled about putting the minimum effort required into whatever task they had been given. They always seemed to have one eye firmly fixed on the Land Girls who worked the fields nearby, and were sometimes heard shouting what were, no doubt, bawdy declarations at the women in their mother tongue. Even Esther was not spared their lascivious glances when she came to check on their progress which, in general, left a lot to be desired. It made her so uncomfortable that she took to asking the foreman, Cary Eden, about their work rather than enduring their scrutiny and calls of '*Ciao, bella signora!*' when she visited.

As time progressed, the locals began to realise that these exotic Europeans were not only hunting their womenfolk but also the estate's game. Muldoon had angrily suggested they reintroduce hanging when he noticed the sparse numbers of pheasant and rabbits in the fields and woods around where the Italians were sent to work. Even some of the other estate workers had come to Esther to complain of their damaged snares and pilfered catches. The birds and rabbits were a much-needed addition to the diet of many of the estate's inhabitants whom Esther permitted to hunt on the land. Had the Italians asked her leave to set snares, she would have readily agreed. But it was the fact that they were poaching animals from her land that really rankled her.

It was, therefore, something of a relief when the war ended and she finally had cause to release the men from their service. However, the German surrender the previous May was not, as she hoped, swiftly followed by the departure of her slothful, thieving workforce. The Italians were the first to be sent home, though her labourers didn't leave until the following February. Their departure resulted in tears from one or two of the local Land Girls, but Esther was glad to hurry the men on their way. There were few enough workers without some of them succumbing to pregnancy.

Yet, once they left, Esther found herself sleepless with worry once again as she tried to come up with a workable solution to their labour shortage. With the influx of German prisoners recently arrived in Britain having waited out the war in prison camps in America, Esther was certain her lack of workers would be short-lived. However, when she met with Donnie McDonald, the local War Ag official, he was initially reluctant to provide her with the men she needed. Kirkmore was outside the catchment area of the main camp and was even too far away from the satellite camps to allow easy transportation of workers to and from their base.

It was all Esther could do not to throttle the grey-haired McDonald at the War Agricultural Executive Committee when he said things like, "You *do* know there are *fuel* shortages, Mrs McAllister?" He had a horrible singsong, condescending voice which he used to explain things to Esther in painfully pointless detail. He treated her as if she were an uneducated street urchin rather than a woman who had run several thousand acres of country estate for the last six years. She understood the difficulties of transporting the men to Kirkmore better than most since she had spent years travelling the roads leading to the estate that snaked through the heartland of Scotland. Yet, she had a solution to that problem too. Just as precisely as he might have done, she explained her plan to house the prisoners at Kirkmore to McDonald.

He had laughed in her face.

She had taken great pleasure in wiping the simpering smile from his cheeks when she presented him with letters of approval for her scheme from the prisoner-camp commandant, various high-ranking officials in Kirkmore and the local member of parliament who also happened to be her husband. She didn't tell McDonald that she had, in fact, forged her husband's signature on his letter but she had been using his name for years to provide the leverage her own could not. Fraser didn't care. He was too busy in London.

The camp commandant had taken a little more persuasion but, being desperate and stressing the need for workers to feed the population of Great Britain, she eventually wore him down. The struggle to find adequate rations for the prisoners as well as work to occupy their time helped to influence his decision. Feeding hundreds of men was always challenging and Esther's offer to take even a few well-behaved men off his hands was always going to be hard to refuse. He understood the difficulty Esther faced and was keen to help even though he thought it highly irregular that he was sending men to live under the employ of a woman. Yet, if determination alone was enough to make something work, then Esther's determination would surely lead to success – that and the fact she would be paying the War Ag £4 a year for the upkeep of each man in her employ. It was then up to the War Ag to pay the POWs what they would in wage coupons which the men could exchange for 'essentials' like cigarettes. And also, not forgetting to keep a pretty penny of Esther's money to pay for the War Ag's 'handling' of the prisoners' affairs.

However, the confidence of the Much-Honoured Esther McAllister of Kirkmore didn't prevent some of the locals from thinking the Germans would revolt and murder everyone in their beds. If she was honest, Esther had to admit that the thought had crossed her mind. But she didn't tell that to the sceptics. She simply hoped their fears wouldn't come to fruition and that everyone would learn to muddle along no matter how odd the situation was likely to be.

Yet up until the day of their arrival, those closest to Esther were still questioning her choice to allow these unknowns into their lives.

Chapter Four

"Are you *sure*?" Mrs Morris asked her, a pained look on her face.

It was the morning of the prisoners' transfer onto the estate and everyone was a little edgy.

"Well, it's too late now," Esther muttered. "We need them."

Though she didn't completely catch Mrs Morris's grumbled reply, the gist of it was that they could manage fine on their own.

"But we're *not* managing fine on our own!" Esther replied, her voice harder and more authoritative than it had ever been with the housekeeper. "We had a whole field of leeks go to seed, some of the potatoes rotted before we even got them out of the ground and we also ended up with a terrible second crop of hay since it rained for two days straight last year before those bloody Italians managed to pick it up. *That* is not managing fine." She hissed out an exhalation through her nose. Then more quietly she added, "You might not want to admit it but there just aren't enough people here to do the work. Especially when so much of the land has been replanted with food crops. Even without everyone leaving, we would have to hire more workers. We need the manpower."

Though she didn't acquiesce, Mrs Morris said nothing more to her mistress. She wanted everything to work out as much for Esther's sake as everyone else's. Though she would never show it, she cared deeply for the girl. Esther's mother had been one of her closest friends and, before she died, Lizzie made the housekeeper promise to help her daughter in any way she could. It was an easy promise for Mrs Morris to make since she thought of Esther as the closest thing she would ever have to her own child. She took great pride in seeing the girl's ascent from poor, simple beginnings to laird's wife.

"The men will probably arrive before I get back from my postal round," Esther informed her as she shrugged on a jacket. "You don't need to go out and meet them. Old Major Brown's overseeing their transfer onto the estate. Unless you want to go out and see them." She grinned at the look of horror on the old woman's face then left with a cheery wave.

Esther stayed away much longer than she usually would have. She stopped to chat with everyone who crossed her path and even rode up one of the estate's braes from which she could view vast swathes of Kirkmore. She didn't want to stand around waiting for the prisoners to arrive. Part of it was because she feared what she might see. Were they going to be wild-eyed young men, half-starved by life in a prison camp? Would they cause problems the moment they set foot on Kirkmore soil? Maybe they would simply refuse to work for her. She didn't know how kind or how severe she should be with them. She supposed Major Brown would be her guide on that. He was a retired army man who lived nearby and had been commissioned to manage the new men and make sure they did exactly as they were told. If they needed any more wardens to safeguard the locals, they were to use the older men from the village who had served during the Great War, many of whom still had their old weapons which they kept clean and well-oiled. And, if they found themselves in the middle of an all-out rebellion, Esther was to provide the

villagers with the contents of the McAllister gunroom. She
prayed to God she would never have to do that.

When she eventually did arrive back at the house
covered in dust and sweat, there was a flurry of activity in
the yard where the men were being washed and deloused.
Rather than ride through the middle of it all on her mare,
she went around the back of the stables to dismount and
wash off her horse. She could have let Alfie do it, but she
was still dawdling. She also wanted to try to gauge the mood
of the twenty German prisoners only a few dozen yards
away before she approached them.

The carriage doors at the opposite the end of the stables
were thrown wide open with the midday sun streaming
down the passage. The figures of many men were silhouetted
in the light, making it difficult to pick out who might be a
guard and who was a prisoner. Several people seemed to be
milling about. Clouds of cigarette smoke drifted around the
heads of some while others stood with their hands in their
pockets which she took as a good sign even though she was
quite surprised they weren't marshalled in neat rows. Then
one man turned. He was very clearly holding a rifle across his
chest. Esther hesitated. Perhaps she shouldn't approach the
prisoners at all. She wondered how long it had been since they
shared a space with a woman. But then she remembered that
many worked as farm labours or builders before coming to
her. They couldn't be that insulated against the outside world.
Yet still she held back.

Suddenly, a black figure appeared, limned by the
sunlight. He was a man of diminutive stature with a slightly
running step. Furtively looking behind him, he ducked
through the door of the stable without noticing Esther
standing midway down the passage. Her stomach dropped
as she realised this was the beginning of the end of all her
hard work and scheming. The men had barely been there an

hour and already one of them was making a bid for freedom. And yet, he had stopped just inside the door. He was standing in slight shadow at the first stable on the right, well within the line of sight of anyone who cared to look in his direction. Peeking into the first stable, he tentatively reached out to touch the pink-and-grey muzzle of the pony whose nose barely reached over the top of the door. The pony sniffed cautiously before shoving its nose into the proffered hand, expecting to be fed.

Bob the pony was an old, rotund little creature that was more like a family pet than a very small horse. He was spoilt rotten by everyone, getting handfuls of grass and windfall apples whenever they walked passed. Everyone, including Drew, Esther and her children had learnt to ride on him, but he also taught them to avoid small stamping hooves and sharp yellow teeth. She wanted to call out a warning to the prisoner ignorantly rubbing between Bob's nostrils but didn't want to cause a commotion by either frightening the man or startling the guard with the gun into action. Instead, she waited with bated breath for the inevitable.

Just as the man's fingers travelled further up the animal's bony nose, Bob's ears flattened against his poll and, quick as a flash, he made a toothy swipe at the man's exposed wrist. Esther expected to hear a shout of pain but, equally quickly, the little man swiped his hand out of the way before neatly giving the pony a chastising flick on the nose. He then spoke in a mild tone to Bob, clearly scolding him in German.

Esther couldn't help but smile. It was obvious the man knew something of horses. She had done the same with Bob a hundred times over the years. Buoyed by the familiarity of the prisoner's behaviour, she approached him. He couldn't be that alien to her.

Hearing Esther coming, the man shrank away from her, bowing his head, and muttered to her in German.

"I see you've met Bob," she said calmly, plucking some hay up off the ground and proffering it to the inquisitive little nose. Both disappeared immediately as the pony ducked behind the high stable door and wolfed down his food. She picked up some more and, rather than hand it directly to the pony, offered it to the man. Tentatively, he held it out only for it to be instantly stripped from his fingers. He chuckled and was bending to pick up more hay when a shadow fell over him.

A tall man with hands in his pockets stood in the arched doorway, black against the sun outside. He didn't look at Esther, instead focusing on the short man at her side.

"*Wie geht's, Max?*" he asked softly.

Max turned his beaming face to the newcomer and babbled excitedly and a little too loudly in German.

"*Oi! What you think you're doing?*"

The two Germans turned towards the voice.

A boy in an ill-fitting private's uniform came hurrying over to the stable, his weapon trained on them but swinging wildly from side to side as he jogged towards them. "Major says no wanderin' or don't you understand plain fuckin' English?"

The taller man glanced sharply over his shoulder at Esther. The movement seemed to unnerve the young soldier who levelled his gun at the German's chest. The prisoner shuffled uncomfortably. His subtle shift placed him between Esther and the private's gun. She wondered if it was intentional.

"Christ, miss, what're you doin' out here? It's not safe, miss. You wouldn't know what this lot'd do." He glanced disapprovingly at the two prisoners. "Best you get back inside now, miss, before the mistress comes looking and gives us all what for." He gave her a winning smile as if he thought she was as young as he was. But when Esther gazed impassively at him, his confidence seemed to slip. "Please, miss," he begged. "I hear the mistress is a hard old nut. I don't want to be crossin' her from the off. Come on, lads," he added. "Hop it!" He edged around them along the front of Bob's stable, gun still wavering until he stood between the two men and Esther.

Max glanced wistfully at the pony before trotting back out into the yard while the other man nodded once to Esther and left.

"*Phew!*" The soldier relaxed, shoulders sagging. "That could've got nasty. You want to be more careful, miss." He mopped his sweating brow with the sleeve of his uniform. "All sorts could – *aaargh!*"

There was a commotion in the yard as civilians and prisoners alike moved to peer into the stables. Esther stood just inside the door beside the writhing private who was clutching his upper arm where Bob had just found some soft, gullible flesh to bite. Raising his weapon, the boy rounded on the pony as if he were about to shoot it.

"*Private!*" Esther's voice was harsh and commanding as she stepped forward to protect the animal.

The private turned to her with a look on his face that suggested he was going to say something rude when he was saved by the old Major.

"*Private Stanley!* What in God's name do you think you're doing?" Major Brown marched in, chest out, eyes narrowed.

"*He bit me! The bastard bit me!*" The boy sobbed dryly, turning murderously on the pony again.

"*Private Stanley!*" The Major's eyes narrowed even further. "We do not use such language in the presence of a lady, *especially* the lady of the house! *Or* threaten her horses. Get back to your position immediately.'

Stanley's face fell in horror as he stared at Esther in her soiled riding garb. This was clearly not what he thought a lady should look like. He went momentarily pale then his white cheeks flooded with red embarrassment, his mouth working furiously but resolutely silent. Tearing his eyes away from the mistress, he scurried back to the yard with the demeanour of a kicked dog.

"Beg your pardon, ma'am," Major Brown said solemnly as he watched the soldier go. "I hope it won't happen again. But with these green boys you want to have as much wits about you as with the prisoners."

"He's enthusiastic, I'll give him that much," Esther answered, following the Major out into the courtyard. "Although I'd prefer it if he didn't shoot my horses."

"Of course, ma'am," the old man agreed dryly.

"Everything is to your liking, Major? The quarters are adequate?" They had been through everything before the men arrived as well as passing a War Ag inspection, but nervousness made her ask again.

"Everything is as it should be, ma'am," he assured her. "And the prisoners have been perfectly pleasant."

"And they know what will happen if any of them attempt to escape?" she asked quietly.

"They know that the escapee will face the severest punishment we can mete out," he replied in a loud voice that rang off the enclosing walls, "and that everyone else will be returned to their POW camp to be held in solitary confinement until the commandant deems it appropriate to reintroduce them back into the camp's general population."

Some of the gathered men looked up but others hung their heads. One visibly flinched.

"They understand then? They speak English?'

"A few do, some better than others. They know enough not to cross us," he said confidently, again making sure everyone heard the last part. Then he added quietly, "Honestly, ma'am, I think they're quite glad to be here. I saw their camp when I met with the commandant." He paused and sucked air in through his teeth, shaking his head.

"Believe me, ma'am, coming here will be like visiting a holiday resort after the accommodation they've been used to. If they have any sense at all, we shouldn't have any problems."

Esther simply nodded. She hoped he was right.

Chapter Five

The prisoners were to be housed in one of the grain barns that had remained empty since the start of the war. The demand for wheat and barley was so great in the cities that the crops were taken straight to the stores in the suburbs. The building was designed to keep vermin out so, with relatively few changes, it was adapted to keep people *in*. Previously, the building housed some of the Italian workers and they – under Esther's watchful eye – had furnished it with the contents of several of the big house's attic rooms where they found a plethora of old chairs and stools as well as a few dozen hospital beds. These had been left from a time when the house was used as a recuperation facility for soldiers injured in the Great War – a time before Esther was even born. She wondered what the men who lived in those beds would say if they knew their mattresses were now to be occupied by the same enemy they had fought against thirty years previously. Said ancient mattresses were themselves horribly musty but, according to Major Brown, no worse than what the men were used to.

At either end of the building, they had installed fat-bellied stoves in an attempt to chase out the chill that seemed to radiate off the walls and also to give the men somewhere to cook. Mrs Coleman had been tasked with making extra bread and so forth for the men – something she was not at all pleased about. But with the enthusiasm of someone who wanted to make something succeed out of sheer force of will, Esther had begged, wheedled and finally guilted Mrs Coleman into doing the extra work. The cook's godson was in the army so by invoking his name and reasonably suggesting that if – heaven forbid – he had been captured by the other side, she would want someone such as herself to feed him, Mrs Coleman finally conceded, albeit with ill grace.

Esther and the Major had anticipated so many potential difficulties that it was something of a shock when none of them arose. The newest residents of Kirkmore slotted into the lives of the others who were already well-established with something akin to ease. Though she had wished for it more than anything lately, Esther was almost unsure what to do when their arrival passed off so smoothly. It was the one variable she had barely given any thought to. With a dazed sense of disbelief, she organized the men into a work party and gave them their marching orders for the days that followed. Within a week, the routine of the men became as familiar to Kirkmore as that of the local workers. While the locals brought the cows in, the prisoners headed out for their day. Rather than frogmarch them down the lanes, Major Brown allowed them to walk in a ragtag bunch just as civilians would for fear that a militant-style order would remind them too much of their army days. They did everything from picking stones to weeding fields to earthing up potatoes. Some of the work they were tasked with could have been done with machinery but with a shortage of fuel and a sudden abundance of workers, Esther thought it better to put them to good use.

What she had not expected was their willingness to put their own time to good use too. The lethargy with which the Italians approached their labours was infuriating to anyone who had an inherited work ethic like Esther's. To a point, she could understand their disinclination to be productive. They were foreign soldiers captured by an enemy who now expected them to work for meagre wages even though the two countries were latterly allies. All they wanted to do was go home to their own *bella signora*s and they made no bones about getting that point across. Esther did hope that providing them with good food and a not-so-meagre wage might encourage their efficiency, but they remained resolutely unconcerned about the work they left undone or did badly.

The Germans were another breed entirely.

Esther had heard stories about the POWs' aversion to farming the land that raised the soldiers who had defeated them. Individuals from several quarters explained how the men had maimed crops, wasted seeds and generally made a nuisance of themselves with little regard for the nation's (and also the prisoners' own) dire need for food. One man in the War Ag told her of how camp labourers had deliberately removed the tops from carrots making it ten times more difficult to remove the veg underneath.

If initial impressions were anything to go by, however, Esther thought her workers did not seem to be the type that would engage in such callous sabotage. She had, of course, warned the foreman, Cary Eden, and Major Brown to look out for any men doing more harm than good but, in the first month of their stay at Kirkmore, neither man had a single incident to recount. Instead, the men worked steadily – virtually silently – at whatever task they were given without so much as a mutinous glance or grumble.

"Maybe they're planning something," Mrs Morris had intoned one morning in the kitchen but a single look from Esther silenced her.

The thing that surprised her most was the fact that many of her new workers appeared to be little more than children.

A few of the boys – for that was all you could call them – didn't even look old enough to shave. Some still had the uneven skin colouring that denoted the last vestiges of teenage acne and awkward, gangly limbs which they had not yet grown into. None of them seemed to possess the bulk necessary to fill the old Allied army uniforms they wore which were dyed maroon. In any case, the clothing each prisoner stood in – whether man or boy – was so ill-fitting it invariably appeared to belong to someone else. Indeed, their clothing did nothing to alleviate the illusion that one was looking at a field of animated scarecrows rather than living, breathing men as they worked their way across the ground day after day. The impression was also sustained by the hush in which the men worked. Whereas the Italians chattered constantly in loud obtrusive voices that carried across open space, alerting everyone to their presence from a distance, Esther couldn't even hear the Germans speak when she was standing in the fields with them. She wondered if it was something to do with the cadence of the two different languages, one low, harsh and guttural, the other almost musical with its unpredictable rising and falling rhythm. Or perhaps it was just the men who spoke it. The Italians were passionate and exuberant in their speech. They gesticulated wildly and often had conversations that rose to such a pitch Esther wondered if the men having them would come to blows. The Germans were so much more reserved, expressing more with their eyes, the way they smoked a cigarette and the set of their shoulders than they ever did with their voices.

In fact, there was something about the eyes of those boys and men that was truly haunting. They were the eyes of men who knew too much, had seen too much. They were the eyes of children exposed to horrors no child should ever face. And they were the eyes of men who had resigned themselves to their fate, knowing that it could be years before they ever saw their homeland again. Perhaps it was those dull eyes which made them appear so compliant. But still she waited for something to go wrong, for some issue to arise that would spell the end of her perfect plan. Yet the only problems they had in the first few weeks after the arrival of the Germans were what one might expect: minor injuries from farming implements, the odd misunderstanding between the men and their foreman and, of course, the Scottish weather.

None of the prisoners seemed to have adequate waterproof clothing so when it rained or even drizzled, they invariably looked like they had been dunked in the lake fully dressed.

Though she could have approached the War Ag or their old camp commandant to ask for extra clothing, Esther decided she would be better seeking out suitable garb for the prisoners herself. She also felt that asking the likes of McDonald from the War Ag would be tantamount to failure. She wanted to appear capable and self-sufficient when it came to running the estate rather than running to someone else when the first challenge arose.

Therefore, when the prisoners arrived back at their living quarters one evening, Esther showed them a pile of old wax jackets and various other coats that she had bought from neighbours or found in the numerous cupboards around the house. She tried to remain matter of fact about presenting her acquisitions to the men. She didn't want them to feel they had to be grateful for what she gave them. It was a case of them needing coats, so she got them some coats.

She also left them a large tin of wax and some cloths. "Some of these jackets are old and need reproofing." She winced a little at hearing how the rolling Scottish 'r' dominated the rest of the word, knowing how difficult some of the men found the local accent. "You must first heat the wax until it is liquid then keep it in warm water while you are using it," she continued carefully. "Make sure to rub it into the worn patches and along the seams, then hang them up to dry." Esther paused and looked around at the expressionless faces in front of her. She knew some of them didn't understand her but hoped others might translate. "I hope they do a better job of keeping you dry than what you have already," she added with a sniff of disapproval at their current garments before turning to leave.

"Mrs McAllister?"

She whipped back around to see one of the older men had stepped forward. It was the first time any of them had addressed her directly. "Yes, Mr …?" She had no idea what his name was.

He smiled slightly at her. "Erich Neuman, madam," he answered with a slight bow. "Thank you for the jackets," he said simply.

Esther nodded once. "My pleasure," she murmured then left them to their work.

Chapter Six

"Bugger him anyway!"

Esther crushed a letter in her fist and threw it across the room towards the fireplace. However, the paper being light and of low quality, it simply sailed over her desk then died mid-flight, landing on the rug in the middle of the room.

"Bugger who, darling?" Caroline asked mildly as she stretched one of her impossibly long limbs toward the paper ball to pluck it off the floor and toss it into the waiting fire, all while remaining seated in her chair by the hearth.

Esther stared at her friend for a moment too long as she marvelled at the way Caro neatly refolded all her extremities back into her armchair. *"That bloody tutor!"* she hissed, dragging her hand through her already tousled hair.

It was a good thing she often tackled her correspondence in the evenings when no one was likely to call since her usual semi-respectable plaited bun was often left in disarray by the contents of the various letters she handled concerning the business of the family and the estate. No matter how often Caro told her not to worry herself so much, Esther couldn't help but agonise over how she managed the estate. She really cared about doing a good job for the perpetuity of the family property and the sake of the people who worked on it. And she would be damned if she handed

Kirkmore back to Fraser worse off than when he left. That was, if her husband ever came back.

"Which tutor are we talking about? And what's he done?" Caroline sighed with exaggerated weariness.

"The one I had engaged for the summer months that was supposed to be coming at the end of next week, who now *regrets to inform me that he has been otherwise engaged,*" Esther hissed in frustration, slamming her fist on the desk.

For months she had been trying to secure a tutor who would teach Archie over the summer. Though McAllister tradition dictated that the boys of the family be sent off to boarding school once they were old enough, Esther had kept Archie at home. Though she never admitted it to anyone, part of the urge to keep her first-born at home was grounded in a hope that he would experience a similar childhood to her own – that his life would not be entirely dictated by the class he was born into. The freedom Esther was afforded running around Kirkmore with all the other children had been the happiest time in her life and she longed to give her own offspring that chance to live a wild and carefree existence. In this instance, the war had been a godsend. Her justification for breaking with tradition was easily explained away as concern for her first-born's safety and, reluctantly, Fraser agreed. However, the one condition he laid down was that extra tuition had to be arranged – a tutor must be employed to teach their son what the local schoolmistress could not.

The problem was that Kirkmore was in the deepest recesses of the Scottish countryside and there wasn't a suitable tutor in the shire who met their needs. She'd spent the last number of years putting adverts in papers, contacting agencies, writing letters, asking for references, hiring, firing and had not yet found one who could teach her son more than she was capable of teaching him herself. True, her Latin was very rusty, but it was considerably better than that of the fool she had hired the previous year. Though he dressed like an Oxford don, Mr Merriweather couldn't even conjugate the Latin verb "*sum*" and, when Archie had helpfully corrected his mistake, Merriweather had insisted that *he* was right and called her son an "impudent whelp" for questioning him.

"I'm glad '*to be*' rid of him," Archie announced to his mother once she had seen the man off. He smiled at Esther, expecting praise for his cleverness but she had turned away, not in the mood for jokes after the failure of another one of her schemes.

It was an additional stress she did not need.

She stood now and began to stalk up and down the study, dragging her fingers through her hair while Caroline looked on.

There was something so masculine about the way Esther behaved, Caro mused as she watched her friend stride across the room, muttering curses about everyone from her husband to the string of useless tutors she had employed over the years. Yet there was also something sensual about the way Esther McAllister moved: the sway of her hips, the musculature of her calves, the elegant straightness of her spine – even the delicacy of her fingers as they combed her scalp once more. She was a woman with a man's cares and, though the pressure she put on herself to succeed was immense, she wore it well.

For the umpteenth time, Caroline tried to fathom why her own husband, rather than her father-in-law, hadn't married Esther Muncie. When she asked Drew that question, he had shouted out a shocked laugh at her directness. "I suppose the old fox beat me to it," he said with a shrug, matching her candour with his own. Caro followed the first question by asking if he loved his stepmother and, though Drew shook his head, he answered, "Of course I love her."

He had paused for a moment before continuing quietly, "I've known her for as long as I can remember. She's my best friend. She's the closest thing I have to a sister. I love her … but not in that way."

Caroline loved her too and thought her friend was wasted on a sprawling country estate in the back of beyond. Esther should have been at the centre of all the social circles Caro frequented in London. Or *had* frequented. She'd hardly seen any of her friends since the Blitz began. Some, like her, had spent the war in the countryside away from all the death and destruction. Others had charged headlong into it. Not all had survived. Even now when the war was over, Caroline still spent half her time in Kirkmore. Going to the cities upset her now because they no longer looked like the places she remembered and loved. More and more she found occupation on the McAllister estate.

But she still felt that Esther deserved more. Watching her, Caro knew that the best thing to do was let her walk off her frustration and mutter to her heart's content without interruption. It was so much for someone so young to contend with, she thought. Esther wasn't yet twenty-eight – younger than Caroline was herself by a few years – but she had already done so much more than Caro ever had or would.

"What am I going to do, Caro?" Esther asked when she finally came to an abrupt halt, leaning on the back of her chair.

Caroline stayed silent for another moment, allowing Esther the chance to start pacing again as so often happened when she got worked up. But she remained where she was as Caro deliberately closed her book.

"I don't know, darling," she answered.

This was how many of their conversations began over the war years. She might not have had the faintest clue how to help Esther, but it seemed talking it through together generally led them to some kind of solution.

"What about talking to the agency again?" Caro offered.

Esther laughed humourlessly. "Those idiots were no help last time. I don't see why things would be any different this time."

"Surely there's someone local who could help you out?"

"We've been through this *before*," Esther snapped in exasperation. "I've been through everyone within a twenty-mile radius and not one of them is what Archie needs."

Caroline considered this, then had a thought. "You haven't been through everyone."

"What?"

"You haven't been through everyone," she repeated. "There are twenty men within twenty yards of the house and you haven't asked any of them."

Esther gaped at her then barked out a laugh. "Very funny, Caro."

"I'm not trying to be funny, Essie. I'm serious."

Esther looked askance at her friend. "You can't be serious," she spluttered. "Most of them haven't got a word of English never mind Latin! And what about mathematics? Geography and history? *English* history. You hardly expect a German to know anything about that!"

"Have you asked any of them?" Caro said reasonably.

"No, I have not!" Esther began to pace again.

"And are you going to?"

"No!" Esther bit out her reply.

"Why not?"

Esther threw her hands in the air. "I don't know, Caro! Because it's a stupid idea?" She stopped and put her hands on her hips, chewing her lip. "Maybe I could send a telegram to the agency again," she said absentmindedly.

It was Caroline's turn to laugh. "You said they were idiots a moment ago."

"Well, what you've come up with isn't far from idiotic

either," Esther snorted.

Caro looked affronted. "Well, if you can come up with a better idea …" She turned back to the fire and cracked open her book.

"I'll figure something out," Esther muttered.

Chapter Seven

A week later, Esther still hadn't come up with a plan to educate her son. Part of the problem was that there were too many other things to think about. The weather picked up enough for the men to be put to work bringing the estate's sheep down off the braes to be shorn and dipped. Much to her delight, Esther discovered some of the men came from farming backgrounds and were no stranger to handling animals. It meant that those who knew what they were doing could instruct those who didn't without also having to overcome the barrier of language.

However, the residents of Kirkmore still remained vigilant when it came to guarding the Germans, especially when they took the prisoners up the hills, for fear some of the men might wander off either accidently or on purpose.

The whole community brought their sheep down off the spring grazing for shearing but, of course, the McAllister flock was the largest. Fraser had put in a permanent plunge dipping-trough in the twenties which every sheep in the district passed through at least once in their lives. Firstly, however, all the flock were run through the river to wash the wool. Esther stayed to oversee this since it was important that none of the sheep were either caught in the current or pushed under by the scrabbling, shoving bodies of their friends. She also worried that there would be friction between the men, local and foreign. But it was a joy for her to watch them all working together, sharing cigarettes and laughing at their misunderstandings rather than cursing each other's differences, all determined to do their job well.

Believing that things would likely get along just fine without her, Esther left the men to their own devices, dropping by to check on progress every hour or so.

When the school day finished, many of the Kirkmore children drifted down to watch the shearing and dipping. They sat atop the walls and gates surrounding the sheep pens, chattering like swallows on a rafter. Archie and Florence were among them: as much part of the village's gang of children as the offspring of the labourers. It made Esther think of her own youth spent in the same way with Drew and all the others. Never had it occurred to her while sitting amongst the other children that she would one day oversee this annual event.

It was late in the afternoon when Esther decided to take her two dogs back to the house. They were getting irritable surrounded by the other farmers' sheepdogs and she didn't want a dogfight to break out in the middle of so many animals and people. Florence slid off her perch and ran over, ostensibly to walk back with her mother but really to play with the dogs. Like her mother, Florrie had an affinity with animals. She loved nothing more than running after every furry creature in the vicinity and attempting to give whatever it might be a good pat or cuddle, whether they wanted one or not.

Knowing their route home, the dogs ran ahead, bashing into one another and snapping at each other's legs in play. Florence scuttled after them, leaving her mother trailing in her wake. As Esther followed her daughter, she spotted a prisoner carrying a crate of glass water bottles on his way back to the plunge pit. She was surprised that it was he and not one of the local men who had been sent to fetch water for the workers but then she recognised him as one of Cary Eden's more trusted prisoners. The dogs paid him no attention which Esther took as a good sign. She always felt dogs were a better judge of character than humans.

When Florrie finally caught up with them, the two hounds were absorbed in a wrestling match not far from where the man walked. Esther was just about to shout a warning not to disturb the dogs mid-game when one of them broke off, running blindly away from its pursuer and straight into Florrie. The dog caught her in the midriff, knocking her flat on her back, then ran off, carrying on with the game. Florence was momentarily silenced by the shock of the impact before she began to scream.

Esther broke into a run, but she was still a distance away. Instead, the prisoner quickly plonked down his crate and rushed over, crouching down beside Florrie. She stopped screaming as he proffered a hand and, rather than shrink from him as Esther expected, she reached out and grasped it. Stunned and hurt, the child sobbed noisily while remaining on the ground. Still too far away, Esther did not hear what the man said to her daughter when he bowed his head to her – long honey-blonde locks beside short, slightly darker golden ones. Watching, Esther saw her usually shy little girl wrap her arms around the man's neck before he stood, lifting her off the ground and cradling her to his chest.

Esther slowed to a walk, disconcerted by the ease with which these two strangers clung to one another. If anyone other than Esther had seen them, they would have thought the pair were father and daughter. She tried to think if there was ever a time when Florrie's own father held her so tenderly.

As Florrie continued to cry on his shoulder, he made soft hushing noises while gently trying to brush the dust off the back of her pinafore.

"It's all right, it's okay," he murmured in subtly accented English. "Nothing broken? Nothing going to fall off?" He loosened the hold she had on his neck so he could search her face. Florence gave him a watery giggle but then dived for his shoulder again as further tears flowed down her red cheeks.

Esther finally reached them, but the prisoner made no move to release her daughter. And, even when Esther placed a conciliatory hand on Florrie's shoulder, she remained resolutely wrapped in the German's arms.

"Oh Florrie!" she crooned. "Jasper was very naughty, wasn't he?" She leant in to her little girl. "Shall we find him and give him a good talking- to?"

Florence hiccupped out a tiny laugh and turned to look at her mother, laying her temple just above the man's collarbone. She wiped her face with a small, slightly grubby hand, her face level with Esther's own. Standing mere inches from the tall German, Esther watched mutely as her daughter played absentmindedly with a small hole in the front of the man's shirt. She could smell the scents of damp laundry, dust and sweat. They were the honest fragrances of the men she grew up with – the smells of happy memories and hard work.

"What's going on here!"

Esther jumped as though she had been electrocuted.

The German whirled around to see Muldoon approaching with a hunting rifle in his hands. He stiffened and, without taking his eyes off the gamekeeper, disentangled Florence's short limbs from his long ones and handed her to her mother.

Muldoon continued to stalk towards them. *"What do you think you're doing here?"* he snarled. "You're not here to stand around idling. You're here to work or you can go back to whatever hole it was you crawled out of!"

"Muldoon!" Esther's voice cracked like a whip through

the stillness of the warm afternoon. "You will not speak to anybody on this estate in such a manner. Do you understand?"

The gillie's eyes remained fixed on the prisoner.

"Muldoon," she repeated coldly.

The gamekeeper reluctantly dragged his gaze away from the German and turned it on Esther. His insolent regard made her bristle as did his throwaway, "Aye, *mistress*," which he delivered before casting one more murderous stare at the prisoner, about-turning and striding off.

Hissing out air through her clenched teeth, Esther did her best not to say something she shouldn't in front of her child and a prisoner.

They both stood and watched the receding figure of the gillie, and finally she felt calm enough to speak.

"Thank you," she said with feeling, turning to meet the man's gaze.

Unlike Muldoon's, his was warm and open despite the cool, dark, blue-grey of his irises. They stood out in sharp contrast against his lightly tanned skin and flaxen hair.

"What's your name, soldier?"

"Petersen," he replied promptly. "Michael Petersen." He inclined his head.

"Well, Mr Petersen, thank you for helping Florrie. It was very kind of you."

"My pleasure, Mrs McAllister." He smiled slightly then looked at Florence – who was now sucking her thumb – and winked.

With that, he picked up his crate of water bottles and carried on about his business. But not before Esther saw the small contented smile that played with the corners of his lips.

Chapter Eight

Two days later, after the workday was finished and, spurred on by her positive encounter with one of the prisoners, Esther visited their barracks with the impassive Major Brown by her side. In her right hand she had a basket of Beattie's finest produce: new potatoes, leeks, carrots and a string of onions from last autumn. In her left, she had half a dozen dead pheasants tied together with string. She and Caro had gone out on a little hunting trip that morning and had come back with a decent bag. When she was dividing up the birds, she made sure to set aside enough for the prisoners. Their first month on the estate was up and she wanted to thank them for their hard work and good behaviour. She said as much as she placed her offerings on the table.

There were murmurs of appreciation from the men as they stood from their chairs and beds before coming over to inspect the produce. The oldest man in the group, who was probably not much more than forty but looked older, made a beeline for the pile of pheasants. Esther knew he was a Bavarian farmer the others called Alt Hans – Old Hans. With surprisingly dexterous fingers, he unknotted the string that bound their feet and extracted a single bird before taking a stool by the stove and beginning to pluck it. He paused, directing two boys to take a bird each, before he began to explain to them how one went about defeathering a pheasant. Though Esther didn't understand a word he said, the meaning of his quiet exchanges was perfectly intelligible to her. She spoke the same language as Alt Hans did: the language of the countryside.

She dragged her eyes from the men gathered around the fire and took a deep breath. Pitching her voice slightly above the growing hum of the men's conversation, she said, "I also have a favour to ask."

Though many of the men had minimal English, her interruption made them pause mid-discussion. With all eyes on her, Esther felt her stomach drop several inches. She fought to keep her nerve and plough on.

"Many of you may be aware that I have a son," she began.

To her right, Major Brown fidgeted. He had made it clear that he was uncomfortable with her plan but had enough trust in her judgement to allow her to take the floor among the men.

"My son needs a tutor who will teach him in the subjects of mathematics, Latin, history, geography and possibly languages too. German, maybe some French." Her words sounded so foolish as they rang in the silence of the room. But she had come this far so she might as well keep going. "I've spent many years looking for suitable tutors and none have lasted the course. If any of you are able and would be willing to help me, I'd very much appreciate it." She finished in a rush and didn't look at anyone, instead focusing on the basket of vegetables on the table. "I hope you enjoy the food," she mumbled before beating a hasty retreat.

Alt Hans was a simple man but someone all of them had come to respect and defer judgement to. He had a sensible head on his shoulders, not often swayed by prejudice or popular opinion. If you asked Hans a reasonable question, he deliberated carefully before giving a reasonable answer. However, his grasp of English was minimal, so he had to rely on the other men to translate for him.

"What did the lady ask?" he asked no one in particular. His eyes never left the breast of the bird he was methodically plucking, a pile of feathers growing around his booted feet.

"She wants to know if one of us could teach her son," one of the men answered.

There was a murmur of surprise from the prisoners.

The man who answered continued, barking out a bitter laugh. "Who does she think we are? Pets to perform whatever trick takes her fancy?"

"She knows nothing of who we are," Hans replied sharply, "because none of us have told her."

"She knows you're a farmer," Max, who had made friends with Bob the pony, spoke in a voice only loud enough for Hans to hear.

"She knows I am a farmer because I told her so," he replied patiently. "But she does not know that you are a stable lad because you never told her. Perhaps she would allow you to work in the stables sometimes if you asked."

"Do you think so?" Max's voice betrayed his wonder that such a thing might be possible.

Everyone in the group noticed the way his gaze and feet lingered every time they passed by the stable block. But he couldn't seem to pluck up the courage to enter through the carriage doors once again. His nerve always failed him since he assumed such a thing would be absolutely prohibited and would result in his immediate expulsion from Kirkmore. And if there was one thing every man was certain of, it was that they wanted to stay on the estate. It was the best place many of them had been for years. Even though the work was hard, at Kirkmore they were afforded the luxuries of adequate shelter, marginally better clothing, much better food and a sense of freedom that was seldom felt by a prisoner. Though always supervised, there was a certain amount of ease with which their superiors dealt with them. They were not press-ganged or threatened with blades and bullets. Their foreman was a genial sort who allowed them breaks during their workday – who never raised the alarm when one of the men walked off to relieve himself. Major Brown – though a stickler for cleanliness and manners – did not lord it over them as other men in his position might have. He was familiar with them, interested in what they said, keen to hear of any problems and, by the end of the second day, knew every one of them by name. Even Mrs McAllister, who they only usually saw at a distance, was kind to them. The only person they experienced any hostility from was the gamekeeper.

Yet some of the prisoners simply resented their situation on principle.

"I wouldn't get your hopes up if I were you, young Max," drawled another man.

Hans' nostrils flared but it was his only outward sign of displeasure. "As long as no one has any objections – yours don't count, Dieter –" he said sharply before the other man could cut in, "I think if we can help Mrs McAllister, we should. She has been very good to us so far and it is only right that we should behave accordingly."

Dieter muttered something that sounded distinctly like the word bribery.

"And so what if she gives us something in return?" Hans called across the room sharply, his temper finally showing. "Bribes you call them? So what? We work for her, she is grateful. She is prohibited from paying us more so she pays us in kind. I see no problem with that. I have spent far too many months hungry and cold and wet to resent what she might give us. And she does not do it because she has to.

She need not give us anything for our efforts. Yet she does because she is a *good, kind* woman."

It was more than he had ever said on any topic they questioned him on, but Hans felt he had to say it. He feared the restlessness of others amongst them and did not want that restlessness and resentment to be directed at Mrs McAllister. He was old enough to know that they had all been dealt a good hand when they were picked to work at Kirkmore. And he'd be damned if he let one hot-head ruin it for the rest of them.

"If any of us can help Mrs McAllister with her troubles, then we should," he said with quiet finality.

It was not until after the men had eaten their supper that one of the group approached Hans.

"Do you really think I should offer to help her?" he asked without preamble.

Hans looked up into the other man's face. "If you feel you can help her, then I think you must," he answered evenly.

"All right then. I'll speak with her tomorrow."

A rare smile tightened Hans' lips. "Good man."

Chapter Nine

Michael Petersen approached Major Brown the next morning and asked if Mrs McAllister was still looking for a tutor.

"As far as I know she is," Brown answered dryly. He still wasn't that keen on the idea, but he wasn't going to prevent anyone from speaking to the mistress either. "I'll let her know if she comes by today."

Late in the afternoon, Esther was standing at the edge of the field observing the men when Major Brown brought Petersen over.

"Mr Petersen!" she said, greeting him with a smile. The Major had already told her that the German wanted to speak with her. She tried not to seem too eager in case he was not what she was looking for. Disappointment and potential tutors for her son seemed to go hand in hand but she wanted to hear him out nonetheless. "What can I do for you?"

"I think, perhaps, I might be able to do something for you," he said hesitantly. "I have some experience as a teacher."

Esther waited for him to say more but he didn't.

Instead, he looked nervously over at his compatriots still labouring in the field while they threw curious glances back at him.

Sensing he wasn't quite comfortable having an audience observing their conversation, she said, "Why don't we discuss it later this evening? When you're finished?"

"That might be better," he conceded.

"Excellent. Perhaps you could bring him up to the house then, Major?"

"Very well."

Petersen didn't look overly enthusiastic about that idea either but nodded. "Later."

'Later' found Esther sitting at a large desk with summer evening light streaming across the floor of the study but not quite reaching far enough into the room to touch her. The desk lamp was on and she was poring over purchase orders from their seed supplier. They still hadn't paid for their spring seeds but, before she did, she wanted to check what was on the paperwork against what was currently growing in the fields. She knew that the carrots were disappointing, but she wasn't sure if that was due to poor quality seed – since she couldn't remember whether they had purchased new seeds this year or whether they were using the leftovers from the year before. There, in black and white, she saw the words *'carrot seeds'* and growled audibly.

"Mrs McAllister?"

Esther jerked her head up to see the tall German framed in the doorway. She often left the door open. It was her way of saying that she was willing to talk to everyone. She also liked to hear the sounds of the house – all the comings and goings. However, she hadn't heard Petersen approach. It surprised her considering he was such a big man. And it was also somewhat disconcerting. It was also surprising that Major Brown had not escorted the prisoner in. She took it as a good sign, however. It meant the Major had real trust in the German. As these thoughts flew through her mind Petersen continued to stand half in shadow, lingering on the hall side of the threshold, his hand resting on the door frame.

"Is this a bad time?" he asked.

Shaking her head as much to clear it as to deny his question, she beckoned him in with one hand while shuffling her papers away with the other. "No, no. Come in, come in."

He crossed the room and stood before her on the rug, feet together, hands behind his back, chest out. His gaze was directed at the wall above her head.

"I meant come in and sit down," she chuckled.

He looked at her, hesitating. "Are you certain, madam?"

"Of course, please sit down. You're making the place look untidy."

He smiled then. An easy, charming quirk of the lips which eclipsed his usually serious, impassive expression. "Thank you, madam," he said as he folded his large frame into a hardwood chair on the far side of the desk. Esther felt momentarily guilty as she leant back into the extravagant depths of her own seat but then she remembered her place. She was in control.

"So," she said officiously, "you think you might be able to help me?"

"Perhaps," he said with a shrug. "I was a tutor before. Many years ago."

"It can't be that long ago. You hardly look older than me," she said sharply.

Humour flickered across his face once more before it was eclipsed by sadness. "War always makes peace feel distant," he said quietly.

His accent was subtle, his words intelligent. They made Esther sit up, curious.

"So you were a teacher, in peacetime?"

"I was an academic – the Greats – a classics scholar," he clarified. "I tutored in the evenings, sometimes weekends. Mostly boys around your son's age and older."

"What did you teach them?"

"A little Greek, more Latin, Greco-Roman history, some more modern history as per my own interests. I had to help a few boys with mathematics and I taught German too. I have only basic French. My knowledge of European geography is good. Or it was before the war. Now I'm not so sure." He bowed his head.

"You say you taught them German?" she asked, confused.

"Yes," he paused. "They were English boys."

"In Germany?"

"No. I was student in England. In Oxford. That's where I tutored as well." He said it as if it were the simplest, most normal thing in the world.

"Oh!" Esther tried to hide the avidity of her gaze.

For years she had paid through the nose to bring teachers and scholars from various towns and cities across the north of the country for her son and not one of them had lasted the course. Yet here was a man sitting quietly across from her who appeared to possess almost every attribute she sought. And he had landed in her lap, hidden amongst a consignment of prison-camp labourers. She wondered what other unexplored talents the men working her fields might possess. But then she checked her own wandering imagination. She was always sure that the next man she hired to educate her son would finally be the right one, only to be disappointed once again. Perhaps employing Petersen would yield the same results. The only way she would know for sure was to allow him access to her son. But a little chill went through her as she suddenly became acutely aware that the man before her was not just formerly an academic but formerly a soldier of some description too. No doubt he was a killer of men. *British men.* And she was about to offer up her British son to him.

Sitting back, she studied him. He met her scrutiny without flinching, his breathing calm. His face was open, his eyes warm and kind. For a moment, she could see the academic instead of the soldier. Or perhaps she simply saw the man. In her mind's eye she remembered the way he held Florence, their flaxen heads glowing angelically as they bent towards one another in the golden glow of afternoon sunlight. He was so gentle with her, so caring. Esther felt instinctively that she could trust him.

"You're ditching tomorrow, are you not?" she asked, knowing the answer already.

The village had asked if the POWs could help clear the overgrown ditches that had been neglected during the war. The trenches had clogged with the detritus of autumn leaves and fallen branches which meant that once the heavy rain and snowmelt came, the water backed up, overflowing its confines. Several houses in the low-lying parts of the village flooded and their cottage gardens had been damaged that spring. It was the last thing the residents of Kirkmore needed when times were tough enough as it was. The ditches needed fixing and Esther was providing the workforce to do it.

"Yes," Petersen nodded. "For the next two days."

"All right. On Friday you'll be working the potato fields behind the garden. You'll be finishing a little earlier and Archie won't have to worry about school in the morning. How about you come in the evening, after you've eaten? Does that sound like a plan?" she asked.

"Whatever you say, madam," he said with a small incline of his head.

"Of course, our arrangement doesn't need to reach the ears of the War Ag or your old camp," she added as an afterthought.

"Of course," he agreed.

"Good! Friday evening then."

She stood and extended her hand across the wide expanse of the table. As Petersen pushed out of his chair and reached to shake it, she wondered whether a stranger bargain had ever been sealed over the desk in her study. Their fingers clasped. She could feel the roughness of his weather-and-work-worn skin. She wondered if he was surprised by the roughness of her own hands.

"Until Friday, Mrs McAllister." His grip on her hand lingered.

"Until then, Mr Petersen."

"Goodnight, Mrs McAllister," he murmured, studying her face in the light of the lamp on her desk.

"Goodnight, Mr Petersen."

She returned to her paperwork after he left. How much longer would she spend poring over it tonight? One thing was for sure: it was neither the first nor the last time such things kept her awake.

Chapter Ten

When Friday arrived, the morning was chillier than it had been during the week. However, as the sun began to climb in the cloudless sky, its unfiltered heat warmed the earth and the people who worked it. The prisoners had all started their day with jumpers or jackets on, only to divest themselves of their outer layers as they travelled further up the field, leaving small mounds of fabric and wool in their wake. By evening, the sun was still glowing with the warmth of the day, calling on everyone to come outside and play.

Petersen was still in his shirtsleeves when he knocked on the doorframe of Esther's study ready for his introduction to her son who fidgeted in his seat, longing to be outdoors.

Archie huffed audibly as his mother stood to greet the German. She threw him a warning glance and he had the presence of mind to drop his head submissively.

"Good evening, Mr Petersen. I hope you're well," Esther said brightly.

"I am, thank you, madam." His regard slid past Esther quite quickly and rested on the boy who resolutely ignored him. "And this must be the young Master McAllister," he said pointedly, forcing Archie to look at him.

The child's head snapped up. "Nobody ever calls me

Master McAllister," he replied unhappily. "They still call my brother that and he's *old*."

Petersen couldn't hide his surprise. He threw a quick glance at Esther who was watching her son. She didn't look old enough to have another child but maybe she was just one of those women who, despite everything, looked younger than they were.

"So, what should I call you then?" he asked, tearing his eyes away from the boy's mother. "Archibald?"

The boy's mouth puckered as if he had just tasted something disgustingly sour. "No one ever calls me *Archibald*," he said witheringly. He shivered with revulsion. "Only my father and only if he thinks I've been naughty." The way he said it made it sound as if he felt distinctly hard done by when his father accused him of misbehaviour.

It was the big German's turn to drop his head but not before Esther saw the smile slide across his face.

"All right. What then?" He was surprised that she hadn't yet intervened as many parents would. Instead, she was giving the boy the chance to speak for himself.

Her child surveyed the tall prisoner looking down on him with lively, expectant eyes. The youngster's experience with tutors had affected his opinion of the breed as negatively as it had his mother. He knew the type well. Whether young or old, their uniform was a tweed coat with elbow patches, trousers with worn knees and a pair of scuffed brown shoes. Also, he was nearly certain that all of them wore spectacles. Yet, the man who stood in front of him in his shirtsleeves looked nothing like what he had come to expect.

Esther surveyed Mr Petersen much as her son did. He stood up straight, casually throwing back his broad, muscular shoulders – not at all like other academics who walked with a permanent stoop from sitting in chairs too long. His face was expressive rather than closed off, radiating good humour rather than the preternatural irritation that clung to the teachers of small, unruly boys. However, even though the German's expression was benign, there was clearly a steel core of discipline that ran through him. He was not someone to be crossed. But then perhaps that was the soldier in him rather than the scholar.

"Why don't you just call me Archie?" the boy said.

"Archie it is then." The prisoner proffered his hand and the boy took it, gawping as everything south of his wrist disappeared into the man's large palm. "But then you must call me Michael. Mr Petersen makes me feel very old."

"But you *are* old," Archie said with a huff.

Petersen cocked his head to one side, examining the boy. "True," he said evenly. "But age commands respect. You would do well to remember that."

Esther assessed the two people in front of her, wondering should she intervene as they stared each other down. Archie seemed to be holding his breath as he decided whether to defy his new teacher from the off. Petersen appeared to be perfectly calm as he held the boy's gaze.

Finally, Archie looked away. "Yes, sir," he muttered.

"Michael, please," the German replied mildly. "Now, I thought we might start with Latin. I'm not sure how much you know so I thought we could begin with a little practical application of the language, if," here he looked to Esther, "Mrs McAllister has no objections?"

"Not at all," she answered, perplexed. She was about to tell him there was a table set up in the library next door for him but the German was already striding across the floor to the French doors leading out to the garden.

"Are you coming?" Petersen asked, looking back to see the boy still standing by his chair.

"Outside?" Archie asked incredulously.

"Of course. I want to test you on Latin nouns. For

instance, do you know the Latin for 'tree'?" He flung open the door and stood to the side to allow the boy to pass.

Archie all but ran out onto the patio. Then he paused briefly, his face scrunched in concentration as he trawled through his imperfect knowledge of the language. "*Arbor*?" he asked doubtfully.

The German smiled. "Very good! Let's see what else we can find."

As Archie hurried off ahead of him, Petersen hesitated at the door for a moment.

"Is this all right?" he asked Esther.

"Just as long as you don't go too far," she said with a tight smile. She had planned to listen in on their lesson through the connecting door between the study and the library but hadn't factored in their little field trip. She felt like she was losing control of the situation already.

"We'll stay where you can see us," he assured her. Then, quietly, he added, "No harm will come to your son while he is in my care. You have my word."

Esther felt slightly guilty that her fear must have shown on her face. Otherwise, why would he have made such a promise? But she was grateful that he made it anyway without appearing offended by her mistrust. Still standing where they left her, she could hear her son's excited falsetto mingled with the much calmer bass tones of his teacher. As the strange music of their voices bounced off the back wall of the house and drifted in through the French doors, Esther began to relax. She dropped her shoulders and sat at her desk. She had enough to do without watching the German's every move. If she couldn't leave them alone together, what was the point of having Petersen teach her son in the first place? However, she could not sit for long and every now and again got up to peer out at the man and boy as they walked among flowers, shrubs and patches of vegetables.

She could not help but watch as they moved about, sometimes one leading the way, then the other, always talking, gesticulating, laughing. Even from a distance, Archie radiated pleasure, having found someone not only willing to teach him but also willing to listen. Esther always thought listening was an important but often lacking skill when people found themselves in the company of children. She could sympathise. In the world of men, women were often infantilized as much as children.

Gradually, the time between getting up to check her son and then sitting down again stretched as Esther found herself absorbed by work. She barely heard Archie as he clattered along the patio before barrelling in the door and skidding to a halt in front of her desk, eyes shining. Petersen's entry was a little more subdued, but he was smiling nonetheless. Esther noted with some surprise that, though the sky behind him was still light, the sun had slid down behind the braes for the evening. She hadn't even felt the air turn chilly, wrapped as she was in a large winter cardigan. Petersen dutifully closed and locked the French doors before coming further into the room.

"I know how to say everything in the garden in Latin now, Mummy!" Archie announced proudly, lifting himself off the floor as he leant his hands against the desk. "Can Michael come again tomorrow?"

"Mr Petersen has to go back to his camp tomorrow," Esther said calmly, trying to defuse some of Archie's energy.

It was as if the boy experienced a power outage. His whole body slumped and the brightness drained from his face. "For good?" he asked in horror.

Michael laughed. "No, Archie, I have to go back to camp to collect my wages. Afterwards, I'm free to teach you again if you and your mother are happy with the arrangement." Here he looked at Esther but it was Archie who answered.

"You can come again tomorrow evening, then. He can come again tomorrow, can't he?"

Esther couldn't deny him. The look of hope on his face made her throat tighten. "If he's free, then of course."

"How about the same time tomorrow?" the German looked between the two McAllisters, unsure which one he was asking.

"Perfect," Esther answered.

"Is there somewhere we can work inside?" was Petersen's next question. He ignored the look of alarm on Archie's face, addressing himself only to Esther. "He knows what everything in the garden is called but I want to make sure he can spell it too," he said a little more sternly, flashing his eyes at his pupil.

Esther smiled. "There's a desk set up next door," she said, getting to her feet.

"I'll show him!" Archie volunteered, heading for the door hidden in the wall panelling to Esther's right.

Both adults followed the boy at a more sedate pace with Petersen pausing at the door to murmur, "After you," allowing Esther to enter the room before him.

All these years later and even when she knew every inch of the house, the library was still Esther's favourite room. She loved the smell of polished wood, the cold stone fireplace and, most importantly, the slightly sweet scent of paper and old leather that almost made her sneeze when she breathed it in. It was an enormous room and always slightly chilly but she didn't care. It was home.

Behind her, Petersen muttered something in German. "It's beautiful," he said in an awed whisper. Without invitation, he reached out and bumped his fingertips along the spines of shelved books. The sheer delight in his face as he turned to Esther was rivalled only by Archie's who stood in the centre of the room, smugly lording it over all he surveyed.

"You like it," Archie said with certainty.

"How could I not?" There was still a hint of distracted wonder in Petersen's voice as he stretched to an impossibly high shelf, pulling a book out. "Sophocles," he crooned, holding the book tenderly in both hands.

"I wish I was that tall," Archie mumbled, eyes still on the gap where the book had come from.

"Come here." Petersen beckoned, putting down his book and heading to another shelf. Archie trotted over and without warning, the German caught him by the waist and lifted him onto his right shoulder. The boy grabbed hold of Petersen's forearms, letting out a little yelp of shock. "Could you bring down the book to your right, please? *Treasure Island*." He sounded perfectly unimpeded by the weight of a not-so-small boy on his shoulder. Job done, he neatly set Archie down again. "Would you like to read the first chapter with me and then we'll finish for the night?"

A smile crept across Archie's face and he nodded enthusiastically.

Petersen steered the boy across to the desk and they sat, companionably poring over their new treasure. Esther slipped quietly from the room back to her study. She left the door ajar so she could hear the slow childish struggle mixed with the assured susurration of Petersen as he took over when her son got tired. When she thought it was time for the lesson to end, She stole back into the library and waited by the door. Petersen's eyes flickered upwards when she entered but he continued to read, his deep voice calm yet animated. However, Esther's attention was focused not on her son but on her daughter.

Florence was standing in her floor-length pale-pink nightdress, half hidden behind the door into the main hall. Her tiny hands were gripping the thick dark wood of the edge just below the lock and her cheek rested on her knuckles. She was completely still, enthralled by the tale that was being told a few yards away. She should have been in bed. Yet Esther couldn't be cross with her daughter for being drawn to the sounds of the German. The colour and vitality he gave the story was captivating: the high, adolescent voice of Jim Hawkins and the heavy drone of Billy Bones.

Esther was sure they had gone much further than the end of the first chapter. Even so, when Petersen's steady reading came to an end and he reached for a fold of paper to mark the page, Archie begged for more.

"Just one more chapter, Michael, please!"

Even Florence came out of hiding to stand a little closer, as if her proximity to Petersen might somehow influence him to continue.

"I think we should leave it for another day," the German said lightly but firmly. "I don't want to lose my voice now, do I? How would I shout at you if you misbehaved when I have no voice?" he added, bumping his shoulder against Archie's.

"But I *don't* misbehave!" Archie replied earnestly.

"Yes, you do!" Florence piped up, making man and boy start. They hadn't noticed her at all. "You fed all your broccoli to Jasper at dinner this evening when Mummy wasn't looking."

Both adults bit their lips as Archie reddened, swelling like an angry toad, his face contorting with rage as he rose to advance on his little sister. "I did *not*, Florrie! It's not true! Tell them!" he said, spotting his mother for the first time but also not wanting to lose face in front of his new tutor.

Florence, to her credit, stood her ground in the face of her brother's indignation, chin held high, fists clenched. "It *is* true and you know it!" she shrilled.

"All right!" Esther's voice was pitched just loud enough for it to brook no argument. Still, she crossed the room with hands held out between her children in case they decided to launch themselves at each another. "Whether Archie ate his broccoli or not is hardly worth an argument. Besides, we'll be having broccoli tomorrow for dinner and Archie will prove how good he is at eating it then, won't he?" Esther smiled kindly at her son, knowing full well that his vegetables had ended up in the dog that evening.

His face fell before he was quick enough to hide his disappointment. "Yes, Mother," he huffed.

"Now – bed! Both of you." She clapped her hands and began chivvying them towards the door. "If you wouldn't mind waiting, Mr Petersen, I'll be back to you in a moment."

Esther found the children's nanny, Mary, at the top of the staircase.

"Oh, you little maggot!" Mary said crossly as she took Florrie by the hand. "We said there'd be no more wandering after bedtime!" She gave Esther a small apologetic smile.

"But I couldn't sleep," Florrie protested

"Well, you aren't going to sleep standing up, are you?" Though Mary always seemed exasperated by the antics of the children, there was a deep-rooted affection there too.

"Horses sleep standing up," Archie offered only to receive a withering glance from the nanny.

Giving both children a kiss on the forehead before Mary began towing them to bed, Esther watched their receding forms head down the long corridor. "Goodnight, sweethearts!" she called softly after them as the three continued to bicker.

Once they disappeared from view, she descended the stairs and returned to the library to find Petersen standing at the far side of the room with his hands behind his back. Craning his neck to see what other treasures rested on the shelves, he did not hear Esther's re-entry. His pale shirt and colouring stood out in sharp relief against the dark spines of the books before him. For the first time since they met, she saw the shape of the man – the physical bulk of him – without any other distractions.

He was tall – but then she knew that already having come only to his shoulder when he held Florence after she fell. What she hadn't appreciated was the breadth of his shoulders. It was exaggerated by the position of his clasped hands resting just below his tailbone and drew the eye to his narrow hips. The maroon trousers that encased his legs were gathered at the waist by a woven belt before sweeping over his hips and dropping straight to the floor without hinting at the shape of his long limbs. However, as Esther's gaze travelled down the length of his body, it was arrested by an angry red slash on the underside of German's left forearm.

The scar cut its way down his arm from elbow to wrist, a long bulging rope of red and white tissue which marred his flesh. She felt a pang of sadness as she compared the damaged left arm with the untouched translucent surface of his right which was webbed only with the cord-like shadows of his protruding veins.

The war. This was what it did to young men. If the slash on his arm was the only injury Petersen carried from the war, he got off lightly. She wondered whether there were more scars hidden under his clothing. So many men and boys were coming home with bodies bearing marks of the violence they had suffered, the violence they had themselves carried out. They covered up what they could, never flaunting their maimed limbs as they tried to forget their war years and pick up what remained of the life they left behind. But many of them were unable to forget. It was their memories that bore the worst scars.

Petersen glanced over his shoulder and spotted the mistress of Kirkmore standing by the door, her eyes fixed on his back. He hastily rearranged his limbs and faced her, the look of a guilty schoolboy clinging to his features. "Mrs McAllister. I didn't hear you coming back." He shifted awkwardly under her scrutiny. "You managed to settle the children, I hope?"

Esther blinked rapidly as if waking from a trance. "Yes, yes, of course." She gave him a smile that didn't touch her eyes then gestured towards the study. "Shall we?'

Petersen again allowed her to pass through the doorway before him – then, once he followed her into the room, waited until Esther gave him permission to sit.

"Well, I think you'll agree that that went rather well," Esther began with airy enthusiasm, her fascination with the contours of his body pushed aside in favour of the business at hand. "I've never seen Archie enjoy a lesson so much."

Petersen gave a small smile, not meeting her eye. "He's a good student. Curious. I find that's half the battle."

"Aren't all children curious?" Esther countered.

He gave a humourless chuckle. "You'd be surprised. It's why I prefer to start with nouns when teaching Latin. Children often get confused and frustrated when you try to teach them the intricacies of grammar. Especially before they have sufficient interest in the language to learn it."

"Indeed." Esther fought to keep the surprise from showing on her face. It was rare that she came across a Briton who could use his own language as eloquently as the German sitting in front of her did. It was also odd to find someone who approached teaching in such an unorthodox way. The educators she previously came across all sang from the same droning hymn sheet and were completely incapable of changing their ways.

"I will, of course, teach him the necessary grammar and verbs in due course." A flicker of doubt passed over his face. "That is, if you want me to continue to teach him."

"Of course I do!" She laughed. "I don't think Archie would ever forgive me if that was your first and last lesson together."

"I'm glad." Petersen dropped his head to hide his relieved smile. Though he enjoyed work on the farm and liked the physical effort it took, he craved an outlet for the knowledge he had worked so hard to acquire. It was as if he and Archie McAllister were destined to meet one another. Though he hardly dared hope, the possibilities of what he could teach the boy had swiftly spooled through his head as they conversed in the garden. He was planning their lessons before they even set foot in the library where their opportunities for study grew even more.

Pulling at his mouth in an attempt to conceal his delight, Petersen realised too late that he was using the wrong hand.

"Does it still hurt?" Esther asked quietly as her eyes lingered on the scar.

The German thought he could hear sympathy in her voice, trace it in her looks. He crossed his arms over his chest, covering the injury. He didn't want her pity. "Not as much as it did," he said shortly.

"We all have scars," she said, her voice far away. "It is how we carry them that defines the way others perceive us and how we perceive ourselves."

"Yes," he said simply.

"Same time tomorrow, Mr Petersen?"

"Same time tomorrow," he answered with a nod.

"Goodnight then."

"Goodnight, Mrs McAllister."

Chapter Eleven

As July rattled on, the rhythm of life at Kirkmore settled into something akin to permanence. The Germans became part of the fabric of the estate as they continued to toil alongside the old hands, making many locals wonder how they ever managed without them. Though no one was particularly vocal about their admiration of their former enemy, the prisoners had managed to win the grudging regard of almost everyone within the first month and a half of their arrival. People were less wary of them and more inclined to attempt conversation even if it was conducted using a garbled combination of gesture and pidgin English. Some of them were even asked to dinner on Sundays after church.

Even the Germans themselves seemed happier. When they set out for work in the morning, they looked less bedraggled, no longer carrying themselves as if they had the weight of the world on their shoulders. Fewer men felt the need to dull their pain with chain-smoked nicotine. There was more horseplay, fewer haunted faces. They talked and laughed more frequently. The food they got at Kirkmore, supplemented as it was by the produce and game from the estate, was the best they had eaten in years. Not only that, for the first time since the war began, they had a safe place to sleep, warmth and the companionship of men who no longer feared whether they would see another sunrise. And, though the work was often hard and monotonous, it gave them pleasure to see that their efforts made a difference. At the end of the day, they could walk back through a freshly weeded field and see the clean brown soil that surrounded the tops of carrots or beets. When they cut an entire field of cabbages and saw them all neatly stacked in crates by the end of the day, each man felt a sense of pride in the work they had accomplished. What they were less happy with was the week of cooked cabbage that followed their harvest and the lingering smell of wet socks that the boiled leaves left behind.

The men were happy to be billeted at Kirkmore. No matter how hard the work was – or how bad the smell of cabbage in their quarters – the freedom they were afforded on the estate was far superior to the unvaried confines of the POW camp they left behind. The security of a good workplace was also preferable to the day-to-day jobs the men had been given on various smallholdings closer to the camp. On these farms, no one cared whether the workers were treated fairly. They sent the prisoners out under armed guard in all weathers with inadequate clothing and often under the supervision of a less-than-sympathetic foreman or indifferent farmer. It did not matter to those men whether the Germans liked them or not, since if there was any animosity between prisoners and landowners they were simply sent back to the camp. That uncertainty ate away at the men's souls, as did the hours of depthless time that stretched out before them. Unoccupied time gave them far too much empty space in their lives to fill with thinking and remembering. And, if there was one thinking soldiers hated to do, it was remembering the horrors of the war they had somehow managed to survive.

But it wasn't like that at Kirkmore and they were grateful for it. Aside from the work – which, given the size of the estate, was quite varied – there were other forms of entertainment that kept them occupied once their workday was over.

Hearing what powerful voices many of the Germans had in church on Sunday (even if they didn't know the words), the local vicar began a weekly singing group where he taught the men the hymns that would be sung in later services. The vicar's wife was even requisitioned to accompany them on an old piano which Esther found in one of the upstairs rooms in the main house. It had taken six prisoners the best part of half an hour, much sweat and some swearing to carry the instrument down the narrow back stairs to their quarters. Only then did they discover one of the Germans was, in fact, an excellent pianist who delighted in playing everything from the popular songs of Glenn Miller to Chopin. Soon, all the vicar's wife did was sit and listen as the men filled the space with music.

On their free evenings, while some men played cards and others read the German books from Fraser McAllister's collection in the library, there was a large group who took to carving wooden toys for the local children as well as various boxes, trinkets and figurines. The beauty and intricacy of their work gave rise to more admiration, as well as multiple gifts in kind from villagers keen to show their appreciation of the prisoners' offerings.

The only real clash that occurred between the new and old residents of Kirkmore transpired on the playing field. It had been years since the area had enough young men to field two football teams. Initially, matches were played with the Kirkmore lads on one side and the Germans opposing. But as they got to know one another better, for the sake of evenly matched teams, they began to mix. At the start of every match, two captains chose their men – just as thousands of schoolchildren did the world over – as the women and children gathered to cheer them on.

Had outsiders been privy to the goings-on of Kirkmore, there would, no doubt, have been hell to pay. Before the prisoners arrived, Esther and Major Brown had both been issued strict instructions that there was to be no fraternisation between the Germans and the locals. Esther was herself warned to keep away for fear the men would be unable to control their long-unsatisfied carnal desires. However, once she encountered the men on the first day, she surmised that the War Ag and camp commandant's warnings came from a lingering fear of the enemy Nazis rather than any true knowledge or understanding of the men themselves. Nothing the prisoners had said or done suggested to her that they were bent on mischief or destruction. All she saw were men making the best of a bad lot while continuing to hope that they might one day be free to go home.

Just as the other men found various pursuits to occupy their time, Michael Petersen increasingly found diversion in teaching Archie McAllister. His initial assessment of the boy as a good student proved correct as they settled down to a more formal education than that of their first lesson. They sat together for hours in the evening as the German awakened the boy's interest in science, history, Latin and German. They also spent entire evenings filling pages and pages with the solutions to mathematical problems taken from a textbook Esther had ordered from Edinburgh especially for their lessons. The French Petersen left to Esther since her knowledge of the language far outstripped his own.

However, it was not just Archie who benefitted from the German's tutelage. Florence was quite taken with Petersen and kept making excuses to come down to the library when he was there. At first, Esther was unaware of the little girl's evening visits to the lessons since Florrie was clever enough to remain out of her mother's line of sight. It wasn't until Esther happened to need some maps of the Kirkmore estate which were kept in the library that she finally caught her youngest out.

Entering the room silently so as not to disturb the lesson, Esther found herself rooted to the spot by what she saw. Michael and Archie were poring over a sum which she was sure was far too complicated for a boy who had turned nine just a few days before. However, while Archie sat on the chair to Petersen's left, Florence was perched on the prisoner's right knee, bending over a sheet of paper, absorbed in her own work with her tongue between her teeth. Though she thought about chastising Florrie for disrupting Archie's tuition, Esther couldn't justify any irritation. She was fascinated by how content the three of them looked together. On tiptoe, Esther edged around the room to better see what her daughter was doing.

On a blank page, Petersen had drawn widely spaced horizontal lines in black pen. At the top of the paper – also in pen – was the sentence '**The quick brown fox jumps over the lazy dog**' in neat easily legible letters. Florence had a death-grip on a pencil and was doing an admirable job of filling the page with her own efforts. The thing that most impressed Esther, however, was that the German seemed entirely unconcerned by the fact that Florrie was writing with her left hand.

Just the year before, Esther and the local schoolmistress clashed when the woman tried to force her daughter to use only her right hand. Though naturally left-handed, Esther too had been obliged to switch to the other hand in school. It wasn't until little Essie came home with welts from the strap on the palm of her sinful hand that Lizzie Muncie finally went to the teacher and gave her what for. As far as Lizzie was concerned, it didn't matter that her daughter was cack-handed as long as her writing was legible. And it most definitely was *not* when she wrote with her right. As a result,

Esther could write passably with both hands but her characters were functional rather than elegant and ladylike.

Finishing the final "g" with a flourish, Florence looked up to seek the approval of her teacher and came face to face with her mother. Guilt made her shrink into herself but, precariously positioned as she was, she began to slide off Petersen's knee. He caught her with fluid ease before glancing up to see what had disturbed her. Esther gave a little questioning quirk of her eyebrows, but he smiled and shook his head. Apparently, he was happy to entertain both children.

Though he didn't always teach her, Petersen seemed content to have the little girl mill about while he taught Archie. The one rule he had was that she was not to disturb them while they were in the middle of something. If she wanted him to give her an exercise, she was to leave a blank sheet of paper beside him on which he would trace another saying for her to copy or some simple sums for her to answer.

For the most part, Esther left them to their own devices. But sometimes her curiosity got the better of her and she was drawn to their strange little collective. She would stand at a distance, noting how Petersen spoke to them and how they responded. Each time the children succeeded in answering a question correctly, she would feel a little thrill of pride at their intelligence. However, she was never effusive in her praise of the children and neither was Petersen which she liked. Equally, she was pleased that he never seemed angry or disappointed when they got something wrong. He simply went over it again, correcting and explaining their faults before repeating the exercise until they got it right. It made Esther wonder what the world would be like if all children were offered such calm encouragement from the people who educated them.

In general, however, Esther dealt very little with Petersen except to ask about Archie's progress or to allow the German to take books from the library back to his quarters for the other men. After their first escapade into the garden, teacher and student very rarely left the library but when they passed through Esther's study one evening on their way out, she felt compelled to follow them. After waiting what she thought was an appropriate amount of time, she too headed outside, following the sounds of their voices through the maze of paths that wound their way through the garden's many vegetable and flower beds. As she approached, she recognised some German words smattered among those in English though she didn't know what they meant.

Rounding the end of a tall hedge, she came upon the three of them kneeling on the grass in front of one of the borders. It was laid out like a bed in a cottage garden with vegetables dotted amongst the profusion of flowers. Glancing up, Petersen silently beckoned Esther to join them, a grin lighting up his face. The three of them were intently focused on a patch of tiny violets struggling not to be swamped by the encircling buddleia bushes. The buddleias were alive with the buzz of insects. Flashes of contrasting colours alerted Esther to the presence of several orange butterflies flitting from bloom to bloom. She came to a halt beside Florence and knelt next to her daughter, her knees cracking in protest.

"*Shhh!*" Archie admonished, never taking his eyes off the violets or, more accurately, the tiny butterfly perched among the flowers.

It was one Esther had never seen before. Its wings which flapped lazily in the still air were an autumnal yellow-orange. Row upon row of black diamonds and zigzags fanned out from its body as far as the edges which were limned in a pearly blue-white. Surrounded by many much flashier members of the species like the Admiral and the Peacock, the unknown butterfly was all the more striking for its lone, delicate beauty. Esther sat in thrall to it just as the others did.

"In German, a butterfly is called *ein Schmetterling*," Petersen informed them quietly.

"Do you know what this one is?" Esther breathed.

He shook his head. "No. I don't know butterflies. I was hoping you might know."

"No, I don't."

They lapsed into a hushed reverence until the insect took to its wings and flew up over the buddleias and the hedge out of sight.

"*Bye, bye, little flutterby!*" Archie sang, jumping up to wave it off.

Florence got to her feet and stood on tiptoe as if she thought she might see over the hedge which was taller than everyone. "*Fly away home!*" she whispered sweetly.

Pettersen's gaze was still on the patch of violets the butterfly had just vacated. "My mother taught me a song about a butterfly when I was a little boy." In a voice barely more than a whisper, he began to sing in his native tongue.

He sang so quietly that neither of the children really heard him. They were too busy combing the border for more bugs to observe. But, kneeling by his side, Esther could hear what seemed to be the soft melody of a nursey rhyme. Even though the words were unintelligible, the gentle ups and downs in his voice were quite soothing until abruptly, mid-phrase, Petersen's breath caught. Looking into his face, Esther was shocked to see it streaked with tears. His skin was pallid, his eyes hollow and full of sorrow. She watched in horror as the man who was usually so cheerfully stoic gasped for breath. He fought the silent sobs as transparent droplets slid down his cheeks and neck into the collar of his shirt. It terrified Esther to see a strong, vigorous man like Petersen dissolve in front of her. Such outpourings of emotion were not meant to be witnessed.

"Archie! Florrie! Go and see if Beattie has any raspberries

for you before he leaves for the evening." She never took her eyes off the German as the two children squealed with delight and cantered off to find the gardener.

Still on her knees, Esther shuffled forward and took one of Petersen's clenched fists in both hands. She could feel its size, its strength, its warmth, as he tightened his fingers trying to suppress his grief through sheer force of will. She squeezed it firmly between her own hands, offering to strengthen his crumbling courage with her own. He choked, breath hitching as his chest rose and fell unevenly. Able to bear it no longer, Esther raised his fist to her lips and kissed his knuckles.

It was a strange thing for her to do. She wasn't normally the type to offer kisses as a form of comfort except to her children. Perhaps it was the fact that the big German seemed to be collapsing in on himself – shrinking, regressing – which prompted Esther to kiss his hand. Or perhaps he was so hell-bent on drowning in his own grief, all she wanted to do was shock him back to consciousness. What she didn't expect was for the air to leave his lungs altogether.

He simply stopped breathing and, panicked at the change, Esther reached for his face with one hand while still holding his fist with the other. "*Shh* …" she whispered. "*Shh* …" She leaned forward, unblinkingly holding his gaze. She had no idea why she was telling him to '*shhh*'. He was totally silent as it was. But it seemed appropriate. "Breathe," she said softly, gently stroking his cheek. "Just breathe." He coughed then began gulping in lungfuls of air. "Good!" she encouraged. "Just breathe. In and out, like me." She inhaled and exhaled to demonstrate, drinking in the scent of the garden. Carefully, he copied her, breathing audibly, his eyes never leaving hers.

Gradually, he began to calm and the air whistled less as he drew it into his nose. Esther gave him a small encouraging smile and withdrew her hand. When she did, he inclined his head slightly and rested his forehead against hers. For a brief moment, he closed his eyes then pulled back.

"I'm sorry," he said, swiping his palm across his cheek to clear the moisture away.

"It's all right," she murmured, looking away. She wanted to take his hand again but knew she shouldn't. She felt unaccountably sad that he no longer needed to leech courage from her touch. The feeling of his skin under her fingertips had been as comforting to her as it was to him.

She gave herself a little shake to clear her mind.

"We should go and find the children." Petersen rose to his feet and proffered a hand.

However, Esther did not see it and, instead, braced her fists on the ground to push herself up.

Together they walked the path to the raspberry canes, maintaining a safe distance between them by hugging opposite edges of the grass walkways. Neither spoke and, though she didn't look at him, Esther saw Petersen viciously scrub his face in her peripheral vision.

She so wanted to take his hand in her own once again. But she didn't.

Chapter Twelve

At the start of August, with Parliament enjoying its summer recess, Fraser McAllister finally came home for a short stay.

Esther hadn't seen her husband in seven months but there was no fanfare for his return. There was no one other than the stable lad, Alfie, at the train station to collect him. When he arrived at the house, he found the children in the lounge with their nanny and Esther in the study poring over letters from various tenants and businesses.

"Still hard at it then?" he asked her mildly.

"Yes," she sighed, barely looking up. "You know how it is."

She didn't see his nod of agreement. He would have offered to help her, but the truth was that he hardly knew how the estate ran anymore. When he first left Esther and moved to London, he had given her the vague directive that she was to "look after the place". He hadn't expected her to take him quite so literally. He especially hadn't expected her to take over from the old farm manager when he retired. He was quite shocked when he got a rather terse letter from Muldoon asking him whether his wife's instructions were to be followed. Curious about what schemes Esther was concocting in his absence, Fraser had ordered his men to follow the lady's commands. He was sure the gamekeeper and Cary Eden would prevent the place going to total rack and ruin so he was inclined to indulge Esther's whims if it kept her happy.

Fraser sometimes lacked judgement. His marriage to Esther, for instance, was an example of a gross lack of judgement. There was nothing wrong with Esther. She was a wonderful, intelligent, pretty young woman. But she was wrong for him and he was most definitely wrong for her.

It was never his intention to marry her as she grew up, but when he saw her laughing and cavorting at the Midsummer dance in the autumn of 1936, he knew he had to have her. It was something primal, an urge he never even thought to curb. And he was usually so controlled, so distant, so uninterested in women. With Esther Muncie, however, a switch had been flicked in his brain and now he lived with the consequences. It wasn't Esther's fault, of course. Her mother had all but led her to the altar, knowing a girl like her daughter would never get such a good chance in life as afforded by marrying the local laird. And Esther tried her best to be a good wife but Fraser knew, deep down, that he had made a mistake by tying her to him when she could have had any man she wanted. If he hadn't wanted her himself, he might have consented to his son marrying her. But his own lust and fear of growing old alone made him act rashly and a wife – more than two decades his junior – was the result.

What impressed him most about Esther, however, was that she did not turn bitter or needy when he began to withdraw from her. Instead, she directed her attentions elsewhere: namely towards her children and Kirkmore. Though she was young and inexperienced, Fraser was amazed when he arrived back from London in late 1940 to discover that Kirkmore was not only carrying on as it had under his guidance, but it was making much more money. Esther, he discovered, possessed a canny mind for business – and she was no stranger to hard work or long hours, which made her the perfect person to run the estate. And though he assumed she would eventually tire of running such a place, that he would have to hire someone to take her place – or better yet finally call his eldest son to heel – Esther's control over the estate went from strength to strength. He was really quite proud of her achievements but, being such a taciturn man, he would never tell her that.

In his eyes, Kirkmore was Esther's more than it had ever been his. As he got older, he also felt more keenly that he would never live up to the example his own father set him. And, as well as his feelings of inadequacy, since his return from the Great War Kirkmore held nothing but ghosts. The living were little better. They were a constant reminder of his failing to bring home their husbands and sons. Though no one really did blame him, he was almost sure they believed it was his fault so many young men didn't come home. And then there were the sprawling fields of the estate which did nothing other than reminded him of the yawning chasm of no man's land during the Great War. It was, therefore, easier to leave Esther in charge, easier for him to leave it all behind, to stay in metropolitan London to do a job he enjoyed and was good at.

But then there was Archie and Florence.

Fraser loved all his children but when he looked at his two youngest, they just served as another reminder that he was an old man or, rather, that he felt like an old man. They were so vibrant and youthful with their shouts and screeches that hurt his head. When they wanted him to run, his sedentary life in Whitehall betrayed him, leaving him out of breath with chest pains. When they asked him to read to them, he invariably fell asleep. And when he spent any amount of time with them, he eventually ended up shouting at them for being too noisy, too boisterous, too fidgety or just too childish. They were a living, breathing reminder of his weakness: his longing to possess the girl who was little more than a child herself when she bore them. He was sure she was ruined for any future men who might consider her once he was dead and gone. He had marred her beautiful body when he impregnated her. He gave her two children while also denying her the possibility of more. He wondered if that was why Esther threw herself headlong into the work at Kirkmore: it filled the gap of the third child she would never have. He also harboured the suspicion that this third child was, in fact, her favourite child.

It wasn't that she lacked affection when it came to Archie and Florence. On the contrary: she was a very loving mother. It was more a case of her spending every waking hour dealing with the estate and its problems rather than her children. Night after night she sat in the study poring over ledgers, accounts, statements, letters and plans while the nanny entertained the children. Mary got them up in the morning. Mary got them ready for school. Mary often put them to bed. And all the while, Esther slaved away trying to make Kirkmore more profitable. Perhaps she avoided her children because they reminded her too much of the existence of their father. But, on the other hand, surely Kirkmore – as a whole – reminded Esther that she was wed to Fraser McAllister. Yet he had his suspicions about that too.

The estate was a constant in his wife's life. Esther Muncie grew up on Kirkmore and even as a child was queen of all she surveyed. Though he didn't often like to remember Esther as a child, Fraser could still recall the way the other children – including his own son – flocked to her, played whatever game she wanted, followed the rules she made up and generally fulfilled her whims and fancies. They were like moths to her bright flame and now, as an adult, she had the chance to live out that fantasy again albeit with an excess of responsibilities attached. In marrying Esther Muncie, Fraser had given a poor, fatherless girl everything she could ever have wanted, except a young husband. Instead, she was saddled with him. Perhaps an old husband was a small price to pay for such riches.

Or perhaps nothing was worth a marriage contract that both parties regretted signing in the first place.

Chapter Thirteen

It caused something of a stir among the prisoners the day the laird arrived in the field unannounced, accompanied by his young wife. As word slid through the line of men, regarding the identity of the stranger, the prisoners continued to throw curious glances in the direction of the couple long after they normally would have lost interest. They tried to be surreptitious with their gazes but, because there were so many of them spread out across the field, there were always at least two men looking at the McAllisters at the same time.

What they saw did little to answer their idle curiosity about the laird and the mistress.

It was clear that, at least in public, the two were not close. Madam, in fact, seemed uncomfortable in his presence. They walked together but separated by a distance of a few feet. Neither of them looked at one another like a husband and wife who had spent months apart. When they stopped to talk to the foreman, she stood at a distance from the two men, one hand wrapped around her lower ribcage, the other clutching the opposite bicep.

And then there was the age difference.

All the prisoners had, at some point, discussed the apparent youth of their mistress and wondered how someone so young found herself controlling an estate the size of Kirkmore. She looked to have more in common with the Land Girls they came across than their idea of British landed gentry. Questions about her age also led to speculations about the age of her husband and why a man who owned such an estate would cede control of such a place to his wife. Initially, many had speculated that the mistress was, in fact, a widow but they were disabused of that notion once Petersen shared the few basic facts he had gleaned from working in the big house. As far as he could gather the current Mrs McAllister was the *second* Mrs McAllister and her husband was perpetually from home – facts that further confused the men's musings.

Unfortunately, the men were offered very little time to observe the owner of Kirkmore before he disappeared back to the main house. His distance surprised them, given that Madam was so often involved in or passing comment on their work. They got used to her presence, so it was something of a disappointment for them to discover that she was an exception rather than a rule. Under her care, they almost forgot what it was to be considered prison-camp labourers – something they had been reminded of daily on the farms they worked on before coming to Kirkmore. Seeing the indifferent attitude of her husband – whose only contribution was to deem their work 'adequate' – the men were increasingly mindful of their good fortune to work under Mrs McAllister.

The one thing, however, that did impress Fraser McAllister enough to deem it a little more than 'adequate', was the improvement in his youngest son's knowledge of Latin and various other subjects.

Every time Fraser came home, he made a point of quizzing Archie on his recent schooling then informing Esther about how insufficient the child's education was. Yet, after just two months under the tutelage of Petersen, Fraser pronounced the boy's education 'good'. It was the best Esther could hope for since Fraser's 'good' was equivalent to most other people's 'excellent.' Even so, when Esther offered to get Petersen so the two men could meet, her husband declined. If he met the man, he might have to praise him for his good work with Archie and, if there was one thing Fraser was loath to do, it was to stoke the fire of someone's ego with praise. Instead, he told Esther to give teacher and student a few days off as a reward for their achievements. Anything else would simply be too generous.

As Fraser's week-long visit drew to a close, just after Florence's sixth birthday, work proceeded apace in the fields with the beginning of the hay harvest. Though much of the rest of the country was unseasonably wet, Kirkmore and the rest of Scotland enjoyed mostly dry weather despite cool temperatures. It meant that, mercifully, they managed to get in their large crop of hay without the rain coming to ruin it.

Before it was ready for stacking, there were several hundred acres of grassland to be cut and turned, mostly by hand since the estate's sole remaining tractor was deathly slow and had an unfortunate habit of breaking down. The Germans were initially quite pleased to see the noisy little metal beast trundle into the field behind them until it sputtered to a halt halfway down the first row. It took the foreman and two of the prisoners an hour to fix the first of its many problems by which point the rest of the men had moved to the next field. When it coughed to a standstill for the third time later that day, the men threw up their hands and left the tractor where it was.

They had considerably more success with the heavy horses and for the first time since the war began, they fielded two teams with Alfie, the stable boy, handling one pair of horses and the diminutive German, Max, working the other.

Esther's earlier suspicion that the man was familiar with horses was confirmed when she watched him guide the team up and down in perfectly straight rows. Perched on the mower's miniscule bucket seat behind the horses, the man didn't look big enough to control the two beasts straining against their harnesses in front of him. Yet, the whole task seemed so easy to him as he chattered incessantly to the horses in his own language while playing the reins in his hands and using his foot to work the long blade of the mower protruding from the right of the contraption just in front of the wheel.

The larger fields suited the horses while the gang of prisoners did the smaller fields with scythes – a job which left many of them hissing in agony as the skin on their hands formed large water blisters which subsequently burst. Seeing the torn, raw, angry flesh on the inside of Petersen's thumb and on the palms of his hands prompted Esther to collect a large bottle of iodine and all the bandages in the house to treat her workers' wounds. The local men had their wives and mothers to offer them physic but, since the Germans had neither, she took it upon herself to make sure the men were cared for. However, there was a practical side to her kindness since the men would be working the fields for several days, turning and drying the grass using pitchforks – wielded by their damaged hands – before it was finally ready to be ricked and stored for the winter.

Despite the condition of their hands, with a combination of the warm, sunny weather and seeing real progress as the ricks grew higher with every hour, the Germans seemed contented. Many of them had been practising their English and were now able to make basic conversation with the Kirkmore labourers. Anything a little trickier was explained using an amalgam of gesture and facial contortions. The other thing that lightened the mood of the whole affair was the children who, now on their summer holidays, often spent much of their day in the fields playing with each other and sometimes including the men in their games. Though initially wary of allowing their children to interact with the prisoners, seeing the joy that lit the foreigners' faces when they saw the youngsters flood into the field soon persuaded the villagers that the little ones were safe in their company. The locals' own lackadaisical attitude to the War Ag's directive of no fraternisation soon spread to their offspring who happily rode on the men's backs or chased them around the hayricks during their breaks. Many of the older Germans had left behind children of their own while those in their teens and early twenties longed for the company of younger siblings they hadn't seen since their conscription.

Esther always tried to make a point of being there to see the men and children charging across the open space once they finished their lunchbreak. They formed teams and devised rules for games that became more elaborate with each passing day. She watched the youngsters screaming and giggling as they were chased, caught and swung up in the air by the bigger men. Jung Hans – 'Young Hans' so-called to differentiate him from Alt Hans – was a boy of no more than eighteen, who looked twelve, and had come out of his shell after months of jumping at every loud noise. She watched as Dieter, the most rebellious of all the men, taught wee Nobby Harrison how to tie his shoelaces as well as how to tell his left from his right. In a strange way, it made her heart swell with happiness to know that without a war, without the suffering that resulted, they would not now be able to experience the joy of togetherness and being alive. Yet, every now and again a flicker of sadness ran through the group of men. As they watched the children gambol about, sometimes a smile would become a little more fixed or wouldn't quite touch their eyes. They were remembering their own families – some of them hundreds of miles away across the North Sea, others no longer living at all. Esther was grateful they never showed their struggle to the children. Mostly, they pushed through or stepped away with an excuse of tiredness. When that happened, they would sit or stand apart, just watching the youth and exuberance of the children, allowing it to lighten their mood, giving them hope for the future.

Though Esther would have liked nothing more than to spend every day of the harvest in the fields, her duties as farm manager often outranked her own desires. She made sure, however, that Archie and Florrie were not similarly tied and allowed them to roam the farm with the other children just as she had in her youth. The end of the harvest was only a day or so away and their summer holidays were drawing to a close so, despite her own confinement to the study, she made sure they took full advantage of their freedom. She loved to see them vibrate with anticipation at the breakfast table before she gave them permission to leave. She also loved the smell of them every evening when they came home: it was the smell of fresh air, earth and sweet, dry hay.

It was, therefore, something of a surprise to her when, midway through one afternoon, there was a clatter of feet in the hall.

"*Mummy!*" It was a child's voice, high and terrified.

Archie.

The fear in his voice propelled Esther to her feet and across the room to where she almost collided with her children who stood hand in hand, pale and shaken. Their freckles – so prominent after a summer outdoors – stood out in such sharp contrast to their pallid skin that they looked like blemishes. The dust on Florrie's face was streaked with clear channels of exposed pinkish-white skin where her tears had washed away the dirt. Her free hand worked a patch of fabric on her dress which had clearly borne the brunt of her worry if the creases in the material were anything to go by.

"What? What is it?" Esther grabbed both children by a shoulder, making them flinch. "What's happened?"

Archie mouthed like a landed fish while Florrie's bottom lip began to tremble. A slow keen began somewhere in the centre of her chest before it burbled from her mouth in a sob just as her tears began to flow again.

The little girl clearly wasn't going to be any help.

Trying to remain calm, Esther focused on her son. "Archie?"

"There's been an accident," he answered in barely more than a whisper.

"What kind of accident?" She raised her voice both in panic and to be heard over Florence's growing wail.

"Erwin, he –" Archie's face contorted, unable to continue.

"All right." She patted him distractedly, hundreds of possibilities thundering through her head at once. She longed to press an explanation from her son but didn't want to distress him further. But she had to ask one more question. "Where is he?"

"They're bringing him up to the barracks." It was what most people called the grain store nowadays.

Esther nodded then turned away from the children and filled her lungs. "*Mary!*" she bawled, her voice reverberating off the thick wood and tiled floor of the entrance hall. It was a moment before the answering call rang down the staircase and was followed by the thump of running feet on carpet. The nanny's head barely popped over the balustrade before Esther yelled, "*Mind the children!*" and took off across the hall to the door.

By the time she reached the bottom of the steps outside, she was running. Usually, physical exertion gave her pleasure but as her shoes dug into the gravel path and slid away from her, all she felt was frustration that her body could not get her to the barracks as quickly as she wanted to be there. Her mind continued to spool uncontrollably as she tried to predict what awaited her once she saw Erwin Riegel.

Like Jung Hans, Erwin still looked like a boy. However, war hadn't touched Erwin as indelibly as it had Hans. The Riegel boy was small in comparison with his compatriots but what he lacked in size, he made up for in activity. He was often the first to join the children in their games and the last to return to work when Cary Eden and Major Brown's patience began to wane. Yet, Erwin was such a wonderfully playful, cheeky boy that no one could stay angry with him for long. Esther wondered if perhaps he had finally pushed his cheek a little too far and come to blows with another man. If so, would that be the end of the Germans at Kirkmore? Her stomach dropped and she almost lost her right foot completely as it slithered through the loose gravel. Or had the boy fallen off a hayrick? Was he even still alive? She shut the thought off immediately. Finally, she rounded the end of the barn and spotted one German at the entrance to the barracks conversing with another who had just slipped out of the door. She clacked across the smooth cobbles of the yard, not even breaking stride as she approached them. One of the men swiftly stepped in front of her, blocking her progress, hands out in supplication. It was Petersen.

"No, Mrs McAllister. This is not for your eyes."

Esther threw him a look that made him step back. "I'm the mistress," she answered coldly. "Everything is for my eyes."

She pushed past the German and through the door. She did not need to look behind her to know that Petersen had followed. Though she couldn't be certain, she thought his hand momentarily brushed her spine, guiding her, supporting her once she saw what was in front of her.

Erwin lay on one of the long, scrubbed tables, ashen-faced and lifeless. For one heart-stopping moment Esther thought he was dead. She felt all the air leave her lungs just as Erwin's rose and fell. The relief that flooded her system made her light-headed but she breathed deeply to steady herself. However, as she continued to evaluate the boy's condition, her unsteadiness remained, keeping her rooted to a spot several feet from the table.

A sheen of sweat coated the boy's exposed skin. By the look of him, she guessed he was in a dead faint but that wasn't surprising when she took in the rest of him. There were two dark patches on the thigh of his right trouser leg where blood had soaked into the material and spread through the fibres. That probably partially accounted for the pastiness of his complexion. However, it was where the blood came from that had surely sent the boy to the oblivion of unconsciousness.

At the centre of each bloody rosette was a jagged spike. A splinter of wood protruded from either side of his leg. The blunt end of the spear stuck out just above the inside of his knee. It was a little more than two inches in diameter and white in colour apart from the angry red stain that coated its bottom edge, dripping a small pool of blood onto the surface of the table. On the opposite side, halfway up his thigh the sharp point of the splinter stuck out a hand's breadth below his hipbone, streaked with the blood of its passage through the boy's leg.

A sharp voice snapped Esther's attention away from Erwin's wounds.

Alt Hans stood at the boy's side, a hand pressing the front of Erwin's leg just below the hip, putting pressure on the femoral artery. With a look of fury at his mistress, he delivered a volley of unintelligible German at Petersen over her shoulder. Petersen answered curtly and the older man hissed out a humourless laugh.

"What are you saying?" Esther cut in. The back and forth was clearly about her and she didn't like it one bit.

"Hans says this is no place for a woman," Petersen muttered, not meeting her eye.

Esther's cold gaze fell on the older German. "Ask him who he thinks sewed and bandaged all the men who came back broken and bullet-holed from the war – because, from what I gather, there weren't many men left to do it," she snapped, striding forward to grasp the boy's hand. "A woman's place can be anywhere she has the strength of body and mind for. Tell him that … and get some cold water and a cloth." She trailed a finger across Erwin's clammy brow then looked around. "Where is Major Brown? And Mr Eden?"

"Mr Eden is with the rest of the men. Mr Brown has gone to fetch a doctor," Petersen answered as he emptied water from a pitcher into a bowl and brought it over to her.

She neatly folded the cloth he also gave her, dipped it in the water, wrung it out then began to mop the boy's face, pushing back his fringe. It was a calm, motherly gesture that came very naturally to her. It wasn't the first time she had sat at an invalid's beside. And she felt responsible for Erwin. It was she who had sent him to the fields to work and this was how he came back.

"What happened?" she asked quietly.

"I didn't see it," Petersen said in a low voice. "But apparently he was standing on top of a hayrick and jumped off it onto a hay bogey. One of the floorboards was rotten and he went straight through it. And that –" he pointed to the enormous splinter "– went through his leg. He fainted when we pulled him back through the hole."

Esther did her best to hide a shiver of revulsion as she tried not to imagine how excruciatingly painful sustaining such an injury must have been – tried not to imagine what it looked and sounded like when the boy had jumped off the rick onto the hay cart. What she needed was something to do. She needed to be useful. She needed to make things better. "Should we try and bring him around?" she asked. She thought having someone unconscious and losing blood was not a good plan. At least if he was awake, they might be able to tell if his condition worsened.

"I think, perhaps, that might not be a good idea," Petersen replied hesitantly. "The pain is, I think, too great for him to bear."

"Boil some water then, Mr Petersen." Esther moved on briskly. "The doctor will have need of it when he arrives. And get the iodine. And a scissors if you have one." Taking a deep breath, she looked at Erwin's leg. The material of his trousers would need to be cut away and she thought it best to have as much as possible done before the doctor arrived.

"Our scissors are not very good, I'm afraid," he said but he went and brought one to her anyway.

She tested them on the edge of the cloth she was periodically mopping the boy's skin with and made a sound of disapproval. "These won't do at all. Would you be able to go inside to the library? There's a sewing box in the far corner with an excellent pair of fabric shears in the lid. Could you get them?"

Petersen hesitated. It was one thing to enter the house when the mistress was there to legitimise his presence. It was something else to wander in, in the middle of a crisis, claiming the absent mistress had sent him there. Then he looked at Erwin and his mangled leg. "Of course."

As he left, the other German who had hitherto remained outside slipped in. His name was Reinhold Teske but the other men all called him Fluss. Taking in the brawny labourer, she guessed that he and Petersen must have carried Erwin up from the field. They were two of the strongest men in the gang. Alt Hans was the patriarch of their pack so it made sense that he was there too. What made less sense was the presence of Jung Hans. Esther hadn't initially noticed him since he was sitting in the far corner of the room and only seemed able to throw the odd, scared glance in their direction. When Erwin – still unconscious – stirred and gave a small cry of pain, the other boy groaned in response, beginning to rock himself back and forth on his stool.

"What's Jung Hans doing here?" she asked Teske quietly. It didn't seem right that such a fragile boy should be present to witness someone else's pain. He was scarred enough as it was.

Fluss's English was basic but he managed a slow concise answer. "They are friends in army."

Erwin's moaning became more frequent as he came around. Esther couldn't begin to fathom what it would be like waking up to rediscover a chunk of wood still impaling your leg. The two other Germans were muttering quietly to one another on the other side of the table while Jung Hans continued to pitch forward and back on his perch. She wished Petersen was there to talk to, to translate what the others were saying. She felt very alone without him. Even when she dealt with the whole group of prisoners on her own, Petersen was always a comforting presence, ready to be called upon to mediate, to explain or even to help her carry the heavy baskets of food she brought the men every now and again.

"Should we hold his leg still?" Esther asked, watching it twitch.

More blood seeped onto the tabletop.

Neither man answered, except to stare at her with incomprehension. She could have mimed her question to them but didn't want to risk hurting the boy by touching him unnecessarily. Watching the blood well forth, she took his wrist and felt for his pulse. It took her longer than she would have thought to locate the radial artery but, when she did, she felt the rapid flutter of liquid rushing through his system. She knew shock and blood loss increased heart rate but she didn't know how to gauge the amount of blood loss from Erwin's pulse. There was a fair amount of red around the entry and exit wounds but she wondered what damage might have been done internally. By the length and the trajectory of the splinter she surmised that the internal injury was just as significant as the external – possibly more so. She shuddered to think what might happen when the wood was removed. Because one thing was certain: the spear going through the boy's leg had to come out.

Eventually, Petersen returned with the fabric shears and Ivor Beattie in tow. The gardener's look of suspicion when he entered the barracks was immediately replaced by one of horror when he took in the scene before him.

"Good Christ!" the gardener whispered, his voice hollow with shock. He removed his cap and began to twist it between his hands. He looked to Esther and jerked his head at Petersen.

"I found the big fella going inte the hoos. I didnay believe him when he said you'd sent him." He turned to the German. "I'm sorry for thinkin' ill of you." He held out his hand, offering reconciliation, and Petersen took it with a grim smile.

"I understand," he said mildly.

Esther took the scissors from Petersen's reluctant hands. Forcing air in and out through her nostrils, she took the end of Erwin's trouser leg and began to cut the fabric up the side of his calf, trying her best not to jostle the material. The boy whimpered nonetheless. His restlessness was more pronounced and Esther thought she heard a few words among the indistinct sounds. Once she cut up the inside leg, past the spike of wood and as far as she could go without revealing his underwear, she moved on to the outside seam.

She had just reached below Erwin's knee when he suddenly woke up.

He gasped like someone who had spent too long underwater and sat bolt upright. Several things then happened at once. He screamed in pain: a piercing, atavistic noise that sounded as if it ripped his throat in two. It made the hairs on the back of Esther's neck stand up. Then he pitched forward to grasp at his leg but shock and light-headedness sent him diving over the edge of the table. He flailed his arms and legs as Alt Hans and Petersen leaped forward to catch him but not before the boy's booted foot connected with Esther's diaphragm. She flew backwards and hit the floor hard several feet away, landing flat on her back.

Erwin screamed again then mercifully went limp once more in a dead faint.

"*Mistress!*" Beattie, a look of abject horror plastered on his face, hobbled forward to pick her up.

Petersen beat him to it.

Esther – completely winded by her fall – was still attempting to grasp how she ended up on the cold stone floor when the German crouched beside her and took her hands in his. Once again, she noted their warmth and the rough, calloused skin that covered strong sinew and bones.

"Est – Mrs McAllister, are you all right?" He tightened his hold on her fingers and braced so she could pull herself up.

Without air in her lungs, she could only mouth soundlessly. Nevertheless, she sat up but in doing so felt the impact of the fall. She grimaced in pain. Beattie hovered by her side, footing uncomfortably, unsure what to do. Petersen made as if to put his arm around her to support her back but she waved him off. He barked something in his native tongue to Fluss who hurried over to the pitcher and brought back a tin cup filled with water.

"Here." Petersen offered her the cup. "It will help you get your breath back."

She took it from him and sipped carefully, feeling her cheeks burn. She was mortified at having been knocked flat. Every conscious man in the room was staring at her as if they thought she might burst into tears at any moment. Putting down the cup, she made to scramble to her feet and found Petersen holding one hand while placing the other at the small of her back. She shrank away from his kindness, bowing her head in embarrassment.

"'M all right," she muttered, putting a little distance between herself and the men once she gained her feet. "Erwin all right?" she asked, squinting at the boy.

"He is … as well as can be expected." Petersen's mouth tightened as he looked across at the boy. "How long before the doctor arrives?"

"Not long," Esther assured him. She was surprised that he was taking so long.

Freddie Robertson. The same Freddie she and Drew had grown up with. The same Freddie whose mother had taken him away from the estate when he was little more than a boy. He had returned as a man and a newly minted doctor – the best in the entire county. The thought that he was coming calmed her, not only because he was an excellent physician but also because – aside from Drew – he was her oldest friend. But then she bit the inside of her lip at the worrying thought that it might not be Freddie Robertson who came at all. If it was Dr Ferguson – the alcoholic septuagenarian, who retook his practice from Freddie Robertson when the younger man went to Manchester to work in an army hospital – Esther conjectured that she might as well get Beattie to remove the splinter. She wouldn't let Ferguson near her horses, never mind a vulnerable, severely injured boy. She hoped to God that Freddie would come.

Pulling herself together, Esther located the scissors which Fluss had helpfully retrieved from under one of the beds. When Petersen offered to finish removing the trouser leg, she gave him a crisp, "No," in reply. She wasn't going to let someone else finish the job she started.

She had carefully cut away what remained of Erwin's

trouser leg by the time Freddie Robertson came hurrying through the door after Major Brown. Relief flooded through her.

Though not much older than Esther was, Freddie had lost a good deal of his dark brown hair to premature baldness. He had aged considerably since the outbreak of war. But war did that to most men.

He took one look at Erwin, muttered "Dear, dear," and examined the wound. "This boy really should be in a hospital," he said disapprovingly.

"If he goes to the hospital, they'll send him back to the camp," the Major answered from the foot of the table, looking queasy.

"So you said in the car," Freddie replied calmly. "Having seen the camp, I can understand why our young friend might be reluctant to return. However, as a doctor, I cannot proceed here without first telling you that the boy should be in a hospital instead of on a table in a barn. These are not conditions I would choose to work in. A lot can go wrong in a field situation such as this, infection being the main worry. But I also have to take into consideration the wishes of the patient or whomever might speak on his behalf in this … situation." Here he turned to Esther. "Mrs McAllister? The decision is yours."

Esther didn't look at the doctor. Instead, she sought out one person among the gathered men. Their eyes locked and Petersen gave a single, definite nod. "We'll proceed here, doctor. I'm sure between us we can do our best to fix Mr Riegel while remaining here."

There was no judgement in the doctor's gaze as he inclined his head in assent.

Fluss had possessed the presence of mind to remove some boiling water from the pan on the stove and put it in a bowl to cool a little. Robertson took it to wash his hands, with a nod of approval to the German.

Hands clean, he crouched by the boy's leg, his nose no

more than an inch away from the skin as he studied the entry and exit wounds. With feather-light touches, he explored the perforated edges while paying careful attention to the amount of blood around the holes. Finally, he closed his eyes. With a careful touch, he palpated the areas around the piece of wood as well as the front of Erwin's leg to better feel the trajectory of the splinter and anatomy of the leg around it.

"Perhaps I'm speaking too soon, but I think our chap here may have the devil's luck. Or maybe a guardian angel." The doctor washed his hands once more. "It's missed the femoral artery which is our main concern with thigh wounds. The splinter is too shallow and there's not enough blood to suggest it's hit a main artery or vein. It may have hit one of the descending branches though." He bent down again to scrutinize the congealed red liquid. "*Hmm*. Perhaps." He turned back to the gathered crowd. "I also think it may have missed the front muscle in the thigh." He drew his fingers down the centre of the leg. "Here's the rectus femoris. I think it's passed behind this and mostly in front of the two vastus muscles either side." Here, he forked his fingers, demonstrating their position. "Caught all of them but not completely ruined any of them. I could be wrong, of course." He shrugged. "But if I'm right, this injury should be absolutely treatable at home, so to speak."

The doctor checked the boy's heart before taking out various bottles of liquid from which he filled several syringes before administering them.

"Really, I would prefer him to have been awake but I suspect he wouldn't like it very much, poor chap."

"He doesn't like it, no," Beattie said dryly. He was standing a good distance away, rocking back and forth on his heels. He looked as if he was on the verge of either coming closer or leaving altogether. "Knocked Mistress flat with all his flailing."

Esther swelled with indignation as she cast a cold glare at the gardener.

"Are you hurt?" the doctor asked her sharply.

"No," she said with a grim smile. "Only a bruised ego."

"Ah, the legendary bruised ego. I'm afraid I can prescribe nothing for that other than time and the silence of all the honourable gentlemen present." He cast a stern gaze over the gathered company, most of whom looked distinctly nonplussed. "Now. I think it's time we got to work on Mr Riegel's leg."

The first stumbling-block was the prodigious length of wood which protruded from the outside of the leg.

"The less we have to draw out, the better," said the doctor. "I should saw off most of the wood but that would be difficult – if not impossible. Too much jostling."

Beattie then suggested his heavy-duty hedge-cutting shears which were used to lop off stray or low-hanging branches. Jung Hans was immediately dispatched to the tool shed with detailed instructions regarding where the implement was kept.

"Could two of you wash your hands, please?" Robertson said. "I'll be needing some assistance."

Esther was beaten to the wash basin only by Petersen. The others stayed exactly where they were, ashen-faced at the prospect of what was about to happen.

"Don't dare ask me if I'm sure," she hissed when she saw him opening his mouth.

A genuine grin momentarily lit his face before he sobered and innocently answered, "I was only going to ask you to pass the soap."

She narrowed her eyes at him since the soap was well within his reach but passed it to him anyway. Unaccountably, she felt the corners of her own lips quirk as they scoured their hands side by side, reddening the skin in the piping hot water.

Jung Hans returned, puffing heavily from his exertion, with two bright patches of colour lighting each cheek on his otherwise white face. He made to hand them to the doctor but was instructed to douse the entire thing in boiling water as Robertson cleaned around the wounds.

"I hope you both had a good breakfast this morning," he commented dryly. "This isn't going to be easy."

Gesturing to Alt Hans, he got the old German to once again clamp a hand on the top of the femoral artery. He also got Hans to put his forearm up the boy's chest to minimise his movement. Petersen was commissioned to hold Erwin's lower leg in case it began to shake or jerk involuntarily while they worked.

"That leaves you, Nurse Muncie," Robertson said with a sympathetic smile. "I want you to stabilize the opposite end of the splinter while I cut it. Can you do that?"

Esther took a moment to answer. She wanted to be sure. "Yes, I can do that."

"I'll do it if you don't want to," Petersen murmured as she took a deep, steadying breath and moved closer to the table.

"No, I'd prefer to have you anchoring his leg," the doctor said. "It will take a great deal of strength to hold him down if he does begin to thrash. Are we all ready?"

Wordlessly, Esther manoeuvred herself into position on a bench by sliding the bottom half of Erwin's good leg off the edge of the table so that his knee and shin where pressed against the side of her chest. She hoped he wouldn't wake up and kick her again.

"All right. Grab hold, Esther." The doctor waited for Esther to reach over and carefully wrap both hands around the wood, making sure she didn't jostle it. "Steady now," he muttered, closing the blades of the shears around the neck of the spike.

Esther felt the wood wiggle in her grasp and tightened her hands. She could feel the sharp edges of the broken wood digging into her palms.

Alt Hans let out a low wail and fixed his gaze on Erwin's face.

"*Now.*"

Though she held on as tight as she could, Esther couldn't completely prevent the spike from moving. Yet, Beattie's steady shears did their job and she heard a little clunk as the end of the splinter hit the floor.

"Well done, everyone. Very good. Now ..." The doctor stood back. "I wonder ..." He fetched a saline drip from his bag along with some rubber piping which he dipped in the boiling water. He pulled out bandages, gauze, packing and – surprisingly – a jar of honey before washing his hands once more. "Really this needs two people." He seemed to be talking to himself.

"What does, Freddie?" Esther asked.

He wore a preoccupied expression which cleared when he focused on Esther. "I'd like to pull out the splinter but I also want to make sure there are no smaller splinters left behind. The best way I can think of doing that is to follow the spike out as far as I can with my finger. And I'll need to wash some saline through while we're doing it too. But that, unfortunately would require at least three hands."

"Could I pull it out?" Esther asked. She felt weary. Her senses seemed to have been calmed or perhaps numbed at some point between the doctor's arrival and that moment. She just wanted the whole thing over and the boy out of pain.

"You could," Robertson said hesitantly. "Do you think you can?"

"I can."

The doctor still looked reluctant.

"Let's just get the damn thing out, Freddie," she said bluntly, holding his gaze.

"All right."

Taking the rubber tube from the water, the doctor connected it to the saline drip. "Hold that up," he said to no one in particular.

Fluss stepped forward reluctantly, his skin an unhealthy grey colour, lips pressed hard together.

"Turn on the tap when I say. Esther, when I say, start pulling. Steady pressure. Stop if I tell you. And whatever you do, keep it on the same plane. No twisting."

"Understood." She gave him one quick, sharp nod and cautiously wrapped her fingers around the wood until she was happy with her grip.

"Good. All right. *Now pull.*"

Throughout her life, there had been many instances when Esther had pulled something that was seemingly inanimate from the depths of a living being. When helping a ewe with a difficult lambing, the constant tension kept on slippery little legs was not dissimilar to that which she exerted on the shaft of the wooden spike. If she told herself she was delivering a tiny lifeform rather than acknowledging the grisly truth of what she was doing, it became more bearable. It wasn't a piece of wood, it was a lamb's foreleg. The small moans of pain were that of the mother. The gore that oozed around it was perfectly normal – the fluid of birth, sometimes clear, sometimes bloody. Once the distress and effort of birth was over, the parent would be up on her feet in no time as if they had done nothing so miraculous as bring new life to the world.

With a kind of crazed calm, Esther drew the blunt, bloodied tip from Erwin's leg with Freddie issuing a steady stream of instructions and encouragement. Meanwhile, he probed the wound with his finger and threaded his rubber pipe after the splinter, washing the small cavity with saline solution until it began to well out the hole around the wood in the opposite side. Finally, with an unavoidable jerk, the splinter came free in Esther's hands followed by a trickle of blood then the steady dribble of saline.

The shaft of wood was so light, Esther reeled backwards slightly, almost toppling off the edge of her bench. It felt so insignificant. Her hands felt so heavy around it. Still suffused with the physical and emotional stress it took to remove it, her skin crawled. The small baton of wood clattered on the floor. Empty of the thing that had filled them, her hands began to shake. She hid them under the table.

The doctor was still exploring the wound. "Can't feel anything," he told them. "That doesn't mean it's not there. If there is anything there, it will likely make itself known within the next twenty-four hours. Swelling and possibly discharge which will mean I'll have to have another poke around in his leg. Our next worry is infection since you can bet that piece of wood wasn't clean. We'll get a bit of penicillin into him and that will hopefully knock any badness on the head." Finally, he finished probing the wound. "Not too much blood either which is even better."

Esther took one look at the doctor's bloodied hands and felt her stomach drop. Whatever he said, it seemed like there was an awful lot of blood to her. Yet, when she forced herself to look more closely at the wounds, she could see that there was only a thin, slow trickle of watery red seeping from the hole closest to her. She supposed the saline solution hadn't done much to lessen the appearance of the puddle on the table that was dripping onto the floor. Unaccountably, she felt the urge to get down on her hands and knees and clean it up. It felt cruel to leave Erwin's drained lifeblood to stain the concrete floor.

Lifting her head, she saw that Petersen was holding his comrade's leg aloft to allow access to the underside of the boy's limb. She watched the doctor clean around the wounds before coating two pieces of gauze in honey and placing one on each hole. They neatly adhered to the boy's leg, leaving Robertson free to use both hands as he wrapped several rolls of bandage around his thigh.

Now Petersen was attempting – rather unsuccessfully – to undo the lace on Erwin's boot. In all the excitement, his footwear had been left on. Seeing him struggle to unpick the knot, Esther wordlessly pushed his fingers aside and dexterously undid it, relieved by the apparent steadiness of her hands. When she looked up, he was studying her. Self-conscious, she gave him a tight-lipped smile.

"Is there somewhere he can stay that's a little brighter and cleaner?" Robertson asked. "Where he can be monitored round the clock? Not that this isn't clean, it's very neat really. But I'm not sure it's quite suited to aiding Mr Riegel's recovery."

"He'll be coming into the house," Esther answered decisively. She was already planning to put him in Drew's old bedroom which was on the same floor as her own. "I can check on him at night since I'll likely be awake anyway."

"Still not sleeping?" the doctor asked.

She gave him a bitter smile. "No."

He shook his head sympathetically. "Dear, dear. Still, I'm not sure having you be solely responsible for him is a good idea. Who knows what might go wrong in the night – or what his needs may be?"

Major Brown spoke up. "He could come and stay with me," he offered.

Esther stifled a titter. The major's wife was notoriously fretful. If she was put in charge of an invalid, the poor woman was likely to keel over from the stress of it all.

"Perhaps not, Major." Robertson apparently had come to the same conclusion as Esther did. Their eyes locked momentarily, and each looked away quickly for fear of making the other one laugh.

"He stays in the house," Esther said firmly. "We'll manage him somehow."

"I could stay with him," Petersen said quietly. "You could lock the door. You have my word nothing untoward will happen." He said it so sincerely. His eyes were solemn and guileless, leaving no one in any doubt that he spoke the truth.

The doctor remained cautious. "It's a possibility."

Esther was hesitant about Petersen's suggestion. Not because she didn't think it was a good idea. On the contrary. If there was anyone she would trust with the health of an invalid, it was Petersen. What made her hesitate was the opinions of the other people gathered in the barracks. Even though both Esther and her German workforce were held in high regard locally, it would only take one misconstrued story for all of them to fall out of favour. And two Germans staying in their very female household was prime fodder for misinterpretation.

"Do you have any medical experience?" Freddie asked, surveying the German keenly.

He shrugged. "A little. My father was a doctor. I know the basics."

Freddie nodded. "Very well then. As long as Mrs McAllister has no objections, I think this arrangement might suit everyone while also making sure it stays Kirkmore business. If you don't want outsiders to know about his injury it's better to keep the whole affair in-house, so to speak."

Esther acquiesced. She couldn't have come up with a neater solution to their problem if she tried. There followed a lengthy list of instructions on how to care for their patient which she only half heard. She was suddenly bone-weary. There were lead weights attached to her ankles trying to drag her feet through the floor. Muttering an excuse, she stumbled from the building, hoping that some fresh air might help to restore her or at least get the smell of blood and fear from her nostrils.

Stepping out, she was momentarily blinded by the evening sunlight – like coming out of a theatre matinee in midsummer. In the confines of the barracks there was no natural light. Illumination came from bare bulbs, giving the illusion that it was perpetually night no matter what time of day it was. She gulped in a lungful of dust-scented air and thought nothing had ever tasted so sweet. Closing her eyes, she inhaled deeply, leaning back against the wall of the grain store. The rough stone wall was cool, craggy and solidly reassuring. She heard the door of the barn creak open but kept her eyes tightly closed.

"Bad day, Essie?"

Freddie's genial voice made her smile. "You could say that." She matched his nonchalance. She loved how calm and mild-mannered Freddie Robertson was. It made her feel safe in his care and it was why she chose him to be Archie's godfather and given him the middle name 'Fredrick'. That, and the fact that he was one of her oldest friends. If her son grew up to be half the man the doctor was, she didn't need to worry about him finding a place in the world.

As if he read her thoughts, Freddie said, "How's my godson?"

"Archie's himself. Up to no good half the time, I'm sure."

Freddie chuckled. "Yes, I was aware of that. I don't suppose he told you about bringing wee Dougie Harper to get stitches in his elbow after a fall."

Her eyes sprang open. "No," she said tersely. "When was this?"

"Last week. But don't tell him I mentioned it. I'm sworn to secrecy." He winked and tapped the side of his nose.

She snorted. "I don't suppose you told wee Dougie's mother then."

"Of course I did. But I swore her to secrecy too. We did a funny handshake and everything."

Esther's smile faded as she thought of Norah Harper. "Poor woman."

"I know."

"Poor Dougie too. He's a lovely wee boy."

Dougie's father, George Harper, had died on the beach at Dunkirk in 1940 before the boy really got a chance to know him. Esther always got angry when she read about the evacuation of Dunkirk as a great Allied success when so many men perished on the beaches of France. Norah's husband was just one of many. Though the locals did their best to help her, many felt poor Mrs Harper would never recover from the loss of her husband. She was such a fragile thing, unsuited to a life of single motherhood, especially when the child in question was a wild and boisterous boy like Dougie. But she did her best and Esther admired her for it. Norah remined Esther of her own mother in a life where there were increasingly fewer reminders of the departed Lizzie Muncie.

"Wee Dougie is a terror and you know it." Robertson's eyes danced with humour. "But he loves his mother so I can't be too hard on him." He leaned against the wall and scrubbed his face with hands that were now mercifully free of gore. "I hear you've got Archie a new tutor too." His voice was casual – too casual.

"Yes."

He waited for more, then tutted. "Oh, come on, Essie! You can do better than that."

"What do you mean?"

He shook his head in exasperation. "He says it's one of the Germans. Dare I ask which one?"

"The one you just made Erwin Riegel's night nurse."

Freddie's eyebrows shot up in surprise. "Oh." There was a long pause. "Well, I suppose he seems nice enough."

"He is," she replied shortly.

Freddie pushed off the wall and stood in front of her.

"You'd want to be careful who you say that to."

"So you're allowed to say it and I'm not?" Her mouth twisted bitterly.

He looked at her grimly. "Frankly, yes." He glanced down, scuffing his shoe on the cobbles. "Come on. I want to get this chap settled in and see if he'll wake up for me before I leave."

Chapter Fourteen

Mrs Morris agreed with surprising alacrity when Esther proposed to install Erwin in Drew's old bedroom. Andrew's former bedroom was anything but grand. It was, in fact, one of the smallest bedrooms on the first floor but it had two large, bright windows and looked out on the back garden. In truth, the room was a bit of a shell since it had never been occupied since Drew's departure. There was, however, a large bed and enough furniture to make it presentable should any guests wish to use it.

Freddie offered to stay in the room with Erwin for a little while in the hope that the boy might wake of his own accord and be lucid enough to tell him how he felt.

Jung Hans also stayed with him, not wanting to leave his friend's side, while the others all headed back to the barracks to clean up the mess left behind.

Esther stopped Petersen with a hand on his arm as he was leaving. "There's no need for you to give Archie his lesson this evening. It's been a hard afternoon and it may be a hard night too."

He shook his head. "If it's all the same to you, Mrs McAllister, I'd prefer to continue with our lessons as normal. It will give me something positive to concentrate on rather than think about what happened today."

She thought about what he said for a moment and, unbidden, an image of her own hand pulling the splinter from Erwin's leg flashed across her vision. She cringed away from it. "All right then." Only then did she realise she was still clutching the German's arm. She withdrew her fingers a little too quickly and felt her skin burn with embarrassment. Her complexion wasn't helped by the look the doctor gave her as the German brushed past her through the door. Freddie had noticed her holding on too.

Ignoring him, she went off in search of the children. When they were bringing Erwin into the house, she had spotted them looking out the window. She wanted to make sure neither of them was too disturbed by the incident and also reassure them that their friend was hopefully going to get better. When she turned the corner to the nursery, both were peeking through the crack between the open door and the frame, Archie's chin resting on the crown of Florrie's head, his arm across her chest. Florrie was clutching a threadbare pink and dirty-white bunny rabbit to her front.

"Is he dead?" Archie asked, throwing the door open. He looked pale, his eyes bright.

"No!" Esther answered, shocked. "Why would you think that?"

Archie looked abashed. "I just thought he looked very white and he wasn't moving – a bit like when we saw Granny," he said quietly.

Esther's mouth tightened grimly. Fraser had insisted on Archie seeing his dead grandmother only a month after his third birthday. Her husband maintained that children should learn to understand death early on in their lives to save later confusion and explanation. However, seeing the corpse of his grandmother did nothing to alleviate Archie's confusion. Instead it only added to it since he insisted, in front of a gathered crowd of mourners, that all they had to do was wake her up. When no one did as he asked them, Archie screamed and sobbed until Esther – then eight months pregnant with Florence – had to half carry, half drag her son from the room until Drew came to her aid. Without a word, he lifted his half-brother into his arms and carried him up the stairs to the nursery. He waited until Esther came and sat on the large, comfortable settee then laid Archie in her lap. Though horribly traumatic for both mother and child, the one good thing that came from her mother's death was the restoration of her friendship with Drew.

When Fraser married her, Drew saw the whole affair as a betrayal of their many years together. He wondered if she had used him to get to his father – if their years of friendship were all a lie. He wondered whether his father planned it all from Esther's infancy – a thought that completely revolted him. And he wondered whether, if he had asked Esther to marry *him*, she would have said yes. Whatever the reasons for their union, Andrew McAllister did not stay at Kirkmore to find out. Having completed his final year in school, he went straight to university without coming home. In three years, she saw her best friend and stepson twice. Both occasions were excruciating in their coldness. But when Lizzie Muncie died, Drew felt duty-bound to return home for the funeral even if it meant another painful meeting with the girl who had once been Esther Muncie but was now his stepmother.

Yet when he saw the frail, drawn young woman who stood so forlorn by her mother's coffin, Drew felt a tug on his heart once more. He remembered her sense of fun, her playfulness, her honesty. He pondered how much of each might be left and what toll her new life had taken on her. All the plans she made for her future – the hopes that she would get a job, be able to live in the city, see the world before she settled down – had come to nothing. Drew always thought she was too big for somewhere as small as Kirkmore, that she deserved to leave its simplicity behind. He encouraged her fantasies and dreams of future freedom. Yet here she was at twenty-one, an orphan, a mother of one and just about ready to burst with the second. Where did the girl he knew so well disappear to? He knew the answer. Esther had been swallowed up by Fraser McAllister. She took on the burdens of Kirkmore without seeing the benefits. Drew's father had woven her a gilded cage, tying her to her homeplace without her even realising it. And now that her mother was dead, her last true connection to the place was severed. Her mother's demise should have signalled the death-knell of what bound her to Kirkmore. Now all it did was remind her that she gave up her chance at freedom before it even began, choosing instead to yoke herself to something that would slowly drain the life out of her.

Sitting in the nursery that day, cradling her son to her chest, she began to weep. She wept for her mother. She wept because she was exhausted. And she wept for the child she had been less than five years before. The child with so many plans for the future who died the day she agreed to marry Fraser McAllister.

Unable to say anything comforting yet also unable to leave, Drew sat on the settee, wrapped his arms around her and her son, and held her as she cried. No one had held her in a long time. Those she knew in childhood now thought her elevated position meant their comfort was no longer of value to her. And the people who now surrounded her did not believe in either showing weakness or pandering to it. Esther McAllister was lady of Kirkmore. She was not supposed to cry. And yet, she did. Clinging to her best friend and her firstborn, she rocked and sobbed until there were no more tears left, until she wore herself out. Purged of the grief that had been building up inside of her for the past four years, her whole body ached around the hollowness left behind. In that moment, she just wanted it all to end. She wanted to be free of Fraser, free of Kirkmore, free of her burdens, of children, of acquaintances, of everything. She wanted to sit in the nursery, close her eyes and never wake up again. She wanted to die, to go back to a life where it was just her and her mother – when life wasn't complicated by so many unwanted additions.

Calling Mary, Drew disentangled Archie from Esther. Then, picking her up, he carried her to her room.

Once he left, a numbness overcame her. In the haze between pain, anguish and exhaustion the last vestiges of childhood expired. It wasn't Esther that needed to die, it was the child inside her clinging to the possibility that things would just go back to the way they were. There was no escaping her position in the world anymore. She was either going to wallow in the perpetual sadness of missed opportunities or learn to accept and thrive in her new life: to make the most of what she was gifted through her marriage, to use her agile mind for something worthwhile rather than self-torment.

She went to sleep as Esther Muncie and finally woke as Esther McAllister.

Her mother's funeral was also the last time Drew slept in his childhood bedroom. On that day it seemed that both of them left their old selves behind and became better people. Esther threw off the remnants of her childishness and Drew buried three years' worth of resentment directed at those closest to him. Each saw this change in the other and, instead of slipping into the old rhythms of their childhood friendship, embarked on a completely new adult relationship. Drew began to write to her separately from his father. When Florence was born, he became her godfather. The wonder in his face when he eventually sat on the settee in the nursery and held his baby sister helped Esther recover her own wonder after the traumatic, difficult birth of her youngest and final child.

Sitting on the settee now with Archie and Florrie after the challenge of mending Erwin Riegel's leg, she closed her eyes and remembered the many times she shared the seat with Drew. After their friendship was repaired, they often found themselves in the nursery again. It held so many happy memories. It was where Florence had taken her first steps, tottering across the floor where they sat six feet apart. Archie had uttered his first swearword in the confines of the room, to Esther's dismay and Drew's unbridled, cackling glee. Here they sat together watching the children play when, one day, Drew leaned in and whispered sadly, "This should have been us."

Once, when he was seventeen and she eighteen, it could have been. Esther had no doubt they would have been a happy, loving couple. Drew, she knew, would be a wonderful father. He was already a wonderful husband to Caroline. But the burning candle of their budding teenage relationship had been snuffed out, melted down and turned into something else. The sexual attraction that existed between the McAllister boy and Esther Muncie was lost to the ether. It was something both of them even spoke to one another about. They loved each other dearly but, neither could muster any more than a brotherly or sisterly affection now.

It was just another indication of how people changed as they grew up.

"So, will Erwin get better, Mummy?"

She looked down at her son. He had the same eyes as his father. But Esther never thought of them like that. She thought he had the same eyes as Drew. She sighed and cuddled both children in her arms. "With luck and good nursing, he should get better, yes."

"It was horrible," Archie shuddered.

Florrie snuffled into her bunny rabbit.

"Did you get the stick out of his leg?" Archie asked.

"Yes, we managed to get it out."

"Was there a lot of blood?" Archie probed in hushed tones.

"There was a bit, yes," Esther answered vaguely. She didn't want the boy to have nightmares. He was only just growing out of the ones that involved her mother's corpse.

"There was blood when he did it too. Michael yelled at me to take Florrie up to the house." Archie paused. "He's never yelled at me before." He sounded hurt.

"I'm sure Mr Petersen was just scared the two of you might see something that would upset you. He didn't mean to do it, I'm sure."

"Why do you always call him 'Mr Petersen'?'" Archie asked, seeming genuinely curious. "He said it makes him feel old."

"I don't know," she said with a chuckle. "Maybe I think it's polite. Or maybe I don't mind making him feel old since it makes me feel a little bit younger."

"But you *are* old," Archie reasoned. "You're my mummy."

"And what, you think all mummies are old?"

"Yes. You have to be a grown-up to have children. Grown-ups are old," he said sagely.

"But I'm not old!" Esther replied in mock indignation. "I'm not even thirty!"

"You're not as old as Father," Archie conceded but he still didn't look convinced.

"I'm definitely not as old as your father," she agreed. "I bet I'm not even as old as Mr Petersen."

"He says he doesn't have any children. So you must be older." Archie seemed to think this was an incontrovertible argument and crossed his arms with a triumphant grin on his face.

Esther thought she might have to agree with him since she couldn't figure out a logical way to counter his point of view. Trying to cudgel her brain into action was becoming harder by the second but, luckily, Florrie saved her from any further conversational sparring.

"Can we go and see Erwin before we eat?" she asked, her voice muffled by a rabbit's ear.

Esther looked at her watch and saw that it was ten minutes to suppertime. "I don't think so, lovie," she murmured, kissing the top of her daughter's head. "Poor Erwin's had a very hard day and I think he'll want to sleep this evening. Maybe if he's feeling better you can see him tomorrow."

Florrie nodded and began to burrow further under her mother's arm.

"Now, I'm afraid we'll all have to go and wash our hands before supper."

She stood and picked Florrie up, hitching her onto her hip. It was rarely she carried Florence nowadays but today made her want to hold her children more tightly. Reaching out, she took Archie's hand and he let her lead them to the bathroom where they flicked water at one another and giggled at the silly, slippery, escaping bar of soap.

Chapter Fifteen

Freddie came down just as they were finishing supper and was promptly seated at the head of the table when Esther insisted he have something to eat before he left. Once assured that Erwin was awake and feeling better though still not ready to receive visitors, the children ran off to play before Petersen arrived. Esther remained behind to keep Freddie company.

"Mrs Morris is sitting with him. He was still quite groggy when I left," he told her while he ate, "but we managed to have a little chat once Jung Hans told him what was going on. I loosened his bandages a little. His leg is quite swollen, so they'll need to be tightened again probably as early as tomorrow. If you want, I can come back and do them. Save the nurse coming and asking too many questions." He continued to eat.

"If you think that's best," Esther answered, standing to pour herself a whisky. She rarely drank but tonight seemed like as good a time as any for a tipple.

"I do," Freddie said happily as he added two extra potatoes to his plate and began mashing them into the gravy.

"Drink?" she asked, still holding the bottle.

Freddie raised his eyebrows but shook his head, attacking his veg with renewed vigour.

Esther sat back down at the table. "Do you always shovel food in like that?" she asked conversationally.

"Yes. Habit, I suppose. When I was at the hospital in Davyhulme during the war you could be doing surgery or rounds for hours. You never knew when you were going to get a chance to eat or sleep. And you'd be guaranteed to get a call the moment you sat or lay down. Most of the staff ended up with stomach ulcers. I was lucky. All I came away with was less hair and the ability to sleep whenever I want to."

"Lucky you," Esther said as she played with her glass. "Being able to sleep, not the hair loss, obviously."

"Maybe the two are connected," he speculated. "Maybe if you shaved off all that lovely blonde hair you'd sleep like the dead."

"I must try it some time," she replied drily.

Having finished his meal, Freddie pushed his plate aside. "You're really still not sleeping?" The professional demeanour was back once again.

"No." She gulped what was left in the bottom of her glass and felt her eyes and throat burn. "Perhaps if I drank more, I might sleep."

He clucked disapprovingly. "Slippery slope, that. Nothing I suggested worked?"

She sighed. In a funny way, she didn't want to disappoint him but she also wanted to be honest. "No, I'm afraid not."

"I'm sorry, Esther."

"There are worse things," she said with a shrug.

"Still, it would be nice for you to get a decent night's kip."

Esther laughed. "Wouldn't it just? But we'll soldier on regardless."

They were quiet for a time apart from Esther again offering him a drink which he declined.

"I'd best be off – my housekeeper will think I'm up to no good," he said with a wink.

135

They both knew old Mrs Gearety sat in the front window of his house with her neck out on a stalk, waiting for him to come home.

Standing up from the table, he stopped, head cocked, and gazed at Esther. "You really did do very well today, you know."

"Oh?"

Archie nodded. "There's not many people who could have stayed upright doing what you did for that poor boy. You really were very impressive."

"Maybe I should become a doctor. I hear they let women in nowadays too," she joked as she walked him to the door.

"You're going to put us men out of a job," he said, shaking his head ruefully.

Esther chuckled. "There's no fear of that. Women are the ones who have to look after the children, or haven't you noticed that?"

"I had, now that you mention it," he answered wryly, turning to her. "Take care, Essie." He bent and kissed her on the cheek. "And call if the boy is in trouble. Any time."

After Freddie had left, Esther ignored his advice about alcohol and poured herself another, more generous whisky since she hadn't really enjoyed the first. The jittery buzz left by the afternoon's adrenalin rush made her feel strange. She wanted to dull the anxiety that crawled through her system, hoping that it would allow her to get on with the work she had neglected during the course of the day. It wasn't an ideal plan but, as she sat at the study desk, she felt the calming effects of the first glass. The other hope was that if she got even a little bit tipsy, she might get to sleep more quickly instead of having images of Erwin's skewered leg keeping her awake.

When Petersen arrived for his lesson with Archie, she barely looked up from her paperwork, knowing that she only had a certain amount of time to be productive before the alcohol fuddled her brain. She was, therefore, very surprised when the German stuck his head around the door to tell her they were finished.

"So soon?" She heard Archie yell "Night, Mum!" as he tore up the stairs. Looking at the clock, she was shocked to see a full hour had passed. "Oh." She cast a confused look over the pile of completed accounts she had sorted through without realising. Perhaps she *should* drink more often. She could hardly remember a time when she was more productive than she'd been in the last hour. But then she couldn't really remember the last hour either. On second thoughts, maybe she shouldn't drink at all.

Petersen still stood in the doorway. That only added to her confusion until she realised seconds had passed rather than minutes. She stood abruptly and felt the room sway a little as she carefully concentrated on what he said next.

"I'll be back in an hour to sit with Erwin," he told her, a concerned look on his face.

"*Nonsense!*" She said it a little too loudly. She was not drunk, merely tipsy, just as she hoped. "Stay in the library if you want. You can read for an hour then go up. Save you going away and coming back again." She had meant to say it earlier but forgot. He seemed unsure. "Stay," she said softly. "I won't disturb you."

"All right. Thank you." He withdrew but left the door ajar just as he did when giving a lesson. She heard him shuffle off across the other room then the occasional sound of him moving the library steps and opening or closing books.

The soft sounds of the house lulled her into a stupor until she realised what she was doing. Snapping herself out of the fug, she crossed the room to the gramophone and turned it on low, hoping the noise would keep her awake. As she walked back to her chair, she couldn't help but sway a little to the music. It was a long time since she had played anything at all. Usually it was Caroline who listened to records since Esther, more often than not, worked in silence. The music did the trick and allowed her to push on through two letters that should have been written the day before. It wasn't until 'A String of Pearls' came on that she stopped and allowed herself the luxury of really listening to the music. She always liked the big band music of the thirties. It made up the majority of her record collection. The classical music was Fraser's and Caroline had managed to sneak in a few jazz records over the years. But Esther's heart still firmly favoured the likes of Benny Goodman and Glenn Miller. If Caro was there, she might have got her up for a little dance, just to remind herself of the joy of movement. She hummed along to the tune, knowing every dip and skip of the piece by rote. Absorbed by the music, she gave a little start when the floor to her right creaked. Petersen stood leaning against the doorframe, looking slightly guilty but smiling nonetheless. He stepped forward and the floorboard under the carpet protested again.

"Sorry," he said apologetically. "I didn't mean to disturb you. I just haven't heard that kind of music for a long time – well, only Kurt's piano versions! I'll leave you alone."

"No!" Esther sat up in her chair. "Please, come in and sit down. There's no need for you to hide. Come in."

He gave a small, shy grin, dipped his head and came into the study. Crossing the room, he came to a halt in front of Esther's desk, his eyes gazing unseeing into the middle distance. "I remember dancing to a song like this when I was still in Oxford, not long before I went back to Germany," he said quietly. "It was a slow dance. 'Moonlight Serenade.' When times were more innocent."

"'Moonlight Serenade' is nothing like this!" Esther scoffed, trying to break the sad tension he had created.

"No, I suppose not." His lips quirked, knowing well that she was trying to lighten the mood. "The same band though, isn't it?"

"Yes."

"Do you ever dance, Mrs McAllister?" he asked, curious.

She looked away. "Rarely." It pained her to admit it. She had once dreamed of music halls stuffed to bursting with young men and women where she might go with friends to find herself a husband. It was what all the girls at her boarding school dreamed of. But Esther found a husband without dances in music halls.

"A pity," Petersen said softly before sitting down in an armchair by the gramophone and closing his eyes to listen.

Esther's pen scratched, the clock ticked and the music played on. When the record played out, she told Petersen to pick another. The soft flip, flip, flip as he sorted through the sleeves was the only sound for a moment until she heard the ceramic hiss of the turntable as it began to spin followed by the catch of the needle dropping on the record. The tinkling of piano keys filled the air, presently accompanied by the dulcet honk of a clarinet. 'Moonglow'. It was a favourite of Esther's from just after her marriage. It conjured memories of a time when she wondered at her good fortune, when she was still relatively innocent of the life she was now wedded to. But mostly she remembered lying on the chaise longue in the sitting room listening to the Benny Goodman Quartet while pregnant with Archie.

Though she was young at the time, her first pregnancy was a happy one with minimal complications and very little sickness. It was also a time when Fraser still made an effort to be her loving husband, to hide the shame he felt for marrying a girl of eighteen when he was middle-aged. He treated her kindly – indulgently – but he also confined her. Initially, she saw it as protectiveness. Later, she realised he did it out of embarrassment. He did not want to see people talking behind their hands when he walked by with his young wife. He did not want to be identified as the man who married the girl who was all but legally his ward – his inferior both in age and social position. But, Esther being the woman she was, could not be caged for long. Once she began to stand on her own merit, to defy him, Fraser was no longer able to hide her. So, instead, he hid himself.

Looking up, she realised that Petersen was hovering a few feet in front of the desk. He seemed unsure of himself which was surprising since there was always an air of self-possession to him. The skin around his eyes wrinkled and his mouth appeared to be working on something that he was unable to utter.

"Would you dance with me?" he huffed out. His eyes sprang wide as if he was himself surprised to hear the words come from his own mouth. "That is – I – eh –" He turned away, taking a faltering step towards the chair he'd just vacated.

But Esther's voice halted him.

"All right."

Had she been completely sober, she would have thanked the German but declined. Not because she didn't want to dance. On the contrary: all she wanted to do when she heard such music was dance. She always gave those few light little rhythmic steps when she was alone. The problem was that she felt she shouldn't dance in company. She worked hard to be taken seriously as a farm manager and thought that, if she danced, it might somehow lessen her authority. They would see her as a dizzy girl again rather than the businesswoman she purported to be. She had to be careful about what people saw her doing. Yet, somehow, exposing herself to Petersen didn't seem so dangerous.

She stood and was glad to find her legs were steady even if her head was a little light. Crossing the room away from the German, she closed the curtains over the double doors for fear someone like Muldoon might be snooping. She felt slightly guilty as she did it, knowing that if what she was about to do was completely innocent, she wouldn't need to hide it from curious eyes. But the guilt wasn't enough to make her change her mind. Turning, she found Petersen looking very awkward, rooted to a spot in the middle of the carpet. Then she realised she probably looked just as uneasy. Perhaps he was having second thoughts.

"If you don't want to –" Both of them spoke the same words in a rush.

They smiled shyly at one another from across the room, like debutants at a party.

"Shall I put it back to the start of the song?" she asked. "It's nearly over."

She didn't wait for a reply. Going to the gramophone gave her an excuse to get closer to him without going directly towards him. Once she adjusted the needle and the first few bars of brass floated into the room, she turned and almost collided with his chest. Concentrating as she was on not damaging the record, she hadn't heard him come up behind her. Automatically, he went to grab her shoulders to steady her but then withdrew before hesitantly offering his left hand, palm up. She placed her fingers in his and he held them lightly as he led her into open space.

Once they were in the middle of the room, the next challenge they faced was what to do with their remaining hands. Initially, Petersen grasped her left hand in a similar fashion to the other so that they were doing an inelegant two-step with bent elbows and both hands at waist height. Feeling how uncomfortable it was, Esther twisted her fingers from his and placed them lightly on his shoulder. Tentatively, the German reached down and softly touched her waist. Slowly, they began to sway more freely.

Though both knew how to dance, they were out of practice. For the first song, both spent the entire time looking down at their feet and, though they were mostly about a foot apart, still managed to catch each other's toes.

"You're trying to lead," he laughed when he attempted to guide her into a reverse turn and found her resisting him. "You don't have to."

She gave her arms a little loosening shake and tried to relax. Closing her eyes, she let her other senses explore in an attempt to stop her brain overthinking the movement required for dancing. First, she heard the music. Had she played an instrument, she could have played the song note for note, she knew it so well. But once she moved past the tune, she caught the susurration of the gramophone needle as it slid over the surface of the record. Though she tried not to flex her fingers, she could feel Petersen's work-roughened left hand in her right and the gentle shifts of the muscle and bone in his shoulder as he guided her around the room. She could smell him too. The overriding scent was carbolic soap but, as he shifted, she got little whiffs of sweet hay dust and the musk of dried sweat. The aroma was familiar, comforting. She leaned into it.

Then he stood on her foot.

"*Sorry!*" he exclaimed as she hissed between her teeth in pain.

"It's all right. My fault." She looked up into his face. It was the wrong thing to do. There was such concern in his eyes. She couldn't look away. She wanted to take his face in her hands and stare into those eyes for hours. But then her eyes drifted down to his lips. His mouth was wide, the lower lip full while the upper was thin but had a distinct angular bow. She moved forward into the space between them. She wanted to taste his lips.

He stepped away. "You're trying to lead again," he tutted playfully.

Esther wasn't sure if he was trying to brush her off gently

or if he really thought she was, once more, attempting to guide the dance. Nevertheless, she smiled at his teasing. But she couldn't look at him, instead casting her gaze on the floor.

Yet the seed was planted.

Energy coursed through her body – all of it directed towards the man in front of her. What contact she had with him wasn't enough. She wanted to intertwine their fingers, to run her hand down his bicep, to feel the sinew and muscle of his arm. She wanted to press her nose into his chest, to drink in his scent until it made her lightheaded. She wanted him to kiss her hair, her eyes, her cheeks, her neck, her lips. And she wanted to feel the length of his body against hers – to have her breasts against his chest, to press their thighs together, to reach up and hold herself close to him, wrapping her arms around his neck.

The first chime of nine o'clock rang out from the timepiece on the mantelpiece.

Her senses came back, crashing into her with the force of a breaking wave. She let him go, knocked backwards, dazed and shaky, trying to quiet the roar in her ears. What was she doing?

Gone were the lulling romantic tones of a slow waltz, replaced by a slightly faster tune. She had not heard the song change. They were no longer dancing to the music, they were dancing for the sake of touching one another. But now the spell was broken and the censorious ring of the clock called them back to reality. They had gone beyond the innocence of what they initially set out to do. There was nothing wrong with a man and woman dancing to a good song. However, when a man and a woman danced for the sake of it – touched because they enjoyed how they felt in one another's arms – that was different. And dangerous.

"I should go up to Erwin." Petersen appeared to be fascinated by the pattern on the carpet.

"Yes," Esther answered shakily. She touched her mouth,

wondering if they had, in fact, kissed. She was sure she could feel the tingling pressure of his lips on hers. Had she imagined it?

Glancing at him, she saw that he was no longer looking at the rug. He gazed avidly at her lips.

"You know the way up, don't you?" she asked him a little too loudly. He had carried the boy up earlier, but the house always looked different in the darkness. "I'll show you anyway."

It took every stoic bone in her body not to touch him as they climbed the stairs. At the door to Drew's old room she stopped. They stood facing one another, both wanting to say something, neither sure what it might be. But they didn't get the chance. As Petersen opened his mouth, the door opened, making them jump apart guiltily.

Mrs Morris cast a curious glance between them before turning to her mistress. "I didn't want the lad to be alone," she explained. "He's been asleep most of the time I've been here. Poor boy," she turned to look back at him, "he's been through the wringer. We'll see him through it, though."

"Yes." It was all Esther could think of as a suitable reply. The housekeeper's homely face had brought her back to earth with a bump. There was more in her world than just herself and a tall, handsome German. There was a sick boy, there were staff and there was Kirkmore. "Petersen will see to him until morning."

"Aye. We've set up a bed in the corner." Mrs Morris raked her eyes up and down the German. "Although I'm not sure you'll fit in it."

"I'll manage," he said mildly. "Thank you." Without further comment, he walked into the room to his comrade's bedside.

Esther shut the door.

"Catches the eye that one, doesn't he?" Mrs Morris murmured to her.

She didn't reply.

Chapter Sixteen

Despite the alcohol and her best intentions, Esther couldn't sleep once she went to bed.

Having locked Petersen and Erwin in the room together, she went back downstairs to finish up the accounts. Though she'd completed most of the filing, there was still the matter of entering everything into the ledger that sat accusingly on the edge of her desk. Though she always meant to write all her credits and debits as they went in or out, she couldn't manage to stay on top of them. There was always something more pressing to do. She would do it tomorrow and tomorrow and tomorrow. It didn't help that it was a task she dreaded the thought of, even if it was quite satisfying to see the neat columns of figures stacked on top of one another. The accounts were also solid proof that the regime she implemented at Kirkmore was successful, despite the doubts of her detractors.

But even the estate's increasing fortunes could not give her satisfaction that night. The figures slid through her brain and, no matter how hard she tried to keep them there, they were gone by the time she tried to write down her additions and subtractions. She closed her eyes and tried to clear her mind by listening to the music. However, as she let the sound wash over her, all she could do was smell hay dust, sweat and carbolic soap. She snapped her eyes open and glanced down at the blank, yawning pages. Cursing the ledger and its empty pages mocking her inability to fill them, she slammed the cover shut and stood to leave.

Though she stalked out of the room on heavy feet, she moderated her tread as she crossed the tiles of the hall to lock the front door before heading up to bed. No matter how bad her day was, she was always careful to maintain the peace of the slumbering house. Tonight especially, she didn't want poor Erwin to wake. She knew from experience how the sounds from the hall travelled up to the first floor of the house: every slammed door, every clacking heel. Very little went on downstairs without someone being able to hear it. Of course, Fraser hadn't cared who heard him. He was master of the house and could make as much noise as he damn well pleased. But the mistress did care who heard and was mindful of it even when she had other things to think about.

Like Petersen.

She didn't intend to dwell on her evening with the German but she couldn't help but feel his touch on her skin. To begin with, it had been soft, hesitant. But as he grew bolder, more comfortable, he took a firmer hold. There was strength in those hands. He didn't need to exercise it for her to know that. Yet, he touched so little of her body, it left her skin burning.

Lying in bed, she tried to concentrate on what it might feel like to have his hands explore her body but her imagination was frustratingly lacking. It went so far then stopped short every time she lost concentration and tried to think about the sensation, the moment when his fingertips finally rested on her skin. It was even worse when she tried not to think about him. Screwing her eyes tight shut, his arresting blue irises glowed from the depths of her internal darkness. His voice whispered through the empty room, making her believe that he was somehow sharing the space with her. Tensing all her muscles, she tried to force him out but he didn't budge. Behind her closed eyelids, his face smiled mockingly at her.

Frustrated, she flipped over onto her stomach and gasped in pain before peeling herself away from the mattress. She had forgotten about Erwin's accidental assault. Her chest ached from the force of the impact and now that she knew it was there again, she couldn't seem to shake the feeling. It also made her aware of the bruising on her backside which she hadn't been so aware of in the comfortable depths of the study chair. Lying on a hard mattress, she suffered for every small movement as she strove to find a comfortable position to stay in. Almost sobbing in exasperation, she suddenly became aware of a moaning sound from the room down the corridor. Totally alert, she stopped moving and concentrated with all her might on the noise from Drew's room, wondering if she should go and investigate. However, there was no call for help and, gradually, the whimpering subsided.

Guiltily, she shuffled down into the bed again. If she thought she had problems, they were nothing compared to what poor Erwin Riegel was suffering. As the night progressed and she finally began to drift in and out of sleep, she was aware of disturbances from the other room as Erwin's pain medication wore out. She wasn't sure if they were sleepless sounds or just echoes of pain-filled dreams. Every time she heard another sound, she wanted to comfort the boy. She felt sorry for Petersen too. Overseeing someone in that state was never going to be easy. But she felt sure Petersen would manage. Nothing seemed to faze him: farming, education, medical emergencies … dancing. And with that thought, sleep deserted her once more.

When the rest of the house began to stir Esther, having

given up on sleep, was already in her window seat, having spent quite a few hours trying to keep herself there. She considered going back down to the study to do more work on the accounts but knew from experience that it was pointless. It would also leave her completely exhausted by noon. She then thought about going to check on the boy since she hadn't heard a peep from the room for some time. What if Petersen had fallen asleep and didn't realise his charge needed attention?

Of course, she couldn't be sure that her concern for Erwin wasn't simply entangled with her desire to be close to Petersen again. She wanted to share a space with him, stand in front of him, to be sure that what she felt was real and that she hadn't imagined the attraction. And it wasn't just about how she felt. She needed to know if her sentiments were reciprocated. It was no use if her emotions told her one thing and his told him something else. Then there was the possibility that the German's interest in her was no more than a means to an end. She had no idea how long Petersen had already spent in captivity with only men for company. What if he was using her to satisfy years of pent-up lust and sexual unfulfillment. It wasn't inconceivable to think that he might string her along, no doubt aware of his attractiveness to the opposite sex. Yet she doubted he was that good an actor. He seemed too well mannered and attentive to her interests to be driven purely by lust. And, anyway, if he had allowed her to continue the evening before, she probably would have ended up on the study floor with him. But he hadn't let that happen.

Eventually, at what she thought was a reasonable time, she dressed and went to check on Erwin. She hesitated, wondering whether to knock, afraid to wake Erwin if he was sleeping. Then she cautiously opened the door a little and peeped inside. Mrs Morris was once again keeping watch over the young man. He was, mercifully, fast asleep and snoring softly.

"Mrs Coleman said she'd prepare breakfast for everyone else first then bring Mr Riegel up a bit to eat afterwards," the housekeeper said by way of a greeting. She was a woman of business, not pleasantries, Mrs Morris. "She said she'd watch the boy for a while in the morning. We'll take it in turns if you like." Her voice was pitched low so as not to wake Erwin but there was also a hint of challenge in her tone. It suggested that she and Mrs Coleman would be caring for the boy during the daytime and there would be no argument about it.

Esther nodded. It was too early in the morning to disagree with the housekeeper. Besides, with all the wild thoughts swirling around her head over the course of the night, she hadn't once thought to come up with a solution for the boy's daytime care.

"Mr Petersen's gone, is he?" she asked casually.

"Yes. Left the moment I arrived after letting me know how the night went. Then he was down the stairs like a shot. For a lad so big, he can't half move. And so quiet too!" She gave a little shudder. "Like a cat burglar. Flew down the stairs and not a creak out of a floorboard or anything. You'd never know he was there unless you saw him." She shook her head. "Any idea when Dr Robertson's coming back, mistress?"

"When his rounds allow, I suppose," Esther answered. "Why? Are you worried about something?"

"No, no. The boy seems to be doing well." She looked at him critically. "Though it's hard to know without opening the bandage. I had a smell of it when I came in though and it seems fine. You can often smell the infection if there's any there."

Esther nodded. She'd come across this pearl of wisdom before though she wasn't sure if it was in a medical or agricultural book. Doubtless the principle was the same for both. "And do you know what it would smell like if it were infected?" she asked. It was all very well to read about it. It was another entirely to have the practical knowledge of such things.

"Oh yes," the housekeeper answered brightly. "I'd know the smell anywhere. It was something we learnt to sniff out when we nursed here in the Great War."

Esther's eyes bulged in surprise. "You were a nurse here? At Kirkmore?"

"Oh aye!" Mrs Morris folded her hands in her lap and sat back, pleased that she could tell the mistress something she didn't know. "I became a nurse in Glasgow not long after the war started. I was a maid in a big house in the city but when the call went out for nurses – much as it did during this last war – I signed up. I thought I'd be able to help. And that I might find myself a handsome young soldier I could nurse back to health." She leaned in conspiratorially. "He'd be forever grateful when I saved him and would propose marriage on the spot."

"And did they ever? Propose?" Bald curiosity made Esther pry. She knew Mrs Morris had never married and that her honorific was given to her as a mark of respect for the position she held within the household.

Mrs Morris laughed softly. "Oh a few, a few. None of them tickled my fancy though. They transferred a group of us out here in '15 and, well, I've been here ever since. I suppose I prefer to keep someone's house rather than try and keep another human being alive. Especially when they have such a terrible habit of dying on you. What we would have given for penicillin," she murmured, shaking her head. "Anyway. I'll manage here if you want to head on down to breakfast."

As she headed along the corridor to wake the children, Esther mulled over what Mrs Morris told her. She had known Margaret Morris all her life, spent hours, days, months, in her company yet never knew how the woman came to live and work at Kirkmore. She knew the housekeeper was from Glasgow since her accent sometimes betrayed her heritage but, other than that, she never spoke much about her life before her time on the estate. It made Esther think: if she spent the last quarter of a century acquainted with Mrs Morris yet didn't really know her at all, how was she to know the mind of Michael Petersen? She couldn't even fathom the people who were around her all the time. Was this German making a total fool of her?

She was quiet at breakfast as she continued to ruminate on everything that occurred the day before. However, when she was almost finished her one and only cup of tea, there was a singsong shout from the hall that swept away her idle thoughts.

"*Hellooo!*"

Recognising Caroline's voice, she and the two children jumped up from the table and met Caro at the door. Behind her stood another figure.

"*Drew!*" Esther nearly knocked her oldest friend flat with the force of her impact.

He stumbled backwards, clinging on to her as she hugged him fiercely. "*Woah now!* Steady on, girl! It's all downhill from here on out if that's the welcome I get. How have you been?" He laughed, extricating himself from her grasp and holding her at arms' length to examine her. What he saw obviously displeased him. His mouth tightened. "God, you look awful."

"Andrew!" Caroline walloped him hard on the arm. "What a horrible thing to say!"

"*Ow!*" He rubbed his arm. "You're bloody dangerous, woman!"

"He probably has a point though," Esther conceded.

"*Drew, Drew, Drew!*" Archie bounced on the balls of his feet beside his brother. "I know Latin now. And some German. And I've been learning about geometry too. And last week, Dougie and I started to build a treehouse in the woods. Do you want to come and see it?"

Not to be outdone, Florence skipped around her siblings, vying for Drew's attention. "I can ride my bike on my own now and Michael said I haven't got a sum or a spelling wrong since the start of August. He says maybe he's making them too easy for me!"

"So will you come down to our treehouse?" Archie asked. "Although it's not really a treehouse yet. Just a ladder. But we made it!"

"And where did you get the wood to make it?" Esther cut in sharply. The local boys were not above pilfering firewood from their own families as well as neighbours when inspiration for a new venture took hold.

"Dieter and Heinz showed us how to split logs with a chisel and hammer one day at dinnertime. They helped us at first but now we do it all ourselves," he said, puffing out his chest with pride. "Major Brown says we're doing a good job. And we even asked Beattie if we could borrow some nails to put it all together."

"But borrow means you're going to give them back," Drew pointed out.

Archie's face fell and Florrie took it as her cue to barge in. "Do you want to see me ride my bike? I can bring it into the hall to show you."

"No, you cannot!" Esther said loudly over the clamour. "Ada and Mrs Morris would have a fit if you left dirty tyre-marks all over the floor."

Florrie looked as if she might cry. Spotting trouble and keen to head it off, Drew swept her up into his arms. "Why don't we cycle out to see Archie's treehouse after Caro and I've had some breakfast? You can go and practise for a while in the courtyard and we'll be out to you in a while."

"I'll go and get Dougie so we can show you the treehouse

together," Archie declared. He was just about to sprint off when he caught a look from his mother. "Is that all right?"

One of the few things Esther insisted on was that they weren't allowed to leave the house until she said so. Though she wasn't always entirely certain where they ended up, she always knew where they were headed at the start of every day. She did worry about what mischief they got up to, but she also thought it important that children with a playground like Kirkmore should have the freedom to explore it. After all, it was what made her and Drew's childhood so wonderful.

"All right, but –" Esther's voice halted Archie mid-step, "go down to Mrs Coleman and get her to put together a basket with some eggs and vegetables for Mrs Harper. Can you do that? *Without* breaking the eggs this time?"

"Yes, Mummy," he answered solemnly before sloping off to the kitchen.

"Norah still struggling?" Drew asked quietly as they watched Archie leave, Florrie skipping after him.

Esther sighed. "As much as she ever did. Some women just don't seem to know how to cope on their own. And her mother died earlier in the year too."

"I heard. I sent her my condolences. I always hate doing that. It seems so inadequate."

They turned and made their way to the breakfast room where extra food had magically appeared in their absence. Esther wondered how Mrs Coleman already knew there were visitors and that they would need to be fed.

Andrew took three rashers of bacon, a generous helping of scrambled eggs and some toast from the rack. Drew always ate when he came home. He was very fond of Mrs Coleman's cooking and she, in turn, was *very* fond of him.

"You're not sleeping again," he stated.

He didn't even look at her. But then he didn't need to. He

knew the tell-tale signs of Esther's insomnia from previous experience. Her face looked pale and there was a false shininess to her darkly circled eyes.

Caro glanced at her sympathetically but said nothing.

Esther hated the fact that she couldn't hide the physical signifiers of her sleeplessness. They were another thing she believed made her look weak in the eyes of others. When she looked so tired, people tended to coddle her, to talk down to her which, of course, never went well since along with the tiredness she also became quite short-tempered. She had no patience with sympathy. It wasted time and energy she could use for something more useful.

"Drew, I haven't slept properly since Florrie was born," she said wearily. "You know this already."

"Yes, but sometimes you're better than others. Most of the time you look fine."

"And we've already established that I look awful at the moment," she answered acidly. "If you must know, one of the men was injured yesterday. Long story but he ended up with a two-foot piece of wood through his leg. If that doesn't give you a sleepless night, then you're a harder man than I am.'

"But it's not just one night, is it?" he pressed, then added, "Is your man all right? Was it one of the Kirkmore lads?'

"No, it was one of the younger Germans. He's doing as well as can be expected, for now."

"And is he in the hospital or at Archie Robertson's?"

"He's in your old room," she told him curtly. "And not to be disturbed. Dr Robertson's orders."

Drew's eyes sprang wide. "Why is he here and not in hospital?"

"Because that's the way of it, Andrew!" Her composure was slipping. She gave him a hard stare.

He gaped at her for a moment. "Christ, it must be bad when you're calling me 'Andrew'," he said evenly.

"Drew," Caro warned.

Esther glared coldly at him. "Nothing is 'bad', Drew. Everything is going excellently well, in fact. But I don't appreciate anyone coming in here – whether they are the heir to Kirkmore or not – and questioning the way I do things. I have never let this family or the estate down before, so what makes you think you need to question my decisions now?"

Considering her for a moment, Drew appeared to be at war with himself. He knew Esther's judgement was sound. She proved it time and again. But he also knew she was running herself into the ground trying to maintain the estate while taking very little care of herself. He worried about her. He worried that Kirkmore would take from her what it could never give back: her youth, her drive, her happiness, her energy. The estate might easily suck her dry without her even realising it. And it could all start with a single questionable decision. Andrew wondered if her choice to put one of the Germans in the house, only a few doors from both her and her children, was the start of her downward spiral. But he knew her well enough to know that if he got into such a debate with her, when she was already desperately tired, things would not end well between them.

"I'm not questioning your decisions, Essie," he said calmly. "But you do have to admit that putting an injured Jerry up in my bedroom is a wee bit odd, no?"

She sighed heavily, scrubbing her face viciously. "I suppose. But I didn't know what else to do with him. He's perfectly harmless, by the way, if that's what you're getting at. They all are."

"If you say so," Drew murmured politely.

Esther's face tensed. She knew he didn't believe her. She would show him. "They're good men and they've done excellent work for us over the last three months. If you're done, I'll take you around to see everything. Then we can head down to the yard where you can meet them. They're covering the ricks and dosing sheep today."

Caro begged off so Esther and Drew traipsed outside to see Florrie on her bike. Then the three of them began a circuit of the estate. Esther had insisted that they either rode or cycled since, she reasoned, there was a shortage of fuel. It was a lovely dry day so, despite some grumbling and a flat refusal to ride from Drew, they set off on bikes to view the estate. On their way, they met Archie on his bike with Dougie riding a lady's bike which belonged to his mother.

The two boys took the lead to make sure the tour took in the beginnings of their treehouse. As they cycled along, Drew did most of the talking. He complemented Florrie on her cycling and praised the neatness of the hedges which the prisoners had trimmed before the hay harvest. He admired the weed-free vegetable fields, the cleared ditches and the shorn hayfields. He really was impressed by what he saw and proud that Esther was commanding such good practice amongst her workers. But he also wanted her to forget the tension of the breakfast room. Bitter experience taught him that if he fell out with Esther, it could take them years to mend fences and he really didn't want to do that again. He was happier in his life knowing he could come and go to Kirkmore whenever he pleased. Not only did it mean he could spend time with Esther, it meant he could catch up with all the trivialities of his little brother's and sister's lives too.

After they reached the site of the boys' new project, praised the work done on the treehouse and the soundness of all plans for its construction, they left Dougie and Archie to continue their labours. Retracing their journey, their slightly depleted group passed the house and carried on to the main yard where the men were working that day. The bulk of Kirkmore's winter fodder was stored around the yard and, when they came upon the ricks, they found several men bustling around the tall hut-like structures, covering each with a length of tarpaulin. There were two others on the ground sewing together more lengths of covering with oversized, vicious-look needles.

Alt Hans appeared to be in charge of the whole operation.

"Good morning, Hans," Esther said brightly as she arrived.

He turned to her and immediately removed his newly acquired cloth cap. Though very few of the men had caps, one of the locals had taken pity on Hans and his burning bald patch during the harvest and donated a spare tweed cap to him. Esther had never seen the German so happy. Now, every time she came anywhere near him, he doffed his cap respectfully then carefully replaced it on his head. He seemed so fond of it, Esther even asked Petersen if he slept in it. Petersen had roared with laughter then informed her that Hans, in fact, slept with it under his pillow for safe-keeping.

"Mistress," he greeted her with a little incline of his head. "We will finish before the rain, no?"

His English was improving apace.

Esther grinned encouragingly at him. "I think so. They look excellent, Hans." He smiled shyly at her praise. "Don't you think so, Drew?" Without waiting for a reply, she turned to the German conspiratorially. "Drew is my husband's eldest son. But don't let that put you off him!"

"Now, don't listen to her! She's very fond of me really. Hans, isn't it?" Drew extended a hand and Hans shook it with a small incline of his head.

"The rest of the men are dosing the sheep, yes?" Esther knew at a glance they weren't all there and, as she scoured the group, she was certain of at least one person being absent.

"Yes, they are with the sheep," he replied, pointing to the far side of the yard behind which were the dipping troughs and a vast field of pens to keep the animals in.

They departed for the sheep pens.

"The yard is very clean," Drew commented as they passed through it.

"The men tided it one afternoon," she explained. It was a rather poor explanation for the Trojan effort the prisoners had put into uprooting weeds growing in the cobblestones, clearing away bits of broken machinery and implements, animal detritus and general dirt. Since then, some of the prisoners were repairing the lime mortar of the buildings and replacing the rotten window frames. It looked wonderful and a few of the men seemed to enjoy the chance to better their skills of stonemasonry and carpentry so Esther was delighted to let them pass odd days improving the place.

"Useful chaps really." He stopped for a moment to take it all in. "With efficiency like this, it's a wonder we managed to win the war at all."

Esther burst out laughing at Drew's dryness. She rarely laughed like that anymore. Yet Drew always managed to shock a laugh from her.

The group of men closest to them, who were working with the sheep, looked up curiously. Though they saw Esther smile or give a humorous chuckle every now and then, none had seen her laugh like this. Their attention was immediately diverted to the stranger beside her who elicited such a reaction. They noted that he was moderately tall, trim and youthfully handsome. The way he looked at their mistress and she at him instantly piqued their curiosity. For some, it brought an abrupt distrust of this new gentleman as their instincts told them to protect Esther. Their feelings weren't so much a slight against Drew as a compliment to Esther. While they were working in a foreign country for a pitiful wage in all weathers, the men truly cared for Esther's well-being since it was so much tied up with their own. Though love was too strong a word to describe what they felt, they respected her abilities, her kindness, and all felt a certain amount of loyalty to her. Any kind of interloper – in their eyes – spelled trouble.

Approaching the hive of activity, Esther and Drew stood leaning against the edge of the pens watching locals and Germans alike as they shooed sheep into the chutes to be checked for maggots and drenched for worms. It was heartening to see that there was no segregation of men about the enclosure. The Germans mixed and laughed and chatted in broken English which was improving all the time. Esther studied the gathering, looking for any sign of animosity among them but could find nothing. If it weren't for the accents and strange clothing the Germans wore, they would have blended seamlessly with the residents of Kirkmore.

Of course, once she made her first sweeping assessment of the work party, her eyes sought out one man.

Petersen was at the sharp end of the operation, wielding a dosing gun that contained the foul-smelling drench. Though she had seen and felt the delicacy of his hands the night before, now she was witness to their strength as he caught each sheep and delivered the worm treatment into the back of their throats before pushing them on and dosing the next one. He hunched over each animal and treated each with such focused efficiency that he seemed oblivious to the world around him. Then suddenly he looked up and unwaveringly found Esther's gaze upon him. When their eyes locked, Esther wasn't sure if her stomach dropped, flipped or jumped to her throat. Whatever happened, she couldn't look away and it seemed he couldn't either. She felt the heat and the weight of his regard deep within her body. There was no mistaking what burned inside him. Esther didn't doubt that her own gaze held similar promise. But then someone called his attention back to the task at hand and the moment was broken.

"Who is he?"

Glancing at Drew, Esther silently cursed herself. Was she really that obvious? Just the day after they first touched each other, she and Petersen were giving themselves away in public. She would have to be more careful in the future. Then she caught herself. Future? What future did she have with the German? What did she want from him? To be held, touched, kissed? Did she want something more? Deep in the pit of her stomach she felt a flutter and knew exactly what she wanted. But it was impossible and she knew it.

"That's Michael," Florrie chipped in helpfully. She climbed to the top of the railings, using Drew's arm to steady herself. "*Hello, Michael!*" she called, waving frantically at him.

The smile he gave the little girl warmed Esther's heart. It was so loving, so easy, there could be no doubt about his fondness for her daughter. Once his hand was free, he waved back.

"Michael's been teaching Archie and me over the summer," Florrie explained. "And there's Jung Hans! Can I go and say hello, Mummy?" Hopping down from the wooden railings, she turned expectantly to Esther.

"Off you go then, but careful and don't get in anyone's way."

They watched her scamper off around the enclosure to see the boy.

"Didn't think you'd let the wee folk near them," Drew commented.

Esther tensed. Her smile slid off her face. "Well, I did and I do and so does everybody else."

"And if everybody else jumped off a cliff, would you do it too?" he muttered, turning away.

"*What?*" she said sharply, making several people nearby look up.

"Come on, Essie!" he hissed, leaning closer so no one would hear. "These men are killers and you're letting your children mosey about with them?" He shook his head.

"Nearly every man who came back from the war is a killer," she answered stubbornly.

"Yes, but they went *home*. They didn't get press-ganged into farm labour in enemy territory. What if they turn on you? What will you do then?"

"If they were going to turn on us, they would have done it by now," she said confidently. She didn't dare to admit that a workers' revolt was something that always niggled at the back of her mind.

Drew snorted, knowing her too well. "That doesn't mean they aren't biding their time. What then?"

"We'd deal with it," she said tartly.

Turning to walk away, she found her arm caught in Drew's grasp. She wrenched it free, furious. They were getting more than curious glances now. Many men – local and German – were openly staring. Florrie, who was chattering to Jung Hans and another young man by the fence, was thankfully oblivious.

"Don't push me, Drew." Esther's voice was cold and livid. "You and your father swanned off and left this place to fend for itself. I've been the one who dragged it back into real profitability while you pair have been off doing God knows what. I know my job and they –" she threw a careless hand in the direction of the workers, "know theirs. The war is over. And yes, they haven't been sent home yet and that's very unfair. But if it's a choice for them to stay here where food is good and they're treated like human beings or go off to some other godforsaken farm or camp, the men would choose here. You can ask them if you want." She crossed her arms and flashed her eyes in challenge.

"The mistress is right, sir." Cary Eden approached along the side of the pen. The foreman had been watching and listening as their voices rose. "I've worked with these men for three months now and I'd trust my own children with them so I think she can too. They're just normal men, sir, and they are grateful to be here where conditions are good. They appreciate it, sir. I know it's hard for you just coming in to understand us all working together like this but … it works," he shrugged.

Esther stared at her foreman. She'd never heard him utter so many words in one go. It was a running joke locally about how Cary ever managed to get through his wedding vows since he was always such a reticent individual. Now Esther knew exactly how he got through them: if Cary Eden thought something important enough, he said it. She grinned at him in gratitude and fought the urge to stick out her tongue at Drew and say, 'I told you so!'

Eden calmly met Drew's hard stare until he looked away with a sigh and relaxed his shoulders. "All right," he muttered. "I believe you. Sorry, Essie," he murmured, sticking out a hand for her to shake.

"We have to stop arguing every time you come back," she said quietly, taking his hand and giving it a strong squeeze. "I don't ever want us to go back to the way we were before."

Drew nodded then, without warning, pulled her in for a bone-crushing hug that almost lifted her off her feet. "Deal," he replied, voice muffled against her jumper.

Mortified by his display of affection in front of all the men, Esther could feel her face glow with embarrassment when he released her. She knew, without looking, that almost everybody was staring at them.

"You've gone all red!" Drew said in a singsong voice.

Esther gave him a cross shove in the chest as she had so often done as a child when he teased her. "Shut up and bugger off, McAllister!" she huffed.

"*Ooo*, Muncie's got a temper!"

Drew crouched and shouldered her back, sending her

flying into Cary Eden who kindly righted her before sauntering off for fear of being caught up in their playful scuffle. Esther cast a ferocious look at Drew who had the good sense to put up his hands in surrender.

"Okay, okay. Truce?"

Cocking her head, Esther turned away as if she was considering her options. She caught Petersen looking once again, his eyes glittering as he watched her. Returning to Drew, she did her best to look innocent.

"Shake on it?" she asked, careful not to proffer her hand.

Luckily for her, Drew was only too ready to extend his own hand. She smiled wickedly before grasping his hand between both of hers. The look of relief on Drew's face quickly turned to one of horror as he looked down to find Esther was in the process of mashing a large handful of dung into his hand. It was worth getting her own hands dirty to see Drew's sudden revulsion.

Cackling wildly, she took off around the sheep pens as Drew's garbled threats, insults and sounds of disgust followed her. The dung handshake which every child at Kirkmore perfected in their youth was something Esther hadn't used in fifteen or twenty years but she was pleased to discover it was still as funny as it had been the first time. The gathered men found it hilarious too, delighting in this show of youthful exuberance and mischief from the lady of Kirkmore. Many also silently vowed to make use of the dung handshake at the first opportunity.

By the time their roars of laughter subsided, Drew had wiped his hand with his handkerchief which he then discarded and was making a valiant attempt at regaining his dignity in front of so many spectators. Esther was a good distance away by then, standing at the opposite side of the pen with two fences and a whole flock of sheep providing a useful barrier between them. She had already washed her hands in the sheep disinfectant which smelt very strong but at least was sure to leave her hands clean. She grinned triumphantly across at Drew who pointed an accusing finger at her.

"*You, Muncie, are for it!*" he shouted across at her before turning and stalking off up the hill back to the house to the ringing sound of catcalls from the Kirkmore men.

Chapter Seventeen

As luck would have it, Drew did not make good on his threat of reprisal. His presence always reinvigorated Esther and delighted her children. He ran around with them, played their games, praised their achievements and generally did all the things their father never did with them. Yet, the contrast between Fraser's passivity and Drew's activity no longer bothered Esther. She was used to seeing it and could accept it now she knew it was never going to change. Once Drew accepted that her decision-making and judgement was still as sound as ever, she began to discuss the estate's business with him. However, she did not do so out of an urge to seek any kind of approval. She did it because, like Caro, he was good at listening to new plans while confirming that her past choices were also sensible. As far as she could tell, Drew had little interest in taking over the estate once his father died. It made Esther wonder why she was putting so much effort into keeping Kirkmore going if it was unwanted. There was no guarantee Archie would want it either when he grew up. She wondered what would become of the place if it was left to either of them. But she pushed that thought to the back of her mind. She had enough things to worry about.

One thing she did not have to worry about was Drew's opinion of Petersen.

If her best friend had disliked the German, Esther would have been totally at a loss as to what her own feelings were telling her. But, on the first night, Drew headed into the library for a book once Archie finished his lesson and never came back. Esther was still slaving over the accounts when she heard the low rumble of male voices mixed in with the lighter tones of Caroline's. Though she could not hear the content of their discussion through the cracked door and was relieved that things were so cordial, she still found their eruptions of laughter distracting. What she would have given to sweep all the pages of numbers onto the floor and join them. She struggled on for a whole hour, watching the clock until she could finally go and collect Petersen to take him up to Erwin's room.

"We'll talk again tomorrow," Drew assured Petersen as he said goodnight.

Esther was careful to close the door to the library properly as she left. "You and Drew seemed to get on well," she said quietly, struggling to keep the envy out of her voice.

"Yes," Petersen answered, sounding surprised. "You know, when I saw you together this morning, I hoped he was your brother."

She glanced at him sharply and had to look away almost immediately. He really did have the most alluring, expressive eyes. If she continued to hold his gaze, she thought she might do something foolish. She wondered if she should even trust herself to be alone with him. "Well, you don't need to worry on that account since he is, in fact, my son."

"Yes, the local men told us that. But he told me now that you were as good as brother and sister. That," Petersen breathed, "was a relief."

Voice caught in her throat, Esther stood dumbly a few feet from the German, captured by his stare. He took one step and was toe to toe with her. She could feel the soft gust of his exhalation on her cheek.

"*Esther* ..." he whispered.

They jumped apart as the door to the library flew open.

"Essie! Caro and I were wondering if you'd have time for a drink before we headed home." Drew didn't seem to register the fact that she and Petersen had only made it fifteen feet across the hall to the bottom of the stair. His expression was guileless as he observed them, his question innocent.

"Yes, all right. I'll be down in a minute. I just want to check on Erwin." She began ascending the stairs.

When she and Petersen reached the door to the invalid's room, they stopped once more.

"Don't drink too much," he said with a grin. "It makes you lose your inhibitions."

"Oh? And how would you know?" she asked.

Stopping at the door, he leaned in so that his breath tickled her ear as he spoke. "Because I saw it last night. It makes you reckless."

She stood on her toes, her lips brushing against his ear. "I don't always need a wee nip to make me reckless." She pulled away and smiled at him, quite pleased to see the effect she was having on him.

Rapping once on Erwin's door, she opened it and ushered Petersen in while Mrs Morris stood to leave. But, as he passed her, Esther felt his fingers brush against hers.

"Good night, Mrs McAllister," he said, his words heavy, full of promise.

"Good night, Mr Petersen," she breathed.

By the time she composed herself and went back down to the library, Esther found Caroline and Drew lounging in the two deep, leather sofas studded with hundreds of buttons that flanked the fireplace. Caro stayed where she was but Drew swung his legs off the seats and beckoned Esther to join him.

"I just have to turn off the lamp in the study," she said, heading straight past the back of his sofa to the connecting doorway. Drew grabbed her hand over the fat, rolling leather back and she got a sudden flash of another hand touching hers only minutes before.

"I've already done it," Drew said, not letting go of her as he dragged her around the end of the settee to sit. "I know you. You go in there and we won't see you for another hour at least. Sit, Esther, put your feet up. You deserve it." He handed her a drink and clinked his own glass against it. "Cheers!"

"Cheers," she murmured, taking a sip. It was a lighter drink than the one she had the night before. Caro always mixed whisky with soda since she thought it much too harsh a drink to have on its own.

"We were just talking about Archie's tutor," Drew said conversationally. "Seems like a decent chap. Very decent, in fact."

"We approve," Caro butted in, eyes sparkling. "We definitely approve."

"Intelligent sort and an Oxford man too." Drew seemed to be talking to himself.

"And so *handsome*!" Caro said baldly. "Well done on that front, Esther."

Drew snapped his head up to look sharply at his wife. "That's hardly relevant."

Caroline rolled her eyes. "Oh, come on, Drew! Even you can appreciate he's good-looking! And why shouldn't she have something male and pretty to look at around the house. Because bulls and rams and dogs just don't really cut it. It's good to have a man's energy in a house."

"As a husband or a brother or a son perhaps," Drew said indignantly. "Having an enemy prisoner about the house for male energy is hardly appropriate. In fact, I would say that's highly inappropriate."

"I agree," Esther answered calmly, though she couldn't even glance in Caro's direction as she said it. "I picked

Petersen for his knowledge and his rapport with Archie, that's all." Or, she could have added, at least it was at the start.

Drew smiled at her approvingly and Caro tutted, disappointed that her fun was to be cut short. Esther was sure this wasn't the last she would hear on the subject of the German. She would have to be careful about how she answered any questions that came her way. Freddie Robertson had warned her about that.

"The hay this year smells good," Drew commented, moving onto less shaky ground.

"It does, doesn't it?" she agreed.

Chapter Eighteen

Unfortunately, Esther struggled to keep the promise she made to herself about answering questions regarding the German. The very next day, Caroline arrived just as Esther and the children were finishing their breakfast, proposing a shooting trip, "Just for us girls." It was the sort of thing the two women did every now and again. Where others might have gone on a shopping spree or to the theatre, Esther and Caro were much more comfortable trudging through the countryside in tweed jackets and trousers. It was something that never failed to amaze Esther – how comfortable Caroline was out in the open tramping up muddy paths since, when Esther met her for the first time, she was the most urbane creature she had ever beheld.

It was shortly after the crushing experience of Florence's difficult birth that Esther found herself in Aldershot, Hampshire, with very little idea how she got there but knowing for certain she wanted to be anywhere but at Kirkmore. There were times when she walked the streets of that new town with no idea where she was going and even less of an inkling as to where she came from. All she knew was that she was there for Drew because Drew was dying just like she had been a month before.

When war broke out, Fraser insisted that Drew did not join the army. He had seen the horrors of the Great War first-hand and did not want his son to share such a terrifying experience. Instead, Drew abandoned an engineering degree at university and joined the Royal Air Force to become a pilot of small aircraft, thinking that being up above the conflict would be safer than being in the middle of it all. He only found out how wrong he was when it was too late.

Sitting at home in a disturbing, disorientating fug, Esther took delivery of a telegram informing her that Plt. Off. Andrew McAllister was gravely wounded and currently receiving treatment at Cambridge Military Hospital in Aldershot, Hampshire. In her addled state, Esther immediately sprang into action and within an hour was on her way to Aldershot.

Her abscondence went against every piece of advice she was given by her doctor to remain at home on bed rest near her new-born daughter to give her a chance to finally bond with the baby after such a long period of time apart. But all Esther wanted to do was extend that time apart. She wanted to avoid the accusatory eyes of everyone who thought her a bad mother for not loving her new daughter and going to see Drew was the perfect excuse. No one could deny comfort to Kirkmore's favourite child when he was so gravely ill, even if it was in the form of the now broken young Mrs McAllister.

Esther had struggled on the journey down south, given that her blood pressure had not quite recovered since the birth and she was still prone to dizzy spells, nausea and cold sweats. She also struggled with concentration which meant she missed one of her connecting trains on the journey down and also misremembered the name of the street she was staying on when she hired a taxi to take her there.

And then there was the hollowness inside her: the terrifying emptiness of a child that had once been one with

171

her body but was no longer there. It felt like some vital organ had been ripped from her unconscious form. Every now and again she found herself absently attempting to stroke her distended belly only to experience the split-second horror and petrified panic that what had lived inside it was somehow gone. Then the memories of cleaving agony tore through her brain reminding her that her child, though absent, was alive and elsewhere. Yet, after such episodes she continued to find herself short of breath with a thundering heart and limbs that refused to stop shaking long after she quelled the torturous memories.

Finally, when she reached Drew, she found something grounding in his familiar presence even if he was swollen, bruised and broken. As she sat by his bedside, clinging to his hand like a dying woman, she guiltily realised that she had come to him as much for her own comfort as for his. She felt as if she were falling apart at the seams and that, by some means, Drew would be the one who could pull her back together again. He was the one remaining constant in her life – the person who had seen her through so much from youth to adulthood and was still there despite all of it. If Drew died, she knew she wouldn't survive it. So she held on, willing him to recover as much for her sake as for his own. And then there was also the comfort of a familiar face that stayed serenely expressionless. In the last number of weeks, she had become so attuned to the looks people gave her and hated every one of them. There was sympathy, curiosity, judgement, anger, disregard, false jollity, contempt, imperiousness and – almost worst of all – pity. It was so freeing to have such a loved face display nothing at all other than restfulness. Other peoples' countenances put her on edge but the tranquillity of Drew's calmed her. She was less on edge and, as she watched by his bedside day after day, Esther slowly returned to herself.

That was when she first encountered Caro.

Sitting in a café near the hospital for lunch one afternoon, Caroline Reeves breezed into the establishment wearing a thigh-length bottle-green jacket and wide, billowing high-waisted linen trousers in the most startling terracotta colour. She had topped and tailed the entire ensemble with a plum-coloured hat and two-tone white-and-tan brogues. Coupled with her height, Esther didn't think she had seen anything quite so exotic as this woman in her entire life. It was, therefore, something of a shock when the woman – who commanded the attention of the entire room – stopped and spoke to her.

"You're with that fellow on Ward Four, second floor, aren't you?" she said without preamble.

"Y-yes," Esther stuttered, stunned that such a creature would even acknowledge her existence, never mind talk to her.

Without further ado, the woman plumped herself down on the seat opposite and gave a dramatic sigh. "There's no one sitting here, is there?" she asked as an afterthought.

"No," Esther replied breathily.

Caroline – for she then introduced herself as such – was there to see her brother who was another injured pilot – "bloody fool" – who had lost the lower portion of his left leg after a mid-air skirmish with a German Messerschmitt. Caro then proceeded to recount her entire life story to Esther as they sat in the café all afternoon drinking cups of progressively weaker tea as the hours wore on. Esther found herself fascinated by the woman's openness but also the strangeness of her life as the only surviving female in an entirely male aristocratic household. That, at least Esther thought, explained the way she dressed, spoke and carried herself. There was something wonderfully irreverent about Caroline Reeves that Esther had only previously come across in men. And then there was the fact that Caro made her laugh more than she was used to and certainly more than she had done in the previous number of months. She possessed a dry wit that Esther found familiar since it was so similar to Drew's sense of humour. She was also well-read, highly intelligent, opinionated and self-confident – all the things Esther wished she was. Self-confidence was something she seriously lacked given her experiences over the last number of weeks and it was not helped by the hollowness at her core. In fact, Esther's confidence had slowly crumbled as she went straight from child and daughter to wife and mother without the chance to consider her own state of mind. Being away from Kirkmore gradually allowed her time and space to redefine herself – to come to a better realization of who she was and what she wanted in life. And, of course, being around someone as easy to talk to as Caro helped enormously.

Outside of the hospital, the two women began to spend more and more time together. They ate their meals together, walked in the grounds of the hospital and even went on a daytrip to Reading to buy some clothes for the winter and provisions for their respective invalids who, despite their initial prognoses, were both doing well. As they walked or sat side by side, Esther unburdened herself of every unhappiness, every embarrassment, every guilty secret of the last four years. It was such a release to unpack these festering thoughts to someone who did not know her past or where she came from. There was such a lack of judgement from Caroline that Esther probably told her more than she should have. But it was so easy to talk to her without fear of getting funny looks. And then there was the benefit of knowing Caro wouldn't just tell her that this was her lot in life, that she should be grateful to be a wife and mother. Because being just a wife and mother was not enough for Esther and it was Caroline who made her see that.

It was one of the reasons Esther would forever be in

Caroline's debt. She returned to Kirkmore rested and rejuvenated, ready to take on new challenges and give her daughter the unconditional love she deserved. Time, distance and a sympathetic ear, she discovered, were great healers.

The other reason Esther loved Caro dearly was because she made Drew happy.

On a day when both women went to the hospital, Caroline found her brother fast asleep and, rather than going back to her hotel alone, she asked if she could sit with Esther and Drew. Esther didn't get a single syllable out before Drew almost shouted that she was very welcome to stay and then tried to sit up straighter which left him grimacing in agony. He had healing burns down his left side which were tight and not yet inclined to stretch when he moved. Seeing his discomfort, Caro had gently put a stilling hand on his shoulder which she kept there for far too long. Esther secretly maintained that, on that day, she watched the two of them fall in love and was quite proud that it was she who brought them together.

Six months later – and fully recovered – Drew was still in the RAF but working as an engineer rather than a pilot. He and Caro married in Kirkmore church on the 28th of April 1941 and since then split their time between the gate lodge and wherever their occupations as writer and engineer took them. By that stage, Esther had taken on the mantle of overseeing the running of the estate, much to the surprise of everyone except Drew and Caro who were always there to give her confidence but also remind her to live her life just a little every now and again. It was something that Caro was especially good at.

That afternoon found the two women marching up the brae at the back of the house to get to good shooting, the dogs passing swiftly back and forth, noses to the ground.

"You're working too hard, you know," Caro told Esther as she watched Jasper and Sadie hunt. "I can tell just by looking at you."

"You always tell me I'm working too hard," Esther said wearily. "And what the hell is wrong with the way I look?" she continued crossly. "That's both you and Drew who've said I look terrible in the space of two days. Thank you."

"I did *not* say you looked terrible," Caro answered, repositioning her broken gun under her armpit. "Drew did, of course, but he can be awfully blunt."

Esther eyed her shrewdly. "So, what you're saying is – while he shouldn't have said it in that way – what he said was true?"

"Well … yes." She caught Esther's expression. "Sorry."

"Drew's not the only one who's bloody blunt as it turns out. Is there a point to insulting me or are you just doing it for your own entertainment?" Just like her relationship with Drew, Esther's friendship with Caroline was a healthy balance of unconditional love and bickering.

"There is a point," Caro said happily. "Sometimes it's better to leave work and come back to it once you're well rested and refreshed. And I know what you're going to say!" She spoke a little louder and held up her hand to cut Esther off before she even started. "You're going to say that you can't leave your work and that there's too much to do and anyway you don't sleep so how could you possibly rest. Yes? So, what you need to do is do something for yourself. Not something for Kirkmore, not something for the children, something for you."

"And what do you suggest?" Esther asked, irritated as she walked on ahead of her friend up a narrow pathway.

"Well, how about a little fun with that rather dashing German friend of yours?'

Caroline walked straight into Esther who had become

rooted to the spot. Slowly, the mistress turned to gape at her friend.

Caro guffawed at her horrified expression.

"*What?*" Esther hissed, casting about to make sure there was no one listening.

"Oh, come on, Essie!" Caro huffed, putting her hands on her hips. "I've seen the look on your face – don't deny it! – and I know you appreciate a handsome man just as much as I do. Even if you are married to an old goat."

"And there's the problem," Esther said simply, trying to keep the sadness from her voice as she gazed unseeing at the gambolling dogs.

Caro scoffed. "And what odds does that make? Your dear, darling husband sleeps with the same woman he's been sleeping with for the past twenty years – don't look at me like that – I know you know as well as everyone else does."

Esther was silent.

Caroline's impassive expression turned to one of horror. "You mean you don't know?"

"I know," Esther sighed.

She had long suspected that Fraser was having an affair (or perhaps relationship was the more appropriate word) with his secretary in London. Madeline Pugh was a sweet older woman – the mothering type, whose husband absconded with a nurse shortly after the Great War without formally divorcing his wife. The woman lived in a kind of limbo, alone yet unable to marry while also struggling to find constant employment and suitable lodgings for a single yet legally married woman. That was until Fraser McAllister offered her secretarial work which gradually extended to keeping his house and latterly keeping him. Mrs Pugh even came to Esther's wedding and gifted her a beautiful set of English lead wineglasses which she later discovered were a very expensive present for a mere secretary.

It wasn't until she made an unscheduled trip down to Fraser's London home and had a little snoop about while the place was empty that her suspicions about Mrs Pugh were confirmed.

At first glance when she entered the secretary's bedroom, it seemed suitably modest and frugally furnished. But something about the space niggled at Esther and made her travel further into the room to investigate. It was then that she noticed the smell of disuse, the must of damp in the air. When she ran her fingers along the surface of the bedside table and the chest of drawers, they came away grubby. The only piece of furniture that appeared to be in regular use was the wardrobe. Clearly, no one had been there for a while. Her suspicions were confirmed when she found a lady's underwear drawer in her husband's bedroom.

Though it hurt Esther a little to discover Fraser's betrayal, she also felt a surge of relief that her failed relationship with her husband was not the only one he had. It liberated her from what she thought of as her wifely duties since someone else was performing them for her. She was freed from the burden of having to find a way to make their marriage work again. And the guilt she felt for failing as a wife also began to recede as she discovered that it was not her fault that her husband regretted being wed to her. However, she was never certain that others knew until now.

"Thank God for that!" Caro squealed. "I thought I'd put my foot right in it by telling you. I was worried you were going to break down in hysterics or something."

Esther eyed her critically. "What could possibly give you the idea that I might be prone to hysteria? And especially over something like that."

"I suppose not," Caro shrugged. "I'll never understand how you ended up *married* to *him*." She shuddered. "I mean, even I think he's old and you're *years* younger than me."

"Only four – well, four and a half – but it wasn't like I had much of a choice. My mother told me I should, so I did. And Fraser was always nice to me and he's not a bad-looking man ..."

She trailed off. When she married him ten years ago, he was an athletic man of forty-four who hunted and went swimming. Now, nearly a decade on, several years of which were spent sitting at a desk somewhere in London, Fraser was ... looser. He was not fat – Esther doubted he would ever be that – but was no longer a muscular man. He was hunched from too much time spent at a desk. His dark-brown hair was now well on the way towards white and his face was greying, drawn tight from too many worries and long thankless hours of work.

Caro scoffed at Esther's defence. "He's no Mr Petersen though, is he?" she said slyly.

"No." Esther didn't go any further than stating that one irrefutable fact.

"Then why not have some fun?" Caro's voice was soft and persuasive.

"Don't you read the newspapers?" Esther asked irritably. "Haven't you heard of the ban on 'amorous liaisons' between British women and Germans? They've even prosecuted some poor girls. Fines of ten or fifteen pounds for some of them. And that's not even mentioning that Doris Blake woman in the paper. I read this morning that she's getting two months in prison and has to pay a five-hundred-pound fine. And her lover is facing a court martial. I can't risk that and neither can Michael."

"*Ha!* You called him 'Michael'!" Caro cackled. "So you *do* care about him."

"Oh, for God's sake!"

Esther stomped off only for Caro to catch up with a few strides of her long legs.

"Doris Blake got two months in prison for leaving the country without permission and stealing a bloody great yacht. And her German chap is being court-martialled for escaping and stealing said yacht. So unless you're planning to hightail it and steal a boat, I think you might be safe enough."

"I'm not *planning* anything," Esther snapped.

"Anyway, neither of you would need or probably want to leave Kirkmore," Caroline continued, undeterred. "There are plenty of nice quiet places you could get to know each other without being disturbed."

Esther rounded on her friend. "*Stop it. Just stop it, Caro.* If this is what you want to talk about I'm going home right now."

The cold, determined look in her eye made Caro hold a hand up in surrender.

"All right, all right," Caro sighed, disappointed. Her mind was running away with her as she figured out how to engineer an affair. She loved to create mischief that was enjoyable rather than painful to the parties involved. She wanted Esther to experience something wild, something pleasurable. She wanted her friend to live a little, to take a chance and not be constantly beholden to 'the right thing', whatever that was. Esther lived the life of a nun. She was devoted to her own kind of god-like structure that ruled over every part of her life. Kirkmore was Esther's god but Caro knew commitment to such an unforgiving deity was not enough for anyone, no matter how much they professed it to be. The simple truth was that Kirkmore would never love Esther back. Only creatures with a beating heart could do that and the best sort of creature to do it, in Caro's opinion, was a man.

Though they continued to hunt for the next couple of hours, relations between the two friends were strained. Esther was much more reserved and monosyllabic than usual, but Caro breezed through, acting as though she were oblivious to the tension, chatting about nothing. She knew Esther would come around eventually and they would resume their normal easy friendship. She also hoped that Esther would come around to the idea of having a little fun with their German acquaintance but, wisely, she said nothing more on that front.

When they arrived back, each carrying a string of dead birds over their shoulders, they entered through the basement door, divested themselves of their hunting clobber and left the birds to Mrs Coleman in the kitchen. Drew was waiting for them when they went upstairs. However, when they entered he paid them no mind. He had found a way of entertaining both himself and the children by setting up a huge, long snake of dominos across the tiled floor in the hall.

"*Stop, Mummy!*" Florence stood at the far side, her hands outstretched as if she thought she could push the grown-ups away.

Esther sank down onto her knees, an eager look on her face. "I remember building these with you, Drew, when we were little. You always made the gaps too big."

Drew appeared quite affronted at her for bring that up. "Well, I've learnt my lesson," he sniffed.

"Are you sure?"

Drew narrowed his eyes. "This one's going to be perfect. Isn't it, Archie?"

With his tongue between his teeth as he arranged the final few dominos, Archie didn't reply immediately.

Florence answered for him. "It'll be the best dominos you've ever seen," she enthused, bouncing on the balls of her feet.

Drew looked a tad worried by her pronouncement but still managed to muster an encouraging smile.

"Ready!" Archie called enthusiastically, hopping up. "I'll go and get Mary and the others so they can see it too." He ran around the edge of the hall and disappeared down to the servants' quarters.

"Can I be the one to start it?" Florence begged. She gave Drew a cherubically sweet smile.

Gravely, he shook his head. "We agreed that whoever won rock, paper, scissors would start it and Archie won. You can do the next one."

Esther could see her daughter eyeing the small, spotted wooden tiles close to her toes. Florrie edged a fraction closer. "Come over here, sweetheart!" Esther extended her arms and her little girl turned and trotted into them. She lifted her. "Look, you can see it all much better from up here."

"And even better from up here," Caro said, taking Florrie herself.

Archie clattered back into the hall trailing Mary, Mrs Coleman and Mrs Morris.

"Right!" he said officiously. "Are we all ready?"

They nodded and stepped back, giving the boy the floor. He got into position, crouching at one end of his snake. *"Right. Three, two, one – go!"*

He flicked the first tile and a satisfying purr ensued as they fell, one after the other. Then suddenly: silence. No more than thirty tiles had fallen when one missed its neighbour. Everyone held their breath, hoping that something would happen, that an errant gust of wind might save the day. But it didn't.

A goose honked amongst the gathered crowd. Or, at least, that was what it sounded like. Everyone turned in Esther's direction with a mixture of shocked, concerned and curious expressions as she doubled over, palm clamped over her mouth, tears welling as another snort escaped from behind her hand. She desperately tried to keep quiet but the battle was well and truly lost once Drew spoke.

"It's not funny, Essie!" he whined, reduced to the small

boy who so often experienced the same problem when the pair had played dominos as children.

Esther's laughter was catching as she subsided onto the floor, rocking herself like a madwoman as tiny shouts of amusement escaped her lips. Mary turned away as the two other servants' shoulders shook with suppressed merriment. Only Caro was unladylike enough to join Esther's raucous cackling.

The children stood and watched, somewhere between affront and genuine bewilderment. Drew continued to sulk.

"Well, I was *sure* it was going to work," he murmured petulantly.

It was enough to send everyone but the children over the edge.

Chapter Nineteen

The hilarity of Drew's and the children's escapades wiped all memory of her conversation with Caro from Esther's mind. She got through several more hours of paperwork and dinner without thinking about Petersen. But, as the evening continued and Archie's nightly lesson drew near, the cogs in her brain began to jam with fragments of her argument with Caro. When Drew popped his head through the study door to tell her that Caro was tired and they were leaving, she almost told him to stay. Yet some part of her let him go. It was the same part that thought more and more about the man sitting in the room next door with her son. When the hour came for Archie to go to bed, she left her work and took him to his room where Florrie was already sitting on the bed waiting for a story.

Over the course of the summer, Esther put her own children to bed less and less. It was always the way, especially around August when she started squaring the year's accounts while also keeping an eye on the harvest. Archie and Florence didn't seem to mind, but Esther did.

Lizzie Muncie was the best example of motherhood Esther knew and, as far as she could remember, her mother had never missed a single bedtime. Of course, Lizzie did not have the same demands on her time that Esther did. But, really, that was no excuse since the mistress of Kirkmore had far more help than her mother ever did. Yet with every bedtime she missed, missing the next one was easier. And the children loved Mary so what difference did it really make if someone else tucked them in at night?

Tonight, however, Esther felt it was important that she was the one to give them their final kiss goodnight. Despite what she previously said to Caroline, she *was* planning something. Yet as the heady lure of waywardness dragged her onwards, she wanted to spend time alone with her children. Though she loved Kirkmore with undying passion, she knew that she would be able to leave if she had to. What she could not leave were her children. She knew that if she acted on the thoughts she harboured, there was the possibility of serious recriminations. Watching Florrie and Archie snuggle into their bedclothes ready for a story, she knew nothing was worth losing them. But then, the daring part of her reasoned, she would only risk her position if she was caught.

That was the thing she was most scared about. She was not scared about approaching Petersen or letting him approach her. In fact, she relished the thought of intimacy with him. But the discovery of such intimacy, the thought of outsiders knowing what she was doing and casting judgement on her, was terrifying. Though she was confident that the locals respected, even liked her, she knew her reputation would not survive a scandal. Had she been a man, they might be more forgiving. After all, the laird of another estate some twenty miles away had been having an affair with his wife's sister for twenty years and no one batted an eyelid. However, his wife's sister was disliked by virtually everyone in the county – though Esther surmised that the arrogance and coldness of the lady in question might have something to do with it. Perhaps Campbell McLaren's situation with his two wives was not the best acid test for how people might react to an affair. Then there was the fact that everyone in McLaren's triangle was Scottish. Though Petersen's English was impeccable, there was no getting away from how German he was. He stuck out like a sore thumb with his height, broad shoulders and blonde hair. While people might one day forgive Esther for cuckolding her husband, she doubted they would ever forgive her if the other party involved was a German. The people of Kirkmore got on well with the prisoners – liked them even – but it only took one misstep and the locals would turn on them. Could Esther risk that? Could Michael? Because if he did, the consequences of his being caught could be severe.

Yet all these considerations were not enough to stop Esther hurtling towards the inevitable. She had to do it. Even if it was just once, she had to know what it would feel like to be touched by Michael. *Michael* – even the way she thought about him now was more familiar, more intimate. Although would it really be only once? Would her curiosity be sated after one experience with him? What if Michael demanded more? He was a constant presence in her life – there every day to teach Archie. Would either of them be able to resist the lure of constant contact? Or what if it all went wrong? How could they face one another day after day if it all came to nothing?

When she finished reading the children their story, she wasn't even sure what it was about. Her mind was elsewhere but, as she hugged and kissed them goodnight, she made a conscious effort to be present, to remember the moment before: the moment when her life was normal. It was the moment before she potentially changed everything. Or perhaps she was blowing the entire thing out of proportion. Either way, she clung to her children fiercely, hoping they would feel the love that she willed out through her fingertips into their small bodies. She prayed they would never know what she was about to do.

Once the children were finally settled, she slid quietly

from their room and down the hall to Erwin's room. The boy was sitting up. He was still deathly pale, but his eyes were brighter than Esther had seen them. There was a tray with the remains of a light meal on the eiderdown.

Mrs Morris was sitting by his bedside knitting feverishly as he slowly read from the day's newspaper. The housekeeper listened carefully as he sounded out each word, gently prompting him whenever he struggled.

"Mr Riegel is practising his English," the old lady told her mistress, not without some pride. "He'll be as good as Mr Petersen soon."

"I'm sure he will," Esther smiled. "How are you feeling this evening, Mr Riegel?"

"Much better, thank you," he said carefully. "I am very tired also." He looked at the housekeeper. "Maybe I stop reading?"

"Yes, maybe that would be a good idea." She folded her knitting into her bag and took the paper. "Do you need to use the facilities or straight to sleep?"

The poor boy coloured slightly and muttered, "I think … facilities."

It took both women to heave him from the bed and to the door of the bathroom. After that, he managed to look after himself though he was still flushed with embarrassment when he opened the door to head back to the bedroom and seemed very glad when he was once more under the covers.

However, before she let him sleep, Mrs Morris quizzed him on his leg. Was it painful, swelling, hot or itchy? Were the bandages too tight or loose? Esther could see the nurse in her and wondered that she had never seen it before. She also saw the cajoling, stern care of a loving mother and felt a twinge of regret that the woman never had children of her own.

"Shall I stay until Mr Petersen comes up? In case you need anything?" Mrs Morris asked as she settled the eiderdown around him.

The boy turned pink again but looked shyly pleased with her concern. "I think I will be … all right. Thank you."

She smiled warmly. "Goodnight, then."

They left him to his own devices.

"You're very good with him," Esther told the housekeeper as they walked down the hall together. "I wonder that you could help fussing over me when I was ill."

Mrs Morris looked surprised. Then her face pinched at the memory of feeling so helpless as Lizzie Muncie's daughter struggled to heal after the birth of her second child. "In all the time I nursed, I never once had charge of a woman. It was always men. I suppose I know what to do with the boy. I've seen such injuries countless times. But with you I was all at sea. I knew nothing about postnatal nursing or gynaecology. We barely covered female anatomy in our training. Though I wanted to, I couldn't help you. But I'll always know how to help men and boys because I really have seen it all before. Whatever injury you can think of, I've probably seen it." Unexpectedly, she reached out and cupped Esther's cheek. "Maybe if I could have found a way to help you, you might be happier."

Esther started. "But I am happy!" she blurted out.

The housekeeper smiled sadly. "If you say so, my dear."

Rooted to the spot, Esther stared after the old lady as she disappeared down the servants' staircase. Did other people really think she was unhappy? She wasn't even sure if she thought of *herself* as unhappy. Yet she knew she wasn't quite *happy* either, though she assumed that was something everyone struggled with. It was impossible to be content all the time. Life always had complications. She wondered if what happened tonight with Michael would bring happiness or further problems.

Still she dithered once she went back downstairs. She gave the library a wide berth and slipped into the study unheard. She thought about writing some letters she had put on the long finger but as soon as she sat down, her legs began a kind of tap dance, refusing to stay still. She considered having a drink to steady her nerves, but she wanted to be completely clearheaded for whatever it was that might follow. She began to pace across the floor but stopped when she found the elephantine clump of her heels unbearably loud as they crossed the worn carpet.

Eventually, she turned out the light, straightened her spine and approached the connecting door to the library.

On entering, she was momentarily confused. The only illumination came from the fire and a single, tall lamp that bowed over the nearest settee.

He wasn't there.

Her heart skittered off in panic as she searched the space for any sign of him. And then, there he was – his long, thin form standing at the opposite side of the room again. His maroon clothing blended in with the dark wood and rich coloured leather of the books. Yet his blond hair caught the light, shining like a beacon in the gloom.

Esther's heart still hammered uncontrollably.

On unsteady legs, she began to cross the room. It took her much longer than it should have. The only acknowledgement of her presence he gave was to turn his head to the side and look at her briefly over his shoulder. Then he turned back to study the bookshelves. Esther's gaze raked over the curve of his shoulders as they had once before when he stood in a similar position. But this time, his hands were in his pockets, dark shirt rolled up over his elbows. Before, she had longed to touch those shoulders.

Stopping only a few inches behind him, she reached up and trailed her fingertips over their broad expanse. He rolled his shoulders into her touch and exhaled. Somehow, she knew without seeing that he had closed his eyes. Growing bolder, she dragged her fingernails down either side of his spine, feeling the muscles that bowed out from his vertebrae like wings folded tight to his body. He gave a tiny shudder and pulled his hands from his pockets. She saw him flex then ball his fingers into fists. Yet his feet remained motionless. When she reached the top of his trousers, hesitantly she hooked her index fingers into the waistband and gently began to slide them towards his hips. Then she slid them around him and took a single step forward to stand flush against him.

Michael grabbed both her wrists, arresting her movement. Though it was not painful, his grip was unwaveringly firm.

Mortified by the fact that he had stopped her, Esther tried to pull away but his hold on her was unyielding.

"Slow," he said hoarsely. "Just wait a moment. I want to feel it. To remember it."

Esther bowed until her forehead rested between his shoulder blades. Her shallow breath made the shirt flutter against his back. She felt every shift, every flex of his body under hers. Deliberately, he loosened his hold on her wrists but did not let go completely. He allowed her fingers to wander around his waistband but every time her hands travelled lower, he tightened his grip and she changed direction. Gradually, he relaxed and let his arms fall by his sides once more. Finally, she wrapped her arms tight around his belly, rested her cheek against his spine and drank in the smell of him with a contented sigh.

She didn't know how long they stood like that. It could have been seconds or minutes before he gently pried her arms away.

"My turn," he whispered.

Letting go of her altogether, he turned to face her and stepped back.

Esther stood as proudly as she could in front of him,

trying not to feel embarrassment for having propositioned him.

His eyes were raking every inch of her body. "I've so often wanted to look at you but always been afraid someone else might see." His words prickled her skin just as much as his gaze did.

Eventually, he took a long stride forward so that they were toe to toe. With one hand, he caught her hip, the other he brought to her cheek, cupping her face, his long fingers threading through her hair. He gave her a crooked smile as his large hand snaked around her hip, almost stretching from one side to the other. He pulled her against him, slid his other hand to the base of her skull, bent and kissed her.

It was a new experience for Esther. When Fraser kissed her, she often thought he didn't want to. It was a duty rather than an act of love. Even the kisses she shared with Andrew before she married were hurried explorations of each other, cut short by the fear of discovery. When she was kissed, she never lost herself in the moment. Her thoughts were never more than a fraction of an inch below the surface, ready to return unaffected once the interaction was over.

But this was wildly different.

Michael's kiss was powerful, possessive. Her eyes flew wide as he parted her lips, sucking the lower one as his tongue met hers. She didn't think she had ever touched someone else's tongue with her own. If she had, she was sure she would have remembered. It was a strange feeling to have something so warm, so alive explore the front of her mouth. She only just managed not to pull away. But as his mouth became more insistent and he crushed her body against his, she lost herself to the sensation, allowing him to guide her. Soon, she could think of nothing except where his bare skin touched hers. All she wanted to do was feel more. That was when she really started to kiss him back. She used his strong frame to push herself up to meet him, standing on the tips of her toes to reach as far as she could, now meeting his tongue with her own as she wove her fingers through his hair and pulled him closer. Her lips were a peculiar combination of numb and tingling yet all she knew was she wanted the sensation to continue forever. Still she couldn't touch enough of him. Though his kiss was the most sensual thing she had ever experienced – including sex with Fraser – it soon became apparent to her that it was not enough. She wanted more of him. She wanted all of him. And he clearly wanted her.

Yet she could not bring herself to break their kiss.

Finally, his lips left hers and he began to kiss slowly, luxuriously down her jaw. But Esther didn't want to stand anymore. She felt heavy in his arms, as if they both might topple over at any moment. She didn't want to have to think about unimportant things like keeping herself upright. She wanted to give herself up to him – to think of nothing other than his touch on her skin.

"Michael," she breathed as he kissed the base of her throat.

He pulled his head back from her with a questioning look. Esther realised too late that her voice cracked over his name. It sounded as if she was panicking. In fact, her whole body shook in his arms. Uncertainly, he began to release her but she held him fast.

"Come to bed with me," she whispered. Her teeth were chattering uncontrollably and she clamped her jaw shut. She couldn't work out if it was anticipation, shock or fear of rejection that was making her so jittery.

Michael cupped her jaw and kissed her deeply but all too briefly.

"Yes," he answered simply.

Dragging him towards the door, Esther carefully looked

out into the hall in case anyone might see them together. Then she remembered there was a perfectly legitimate excuse for her to lead him up the stairs, just as she had done for the last two nights. Turning back to nod at him, she let go of his hand but not before giving it a promising squeeze. She stepped into the hall boldly and strode across with Michael in her wake. Or, at least, she thought she did. He moved so noiselessly she had to look over her shoulder to check he was still there. He was walking far too close to her should anyone see them, but at this point she didn't care.

Rather than cling to the banister and risk him chasing her trailing fingers, she walked up the centre of the red carpet, her legs steadying with every step, her confidence growing with the elevation as she stood tall and allowed her hips to shift from side to side. She was testing out her own allure, wondering if Michael watched her swaying hips yet also hoping it didn't look like she was trying too hard. Glancing back, she realised he was still standing halfway down the stair, his eyes shining and hungry in the feeble light of the hall. With silent bounding strides, he took the stairs two at a time and was suddenly behind her, hands on her buttocks, his chin on her shoulder.

"Do you expect us to make it as far as the bedroom?" he asked, flexing his fingers in her soft flesh.

She pulled away from him and stepped up onto the landing, casting her eyes up and down the corridor. She was petrified someone would see them. "I have to check on Erwin," she said unsteadily as she hurried to the boy's door. If she stayed close to Michael, she knew they really wouldn't make it as far as her bedroom.

Erwin was fast asleep. However, Esther walked up to the side of his bed to be absolutely sure the small snuffling noises that emanated from his prostrate form were snores rather than sobs. Standing over him, she recognised that she and Michael were now free to proceed as they intended. The last obstacle in their path was removed and all that remained was a short walk to the room at the end of the corridor. Her whole body began to hum with a mixture of anticipation and outright terror. She was surprised no one else could hear it. Turning, she saw Michael silhouetted in the doorframe, patiently waiting for her. She nodded to him once and began crossing the room towards him. Rather than meet her, however, he stepped aside without touching her. Even when she closed Erwin's door, he didn't make any move towards her. Instead, he stayed a respectful distance away, only moving to follow her as she treaded the familiar path to her room.

It was dark when she entered. The curtains were closed and the fire had burnt down to ashes. Knowing the space well, she crossed swiftly to her bedside locker and turned on the lamp. The blackness of the room was immediately bathed in a pleasant golden glow. There was a moment of silence before the door closed behind her with a soft snap and the key turned in the lock.

Turning slowly to face him, she tried to take a deep breath but it caught in the back of her throat. He still stood against the door, watching her.

"I haven't done this in a long time," Esther said.

"Neither have I," he admitted quietly.

"I … don't even know if I still can," she whispered.

She hadn't thought about that until now. What if she couldn't do it? What if it was too painful for her to bear? Would Michael be angry with her if she stopped him? Would he let her? Somehow, she thought he would.

"I don't know if I can," she repeated. "But I want to try."

He nodded and cautiously stepped forward, catching both her hands in his own. He lifted one then the other to his lips and kissed her palms.

Slowly, awkwardly, they began to undress each other.

Both fumbled with the buttons on the other's shirt. When it came to removing Esther's shoes, she bent down and untied them herself while Michael stripped off his socks and trousers. Automatically, he folded them and looked around for somewhere to put them. Esther stifled a titter.

"Old habits." He shrugged shyly with a smile. He seemed self-conscious standing in front of her in nothing more than a vest and his underpants.

This time, Esther took *his* hands and placed them on her hips, inviting him to remove her skirt. Gently, he ran his fingers around her waistband just as she had earlier. Finding the clasp, he slipped both hands inside the skirt and slid it down past her hips so that she was left in nothing other than her bra, knickers, suspender belt and stockings. Michael's fingers trailed down her thighs and, one by one, he unclipped the clasps that held up her stockings. Kneeling before her, with feather-light brushes he rolled first one then the other down her legs until they were two silky puddles under her feet. She struggled to keep her legs from buckling as he dragged his fingers back up, tickling behind her knees.

Slowly, he stood to his full height once more. Gazing down at her with ardent eyes, he seemed much taller beside her when she didn't have any shoes on. She could feel the gusts of his breath on her face just as she felt them on her belly when he knelt to remove her stockings. It made her exposed skin prickly. She inhaled sharply, making her chest rise and fall. They were so close her breasts brushed the top of his abdomen.

With two fingers, he started at the base of her throat and traced a line down her breastbone over her bra, to the soft flesh above her navel and further down to the belt. Sweeping his hands around to the clasp, he undid it and threw the garment aside. Catching her waist, he pulled her close and kissed her deeply, pressing his body into hers. He seemed to be all around her, invading her, making her feel small. Yet, though she felt petite beside him, she was not scared. Instead, she felt loved, desired, sensual.

Wanting to be closer still, she peeled off his vest to expose the pale expanse of his broad chest. For the first time she noticed the prominent muscle linking each shoulder to his neck and the hollow above his collarbones. As her fingertips traced his torso, she felt the bump of ribs stretching the skin. Though he was muscular, Esther had never realised how slim he was.

"You're so thin," she murmured, stroking his stomach.

"So are you," he countered, gliding his fingers over the exposed ribs below her bra.

"I eat plenty."

"So do I." He grinned down at her, mocking the hint of irritation in her voice.

"I just don't sleep," she muttered.

Michael leaned in close. "Well, I certainly hope you don't sleep tonight." His grin became more wicked, his eyes darker.

He kissed her again and, when he pulled away, her bra fell to the floor. Suddenly self-conscious, Esther found herself exposed to his hungry eyes. Sensing her embarrassment, Michael stepped back, removing his own underwear so that he was completely bare before her. Though his arms were loose by his sides, he stood proud, unabashed in his nakedness. Drinking him in, she understood why. He truly was a fine figure of a man.

Taking a deep, steadying breath, Esther reached down and undid the three buttons at her left hip and let her final covering slither down her legs onto the carpet. As she did so, she prayed to God he would not notice the scar that sliced up the midline of her abdomen.

No sooner did she feel the waft of air from her falling

knickers but Michael was pressed up against her, kissing her untidily, thoroughly, walking her backwards towards the bed. When her legs hit the edge, their bodies collided, pressed closer still. Esther leaned back in his arms and allowed him to guide her onto the coverlet. He climbed onto the bed, straddled her and took both her hands in his. But she didn't want him to hold her hands. She wanted to touch him everywhere. She wanted to feel the lines, the dips, the contours of his body. She wanted to feel every inch of him with every inch of her own body. She wanted it to happen. God, did she want it to happen! He released her hands and, as they moved against one another, it was abundantly clear that he was still absolutely ready for it to happen too.

"I don't know if I can do it still," she gasped, terrified that, after all this anticipation, her body might let her down.

"Just tell me what to do," he told her in between kisses, fondling her breasts.

She pushed one of his hands lower. "Touch me."

Though the skin on his fingers was rough, she barely felt it. She need not have worried. Her body was clearly ready for him. He stroked her nonetheless and her spine arched into his touch. A single finger slid inside her and she felt the tightness of her neglected body yield to him. No one had ever touched her so intimately only for the purposes of pleasure. His finger curled within her and her spine bowed again. It was as if the whole world momentarily disappeared and all that existed was the connection between them. But it wasn't enough.

Watching him down the length of her body, their eyes met and she gave him the briefest of nods. He withdrew his hand and, for a moment, she felt the ache of emptiness before he pressed against her and slowly slid inside with a gentle thrust of his hips.

Esther cried out and his eyes flew wide, scared that

someone would hear them. But she didn't care. All she wanted was for him to do it again. He obliged. She bit down on the fleshy palm of her hand to stifle the cry that was a heady mixture of pain and pleasure.

His movements became more urgent. Though he tried to control himself for her sake, it had been too long. He couldn't help himself. He had dreamed of seeing this woman laid bare in front of him. But nothing in his imaginings had prepared him for the way she quivered beneath him, jostled by his every thrust, squirming to get away yet also fighting to take him deeper and deeper inside her. The sight of her clutching ineffectually at the eiderdown with one hand while she emitted muffled exclamations around the other was enough to send him wild. He couldn't have stopped himself even if she begged him to. And then he began to feel his climax coming. No, he thought. Please, no. Just one more minute. Just a little bit longer. Just let me have her for a little longer.

Esther felt it too. She tried to cling tighter, to will him that bit further. But all her attempts did was bring it to a close more quickly. All too soon, he was pulling away from her, leaving her feeling empty once more and unsatisfied.

"No," she urged, clutching at his back. "Don't leave me."

Michael hesitated then reached beneath her, dragging her into his arms. Rolling onto his back, he cradled her to his chest, stroking her spine. He kissed the crown of her head, entwining his legs with hers.

Esther lay still in his embrace. She wasn't sure whether she wanted to cry or hit him. Yet it was still the most fulfilling sexual experience she had ever had.

With Fraser, sex was always a necessary evil. After they married it took him weeks to even share her bed, never mind consummate their marriage. From reading saucy ladies' magazines and her mother's embarrassed instructions, Esther had a vague idea how to please a man but all her attempts to engage him were futile. When Fraser finally came to her, he didn't want to be touched. He closed his eyes and, much like Esther, waited for the whole sordid business to be over. Once his duty was performed, he returned to his own bed, leaving Esther cold, alone and convinced she was doing something wrong. Not that she was given many incidents to dwell on. It took three encounters before she fell pregnant with Archie and, when she did, Fraser refused to touch her. It took only one for Florence's conception and that was the last time she had ever been touched by a man who wasn't a doctor. She saw a lot of doctors when Florrie was born. The sum total, therefore, of all her sexual encounters numbered four. But not anymore, she thought. Now they numbered five.

His hands languidly wandered over her skin as she ran her fingers through the smattering of curly blond hairs on his chest. There was something surprisingly comfortable in their shared silence.

But it didn't last. He was stroking the side of her belly when, without warning, he sat bolt upright with a look of absolute horror on his face.

Esther asked herself what she had done wrong. As his eyes roved up and down her body, the illusion of contentment shattered. What was it about her that so appalled him?

"You're – you could be – I didn't – what have we done?" he choked.

Esther mouthed ineffectually at him. What had she done wrong? She reached for a blanket from the end of the bed to cover herself as his face began to swim before her. She bowed her head to hide her face. "Do you want to go? You can go if you want."

His sorrowful expression turned aghast. "No! No, that's not what I meant. I meant … what if you have a baby?" he whispered, his fear evident.

Esther swallowed shakily. A mixture of relief and absolute sadness washed through her. "I can't," she finally answered.

"Can't?" he said, confused. "But you already have two children."

She dropped the blanket, took his hand and pressed it to her lower abdomen. He yanked it away but she held fast. "No. Feel it." She guided his stiff fingers along the ridged scar rising up her belly. She had never shown the scar to anyone but, right now, she thought it was necessary to expose the thing she most hated about herself to the man before her. "I can't have children anymore." She said it as calmly as possible, though the tears continued to leak from her eyes as they always did when she confronted that horrible truth. "I can't have children anymore," she repeated, meeting his sceptical stare for emphasis.

Still he was puzzled. "Why not?"

"They took my womb," she replied quietly, her tears cold as they spotted her exposed flesh while she stroked the skin above where the organ once lay. When it first happened, she lay for hours caressing this one small patch of flesh, knowing that it would never swell with life again. If she pressed hard enough, she believed she could feel the hollow cavity inside her where it once rested. It was such a desolate feeling she had to condition herself not to touch her stomach at all. But now, she was strangely appreciative of its loss. It made things slightly less complicated than they already were. And yet, a small, stupid thought still whistled through her brain: she would never bear Michael's children.

His hand clenched over hers. "Took? Why?"

"My uterus ruptured during Florrie's birth. They couldn't stop the bleeding. They did the only think they could to save me. I sometimes wonder if they should have let me go." Tears continued to slide down her cheeks.

Michael caught one with his thumb. "Don't say things like that," he pleaded. "Life is a gift. I've seen too many lose theirs. Don't throw it away. There's always something worth living for. Look at me. I was – I am – a prisoner of war. For the last three years of my life I have lived in overcrowded barracks, been eaten alive by lice, seen what war does to good men. And then one day I was picked to travel to an estate in deepest Scotland. I breathed fresh air, I was treated like a human, not an animal. And then there you were – talking to poor, shell-shocked Max with a smile on your face and an open heart. I thought my life was over, that I would die a prisoner of the British government, that I would never talk to, never touch another woman again. And then I *saw you*. You were – you *are* – so beautiful, I couldn't look away. I wasn't even sure you were real." He cupped her cheek in his palm. "I came up to you. Do you remember?"

Esther cast her mind back to that first day. Was it really only three months ago? "That was you?" she said incredulously.

He laughed in relief and kissed her forehead. "Yes! And that stupid private came waving his rifle in our faces. I was so afraid he was going to shoot you before I even got a chance to speak to you."

Remembering more, Esther sat up straighter. "You moved between us to shield me. That was you?" she said in awe.

His large hands ran down her arms and caught her waist, heaving her into his lap. He cradled her to his chest. "I knew I had to keep you safe. I don't know why. I just knew. I don't even know if I wanted to make love to you at that point. I just knew you were important to me."

"Maybe because I was the first woman you laid eyes on in God knows how long," she joked.

Michael hooked her chin on his finger. "I had seen women. Just none as extraordinary as you are. And I did not dare hope that you might have any regard for me. If I could have watched you from afar for the rest of my life, it would have been enough." He looked away, shook his head and laughed.

"I'm a terrible liar. I could not have watched you for the rest of my days. It would have killed me. It nearly did kill me when I discovered you belonged to someone else."

"I belong to no one," Esther answered him quietly.

"No," he kissed her slowly on the mouth. "You are uniquely your own creature."

They were quiet for a time and, without asking each other, slid under the eiderdown and lay still together. She cuddled into his chest, enjoying the feel of a man's arms around her. She loved his masculine smell, the feel of his softly curving muscles and the smooth warm skin that covered them. Yet, not knowing one another's bodies, they found the need to make subtle shifts to avoid each other's boniness. Young motherhood had not made Esther soft around the edges. Instead, she was now lighter than she had been in her teens though marginally heavier than what she was during the war. Though Kirkmore was never short of food – even during the worst months of the war – the stress of keeping all the wheels turning meant that, though she ate, she never seemed to put on weight. Her mind and body were simply too active. And, of course, the insomnia didn't help.

"Why did you marry him?"

"Fraser?"

"You were married to someone else?" he teased.

Esther poked him in the ribs. "No." She didn't answer straight away. Having spent years trying to explain the decision to herself, she was still unsure whether she had come up with a suitable answer. "I think I did it to please my mother," she finally answered.

"You think?"

She nodded into his chest. "When I look back on it, it's like watching someone who wasn't me. I wanted to please her. It was always just the two of us. My father died in the Great War before I was born. He was part of a company of

Kirkmore men under Fraser McAllister so when the war ended and he came back, he supported the widows and their families. But the others all eventually moved away. Mum and I were the only ones who stayed. Fraser gave my mother a good job and a home and he gave me an education. I'm the daughter of two labourers. Most people can only dream of the privileges I was afforded. So when Fraser asked me to marry him, I suppose I thought it would be ungrateful to say no. And though I think my mother was disappointed at first that he didn't ask her, I think she was proud that of all the women Fraser McAllister could have chosen, he chose me."

Michael shifted, the better to look at her. "That doesn't sound like a good enough excuse to spend the rest of your life with someone."

Esther shrugged, not meeting his eye. "I was eighteen, planning to go off to Edinburgh to teach. But I didn't want to leave home. And then Fraser came along and offered me everything I could ever want."

"But do you love him now?"

"No," she answered without hesitation. "I respect him and he respects me, I think. But you don't need love to be happy. Sometimes you're better without it. Loving my father made my mother miserable when he was gone. No one ever lived up to what she felt for him. When she got sick, I think it was a relief for her. I was taken care of so she didn't have to try anymore."

"Your mother is dead?" Surprise made his question blunt. Esther was still a young woman. It didn't seem right that she should be an orphan even if she was a married mother of two children.

"In the summer of nineteen-forty. Cancer. Just before Florrie was born."

"I'm sorry." He squeezed her gently and stroked her back.

"I could have done with her after what happened with Florrie," Esther mused. "She was so good at helping me after I had Archie." She paused. "She was also the one who sent me to hospital in Edinburgh for both births. I suppose, being my mother, she knew how difficult it would be for me. None of us would be alive if it wasn't for her insisting I didn't just rely on Freddie Robertson."

"Oh?"

"Yes." Esther's hand drifted towards her belly, but she stopped it.

Michael's hand snaked around her waist and held hers firmly against her stomach, anchoring her.

"Both births were difficult. I was underdeveloped as a teen so Archie was born by caesarean. When Florrie came, the doctors hoped I would manage a natural birth but then my womb ruptured along the old scar from Archie. It's rare – very rare. Yet, in a way, I suppose I'm grateful it happened. I wouldn't be the person I am today without it."

"But you might have more children," Michael said bluntly.

She stared at him for a moment then gave a small, bitter smile. "Oh, I doubt it."

Michael raised a quizzical eyebrow.

"My husband hasn't shared my bed since the year we married. My God, it's been almost ten years."

Michael was confused. "But Florence …"

Turning onto her front and folding her arms over his chest, Esther propped her chin on her linked fingers as she decided whether to tell Michael the truth. In such an intimate situation, it seemed truth was necessary. "Florence was the culmination of a drunken argument in the study. Strange how such a beautiful child could be the result of something so loveless."

"He hasn't touched you in six years?" Michael said incredulously. She shrugged but then stayed perfectly still as his hands ranged down her back, her buttocks, her legs. "How could he resist?" he asked in wonder as he rolled her over onto her back and hovered above her, drinking her in with shining eyes.

Esther glowed with happiness. "Again?"

"Unless you object." He smiled knowingly.

She reached up and took his face between her hands and kissed him slowly. "How could I resist?" she smiled.

Chapter Twenty

Esther lay naked in the overly hot confines of her bed. The sheets still retained his warmth as she watched him dress. She was wishing that he didn't have to leave. Her bed felt empty without him. However, she still enjoyed seeing his lithe form move back and forth across her room in the soft light of the bedside lamp. He was so unselfconscious, so calm. It was as if the whole situation was normal. Yet, for them, it somehow was. They should have feared discovery, felt guilty, awkward, but they were none of these things. Neither of them could stop smiling. Esther wanted to laugh out loud and, feeling completely comfortable in his presence, she did.

"What?" he asked, poking his head out of the neck of his shirt. He looked down at himself, wondering if she was laughing at him.

"Nothing. I'm just happy." She threw her arm across her eyes and chuckled again.

The bed sagged as he sat down beside her. "So am I," he told her, pulling her arm away. Stroking her cheek, he leaned down and kissed her slowly, lovingly. Then he turned and began to pull on his socks.

She sat up and rested her chin on his shoulder, wrapping her arms around his waist. "I wish you didn't have to go."

He sighed and rested his cheek on the crown of her head. "I'll always have to go," he whispered.

"Do you want me to check there's no one in the hall?" she asked as he continued to dress without dislodging her.

"Is it likely someone will be out there?"

"No," she said. "The house is always quiet."

"Then I think I'll be all right." His smile didn't reach his eyes now. Both were now anticipating the moment he stood, crossed the room and left. "I'm not going far." He kissed her forehead. "You should get some sleep."

Esther laughed humourlessly. "I don't sleep."

"Maybe you need to do something to wear you out." He grinned wickedly.

"Maybe I should find someone to help me with that." She slid her hands lower and he groaned.

"I have to go," he said raggedly.

She withdrew her hands. "I know. Go, before you can't leave at all."

Once he was gone, Esther got up and went to the bathroom. She looked at her naked self in the mirror and was surprised to find a familiar face looking back at her. She felt so different. Her body ached in unfamiliar places yet she also felt loose-limbed and slightly giddy. It was a totally foreign bodily experience. Was this what she had been missing for ten years in a loveless marriage? Or did the whole affair simply seem so special, so heightened, because it was forbidden? Throwing water over her face, she scrubbed vigorously at her skin. Not that anyone would see her in the early hours of the morning but somehow it seemed important to wash all traces of the night's activity from her body. Taking a facecloth, she washed herself all over, liberally using some lavender soap that Caro said was good for sleeping. But she couldn't have cared less about sleep. All she wanted to do was wash away the mingled smells of her own body and Michael's. She found his scent intoxicating – but she knew she couldn't smell of him when she left the room in the morning. Better to remove it now than to indulge in it for the next number of hours.

However, once she was done and climbed back into her bed, she found his lingering scent on the bedclothes. Panicked, she threw them off and dithered about the room, wondering if she should strip her bed or open the windows. But then she made herself stand still. She breathed deeply and smelt the familiar aromas of her room: firewood, smoke, lavender, the fresh soap used to wash her clothes, the linseed oil polish Ada used to shine the wooden furniture. She was overthinking things. Turning off the light, she slowly clambered back into bed and sniffed the sheets. There was no doubt that they smelled of Michael, but it wasn't half as strong as she initially thought. Searching for a patch of eiderdown that retained his scent, she pulled it close to her nose and breathed a deep contented sigh before closing her eyes and slipping into fitful dreams about touching bodies and whispered confessions.

Chapter Twenty-One

Esther was in the window when Beattie entered the garden gate. She had not, however, been there for very long. She was tired and her body ached, protesting at its unfamiliar use but she thought – this morning of all mornings – she had to be in the window before the gardener arrived. She was petrified her absence would lead to talk and talk to questions or suspicions.

After receiving Ivor's nod, she dragged herself off the window seat and headed to the bathroom. Carefully, she examined her body in the mirror, making sure there were no visible marks from the night before. Not that anyone would see her body but she was remembering a piece of her mother's wisdom. Lizzy insisted that one must always wear clean underwear – "for fear you're hit by a bus or some-such". Since then, Esther always wore clean knickers. Finishing her inventory, she concluded that, in the unlikely event she *was* hit by a bus, she could be confident that her skin was clear of any marks from her night with Michael.

Once dressed, she opened the windows to allow the chilly autumn air to flood the room and clear the languorous cobwebs from her brain. There was a smell of moisture in the air, a promise of rain. The familiar scent grounded Esther after her otherworldly night. Confined to her room, she could have believed that her whole life had changed with the events of the previous evening. But the cold wind blew away her skewed perceptions. Like a drunkard now sober, she recognised that there was more to life than a few hours spent with a man. The rest of her life was waiting to meet her outside of the four walls she stood between.

All she had to do to reclaim it was cross the threshold.

It surprised Esther how easily the change in her relationship with Michael fitted into her life.

At first, she was constantly on the lookout for suspicious glances from the staff. Would Ada notice the male scent in the mistress's bedroom that was so noticeable to Esther? Had Mrs Morris made an impromptu visit to Erwin in the night only to discover his carer was absent? What if she or Michael accidentally let something slip in conversation either with each other or with the rest of the Kirkmore residents?

Yet for both, the hardest part of keeping up the pretence of mistress and subordinate was not calling the other by their Christian names. For Esther, it was slightly easier since she could turn the start of 'Michael' into 'Mr Petersen' but he had to be much more careful. Generally, however, they came to an agreement that they should keep their public encounters to a minimum and were able to avoid one another. If they needed to talk, they saved whatever it was they wanted to say until they were alone. They found they had ample opportunity to do so since poor Erwin was bed-bound much longer than Freddie Robertson initially hoped he would be. Fortunately for them (though unfortunately for Erwin), the boy began to sicken a little over a week after he sustained his injury.

The first indication that something was amiss came when he complained that the room was too hot though everyone else found it pleasantly warm. Though Mrs Morris had her suspicions that the boy's symptoms were worrying, she opened his windows for half an hour in the hope that his illusion of warmth was simply a passing fancy. However, when his temperature began to climb and he began to sweat, the housekeeper thought it best to call the doctor.

Esther got quite a shock when she arrived home from a ride to see the doctor's car in the yard. Abandoning the mare with Alfie, she ran into the house, taking the stairs two at a time up to the boy's room.

"What's wrong?" she asked breathlessly as she caught herself on the doorframe of the room. "What happened?"

"I hope you don't mind, mistress. I thought it best to call the doctor," Mrs Morris said, standing back to allow Esther a place at the foot of the bed.

"Yes, yes, of course." Esther waved a gloved hand dismissively only to see the tan-coloured stains of earth from the horse's coat on the black leather. She dropped her hands, thinking that her dirty clothing was not appropriate for a sickroom. She didn't dare look at her boots or think what muck she had dragged onto the carpets upstairs. "Has the wound become infected?" she asked, alarmed at the shiny redness of Erwin's face.

"That's what I thought," the housekeeper answered, chewing the inside of her cheek. "But we've been so careful with it."

"Even when you do your best, sometimes it isn't enough," Freddie Robertson murmured unhelpfully. Yet when he straightened up from examining the boy, he didn't look particularly grim. "Luckily for young Erwin, however, I think the wound is continuing to heal nicely. I suspect this fever might be something called serum sickness. I'm not sure if you're familiar with it."

Esther looked nonplussed but Mrs Morris nodded, relieved. "I remember a boy had it when I was nursing here."

211

"I've seen it twice," the doctor observed. "Both men I saw reacted to penicillin. Rare enough. Easy to mistake for infection too. But both made full recoveries so – if I'm right – I think Mr Riegel here will be fine too. It's just going to take him that bit longer to get better, unfortunately." He turned with an apologetic smile to his patient and spoke more slowly so he would understand. "Erwin, you will be all right. It's not serious. But I'm sure you won't mind being here for a little longer. By the looks of things, you're well cared for." He grinned at the two women.

Erwin's prolonged illness gave Esther and Michael one more precious week together before they lost their excuse for him to spend the night in the house. After the first night, there didn't seem to be a question that there would be a second. As they kissed, touched and made love, both felt more alive than they had in years – in Esther's case, possibly in her entire life. Slowly, they got to know the rhythms of each other's bodies. As a relative novice at sex, Esther quickly discovered the joy of intimacy with a loving partner. She discovered what she did and didn't like. And she realised that she was, in fact, quite good at sex if Michael's reaction was anything to go by.

Afterwards, they always talked. Sometimes, it was about what they did that day or something funny they heard or saw. Other times, they talked about their lives and their experiences of the war.

"How did you get the scar on your arm?" Esther asked him one night as he lay with his arms above his head.

Michael glanced at the angry, jagged slash and dropped his arms to hide it. "I did it when our plane crashed here in Scotland. I caught it on a piece of metal when I was climbing out."

Esther frowned. "Looks a bit more serious than that to me," she said as she picked up his arm and ran her finger down the raised pink flesh. It was smooth but also strangely puckered in places. "Did it hurt?"

"Of course. But I had other things to worry about so I had to keep moving."

"Did you try to hide?" She was anxious to discover all she could about the man currently sharing her bed. There was a part of her – a part she had quashed early on in their association – which told her she needed to know more about him before getting close to him. But she had ignored that advice and trusted her instincts about his character. So far, they had proved correct.

"No," he said a little indignantly. "My pilot, Albert Stallman, was badly injured. I had to get him help. Though I do sometimes wonder why I bothered."

Esther was about to ask him why when he continued.

"We didn't get on very well. He used to try and rile me, calling me Tommy in front of all the others in the crew."

"Tommy?"

"Apparently I used to talk in my sleep. In English. Albert decided I must be a British spy. He thought it was funny to nickname me Tommy." Michael grimaced. "It didn't endear me to others."

"Oh." Esther trailed her fingers across his stomach. "Did he live? Your pilot?"

"I think so. He had a fractured skull and some swelling on the brain but they managed to reduce the pressure. He was beginning to recover when I was transferred to a prison camp. From what I heard, he was among a group of wounded men sent back to Germany in exchange for British soldiers at the start of '45. But I don't know for sure."

"And was it only the two of you?" she asked tentatively.

Michael sighed heavily. "No. There were five of us. Albert and I were the only ones to make it out alive. The lucky ones."

"Is it not a bit strange to think you were lucky? You ended up a POW. You're *still* a POW." She continued to run her hands over his torso.

"I could be dead," he interrupted mildly. "I could be many things. I cannot say I was happy about being a prisoner. I hated the camps. Everyone does. I spent almost three years moving from camp to camp until they sent me here." His eyes became unfocused as he continued. "You cannot comprehend the relief I felt when we came here. The work is hard but suddenly I was Michael again. I had forgotten what that felt like."

"I think I might understand that too," she mused. "I'm not sure I ever knew who I was until after Florrie was born. I was someone's daughter, someone's wife, never just me."

Michael nodded. "I had that when I went to Oxford. I had always been Dr Petersen's boy, Gerhart Petersen's brother. When I came to England, I was just Petersen. Nobody knew my family. They had no expectations. I had to make my own way. It was a strange feeling but it was liberating."

"Why did you leave?" Esther asked. "I mean, I know they arrested Germans living in Britain at the start of the war but most of them were released and allowed to carry on as normal, weren't they?"

"I think most of those allowed to resume their lives were Jewish refugees from Germany. People like me would have been considered much more suspicious. I was an academic in an ancient, world-renowned British institution. Who knows what undue influence I might have had over the up-and-coming young men of the ruling classes? And then there was my family back home in Germany." The skin around his mouth and eyes pinched. It seemed as if he was remembering something painful. "They were not the sort British authorities would think kindly of."

Esther waited for him to say more but he didn't. "Oh?" she said with only the slightest inflection. If he didn't want to answer, Michael could deliberately misunderstand her.

He cuddled her tightly. "My brother was a commander in

the SS and my father was a prominent member of the Nazi party. He moved to Berlin to act as personal physician to quite a number of disreputable men. They insisted I do my bit for the party. My options were to spy in Britain or come home. I would not become the former so I chose the latter. It broke my mother's heart."

Out of all he said, it was this that appeared to grieve him more than anything else.

"She hoped I would stay away from all the madness. Instead I walked straight into it. She was so upset with me. I suppose having been through another war and losing two brothers, she didn't want the same thing to happen to us. I thought she would be happy to have me home after so many years. But she couldn't even look at me. If she had, I suppose she would have seen that I felt the same way as she did. I did not want to be there. If I thought I could have stayed away, I would have. Maybe I could have if I thought it through. My brother and father treated me like the prodigal son returned," he said bitterly. "Of course, Gerhart wanted me to join the army so I could be an SS man like him and Papa offered to find me a place in the government where my English would be useful. But that all felt too close. Flying in a plane was the only thing that felt far enough away. When I was above it all with nothing but the sound of the engine, it felt almost like the war below didn't exist."

"Except every bomb you dropped just perpetuated the problem."

"Yes," he agreed. "Do you know, it was almost a relief when I knew we were going to crash. Crashing meant either death or capture. In a strange sense it meant I would be free. My part in the war would be over. I would no longer be choosing a side every time I strapped myself into that damned Heinkel bomber. I was not for or against anyone. I never was. How could I support the Nazis? But also, how could I turn my back on my family, the country of my birth?"

Michael rubbed his face viciously. He left his arm over his eyes and pulled Esther closer still.

"What happened? To your family?" she asked. She felt his body tense underneath hers.

"My father died of a heart attack the morning after his house in Berlin was destroyed by a bomb. My brother was killed in action." Here he stopped. Esther felt his chest rise and fall in a sigh. "I don't know what happened to my mother. I've written to her a dozen times and never once received a reply. I wrote to our neighbours too and nothing. My hometown is now under the control of the Soviets. I have no idea if she is alive or dead, whether she was killed in the war or taken east to one of Stalin's work camps. I pray to God they would not be so cruel as to do that to her."

He fell silent once more, dwelling on the potential horrors his mother was facing alone. Or perhaps she was dead and gone and saved from such pain. But if she was dead then she died alone, without her family beside her. In either case, it hurt his heart to think of his mother's suffering.

Clinging to Esther, he knew he couldn't think about his mother anymore. He wanted a distraction – to forget. Trailing his fingers down her spine, he cupped her buttock. "Again?" he whispered, a note of pleading in his voice.

She shifted above him, pushing herself up by placing a hand on the centre of his chest. She knelt, her feet at his hips, then leaned over him to kiss his mouth slowly as she gently moved her body against his until he was ready. She had only taken this position once before and he had held her hands. It felt uncomfortable for her to have nothing to hold onto. She pulled him up off the mattress so they sat nose to nose.

"Make me forget," he begged.

She reached forwards and nipped the lobe of his ear. "I will," she promised.

Chapter Twenty-Two

After three weeks, Erwin was finally well enough to return to his barracks. Dr Robertson gave the boy a thorough once-over, declared his recovery remarkable and said he was ready to tackle some work that wasn't overly strenuous.

Mrs Morris rooted out a cane to help him walk since he still had a severe limp. Though hunched with the effort of healing such a major wound and pale-skinned, his old cheerfulness was slowly returning. He was nothing but grateful for the care he received and was keen to be of some use once more. However, the doctor gave him strict instructions not to overexert himself. The last thing everyone wanted was for Erwin to irritate the tender wound and end up bedbound once more.

Cary Eden was, therefore, put in charge of finding him jobs that could be done sitting down. Given the time of year, there was no shortage of things for him to do, from sewing grain sacks and straw rick-covers in preparation for harvesting the cereals to sorting the potatoes that the men were currently digging up. These jobs, however, were too much for one man – especially one still recovering from serious injury. Erwin, therefore, found himself surrounded by a large number of women – both local and a few of the remaining Land Girls – who took great pleasure in teasing and fussing over him. The other Germans also took to teasing him mercilessly for being the only man among so many women but it was a light-hearted, well-meant joshing which everyone, including Erwin, could laugh at.

Yet, the boy's good fortune not only extended to the female company he kept. As autumn wore on, the weather began to turn. A day didn't go by without either mist or rain soaking into the men's clothing, leaving them cold and miserable as they worked the increasingly claggy earth. Though excellent for growing feedstuffs, the water-logged brown soil became a bane of their lives as it adhered itself to their boots. It weighed down their feet, slowed their progress and followed them everywhere. Soon, every floor they traversed was covered in a fine layer of partially dried mud that was either ground to a fine dust or remained slippery as a banana skin lying in wait to send anyone who was in a hurry skiting across the floor.

It pained the Germans to see their immaculately kept living quarters sullied every time they crossed the threshold. They did their best to clean up after themselves but a combination of the numbers of men, the sheer volume of dirt and exhaustion always seemed to thwart their efforts.

Though they tried to clean the heavy work boots in the grass or with sticks as they walked back to the barracks, they were never able to remove all of it. Ideally, they would have left their boots by the door but, given the coldness of their quarter's stone floor they kept them on until it was time for bed. At that point, their footwear and their socks – which were always wet through – were placed around and hung above the two stoves in the vain hope that they would be dried out by morning. However, this only created more dirt as the clinging earth turned to dust and coated the floor.

But it wasn't just the muck. With damp soil permanently stuck to their boots, many of the men's feet began to turn red. The numbness that a few them experienced in the winters of the war in Europe provided them with the first warnings that, unless something was done and soon, they might start to smell the sickening tang of necrosis. Alt Hans and Michael were, therefore, dispatched to the mistress to find a solution to their predicament.

Since Erwin's departure from the house, Esther and Michael had hardly seen each other. The children were back at school and Esther thought it unfair to overburden Archie with schoolwork and lessons after hours, at least for the first week or two. Their only encounters had occurred in the presence of others and were always about business. Having a purpose made their meetings bearable since they had something else to think about other than the memories of their nights spent together. Yet it was still hard for Esther to meet Michael's eye when the two men approached her in the yard at the end of their workday.

"Good evening, mistress." Alt Hans spoke in careful yet heavily accented English, pulling his cloth cap from his head as he came towards her.

"Good evening, Hans. What can I do for you?" They very rarely came to her unless there was a problem but she was glad they felt they could.

It was Michael who answered. "We were wondering if it would be possible for you to supply us with some talcum powder for us to use on our feet. Our boots are not designed for bad weather and I'm afraid some of the men might be showing the early signs of trench foot."

"Good Lord! That's the last thing you need. Will I perhaps get some tins of Dubbin too? It might go some way towards sealing the leather a bit better."

Hans looked politely interested while Michael nodded. "Yes, that would be excellent. Also ..." he hesitated.

"Go on.'

"Would it be possible for us to exchange some of our ration coupons for wool and knitting needles? I know we're not really supposed to have other clothing in case we escape but we would like some warmer clothes as winter sets in. Most of us can knit – we learnt in the camps – and it would be something to occupy the evenings as well as keep us warm. That is," he added, "if you think us trustworthy enough."

She wondered a little at the last part of his speech. She certainly trusted him and had shown it in their nights together. Or perhaps he was simply being deferential for the benefit of anyone else who might be listening.

"There's no need for you to use your coupons," she answered briskly. "They probably wouldn't allow you anyway. How about I get you a dozen cones of wool and root out some needles and patterns? There are plenty of them in various cupboards in the house. And since I trusted you enough to give you wax jackets at the start of your tenure here, I don't think I'll have any problems with you having some new knitwear."

"Thank you," Michael said simply. He studied her face for some sign of their connection but her mien was showing nothing but benign interest.

"Will that be all?" she asked, making sure that her gaze didn't linger too long on either of the men.

Alt Hans nodded. "Yes. That will be all. Thank you."

"I'll do my best to have everything for you by the end of the week," she said then turned about and walked away.

True to her word, Esther arrived into the barracks one evening accompanied by Archie who insisted on helping her to carry down all the supplies to the Germans. Really, all he wanted to do was talk to Erwin, Michael and a few of the others who he hadn't seen since starting the new school year. Soon, he was sitting by the fire below a washing line of socks chatting about his first month back in the classroom while

Esther handed over her purchases. One of the men, Erich Neuman, who was particularly good at carving and other handcrafts, was the first to make a beeline for the wool. His eyes lit up when she produced a booklet of jumper patterns. He picked them up and hurried over to a stool where he sat feverishly flicking through the pages with the enthusiasm of a little old lady.

Reinhold Teske and his friend Bruno were already heating water to clean their boots in readiness for a coat of Dubbin wax. Meanwhile, Max had commandeered a cone of mealy brown wool and two short wooden needles and was already casting on a row of stitches with a dexterity Esther had previously seen only in Mrs Morris.

Yet, above the excited clamour, Alt Hans' voice still rang out clearly. "Thank you very much, Mrs McAllister. We are very grateful."

An enthusiastic murmur of agreement and thanks rippled across the men who all looked at Esther standing awkwardly in the middle of the room.

"Not at all," she muttered, feeling her skin colour under so much scrutiny. "It was my pleasure. I'll leave you to it." She beckoned to Archie. "Come on." He turned to her with a protest on his lips but she cut him off. "Now," she said with only the barest hint of authority in her voice. It was all she needed to use. Dragging himself off the stool, Archie reluctantly followed her to the door which she held open for him – but he stopped just short of her.

"Mummy, can Michael start giving me lessons again?" he asked hopefully.

Looking at her boy's fervent face, she scanned the room looking for Michael, having previously made a conscious effort not to seek him out. He was sitting by the nearest stove, eyes boring into her. He gave one sharp, subtle nod then looked away.

"Yes, I don't see why not," she answered, lovingly ruffling her son's hair as he passed out by her.

On the 1st of October, Archie's lessons with Michael resumed.

At breakfast, Esther received a telegram from Fraser. All it said was '*Happy Anniversary*'.

Until she opened the envelope and saw the message, she was unaware of the day's significance. She was surprised by her own forgetfulness since, in previous years, she always looked on the date with an impending sense of doom. The day of her wedding was not something she ever celebrated but it was also something she could not ignore. Yet this year, on the morning of her tenth wedding anniversary, her attention was wholly consumed by thoughts of another man. *The* other man.

As she had sat in the window that morning watching the sun rise, all Esther could think about was when she would see Michael that night. She thought about telling Archie that his tutor couldn't come for their lesson and instead spend the time with Michael herself. But it was too risky. Archie was prone to wandering the house in the evenings and it wouldn't do for him to discover his mother was lying to him. Esther always did her best to tell her children the truth and expected them to show her the same courtesy. She did not want her affair with Michael to turn her into someone she loathed. Her relationship with her children was more important than what she had with Michael. She did, however, have to keep reminding herself of that. It was just so easy to get caught up in the lust and emotion of it all.

After receiving her husband's telegram, Esther found it hard to concentrate on anything. The children babbled happily over breakfast but she heard none of it. When they spoke to her, she gave them vague answers that had nothing to do with what they said. She had no memory of seeing them off to school but knew she must have since they were no longer in the house. Eventually, she found herself sitting behind her desk in the study, Fraser's note in front of her.

The two words were so forcefully imprinted on the page, she could feel the ridges of the letters through the back of the paper. Staring at it until it became unfocused, she wondered if, in fact, it was Mrs Pugh who sent the note. Often, it was she who handled Fraser's correspondence even to his family. But there was no punctuation, no endearments and Esther knew such simplicity, such bluntness, was not the lady's style of communication. Mrs Pugh always managed to make Fraser appear more caring than he ever made himself seem. Esther had come to recognise the birthday cards written in the other woman's hand – the curling warmth of '*All my love*' and the neat little line of hugs and kisses with Fraser's scrawling signature sandwiched in between. But above that, there was always some little line wishing them a lovely day or congratulating them on achieving another year. Esther could not help but be grateful to the lady for her efforts. Every year she saw the delight on her children's faces when they saw the secretary's brightly coloured envelopes among the off-white of all their other cards. The kind sentiments in the words she wrote to them always made them feel a little more loved and – in Esther's book – anything that did that was worthy of her good opinion.

Sitting with the anniversary note before her, she was all the more thankful that Mrs Pugh was the one who wrote to the children. Though he obviously took the time and effort to send it to her, there was no affection in the words. All the telegram betrayed was a sense of duty rather than love. Though she did not expect any fondness from her husband – it would have thoroughly shocked her if he sent her something with even the barest hint of affection – it saddened her to realise that, after a decade of marriage, all that passed between them was a telegram with the words *'Happy Anniversary'*. It made her wonder whether they could have done anything differently. Was there any way they could have salvaged their marriage? Or had they always been doomed to fail? Perhaps it was fate that, despite being ill-suited to one another, they were destined to marry. Perhaps Esther could have done nothing about it even if she had the inclination to reject him. Yet, while the marriage itself did not give happiness to either, the position it put them in allowed them to be versions of themselves that they were contented with. Fraser got to be the politician in Whitehall and she got to run Kirkmore. There were worse outcomes to loveless marriages, Esther thought. She knew she was lucky but still she sat and stared at the telegram.

What would she feel if today was a celebration of ten years with Drew or ten years with Michael? Certainly more than she felt now. She sat back and mused over the life she might have led with Drew. Both of them would have lived in Edinburgh while he studied for his engineering degree. They would have had a tiny flat up some narrow stairs with a cantankerous landlady. In the evenings, Esther would always have his dinner ready when he came in. Afterwards, the record player or the radio would be turned on and they would sit in companionable silence as they listened to the music or perhaps a play. Once the war started, she would have stayed safe at Kirkmore while he went off to do his bit fighting the Jerrys. It was easy to imagine rushing to his bedside when he was injured since she had done that anyway. Then, when Drew was demobbed, they would have decided it was finally time to settle down and start a family. It really was an idyllically neat visualization. It was also likely to be very far removed from the truth of how their marriage would have unfolded. And then there was the fact that she wouldn't have Archie or Florrie or even Caroline in her life without things panning out the way they had.

Still staring at the two words imprinted on the cream-coloured paper, Esther attempted to ponder what her relationship with Michael might look like if it began ten years ago but couldn't form anything substantial. While the imaginings that flitted through her head regarding Drew were like coloured photographs seen at a distance, there was nothing but grey shadows that cringed away from the light when she tried to drag them into some semblance of a past with Michael.

Had she met Michael as a green girl of eighteen, she likely would have found him intimidating. He was tall, broad-shouldered and a foreigner to boot. There was also a confidence to him that made her sure he was no stranger to the interests or the company of women. How could she as a clueless girl have prevented him from wandering? There were always creatures far prettier and more adventurous to fill a vacuum created by an innocent little wife in the life of a handsome and virile young man. She was in no doubt that a hasty early marriage to her would have made a first-class philanderer out of Michael Petersen. She did not need to know the details of his past to know he had slept with his share of women. His understanding of her body when they had sex left her completely certain of that. It also made her wonder if, perhaps, all his attention was just a means to an end. Did he really care or was he just using her for sex until a better candidate came along? Or had he now, at the age of thirty-four, grown out of his need to sleep with every pretty woman he came across?

For the rest of the day, Esther thought of the three men in her life. She weighed up what each of them meant to her, she tried to guess what she meant to them and she wondered what shape the next ten years with each man would take. With Drew, it was simple. He was her best friend and she knew that their friendship would last no matter what happened. Or, at least, she hoped nothing would change their love for one another.

As she thought about it some more, she had to admit that their friendship changed before so there was no guarantee it wouldn't do so again. But now he had Caro to help keep his ship steady and Esther was positive Caro would always be on her side. After all, it was she who encouraged Esther to have an affair with Michael in the first place.

But while she was confident of a secure future with Drew and Caro, there was no certainty of her time ahead with either Fraser or Michael. Regarding Fraser, they didn't really spend any time together as it was, so it was hard to imagine any kind of togetherness over the next ten years. It was even harder still to envisage what might happen with Michael.

There were so many variables in his life that she couldn't predict. He might stay indefinitely as a POW at Kirkmore. There was a possibility that the prisoners would move on to a new farm. And then there was the inevitability that he would eventually be sent home to Germany just like the Italians who had been repatriated. But what if he chose to leave her? Even thinking about it made her heart flutter unhappily. Yet the likelihood of Michael staying at Kirkmore was slim. He was a scholar, a city-dweller. What hold could an estate in deepest Scotland have on him? And even though Esther hoped he might stay for her, there was no guarantee he would stay forever. Such isolation was bound to make him restless, make him resent her and eventually he would leave anyway.

By the time evening came, Esther had cogitated herself into such unhappiness that she barely acknowledged Michael when he poked his head in the door to let her know he was there. The warmth of his smile and the tenderness in his eyes were completely lost on her. Had she looked up to meet his gaze, she would have seen his ardour written all over his face. Instead, she buried her head in her work until Archie and Florence burst in to kiss her goodnight. Leaving her work behind, she followed them to their rooms and saw them safely tucked up in bed, read them a few pages from their current book and left them with the door ajar. When she got back down to the study, Michael was sitting on the edge of the desk, Fraser's telegram in his hands. She closed the door with a snap behind her.

"Happy anniversary," he said without inflection.

Still holding onto the doorknob, Esther tried to gauge whether he was mocking her. She decided he wasn't. "Thank you," she said, equally toneless.

"Ten years, yes?"

"Yes."

Nodding, he carefully replaced the note. "I wonder where we'll be in ten years' time."

Esther's eyes widened in surprise. "I've been wondering that all day," she blurted out, immediately cringing into herself for admitting it out loud.

He didn't seem to notice. "What *will* we be doing in ten years?"

"I don't know," she admitted, looking away. "All I came up with was that we'd be apart."

"Why do you think that?" he asked, pushing off the desk, but rather than coming to her he turned away and approached the patio doors.

"Because what could possibly hold you here?" she asked, crossing to her desk.

"You could."

Again, she tried to determine what was behind the words he spoke. "I don't think so," she said stubbornly to the back of his head.

"Why not?"

She gave a single humourless, "*Ha!*" and remained silent.

"Why not?" he repeated, turning to face her.

"Because there's so much more to your world than Kirkmore," she replied simply.

"You don't know that. There is very little of *my world* left," he said mildly. "I have no home, I have no family. What else is left for me other than living on this estate?"

"You have an education. You have your work. Why wouldn't you return to Oxford when all of this is over?"

"Will it ever really be over?" he asked sceptically. "Do you think people will want a German academic who spent four years dropping bombs on their country to teach them about Greek and Roman mythology?"

The thought hadn't crossed Esther's mind.

"And, besides," he continued, "what makes you think I want to go back to that life? The truth is, in *my world* as you put it, I was tired of study, of translations and interpretations and papers and writings. I just didn't want to admit it, since I had been so adamant I was going to spend my life living and working in Oxford. I could not let my family see I made the wrong decision. I could not crawl back to them and tell them I was weary of college, that they had wasted their money to give me an education I no longer wanted. For a year and a half, I struggled with my desire to leave it all and then war was declared, and I had my escape."

"So you don't want to teach anymore? Not even in Germany?"

"One would think you wanted rid of me," he smiled. "No. I no longer wish to teach – at least, not in a university. Perhaps one day I might return to education but for now I am happy to work the land."

"Not for long," Esther muttered. "You've never experienced a Scottish winter. If there's one thing to cure you of your romantic notions about working the land, it's spending your days soaked to the skin or freezing cold, getting chilblains on your hands and nose."

He looked at her sadly. "I may have spent most of my adult life reading stories of heroes and villains, but that does not mean I am blind to the difficulties of real life."

Neither spoke for a time. Esther began to fiddle with the detritus strewn across her desk.

"I know what you're trying to do," he said finally.

"What?" she said sharply, looking up. She wasn't aware she was doing anything.

Slowly, he came towards her. "You're testing me. You're trying to frighten me away. You worry that if I stay for the wrong reasons, I will fall out of love with this place, that I will stop loving you. It scares you to risk your own happiness on someone else's decision to stay or go. If you push me away, then it's your decision." He stopped directly in front of her, reached out then thought better of it. "You want to stay in control."

Esther stared up at him for a moment before snorting incredulously and walking away to the other side of the desk. It was too hard to resist the urge to touch him when he stood so close. Yet, even though she wanted to answer him – to tell him he was wrong – she did not because she knew, deep down, that he was right. She did not dare hope that Michael would willingly stay at Kirkmore, no matter how much she wished he would. There were far too many obstacles in their path to think it could possibly all work out. She was the wife of a laird, managing three and a half thousand acres of land and he was a prisoner of war. They were doomed to fail.

Eventually, she spoke. "You call it control. I call it self-preservation. I have too much to lose if things go wrong. There are too many people who rely on me: my children, the people who call this place home. I can't risk their future for the sake of my own happiness." Michael began to speak but she held up her hand to stop him. As she spoke she realised that she was coming to a conclusion. She barely had time to arrange the words that came from her mouth before they were hanging in the air between them. "We had three weeks together and they were wonderful. I can honestly say I have never felt happier. But being apart from you has given me perspective." She felt a lump rise in her throat, pressing painfully on her windpipe, but she had to finish. "No matter how much we want to, this can't continue."

The silence between them made her skin crawl. She did not want to be the first to look away as his eyes bored into hers but she had to. Her lower lids stung with the threat of unshed tears. Was she really doing this? Had she really made such a final pronouncement on her future without first thinking it all through? Perhaps it would have been better if she had given it careful consideration. Or perhaps she would simply have talked herself out of ending it before their relationship grew into something that was impossible to untangle. But that didn't matter. She had said it now.

Still he stood in front of her, the desk between them, hurt written all over his face as he mouthed soundlessly. Eventually he found the words. "You're … you're finishing this? After all I have said?"

She couldn't answer him. He waited for much longer than was comfortable for either of them then, eyes shining, he stood ramrod straight, focusing on a point above her head before turning about and leaving the room without another word.

It wasn't until he left that Esther realised he had admitted to loving her.

Chapter Twenty-Three

After she had effectively dismissed Michael, she worried that he would cease his tuition of Archie but the next evening she heard the murmur of their voices in the library next door while she tried to concentrate on her meeting with the head of the parish council, Bob Wardle.

Bob was a retired civil servant who thought wearing a tweed coat and mustard-coloured waistcoat made him look every inch the country gentleman. He exuded pomposity to such an extent it seemed to strain the buttons on his already well-stuffed clothing. Mr Wardle also felt it was the duty of a gentleman such as himself to provide some order for the rabble of locals who clearly lacked the necessary cognitive powers to plan anything as well as he could. Esther was meant to be organising the annual harvest thanksgiving dance with him but, as Bob Wardle droned on without apparently pausing to breathe, she lost interest in his plans and found herself straining to hear the content of next door's conversation. When Mr Wardle finally drifted to a halt, she hadn't the faintest idea what he had said to her over the past half hour. However, since Bob had organised the previous half-dozen dances, Esther veiled her lack of concentration by simply agreeing to what he told her. Yet as she reached over the desk to shake his hand, the old man continued, this time asking several questions that required answering, meaning she had to concentrate. Eventually, however, Bob seemed satisfied and only interrupted her twice more while being shown to the door before she finally closed it firmly between them.

Once Esther was alone, she gave her senses free rein to explore the house but, instead of hearing the movement of other human beings, the silence stretched further and further as she strained her ears to perceive even the slightest shift in the air. It was eerily quiet. A chill shivered over her skin as she became aware of how alone she was. It was a crushing realisation. This house was too big to be alone in, she thought, as she crossed the hall and climbed the stairs in search of some life.

Reaching the landing, she was met by the sound of thundering paws as the dogs cantered along the corridor. Sadie, the older dog, skidded to a halt at the sight of her while Jasper continued to bite at his playmate's neck and ears. The dogs weren't supposed to be upstairs and Sadie knew it. That, however, did not stop the children from sneaking them up every now and again, especially when they thought their mother wouldn't notice. Yet tonight, rather than scold children or animals, Esther collapsed cross-legged on the carpet and called the dogs to her. They came willingly, tails wagging and tongues lolling. Sadie immediately lay down beside her with a grunt while Jasper fussed around them trying to shove his wet nose in her face. She was still rubbing Sadie's belly and Jasper's silky soft ears when Mary arrived on the scene ten minutes later.

"Are you all right, mistress?" she asked, looking worried. It wasn't every day she saw the lady of Kirkmore sitting on the floor cuddling two dogs.

"Do you know, I'm not even sure anymore,"Esther answered vaguely without looking up. Pushing herself up off the floor, she smiled at the nanny's confusion. "I'm all

right, Mary," she assured her. "Sometimes I just have to …
not be the mistress of Kirkmore."

Unbidden, a flash of one of her nights with Michael burst
forth before her eyes, obscuring the sweet young woman
standing in front of her and reminding her of another time
she didn't behave like the estate's mistress. She hid her
grimace of unhappiness by bending to the dogs.

"Shall we all go to bed now, yes?" she asked them.
"Goodnight, Mary," she added, turning and walking away.

She havered about bringing the dogs to her room but
couldn't bring herself to bend her own rules. As it was, she
had to go downstairs anyway to turn off the lights so she
brought them down to their room near the kitchen while she
was going. Yet once she was there, she found herself sitting
on the floor again, cradling the dogs to her, seeking the
comfort of their warmth, their somnolent vitality. She
wished they could hug her back.

When she finally left them, she wandered the house,
checking each room for no reason other than to do it,
switching out lights as she went. Of course, Mrs Morris
could have done it, just as she could lock the front door
every night. Esther, however, always thought that it should
be her job. But, tonight, the lock was stiff in the door. The
screech as it finally yielded stabbed at her ears as it
reverberated in the vestibule. Yet it was the quiet that
followed that hurt most.

For the first time in her life, Esther wondered why she
stayed. What was it about Kirkmore that made her want to
be there? Was it just a case of the place being familiar?
Perhaps she was still keeping her mother's dream alive even
though the woman had been dead for half a dozen years.

Though Esther had always treated the main house as a
place to run in and out of with Drew, making a trip to the
"big hoos" was an event for her mother. If she closed her

eyes, Esther could see Lizzie clutching her handbag as she gazed in wonder at the tiled floor, the wood panelling, the paintings, the ever-staring stags' heads. For Lizzie, the pinnacle of grandeur was epitomised by everything about the house. In her opinion, there was nowhere better in all the world. But, then, Lizzie Muncie had never seen the world.

Esther was hardly any better. Never in all her life had she left the island of Great Britain. Of course, she visited some of the bigger cities every now and again – though, since discovering her husband's relationship with his secretary, she was much less inclined to go to London. She had been to Hampshire to see Drew while he was recovering in hospital and she had honeymooned in Scarborough with Fraser. Otherwise the whole of her universe consisted of nothing other than the stretches of ground between the outer reaches of Kirkmore. There was no way for her to tell whether the estate really was the best place in the world when she had nothing to compare it with.

Yet, considering what had happened elsewhere over the past seven years, Esther pondered whether the rest of the world was, in fact, worth seeing. Kirkmore had remained virtually unscathed by the war, given it was several score miles from any major industrial centre. The only way they saw the war was in the people who came back, some whole, others not, all scarred by the inhumanity they witnessed. And then there were the people who didn't come home. The voids in families that waited in perpetuity to be filled. They were strange absences that Esther thought might be filled if someone went and looked for those that were missing. It seemed unreal that they would never come back. More like they were hiding, waiting to be found. It was as if they were simply playing an interminably long game of hide-and-seek – just as they had when they were all schoolchildren – and the lost boys where the ones who managed to find a particularly good hiding-place. Was the world that swallowed these boys whole really worth seeing? Or was Kirkmore truly the best, safest place to be?

Passing into the study, her eyes fell on the portrait of her two children on the desk. When she thought about the safety and happiness of the children, she knew from her own experience that Kirkmore could not be bettered. It was strange to think how a happy child's curiosity, that stretched no further than the bounds of their known universe, could morph into discontented restlessness in adulthood. But then perhaps her unhappiness was more to do with the position she now held. As a child, she was responsible for nothing. Now, it seemed she was responsible for everything. Perhaps her urge to leave was no more than a longing to escape the never-ending responsibilities she bore.

Musing further on the subject and unable to shake him from her mind, Esther realised Michael's relationship with the estate was similar to that of a child's. The place was a haven, untouched by the outside world. It was still new enough to him to be curious and wonderous. He wanted to stay because he was happy to work the land without having to think about anything greater than the task in front of him. He got up, did his day's work then ate dinner and went to bed. At Kirkmore, his was an uncomplicated existence. He was at the bottom of the ladder whereas Esther remained isolated at the very top. Their experiences of the place, therefore, were wildly different. If he stayed, she asked herself whether their experiences would grow closer together. Maybe, the more Michael came to know the estate, the less idyllic it would appear. She supposed that was what she had warned him about. The land was unforgiving and he had only seen it at its best over a particularly good summer.

But what if he stayed and *didn't* fall out of love with the place? He would not be the first who found themselves in the depths of Scotland and decided to stay – to make a life for themselves. For the likes of Mrs Morris, Kirkmore was a place that could not be bettered. Yet the housekeeper was so homely she seemed to fit perfectly into her surroundings as if the ground itself had offered her up. In comparison, Michael Petersen was otherworldly. Tall, blond, blue-eyed – the ideal Aryan. He was at odds with rustic, verdant Kirkmore. He shone like a luminous white beacon on a dull day: bright, unmissable and thoroughly out of place. Yet, now Esther couldn't envisage a Kirkmore without him. In the last five months, he and the other men had become part of the landscape, even if they were a somewhat curious addition in their donated work clothes and mismatched army-issue uniforms dyed maroon.

As it had so many times in recent weeks, her vision was obscured by an image of Michael's uniform strewn across her bedroom floor. Alone in the study, Esther sat in her chair, leaned back and closed her eyes, allowing the memory to play out like a movie at the pictures.

She'd sat cross-legged on the bed in her nightdress as he undressed, dropping the clothes where he stood as he came towards her. Earlier, she'd had a bath while he sat fully dressed on the toilet as she washed. Both had agreed that he couldn't join her in case anyone noticed the scent of her soap on his skin. It was all quite domestic and familiar as he leaned against the cistern with his hands in his pockets, talking casually but watching every movement her body made with hawk-like intensity. Her bare skin burned with such happiness and confidence she was sure the water was heated by her warmth. When she finished, he dutifully wrapped her in a towel but otherwise did not touch her. He was toying with her and she knew it.

Waiting for him to undress in the bedroom, her body still glowed from the heat of the water and his gaze. But when he was finally, gloriously naked, he stopped short.

"I can't touch you," he murmured sadly. "You're too fresh, too clean." Without further comment or even allowing Esther the chance to reply, he turned about and disappeared into the bathroom. Curious, she followed to find him quietly filling the bath. Playing along, she sat on the toilet, reversing their roles as he began to vigorously scrub his skin with nothing more than water and a flannel cloth.

From a distance of a few feet she saw his body from a different perspective – the bumps of his spine, the muscle and sinew that wrapped around his shoulders, his long, hard legs with their dusting of fine golden hair.

"You cannot fathom the joy of a proper bath after almost ten years without one," he said quietly, his eyes aglow with contentment.

He had come to bed with her after that, skin still damp and slightly red from scrubbing. Soon the damp of water was replaced with sweat and the colour of his skin shone just as brightly as her own. Afterwards, he joked that they needed another bath. Esther told him they couldn't since he had used up all the hot water. That made both of them laugh. There was something so familiar in teasing one another about the use of the bath. But what followed was a melancholy silence as both realised it was a false domesticity. They were playing at having a life together in the few short hours where Michael shared her bed. Those moments together were fleeting but wonderful.

A dry sob reverberated around the empty study. Esther opened her eyes as the pictures faded from view, bringing her back to crushing reality. Was that really it? Was it all over? Was she going to live the rest of her life without experiencing his touch? She finally felt she understood what she was throwing away. Before, it had almost been easy to think she could live without him. Abstinence was something she was achingly familiar with. She told herself she could live with it again. But it was easy to abstain from something that was never pleasurable in the first place. However, when she made love to Michael, she never felt more alive. Blood rushed through her veins, her skin tingled and every nerve sang as it responded to every movement he made, every touch he bestowed upon her. How could she deny herself the chance to experience such a sensual, vivid, sweaty, animal reality again? As she thought about its absence, it felt like something was trying to pull her insides out and drag them through the floor. She wanted Michael to come to her now. She didn't care if he was angry with her. She would take it if it meant he would hold her again, intertwine their bodies, love her until she was so senseless she had no idea whose limbs were whose. That was the feeling she craved. The feeling that was nothing other than physical when her mind was completely consumed by him – when there was nothing in the world except the two of them yet that was enough because it was everything.

And he said he loved her.

While she pushed him away, he told her he loved her and she never even noticed. How could she have let that slip by her unquestioned? No wonder he no longer wanted to see her. No wonder he was hurt. No wonder he was angry. He had professed love and she was so hell-bent on getting her point across that she didn't even listen to him. He told her he wanted to stay yet she was so sure that he didn't that she dismissed his arguments without even considering them. She was denying them both the opportunity to make their relationship work because, in her mind, there was no way it could. It was how she made all decisions: if she could see something working, she went ahead and did it. If there was a strong possibility of failure, she did something else. If she'd had the sense to do that at the time, it would have helped her to decide against marrying Fraser. But this wasn't business. This was something entirely different.

Her relationship with Fraser had coloured her view of love muddy-brown. Love for a man – either emotional or physical – was something she didn't really understand. Now, her feelings were confused by loneliness, a recently discovered enjoyment of intimacy and fear of what it would mean to continue either with or without Michael. Would he even want to spend time with her after she pushed him away? Or would it be easier to simply continue living one day after another, deprived of each other's company until it no longer hurt?

They were questions she had no answers to. Frustrated and alone, she went to bed. But she couldn't sleep. For hours she tossed and turned, trying to get comfortable. She stretched out her toes until they reached the foot of the bed. She turned on her side and curled up in a ball, hugging her knees to her chest, but it didn't help. She felt cold even though Ada had put a warming jar in the bed to take the iciness out of the eiderdown and mattress. Wrapping herself tightly in the bedcover, she tried to seal the warmth of her body in a tight little cocoon but, before long, she felt far too confined by the material folded around her. Desperate, almost feverishly fatigued, she reached out to the other side of the bed, seeking the comfort of another body, but the mattress lay cold and empty.

For the first time in her life, Esther was disappointed to find there was no one there.

Chapter Twenty-Four

The harvest thanksgiving was always a big to-do in Kirkmore. Though it was organised by the parish council and presented as a religious festival – with a well-attended church service forming part of the celebrations – it was the much more pagan element that locals always looked forward to. The indoor picnic (as Bob Wardle dubbed it) in the parish hall was followed by a dance where anyone who could play a musical instrument (and a few who couldn't) brought them along and spent the night giving the gathered crowd something to dance to. Young and old attended with the extremes of each age usually found asleep in one corner or another midway through the night. Everyone, no matter their youth or dotage either clapped along to the music or got up and danced. Grannies forced reluctant male relatives to guide them around the floor while little girls stood on their daddies' feet until they got bored and ran off to play with schoolfriends. There was also usually a healthy amount of speculation on the pairings that formed as the night progressed: those that stayed the course of the event and those that broke up (sometimes quite publicly and acrimoniously) before the evening was over. Indeed, over the years there were many marriages and births (one often following hot on the heels of the other) that were the result of harvest thanksgivings.

Since the start of the century, however, various conflicts and contagious illnesses left the area with a disproportionate number of women to the local men. The year before, much excitement ensued when rumours had circulated that the Italian workers were to attend the celebrations. The local lassies were less pleased when they heard that the Land Girls would be in attendance too. However, all excitement was short-lived when the parish council decided the Mediterranean men would not be granted admission to the dance. There was considerable disgruntlement among the Italians too who were already making plans about which girls they would dance with. But the council were well-respected and, despite some half-hearted protests, their inference that the men were far too lascivious for Kirkmore's simple little gathering could not be argued against. However, while the virtue of the native women and girls was saved, poor Esther had a terrible time of it trying to make the Italians work after breaking the news to them. She wasn't sure if they were more angry or hurt not to be invited but, whatever they felt, it was not conducive to a healthy work ethic. She was, therefore, quite surprised when the parish council sent an invitation via the vicar to all the German prisoners of Kirkmore. Yet she could see why.

Though residents were initially highly sceptical about having the 'enemy' in their midst, over the summer the men had made themselves so agreeable to those living on the estate and in the village that everyone now seemed rather fond of them. The men were excellent labourers who took great pride in doing a good job. even though they received only a small amount of the £4 Esther had to pay the War Ag for their upkeep. They were well-mannered and, as the season progressed, became quite friendly. And they loved the children, taking every opportunity they could to play games with them or make small carved wooden or metal toys for them.

Also, as luck would have it, restrictions on communication with POWs across the country were being lifted, which meant their harvest thanksgiving would be above board. Not that it had previously mattered to the locals. They had been 'communicating' with the Germans for months. However, for something as public as the dance, they were quite relieved the men could come without flouting any laws.

Esther, however, didn't know what she felt. Being at the dance would mean she would be in close proximity to Michael for several hours under the watchful eye of every lang-nebbit – 'nosey bugger' to Caro – in the parish. Yet, there was no question about whether she would attend the event. It was a party she organised and paid for in conjunction with the local church. There would be more talk if she was absent than if she drew curious eyes on the night. Unfortunately, this meant that she spent an unhealthy amount of time in the days leading up to the dance thinking about what might happen when she came face to face with Michael in the confines of the church hall. However, there was the possibility that they would have absolutely no contact at all if he wanted to avoid her – something he was clearly doing at the moment.

Though he came to give Archie lessons several nights a week, Esther had only heard Michael's voice. He no longer said goodnight to her before leaving and she no longer went into the library when he was there. Besides, while contact between prisoners and civilians was now permitted there was still a blanket ban on 'amorous liaisons'. And yet, that hadn't stopped Esther and Michael before. They were, however, still unlikely to give any public indication of their relationship, even if it was over.

But it wasn't just herself she worried for. Esther also worried that the excitement of the event might cause some of the local girls and the German men to lose the run of themselves and do something inappropriate. As someone only recently introduced to the joys of intimacy, Esther could hardly blame either sex if they longed for a loving touch. What was to say the local women did not pine for the same things Esther wanted? There were many unmarried women in the area. Others were either waiting for the return of their husbands or knew they were never coming back. Norah Harper was one of the women who fell into the latter category but Esther supposed she wouldn't be falling for a German any time soon. She was still grieving and would likely do so for a very long time. Esther wasn't sure she had even seen love like there was between Norah and her husband. She didn't know if that made Norah lucky for having him or unlucky to lose him. Perhaps she would have been better off if she had not met him at all.

In her bitter moments, Esther thought it might have been better if she had not met Michael Petersen. But these thoughts were fleeting. She could not seem to muster regret since, every time a remembrance of him came unbidden to her head, she fought the urge to smile. Not one memory of her time with him was bad. He was always good, always kind, clever, making her laugh, helping her feel like she was beautiful, desirable, intelligent – worthy of love. How could she not want to spend time with someone who made her believe all those things?

How could she not care for someone who seemed so sincerely good?

When the day of the dance arrived, Esther suspected she was the only person in a ten-mile radius who was not in a state of unbridled excitement. To her surprise, even Norah Harper was bright-eyed and red-faced when they met in the morning at her garden gate.

"Dougie's so excited about tonight!" she gushed without preamble when Esther handed over her post.

Esther smiled, knowing that the widow was using her son as an excuse to look forward to the event herself. In her less self-assured moments, she did the same thing with Archie and Florrie. "I'm glad to hear it. Archie'll be there to keep him company."

However, a look of concern slid over Norah's face. "Do you think …" she asked, stepping forward, "do you think it'll all go off all right? That your boys will behave? They do seem lovely," she continued quickly, "but I'd just hate to see them lose the run of themselves and do something silly. Because if anything happened that would be the end of them here, wouldn't it? I'm not sure we could do without them now. And Dougie would miss some of them something terrible."

The smile on Esther's face became very fixed. She felt a definite protective instinct towards the men and, though she liked Norah a lot, it still wasn't nice to hear somebody else voice the same doubts she had herself about the Germans' ability to behave appropriately. She knew it was ridiculous but she felt it almost as a slight on her own character when her men were slandered or questioned by others. But there was also the rankling worry that Norah's anxiety was not unfounded. What if the men did lose the run of themselves? They would all be forced to return to their prison camp or worse. Esther would lose almost her entire workforce overnight just as root-vegetable harvesting season arrived. There was work for more than twenty men all the way up to Christmas and more beyond. If she lost her workforce and the trust of the War Ag, it would be an utter disaster for the estate. She would lose an entire harvest to frost and rot. All her carefully calculated sums that guaranteed Kirkmore stayed in the black would fall apart and slide the books into red. She would lose the respect of the locals, the wider agricultural community and Fraser's trust in her to run the estate efficiently. And she would lose many friends whom she had come to like and respect over the last five months.

And she would lose Michael. She couldn't bear to think about that.

Chapter Twenty-Five

In the evening, when the church service was over, there was a rush of women and children who almost passed out the vicar in their eagerness to make it out the door and across the road to the village hall. Though all the chairs and food-laden tables had been laid out before the religious service began, the women still needed to put water on to boil for tea and coffee.

Almost everyone in the village had donated a small amount of their own tea ration so no one would have to go without, while Bob Wardle's wife was providing her homemade chicory coffee. Betty Wardle had become such an expert at making the stuff that most residents now brought their own home-grown chicory roots to her for mincing and roasting. Even Esther, who had tasted some quite expensive coffee that Fraser had brought back from Harrods in London couldn't fault Betty's recipe.

The children, on the other hand, had only one thing on their minds: food. While their mothers, aunts and grandmothers fussed over simmering water and the correct allocation of teacups to each table, they were already parked on their seats chewing vigorously from plates loaded with sandwiches and cakes. Their ecstasy was amplified when they were each presented with a teacup full of milk which further added to their sense of importance. They slurped noisily from their cups, many sticking out their little fingers in imitations of elegance. Although the illusion was rather ruined by the residue of crumbs and jam on their faces and hands.

By the time the first flush of excitement had worn off and the children's appetites were satisfied, the rest of Kirkmore began to file into the hall. A number of the sterner women were dispatched from the kitchen to chivvy the children out of the way and up onto the raised stage at the end of the room where they could be kept an eye on. Meanwhile, another army came in with cloths to wipe the tables and lay out fresh food platters and clean crockery.

The children's falsettos were drowned out by the deeper rumble of the men and women as they settled in their places to eat sandwiches, queen cakes, jam scones with cream and a variety of apple desserts. The last of these was the cause of much hilarity to the gathered crowd since everyone seemed to have had the bright idea of getting rid of their glut of apples by feeding them to everyone else.

The Germans were under the supervision of the vicar and Major Brown who steered the group to a separate table at the far side of the hall. Swept up in the gaiety, they laughed and joked with each other and some of the local men but Esther noticed they barely looked at the women. Betty Wardle had taken it upon herself to prevent any fraternization by instructing her somewhat reluctant husband to warn the men off the village's womenfolk. By means of some careful choreography Mrs Wardle also made sure that the Germans were only served by the elderly ladies of the parish. Indeed, she almost shouted at Esther – who was wielding a teapot for the evening – when she approached the Germans' table to refill their cups.

However, as the gathering settled and the platters of food emptied, the men began to change tables. They squeezed in between Esther's labourers, called them over to their own tables and watched, quite unconcerned, as the children skulked down from the stage and re-established the friendships they had formed over the summer in the fields. Esther wasn't sure who was more excited to see whom as voices rose and the laughter swelled, reaching the rafters, filling the room. There was particular excitement surrounding Erwin Riegel who had become something of a local hero after his gory accident. Everyone was delighted to see him and he elicited a particularly loud cheer when he stood up and walked about with only the slightest hint of a limp.

When the time came to dismantle the tables and put them in the storeroom under the stage, the Germans were the first up to help, though they were still careful only to engage with the men and older women. They even seemed to be avoiding Esther under the hawk-like gaze of Mrs Wardle.

However, once Mrs Wardle disappeared into the kitchen to supervise the washing-up, the men began to mingle more thoroughly, their uniforms marking them out from the crowd.

It wasn't long before the musicians took their place on the stage and call for order. Knowing the run of things from previous years, the well-established couples took to the floor and, taking their cue from the accordionist, formed up to dance an eightsome reel.

The Germans all stood to the side where Mrs Coleman took it upon herself to call out the steps.

Initially bemused and somewhat concerned by the bodies flying in every direction, the Germans were soon laughing and clapping along to the music, fascinated by the speed and complicated-looking twists and turns of the dance. Yet the more they watched, the more they began to see the pattern, how many spins before swapping partners, which foot to go forward on. They also saw that part of the beauty – part of the fun – was the fact that it was imperfect.

There were forgotten steps, wrong turns and missed grips but it made the dancers laugh to see each other making mistakes. As the music continued and couples became fatigued, the children began to take their places, matching the adults step for step with their boundless energy.

"They boys should learn some traditional Ceilidh dancin' while they're in Scotland, should they no'?" roared Emun Murray who was one of the local farm labourers.

He was quite fond of some of the men, having spent much of his summer with them. Breaking away from his partner, he began dragging the Germans onto the floor, putting them into groups who knew the steps. Others soon cottoned on to the idea and reached for the men closest to them so there was suddenly an overabundance of men in each set. But it didn't matter. There were women dancing with women so the men paired up and danced together as well.

Mrs Wardle got quite the shock when she walked in and almost collided with two tall Germans spinning frantically arm in arm. By the time the final musical notes droned out across the hall, almost everyone who could stand was on the dancefloor cheering uproariously for the start of the next one.

It was glorious to see everyone so happy. Not even Betty Wardle with her sour puss could dampen their spirits. Buoyed by the eager crowd before them, the musicians played faultlessly, attempting much more complicated pieces than they usually did and generally enjoying themselves as much as the dancers did. When they finally had to take a break to massage their overworked fingers, there was an outcry from the people on the floor. However, Kurt Vogel who was the accompanist for the Germans' choir practice was quickly called upon by the vicar to give the gathering a few tunes on the piano in the corner.

Those who had not heard him play previously stood in awe as his fingers danced across the keys, somehow making even the slightly out-of-tune piano sound wonderful. He gave them a fine mixture of Glenn Miller and Gershwin but never played anything slow enough to encourage intimacy among the couples still energetic enough to continue dancing. However, he needn't have worried since the pairs still on the floor were mostly made up of children and the Germans who were among the few who could keep up with the vivacity of youth. There were still a few Kirkmore residents who were managing to go toe to toe with the youngsters but most of them were late starters since they had been in charge of the food and drink earlier in the evening. Esther was among them and, to everyone's surprise, so was Norah Harper who spent much of the evening being chaperoned by Dieter Scholzen who looked a little mystified himself. The only other person she had danced with throughout the night was Dougie who was currently spinning Florrie in dizzying circles as she giggled and gurgled joyfully. Esther, meanwhile, tried and failed to steer Archie around the floor in some semblance of orderly steps but all he wanted to do was spin in circles too.

"Archie, we're going to crash into someone!" she laughed as he swung wildly away from her and dragged her in the wrong direction. Staggering a little, she bashed into very a solid object. "*Oh! Sorry!*" she said, looking over her shoulder.

Her smile faltered somewhat when her gaze rose to see Michael looking down on her. His eyes seemed distant, hurt.

"Sorry," she repeated as Archie swung their linked hands back and forth, continuing to dance on without her.

The pain in Michael's face seemed to clear a little. He regarded his pupil. "Archie, don't break your mother," he admonished gently. "She's important. Here –"

Without further ado, he took Archie off Esther's hands and gave her the little girl he was dancing with, oblivious to the very disappointed look on the wee lassie's face.

Silencing Archie's protests, he began an ungainly sort of Gay Gordon with the boy. Soon, they had every pair on the floor following their lead as they danced the traditional Scottish jig to a particularly happy song by the Gershwins that several bystanders were singing along to.

By the time the musicians returned, everyone was out of breath from the dancing, singing and laughter. It was, therefore, not without cause that they began the slower section of the night's entertainment since everybody was now too tired for the livelier tunes.

Gradually, people began to drift in and out for fresh air, cigarettes and to use the outdoor toilet. The room had also become quite hot with so many bodies exerting themselves in a confined space. Despite the cavernous ceiling interspersed by the rafters holding up the peaked roof, the windows were cloudy with condensation and when the two small doors were opened, steam billowed out, shimmering in the light as it purled and rose into the darkness.

Feeling her light dress stick to her back, Esther was one of the melee who slipped outside to cool down in the night air. Stepping out into the pool of light cast by a pair of lanterns hanging either side of the door, she saw groups of men and women laughing and chatting in the slightly quieter atmosphere outdoors. She could hear a party of children playing and shrieking on the steep grassy mound just beyond the glowing ring of light. Automatically, she scanned the crowd to make sure none of her Germans were doing anything untoward but everything she saw seemed to be good-natured. She felt somewhat guilty for doubting they would be anything but. She was also surprised to find that her guilt was mixed up with another feeling: she craved a cigarette.

There were very few occasions on which she allowed herself to smoke. She disliked how the smell clung to her clothes and hair. It also reminded her of a particularly nasty teacher she had in boarding school with stained fingers and teeth who constantly dragged the fug of her Sweet Afton cigarettes and a hacking cough around the corridors with her. But sometimes Esther just needed a cigarette. Usually, she allowed herself one on special occasions like Christmas and her birthday. But this year, Michael had been in her bed instead and he had driven all thoughts of tobacco right out of her head. Yet now, all she could think about was the first delicious tang of smoke as it slid down her throat and into her lungs.

Approaching the nearest group from which smoke was rising, Esther tapped one on the shoulder. "Pardon me but does anyone have a cigarette?" she asked.

Before the circle even had time to pat their pockets to find a packet or a tin, a voice behind her spoke. "You can have one of mine."

Esther did not need to turn to know who stood behind her. She was sure she would recognise that voice until the day she died. Smiling in thanks to those she had asked and waving them off, she faced him, chin up so that she looked him directly in the eye. Though she tried to look unconcerned, she wasn't entirely sure she succeeded.

"Thanks," she said as he handed her a cigarette. She ran it under her nose and her mouth watered at the slightly sweet smell of tobacco.

Michael watched her carefully for a moment then produced a card of matches. Striking his match, he cupped it in his hands to light his own cigarette but didn't extend the little ball of light towards her. Instead, he held it close to his chest. Knowing what he was doing, Esther felt the urge to let him burn his fingers on the flame but she also fought the very powerful urge to move closer to him. Taking a step forward, she told herself she was simply getting a light for her cigarette. However, just before the end caught and glowed red, she took a deep breath, trying desperately to find Michael's scent through the fog of smoke. But it wasn't there. All she caught was the smell of cheap tobacco.

"I didn't know you smoked." She pitched her voice low, making sure no one in the vicinity would hear her. Though she was conditioning herself to avoid memories of their time together, she allowed her mind to spool back in search of the clinging stench of cigarette smoke on his clothing. Yet all she could find was the smell of earth, hay dust and sweat.

"I don't," he said shortly then, seeing the questioning quirk of her eyebrows, shrugged. "Usually," he amended.

There was an awkward silence while he seemed to be deciding whether to stay or walk away from her.

"You know how to throw a party," he observed, fixing his feet and taking a long drag. He held it for a moment then exhaled, his shoulders lowering mechanically as if a hand was forcing them lower than they wanted to go. He was trying to appear nonchalant but the tension in his jawline gave him away.

"Oh, I didn't organise it, the parish council did," Esther answered.

"I meant Kirkmore knows how to throw a party."

Esther felt the colour rise in her cheeks, flustered by her misunderstanding. "Oh. Right. Sorry. Yes." To cover her embarrassment, she took an equally deep drag on her cigarette but being so unused to smoking it caught the back of her throat. Fighting for breath, she began to cough and splutter, her eyes streaming.

"Are you all right?" he asked coolly. He didn't show any concern or even offer her a helpful pat on the back.

"Yes," she croaked, throwing an angry glance at him. She knew he was being deliberately cold. She couldn't blame him. But that did not mean his indifference wasn't hurtful.

He had the good grace to look abashed. "Perhaps you

should take a little fresh air," he suggested. "Clear the lungs and start again."

Without another word she turned away from him, heading towards the children's voices and the hillock of grass. There was no point being near him if he was upset with her. It was late, she was tired and she couldn't face the discontent that radiated off him. The best thing to do was leave him alone. Although she did wonder why he had approached her in the first place if he did not want to be around her.

She was surprised therefore, to hear the gravel crunch a short distance behind her as she walked out of the pool of light. Just like the sound of his voice, she could recognise the tread of his step. Where once it would have heated her blood to know that he was following her, now it made the hair on the back of her neck prickle. It was quite a relief, therefore, when his footsteps began to fade and she heard one of the children call his name. Out of the corner of her eye Esther saw two boys run towards him. Flicking away the butt of his cigarette, Michael crouched, gave a roar then bounded forward and caught them both, lifting them off their feet and swinging them back and forth as he trudged up the hill with them. They squealed in delight, alerting their friends who all came tumbling towards him and latched themselves on to whatever piece of a limb they could find.

Relaxing slightly, Esther stopped, put her cigarette to her lips and sucked in a lungful of smoke. It itched her irritated throat a little but she held it until she was almost sure she felt the nicotine seep into her bloodstream. Casting a glance over her shoulder to make sure no one was watching, she slid away from the hum of voices, the damp grass hissing slightly under her feet. Even the children were beginning to sound distant.

On the other side of the mound bordering the roadway was a retaining wall which, as a child, she had often sat atop with friends and a bag of penny sweets from the local shop. When they were little, it often took a couple of attempts to reach the top from the pavement four or five feet below but that was part of the fun of sitting there. Some, like Esther, were agile enough to take a run from the street below and pop themselves up in one swift movement but others needed a hand or a leg-up. Yet once they were there, they felt so important sitting on high, their backs to the grassy hillock, observing the comings and goings of the street before them. Sometimes, they would lie back on the sloped grass that met the top edge of the wall where they sat while their spindly legs hung down over the side where passers-by could easily give their knees a cheeky little squeeze as they walked along.

It was here that Esther sat, her back hunched against the gathering on the other side of the hill, the remains of her cigarette still between her fingers. She was desperate for solitude after her encounter with Michael. She couldn't go back to the crowd and pretend that everything was all right – make small talk about the state of crops and how the root vegetables were coming along nicely. She didn't have the energy to feign interest and enthusiasm. She couldn't do it anymore. Not when she was struggling to keep herself from falling apart.

Tonight showed her how hard it really was to act normally. It had taken everything she had to play along. And the horrible thing was that it was a part she had played before. For years she pretended to be the happy wife, the mother, the lady of leisure. But it was a part she struggled with – it was not written for her. Now she was experiencing a similar feeling. Something offstage made it virtually impossible to go on stage every night and perform her role even if her current role was a more comfortable fit, even if she was born to play it. She knew she had to fix these problems. They were affecting her ability to perform for the gathered audience. Yet she wanted to face these issues even less than she wanted to go back to the crowd and play her role again. Right now, she was hiding. She was in the wings, avoiding both worlds since she didn't want to face either of them.

She nearly pitched headfirst off the wall onto the pavement below when Michael plonked down beside her.

"Jesus *Christ*!" she hissed, clutching her heart to prevent it from hammering out of her chest. "Whatid ye do that fer?"

"You go very Scottish when you are angry. Has anyone ever told you that? Cigarette?"

As she slowed her heartrate, he offered her the box then took one himself, pulling it out with pursed lips. It drooped from the side of his mouth as he proffered a lit match to her before lighting his own.

They sat smoking in silence for a time until a rumbling chuckle began to build in Michael's chest.

Esther glared at him. "What?"

He gave a little titter then shook his head. "You were swinging your legs," he answered, pointing to the limbs in question with fingers paired around his cigarette.

She looked away, tensing her calves against the wall to stop them moving. Almost immediately she began to feel the start of cramp creeping up from her ankle. Disgusted, she released her leg. It wasn't worth the pain.

"You can keep doing it if you want. I won't tell anyone," he whispered, leaning close to her ear, the smell of his tobacco mingling with hers.

Unbidden, Esther's shoulders rose towards her ears.

He pulled away. "If you want me to leave, I will."

She kept smoking. "I don't know what I want anymore," she said finally.

"Well, *that* is quite obvious," he replied.

She thought he might say more but he didn't. She couldn't

think of anything to say either. Everything was either too trite or too serious to broach sitting on a wall in the dark.

"What happened to us?" he asked so quietly she could have ignored him. "It was so easy before."

"We were in our own little cocoon," she said softly. An image formed in her head as she said it. "Do you remember those butterflies we saw in the garden with the children?" He nodded. "Back then we were just new-born. The caterpillars finding their feet."

"Caterpillars have many feet," he said, not quite hiding the amusement or the exasperation in his voice. He didn't like it when people spoke in riddles but she seemed so earnest – as if this was the only way she could explain herself.

Esther ignored his comment and continued with her idea. "Then we came together, wrapped in our tight little cocoon, sealed off from the outside world. We thought of nothing but each other because that was all there was in our own little space. But eventually we had to emerge, face the real world and, in the real world, people notice things. Two butterflies dancing around each other are bound to catch the eye," she finished, reaching out to pat the back of his hand. She wanted to leave it there but pulled it away.

"You certainly catch the eye," he murmured, gently running his index finger back and forth along the length of her upper arm.

It felt like all the heat in her body flooded to the point where his skin touched hers, leaving her extremities achingly cold. "You're not exactly inconspicuous either," she muttered, warring with the contradictory impulses to move closer and pull away. She did neither. "Are there lots of men who look like you where you come from?"

"Like me?"

"You know – tall, blond. Aryan is what your people called it, isn't it?"

He thought for a moment then decided to answer her question truthfully. "Not all Germans fit the blond and blue-eyed Aryan ideal. Where I came from there were more brown-haired boys than anything else. My brother had brown hair. I was the odd one out. I was tall too, taller than most in the same way I'm the tallest of all the prisoners. The people of Germany are much like the men here at Kirkmore – all different but similar." He paused. "But I suppose, physically at least, I fit the ideal."

"But not in other ways." She knew him well enough to be sure he wasn't a Nazi. She was quite certain none of the men were. They were nothing other than the victims of circumstance. Their country went to war, so they did too.

"Well, considering one of my closest friends in Oxford was a Jew, I think it's safe to say I didn't prescribe to my government's way of thinking."

His face twisted as he remembered the footage all the Germans were shown in their camp one evening before they came to Kirkmore. The black-and-white moving pictures of huge eyes in hollow skulls that were seared into his memory forever. You could barely tell if the poor creatures were men or women. Their ages were unknowable. All looked ancient, stretched to their very last breath. Over and over again he saw the Star of David and all he could think of was his friend Daniel who wore the symbol on a chain around his neck. For him, it was a badge of pride. For the poor wretches in the camps, it was their death warrant.

When General Jodl surrendered in May of '45, none of the men cried. To them, it was just another day among many. But on the night they were shown the recordings of the concentration camps, he heard men sobbing in their beds once the lights were extinguished.

"God, what have we done?" he sighed, collapsing back onto the grass behind him, his forearm over his face.

"Which part?" Esther asked, turning to look at him.

"All of it. What my country did. It makes me ashamed. And to think of those poor people from the concentration camps makes me ashamed for thinking I was suffering. I thought no one had suffered pain like mine when you sent me away. But now I know I was just being foolish. What you said to me hurt. But it won't be the death of me."

"We are two fools," she said softly.

"We are many things, but I do not think either of us is stupid. If we were a little less clever, we might not care so much. We would not see the problems, we would not fear the consequences. All we would have to worry about would be each other." He reached down and took her hand in his, lacing their fingers together.

"If only it were that simple."

Michael sat up and cupped her face. "What if it was? If we are clever enough to see the problems, why can't we be clever enough to see the solution? What if we could have those two sides to our lives? You the mistress of Kirkmore and me the labourer but also you Esther and me Michael. Just two people who care for one another." He paused. "Who love one another."

Esther closed her eyes as his thumb caressed her cheek. "What are we doing?"

"Taking the opportunities fate gives us. We can make this work," he said, gaining enthusiasm. "We would have to be careful of course, but we can do that. We can."

She began to shake her head. "You'll know Orpheus and Eurydice," she said sadly. He looked taken aback. "You're not the only one who's read the myths. I just read it in English."

"We are not characters in Greek mythology. You have not died and gone to the underworld. I don't have to bring you back."

"But he *didn't* bring her back, did he?" she insisted. "He

condemned her for all eternity because he couldn't bear to not look at her. Can you bear to not look at me? Give no hint there is anything between us when we are surrounded by other people?"

"I don't know. Will you at least let me try? And if I fail ..." He closed his eyes and hung his head. "If I fail, you can send me away."

This time it was Esther who curved her hand around his cheek. "Please don't make me do that," she begged, resting her forehead against his. "All right. We'll try."

Michael's hand shot up and grabbed her wrist. He squeezed it, then kissed the vein running up the inside. Unconsciously, both inched forward until their lips met. When they touched, Esther immediately felt relief wash through her as if a weight she didn't know she was carrying slid from her body. His kiss felt so familiar yet in it she also experienced the pang of its absence. This was an intimacy she had done without for weeks. And for what? Though she knew their separation was likely the right thing to do, it made them miserable. Was the risk of getting caught outweighed by the joyous feelings she experienced now that she was back in his arms?

She certainly hoped so. She was committed now and to hell with the consequences.

Chapter Twenty-Six

Even though Kirkmore had celebrated its harvest in October, there were still fields of root vegetables that needed gathering. Luckily, the rain of the first two months of autumn had abated somewhat which made life a little easier for the workers. The carrots were already out of the ground and Edwin Riegel, along with a few others, had spent two days reburying three-quarters of the crop in sand to preserve for the winter.

When November arrived, there was an unseasonable warmth in the moist air which created a thick fog over the land and obscured the hills from Esther's view every morning. It swallowed the men as they walked the lanes to work and conjured them up again when she dropped by to observe them. Voices and the sounds of labouring men echoed in the silence which muffled anything more distant. There was something slightly eerie about the dark, spectral figures that drifted in and out of the grey mist, moving up the rows of vegetables in uneven lines. It was the perfect weather for desertion but, much to everyone's relief, all the men stayed where they were amid a blanket of tiny water droplets. However, many of them no doubt wished they had taken their chance to escape given what followed.

The second week in the penultimate month of the year gave Kirkmore some of the worst weather Esther had seen in years.

She had vague memories of weeks of rain when she returned to the estate with Drew once he recovered from his injuries but, at the time, the weather did not concern her quite as much. Back then, Mr Cartwright was still the farm manager and the adverse conditions were his to deal with. Trying to manage the root- crop harvest of '46, Esther wasn't surprised that Cartwright had retired after the winter of 1940. Much like in September, the earth once more turned to mud as the rain persisted, sticking to the soles of boots and clinging desperately to the vegetables purloined from its depths. The labourers' movements became stiff and their work rate decreased as they battled against the weather and bodily fatigue. Hands became chapped and sore, with muck permanently encrusted in cracked knuckles and around broken fingernails. Perpetual backache was another issue for the men working in the cold, wet fields, constantly bending to dig then pull beets, swedes and various other tuberous vegetables.

The sickly-sweet smell of damp permeated every corner of the main house but was even worse in the men's barracks. The dust of dried mud also returned to tickle the nose and colour everything with hints of brown. Drying out clothes became an impossible task with only two stoves which were already struggling to heat the cold room. Thinking it through, Esther came up with the idea of hanging all wet clothing in the boiler room of the main house which had been converted into a wood-burner midway through the war.

After every workday, a bedraggled huddle of men trailed over to the servants' entrance to hang up coats, jumpers and sometimes trousers on hastily erected bars and hooks around the room. Most couldn't even smoke to better their mood since their packets of cigarettes were soggy, papery lumps by the end of the day. The men with metal tobacco tins became exceedingly popular as it was to them everyone flocked while they idled in the warm underbelly of the house. It always took a good fifteen minutes for them to hang up their clothing since they dawdled in the luxury of heat, trying to loosen taut muscles and stiff bones. On particularly bad days, some of them took off their boots and socks to dry them as much as they could near the burner's hatch which glowed gold when opened, running at full blast just to try and keep everything dry. The worst part of it all was coming back to their clothes the next morning which, though dry, were crusty and foul-smelling. However, since everyone was in the same boat, the men complained very little. The saddest thing of all was the fact that their high spirits from the summer were washed away along with vast amounts of topsoil that turned the rivers around Kirkmore a dirty, sandy brown.

Many of the vegetable crops had been planted in the alluvial soil along the banks of the rivers. In the spring, they often flooded the plains on either side of the banks as the rain flowed down from the braes to the sea. For hundreds of years, the people who lived on the banks sowed their crops in the richly fertile earth by the river and the current residents were no different. The issue was that, with the heavy rain and rising water level, the fields were in danger of flooding before the vegetables were harvested. If that happened there was the possibility that the crop would be washed downstream or that flood water might stay indefinitely and rot any submerged vegetation. They could have risked it in the hope that the worst might not come but everyone agreed that, with food shortages and rationing still dictating diets around the country, it was of paramount importance to save every last bit of food they could find.

The Germans were in the fields at the crack of dawn and did not leave in the evenings until it was full dark. However, they were not alone. Almost every inhabitant of Kirkmore was there to help out, once more tapping into the gung-ho attitude that had been so prevalent during the war.

Esther was one of the first to don her boots and mackintosh to help the efforts. She thought it quite fitting that she should help in such a dire time of need. Local labourers turned out in force and brought their wives along with them. They even took their children out of school to lend their small hands to the task. Indeed, the schoolmistress's classes were so denuded of pupils, she turned up on the second day to deliver the remaining children to the workforce and also to be of whatever use she could herself.

The older members of the community who were fit and more accustomed to physical labour found occupation sorting all the gathered vegetables in the storage barns, which helped to make room for the next load that came in … and the next and the next. Those less mobile were put to work by Mrs Morris and Mrs Coleman who set up a dining area in the main hall of the house to feed all the workers. Soups, stews, freshly baked bread, scones, jam and chicory coffee were in constant supply – as were the hungry mouths to eat and drink it all. Nobody cared that the floors were soon filthy with mud and wet trailed in on feet and clothing. There were more important things to worry about than a muddy floor.

Everything that could be used for either human or animal consumption was saved. Turnips (or 'neeps' to the natives) along with sugar beet and chicory were pulled up by the vanguard then others came along behind them to brush off mud and cut off the tops, with the children then collecting the leaves. The tops of the parsnips were the only leaves not passed on since they were poisonous to livestock. The rest were fed directly to the animals who had taken to lining up along the paddock fences near the yard where they would bawl until they were fed. Every day the bags of tops had to be spread further and further along the fence since the ground where the cattle and sheep collected quickly turned to knee-deep mud once they had footed about for a few hours as they fought for the choicest leaves.

Seeing all the people come to her aid made Esther quite emotional. The other thing that affected her was the bone-aching tiredness of physical work. Even the men who were used to it struggled to keep going. But there was such a collective urge to succeed, people simply put their heads down and kept going.

What made it all slightly more bearable for Esther was the fact that she and Michael always managed to work side by side. He pulled the vegetables while she cleaned them and cut off the tops before putting the roots in sacks ready for collection. Archie brought up the rear, helping his mother to bag the roots while also gathering all the greenery for the animals. Esther was amazed by the boy's stoicism as he trudged the muddy fields, hunched against the rain in his oversized coat with only as much complaint as the adults. At some point in the day, most of the other children were sent to sit under a tree or ditch for half an hour so they would stop irritating their parents whining about the cold or the hard work. Esther could hardly blame them. She would have quite liked to join them herself on a few occasions. But Archie was so steadfast in his work, it gave Esther the determination to continue as well.

There was also no doubt that Michael helped both of them too. While others worked in morbid silence, focusing all their energy on the task at hand, Michael used the hours they spent together to teach Archie and tell stories of Ancient Rome and Greece. He spoke of novels and plays, recommending which ones the boy should read and which were boring. On one occasion, he and Esther had quite a disagreement over the best Shakespeare play. He advocated

Hamlet while she, as a committed Scotswoman, told Archie that he would be better to read *Macbeth* first.

"You can't possibly tell him *Macbeth* is a better play," Michael said placidly, his voice sounding somewhat distant as it was swallowed by the pattering of rain.

Taking the opportunity to stand up straight and stretch her back by putting her hands on her hips, Esther swelled indignantly. "I'm not saying *Macbeth* is a better play, I'm saying it's the better one to start with. It's much shorter that *Hamlet* which, by the way, is bloody long. And what's wrong with *Macbeth* anyway? It's an excellent play!"

Catching the eye of a local labourer working the next row who was grinning at their little tiff, Michael winked. The man's grin grew wider and he winked back, shaking his head.

"It's all right, I suppose, if you're Scottish," Michael replied, hiding his grin behind the hood of his coat.

Esther's cutting knife went a little awry and she accidentally removed the top of the root rather than just the greenery. "Dammit!" she swore. "What's that supposed to mean?! 'If you're Scottish!' Its being Scottish is neither here nor there. It's got witches and a ghost, magic and battles. There's love and loathing and murder and real cunning. And then there's justice in the end of it all."

"There's all that in *Hamlet*," he said evenly. "I admit, without the magic and witches. But there's everything else and an excellent play within the play which I found very entertaining when I saw it."

"You've seen it?" Esther said, momentarily distracted.

"Yes. It was very good but very long."

"*Ha!* So you *do* admit that it's long! And besides, where's the love in *Hamlet*? He's awful to the women and then everybody dies in the end. That's not justice, it's a bloodbath."

"*Does* everybody die in the end?" Archie asked.

"Yes!" Esther said before Michael could answer.

"Don't have to read it then," he muttered.

Esther threw a triumphant grin at Michael who quickly countered with, "Everyone dies in *Macbeth* too, so you needn't read that either," which wiped the grin clean off her face.

Several of the people around them who had been watching proceedings chuckled along with Michael when Esther replied by sticking out her tongue at him. In the few days they all spent working side by side, their mistress had become a less remote figure. They remembered that she was one of them – that her childhood and adolescence was spent in the fields alongside them. She worked as hard as they did, spoke like they did and they rediscovered her often buried sense of humour. Indeed, the latter was something she was finding again herself. Living as she did in isolation was not conducive to high spirits. But working with others – spending hours in their company – reawakened her giddiness, her sense of fun, much as Drew's visits did.

Midway through their fourth day of the harvest, they finally removed the last of the crop from the low-lying land by the river and not a moment too soon. The river had chased them across the fields as it breeched its confines, lifting the loose soil off the surface and turning the water brown. Esther shivered to think what the ground underneath would look like once the water receded but also worried about where all that earth would end up.

The answer came sooner than she expected when the ditches around the estate and village began to back up, threatening to flood homes and gardens just as they had in the spring. So rather than finish on their half day and have a rest, the bedraggled residents set off down to the village to save their own homes and gardens from ruin. Again, they worked in teams with Major Brown distributing groups to different areas around the village, some for the purpose of protecting houses, others to keep roads and laneways clear.

By dark, the ditches were clear and the water was free-flowing – in some places several feet below where it had been just hours previously.

If the people of the Kirkmore were bedraggled on the way to the village, it was nothing compared to the shattered crowd who shuffled back to the big house for food in the gathering darkness. Seeing how much the children were flagging, Michael crouched in front of Archie and gave him a piggy-back. A few of the other Germans and some of the local men did the same but most were too tired to consider offering. Even Michael who was so lean and strong was beginning to waver and scuff his feet by the time the house came into view. Wordlessly, Esther stopped him and pulled her son off before both ended up on the ground.

She nearly cried when they finally entered the hall of the house and were hit by the blast of warmth and the heavenly smell of cooked meat in thick gravy. She wasn't the only one. The people maundered in and found a seat as if they were in a fever dream. No one cared who they sat beside. All they cared about was either sleeping until they woke or securing some form of sustenance to keep them going a little while longer.

On the tables were great vats of stewed meat and vegetables, all of which came from the fields of Kirkmore, including the beef. At intervals along the centre were tureens of mashed potato, soft and creamy having been laced with butter and milk. Alternately, diners could help themselves to hulking great loaves of brown bread also made with the wheat from the estate. It was enough to make the vacant faces – young and old – brighten as rich, warm food was ladled onto their plates. Their stiff bodies became more animate with every mouthful and soon they were stretching across one another to reach potatoes or bread and filling their neighbours' mugs with cider from the jugs that were the crowning glory of each table. It didn't matter who the person next to you was. Man or woman, German or native, everybody apart from the youngest in their company had a wee drinkie.

By the time trays of jam scones and buttered fruitcake were brought out along with some chicory coffee and weak tea, everyone was slowly leaving their weariness behind along with the sodden clothes they had stripped off and dumped on the floor behind them. What replaced it was a happy somnolence which made them eat and drink very slowly as conversation was replaced by a rumbling contented murmur. Once they ate their fill, many simply put their heads on their folded arms and slept seated at the table. Seeing that the gathered group would likely be there for some time, Mrs Morris removed their piled coats along with some of her helpers and brought them down to the boiler room to dry out.

Taking it all in, Esther imagined this was what a medieval banquet must have looked like. They had all just returned from a great battle, victorious but bone-weary. Yet these brave soldiers had not fought against an enemy army. They had battled a much more powerful foe. The elements were cruel, they knew nothing of mercy, but somehow the people of Kirkmore triumphed. Yet it had taken its toll. Some looked as if they might weep from tiredness or relief. But all had pushed through their confused emotions to focus on the meal in front of them. Esther had always found food was good at restoring people to themselves. Now, with only a scattering of crumbs dusting the tables, the warriors slept in the clothes they had fought in.

Compelled by some unknown urge, Esther stood and began to walk amongst her men and women. Not only did these people fight for the food on their table, their land and their homes, they fought for her. Every single person in her presence could have refused to come to her aid. Instead, they came in their droves and proved to her that she didn't love

Kirkmore just for the sake of her mother. The people made her love it too. They were the sort who closed ranks when they saw trouble brewing. She was theirs and they were hers. They protected each other and, somehow, it all worked.

Movement to her right caught her eye as a tall, blond figure unfolded himself from one of the low benches. Yet there was still a slight hunch to his back when he moved off.

Michael looked almost lost as he drifted from the hall towards the lavatory down a side-corridor. Watching him absentmindedly, it made Esther question how far the loyalty of the locals would stretch. Would they forgive her if they discovered she had slept with one of the German prisoners, breaking all the rules of fraternisation as well as the covenant of marriage? Casting about the people in front of her, she guessed at least half would turn against her. They were good people who believed in law and common decency. They would never understand that a wealthy, liberal husband did not breed a happy marriage. They would never understand how it felt after ten years of marriage to finally have your sexuality awakened by someone other than your spouse.

Crossing the hall, Esther quietly disappeared into the breakfast room which was uncomfortably dark and empty. She was used to it being bright and full of the smells of toast, porridge and fried meat on the weekends. She crossed the room to the door on the other side and slipped out along the corridor just in time to meet Michael coming out of the bathroom.

"In here," she whispered, ushering him through the door to an oversized lounge. She made sure no one had spotted them before she followed him inside.

Michael was standing just inside the threshold, allowing his eyes to acclimatize to the darkness. Esther locked the door behind her then slipped past him and felt her way to the mantelpiece where she knew there would be a card of matches and a few candles. There were some in every room in readiness for times when the power failed. Lighting two, she turned to see Michael still rooted to the spot where she left him. It reminded her of the first time he came up to her bedroom. Now, however, there was no mischief, no anticipation in his eyes. They were glazed, looking but not really seeing what was in the small pool of light cast by the candles.

"Come and sit down," she said, pulling cushions off a settee and dropping them on the floor. She sat down on one. Both of them were dirty and she thought the cushion covers would be easier to clean than the fabric of the seat.

"Esther – I can't. I'm too tired."

"So am I," she smiled sadly. She couldn't help but feel it was a wasted opportunity. "But sit with me for a while. Just the two of us."

He crossed the room as if there were lead weights attached to the soles of his feet. When he collapsed on the floor beside her, Esther cuddled into him, enjoying the familiar feel of his body close to hers. His clothes had the horrible sweet tang of dried damp and cold sweat but she stayed where she was, unsure when they would get such an opportunity again. It was the first time since the dance that they were intimate with one another. Of course, they had stolen small touches disguised as common courtesy when working side by side in the fields but outside there was no opportunity to cradle each other's bodies as they did now.

"Imagine if we could do this without needing to lock the doors." Michael spoke into her hair, his voice slightly slurred and much more Germanic. When he was tired or very relaxed, Esther had noticed that his precise English slipped.

"I wonder if that'll ever happen," she mused.

"Maybe one day. But for now –" he kissed her temple and settled contentedly against the front of the settee, hugging her tight to his chest "– this is enough."

Chapter Twenty-Seven

After the shock of one of the wettest Novembers in living memory, it seemed the end of the year could not come soon enough. The cold and the wet and the panic of the root harvest affected everyone at Kirkmore. It had taken an emotional toll, leaving everybody perpetually tired but it was the physical damage it did that was most worrying. The last month of the year started with a spate of colds and chest infections which meant Esther saw more of Freddie Robertson than she had in years. Dieter Scholzen developed a bad case of pneumonia which was so worrying the doctor had him moved to the surgery where a nurse could keep an eye on him during the day and Freddie himself at night.

Yet, what was most shocking of all was the fact that Norah Harper made daily visits to the doctor's house and spent several hours by the German's bedside, talking with him and feeding him when he was too weak to do so himself. It was the cause of much talk around the village but, having been a figure of pity for so long, no one was going to tell Norah what she was doing was wrong. Besides, on the surface, really all she was doing was performing an act of charity by being kind to a sick man. But things between Norah and Dieter went much deeper and everyone knew it.

Aside from sickness, the other issue that dogged the

workers was physical injuries. In the space of a month, there were two back spasms, a broken finger, three sprained wrists and a twisted ankle that developed such a serious swelling everyone except the doctor was convinced it was broken. Injuries were not uncommon when people were engaged in physical work but there were more this year than Esther could ever remember seeing previously. She put it down to a combination of elements. Firstly, the men had overexerted themselves to save the crops from the flood waters (which had still not abated by the middle of December). Their bodies simply couldn't keep up with the workload, so they gave up. Another problem was the men were using their bodies differently in attempting to protect minor hurts which then resulted in more serious injury, namely the two back spasms. But what caused most harm was the damp and the cold which contorted muscles and slowed the natural healing process that had served them so well throughout the summer.

Cold air from Europe blasted across the Scottish countryside, freezing the ground and stripping the last leaves that had clung so valiantly to their trees. It froze the air and filled the lungs with what felt like tiny shards of ice. Even the simplest tasks left the fittest workers short of breath. All the small aches each person carried were exaggerated. Indeed, poor Erwin Riegel ended up reverting to walking with a severe limp after several months of improvement.

In an attempt to save themselves further pain, Alt Hans dispatched Michael to ask if the mistress might give them some materials to better draughtproof their quarters on their next Sunday off. Instead, Esther allowed them to take the next day off work to improve their lodgings and also suggested that every day one person be designated to keep the stoves going in the barracks. Though the day was cold it was, thankfully, dry. The prisoners, therefore, spent their time cementing over cracks in the walls and around the whistling door that kept them up at night. They also fixed a few holes in the roof that they had kept buckets under for weeks. Bedding and clothing was aired on strings that zigzagged across the yard as they attempted to eradicate the smell of damp but also give them a hint of fresh Scottish air rather than the must of fabric that had been lived in too long. Finally, they cleaned the place from top to bottom with Borax powder donated by Mrs Morris and great basins of hot water so that, for the first time in months, the place was as clean and tidy as they could make it. For a final flourish, Max and Rienhold disappeared into the fields and returned rather pleased with themselves bearing several strong-smelling branches of an evergreen tree which they placed about the room.

"It is almost *Weihnachtszeit* – Christmas," Fluss shrugged.

Flagging spirits began to revive at the prospect of the holiday. As more candles began to burn on the Advent wreath in the village church, their outlook became marginally brighter despite the adverse weather. Yet, for many, it was still just another Christmas away from home. Most had not celebrated amongst their families since before the start of the war and were inured to the fact that they were not at home. But the younger boys like Hans and Erwin could not hide hints of unhappiness. They were still not used to the separation, given that not so long ago they were children enjoying the wonder of Christmas as innocents rather than hardened adults.

Yet Kirkmore did its best to improve the men's outlook, with the vicar especially making a point of including the men in all the church celebrations. He consulted them on what German celebrations entailed and tried to add some of their traditions in his own services. However, the best thing he did was get them to sing traditional English carols alongside their own German ones. Their version of 'Stille

Nacht, Heilige Nacht' even resulted in a round of applause and cheering from the crowded church with many declaring it better than the English version. The locals took to wondering what they could do for the prisoners to make their Christmas at Kirkmore better than the ones that had gone before. Even Betty Wardle made an about-turn with her opinions, to become one of the strongest advocates for the men. She wanted to have a community celebration in the village hall and invite all the men but, much to the lady's disgust, Mrs Morris and Esther had beaten her to it.

Esther was adamant that the men should celebrate Christmas in the main house because she felt it was her duty, not the village's, to afford the men the best Christmas she could. The other benefit of having the men in the house was that she would be close to Michael. It also gave her something to think about that wasn't to do with the business of running the farm. For once, she got to sit down in the study and plan something with her children who both got very much behind her plans to have as lavish a Christmas as they could within the confines of ever-present rationing. Florrie turned giddy with anticipation, running and skipping wherever she went, unpacking the house's finest cutlery and tableware from its cupboards and spreading it across the floor to decide which crockery would best suit the occasion. Archie, on the other hand, was more interested in which Christmas tree would serve the main hall, insisting that his mother come out to the woods with him so that they might discuss which one would suit. However, Esther did spoil his enthusiasm somewhat when she explained that the biggest tree on the estate was quite lovely but that they wouldn't be able get it through the front door, even though the door was very large.

Eventually, however, a suitable tree was found. On the morning of Christmas Eve, Archie gleefully watched as

Fluss and Erich Neuman felled it then brought it into the house which was a six-man job that left pine needles everywhere. There then followed a long and involved discussion about how to secure the tree which involved wooden supports and wedges that were cut and shaped especially for the tree. Esther had expected the men to lose interest in the whole affair quite quickly but the more the day wore on, the happier they were. It seemed that every German in the place came in at some point to observe the progress or pass comment. For the entire day, doors slammed shut and fires sputtered in the draft as people drifted in and out of the house. Finally, as it began to get full dark Esther brought all the men into the hall where they helped the children, Mrs Morris and Ada decorate the tree and the stairs with ribbons, holly, ivy, various shiny baubles, woven straw stars and some wooden ornaments the men had carved themselves. When they finished, the men lined up as they did in church and sang carols in English and German with members of the household joining in when they knew the words. Florrie and Archie impressed everyone by bursting into word-perfect renditions of 'Stille Nacht.'.

"You've taught them well," Esther said quietly to Michael as they milled about drinking mulled wine Mrs Coleman had prepared before all going to bed.

"They are good students." Michael shrugged but smiled happily at the compliment. "I love your family very much."

"And I love you," she whispered back.

Chapter Twenty–Eight

Christmas Day dawned bright but cold.

Rather than sit in her window when she woke, Esther went straight down to the kitchen to help prepare the food. As she walked along the passage, her mouth began to water with the scent of gloriously rich cooked food. Muldoon (who was thankfully visiting his sister for the festive season) had killed two twenty-pound turkeys for the table, which had been stuffed the day before with breadcrumbs, onion and herbs and were already cooking in the oven. Cary Eden and Kirkmore's village butcher had killed one of the pigs a few weeks before and made trays of rashers and sausages for breakfast. There were eggs from the hens, homemade bread and butter and tattie scones from Kirkmore potatoes. In fact, almost everything they were eating – whether meat or vegetable – came from the farm and fields of Kirkmore with the men having harvested the vast majority of what they were going to eat.

Only the puddings were letting them down on the self-sufficiency front. The alcohol, spices and dried fruit were all bought with ration coupons Mrs Coleman had been saving for months beforehand. Being an excellent cook, she seemed to know instinctively – before Esther even knew it herself – that there would be many more people at the dining table than there had been in previous years. Rather than complain about the extra workload, she had risen to the challenge, employing a local girl to help her in the run-up to the big day but otherwise doing most of the preparations herself. For years she had been wasted as little more than the family cook but now she was given the chance to shine and intended to do so. However, that did not stop her looking distinctly frazzled when Esther entered the kitchen to offer her services.

"*No!*" the cook almost shouted. "*We're fine!*"

Effie Cotter, her teenage helper, had not hidden her disappointment when Esther was dismissed. There had been a momentary glimmer of hope in her eyes when she thought someone was coming to her rescue. Esther gave her what she hoped was a sympathetic look and the girl smiled glumly back, shaking her head and further dislodging tentacles of curly red hair from under her cap.

Not willing to upset anything, Esther went up to the main dining room which had not been used since her wedding over a decade ago. Again, she thought Mrs Morris might resent having to prepare such a big room for individuals who were essentially farm labourers, but she had not uttered a word of protest. She seemed quite glad to return the house to its former glory even if it was just for one day. What Esther could see of the mahogany dining-room table was burnished to a bright red under the heaving place settings Florrie had chosen. Mrs Morris and Ada had even allowed her to help them set the table – much to her delight – while Archie oversaw the erecting of the tree in the hall. In fact, the children had been involved in all aspects of the preparations since Mary, their nanny, had gone home to her family for the holiday the week before. Once they got fed up following Esther around, they usually found their way below stairs to 'help,', the kitchen, of course, being their favourite haunt for obvious reasons.

When the men finally arrived, Esther was pleased and slightly embarrassed to see that every single one of them was wearing the clothes she had given them the night before. In proper German tradition, she handed over her gifts to them on the eve of Christmas rather than the day itself.

She had taken a trip to Edinburgh while the weather was amenable and was tasked with collecting clothes for the men from an army surplus shop in the city since they had earned enough coupons to exchange for much-needed clothing. However, seeing how cheap the clothing was, Esther had bought extra for each man and twenty-five pairs of boots in various sizes. She had worried that they would take such a practical gift the wrong way – thoughtless perhaps. So rather than wait and see them opening their presents, she left a package on each man's bed while they were all in the main house admiring the tree. The boots she had left in boxes beside the table. (She had initially left them on the table but immediately removed them as the old superstition about shoes on a table came to mind).

It was wonderful to see them all dressed in decent, clean clothes for once. They were all very pleased with themselves and kept fixing their waistbands – many of which were still held up with string – and fiddling with their shirt cuffs.

As they milled about waiting to sit down for breakfast, Esther got a glimpse of the men they really were rather than the ragamuffin band they usually formed. She was also glad that they did not come up and thank her for the gifts individually. Instead, Alt Hans, who held his new cloth cap in his hands, approached her in a very formal, grave fashion and thanked her on behalf of all the men. The others looked on, grinning as Esther turned pink and mumbled some form of 'think nothing of it' that she wasn't even sure he understood.

Soon, however, the embarrassment was over and the feasting began with everyone sitting down to a beautiful fried breakfast including, eventually, Mrs Coleman and Effie who only went up to the dining room when Esther ordered them out of the kitchen and promised to hold the fort with Mrs Morris in their absence.

"Do you have any idea what to do in here?" she muttered to the housekeeper as Mrs Coleman scurried off down the hall.

"Not the foggiest," Mrs Morris said brightly. "I was just about to ask you the same thing." Then she added dryly, "I suppose if anything catches fire, we should probably put it out."

Luckily for everyone, nothing ended up burnt to a cinder and their Christmas dinner later that day passed off without a hitch. Afterwards, everyone gathered in small groups about the room to play chess, draughts and various games of cards. The children along with some of the men took up residence on the rug in front of the fire with the hand-carved farm animals the Germans had made for them as presents. During the meal, the small figures had been passed around the table for the admiration of everyone.

Caro and Drew had come down from Edinburgh late the night before. They had been waiting to give Fraser a lift but he had telephoned very late in the evening to say that there were delays on the way up and that he had turned around and gone back to London to spend the holiday at his club in town. Though she didn't admit it to anyone, Esther was exceptionally relieved to be spared her husband on a day of such unbridled gaiety. She knew, had he been there, he would have soured the mood.

At some point, the patio doors were opened and many of the gathering began to file out to smoke some of the cigarettes Drew had brought down from the city as a present. Soon Archie was in the middle of it all, organising races around the garden and offering to show them Ivor Beattie's greenhouse.

All the goings-on outside along with the activities inside meant no one noticed when two of the party disappeared.

The rest of the house was completely silent as Michael and Esther ascended the stair to her room. He held her hand as he trailed after her, taking her all in. He enjoyed the way a loose strand of hair curled at the nape of her neck and bounced with every step she took. His eyes raked down her body to see the way her dark- green dress clung to her waist then belled out over her hips. Below the hem of the dress were her beautifully curved calves with the seam of her silk stockings sliding over the swell of muscle. Yet, again and again his eyes returned to the dress.

That dress had tormented him the entire way through their meal. It clung to the edge of her shoulders then flowed across from either side to meet at her breastbone. But, really, he wasn't looking at the dress. What he was looking at was her smooth, straight collarbones just waiting for him to run his fingers, his lips, his teeth along. His eyes roved across the dress impatiently as he tried to find a button, a clasp, a zip so that he knew what to reach for the moment they were alone together. Yet he couldn't seem to locate any of them.

When Esther closed the door behind them, she made sure to lock it. She had barely turned the key when Michael pressed up behind her, catching her around the waist with one hand while the other dipped under her dress to trail his fingers up the seam of her stockings. He found the bare flesh of her thigh and followed it around to her hip, pulling her back against him. His cheek brushed her ear as he dropped his lips to her bare shoulder and she cocked her head to the side allowing him to kiss and suck his way across the exposed skin. Momentarily, his tongue lashed out and tickled the hollow above her collarbone. She flinched and went to pull away but he held her fast with rigid fingers that dimpled her skin.

"No, you don't," he breathed, gently nipping her earlobe. "You don't know what watching you in this dress has done to me."

281

"Yes, I do."

She leaned her head back against his shoulder then took half a step back. He grunted and tightened his hold on her even more. She pushed at his arms which were like iron bands around her but he wouldn't budge. Carefully, she found his toe with the heel of her shoe and pressed. And just like that, his hands were gone. Yet before she could turn or even take a breath, both his hands were on her shoulders – then they were gone and so was her dress. With a small *'ping'* as some small seams burst she found the top of the dress bunched around her waist.

"*Don't rip –!*"

She got no further. Michael gave another swift tug and she heard more stitches burst and the dress was suddenly a green sea pooled around her feet. But she didn't have time to chastise him for ruining the garment as, with a squeal, she was lifted off her feet and borne to the carpet in front of the fire. As he dropped her on the thick shag-pile rug, she vividly remembered a conversation four months before when they had joked about having sex here.

"But it would have to be in daylight. I would want to see you," he had said and she laughed, knowing it would never happen.

Now, he was proving her wrong. She sat back, supporting herself with her hands stretched out into the carpet behind, wearing nothing more than shoes, stockings and knickers. She breathed deeply, flaunting her breasts as he stood and stripped, eyes fixed hungrily on her body. When he was completely naked, he fell to his knees and crawled towards her, shoulders shifting from side to side with leonine ease. Esther registered nothing other than the fact that he was thinner than ever, before he parted her legs and kissed the soft flesh of her thigh above the seam of her stocking. She watched as his hand grasped her ankles then travelled slowly up her calf to the back of her knee. His fingers teased the sensitive skin before skimming up over the curve of her thighs to meet between her hips. Taking the fabric of her underwear in his fingertips he pulled gently but they were caught by her stocking garters.

"Tear them," she ordered him.

He smiled wickedly at her and she braced herself for a small amount of pain as the material strained against her skin but there was nothing other than the sound of fabric being rent asunder. She followed his hand as like a conjurer he pulled her underwear free, dangling it provocatively on the end of his finger. Throwing it aside, he began a trail of kisses up her body, leaving her flat on her back and gasping for breath. But she grew impatient with his teasing. Wrapping her legs around his hips, she pulled him to her. He didn't need any more encouragement than that. Folding her tightly in his arms, he rocked gently at first then more insistently but never let her move. She was completely cocooned by his body, only able to move her legs and her fingers which grasped handfuls of the soft carpet. She wanted to grab his arms, run her nails across his back but all she could do was worry fistfuls of the rug. She tried to be quiet but, near the end, neither of them were.

When it finished, he collapsed on top of her, his full weight trapping her so that she – already breathless – struggled to breathe even more. Luckily, however, he rolled off her before she began to panic. After the heat of his body wrapped around hers, the sudden exposure to the cooler air of the room was a shock. Goosepimples stippled her skin and she shivered.

"Cold?" he asked, running the back of his hand down the length of her arm, making all the hair in its wake stand to attention.

Esther turned to face him, hooked her foot (which had at

283

some point lost its shoe) over his hip and swung herself upright, forcing him onto the flat of his back. "I know a way to warm up," she hummed.

Leaning down, she began to kiss his chest just as he had kissed hers. She licked her way across his smooth sinewy pectoral muscle to his right nipple. Realising she was copying his earlier exploration of her breasts, he put his hands on her shoulders to push her off. No woman had ever done this to him and he wasn't completely sure he would like it. But Esther ripped his hands away and pinned them to the rug either side of his head. She kissed and licked and then bit the small red button. A guttural sound escaped him and his knee jerked up, hitting her in the backside. But rather than be dislodged, Esther gripped his waist between her knees and continued with her gloriously slow torture until it was he who was squirming underneath her.

Eventually, she pulled him up into a sitting position so that they were nose to nose and she kissed him for all she was worth.

"Pull up your knees," she instructed him raggedly as she took him again.

Initially, she allowed their chests to rub against one another, against their already sensitive nipples. But then she leaned back into his thighs, relishing the feeling of their connection yet wanting more of it, wanting to pull him deeper still.

"*God, I love you!*" she gasped out as his head dropped to her chest and she arched her spine to meet him.

Chapter Twenty–Nine

She couldn't wear her green dress back down to the party. The seam beside the zip had burst when Michael pulled it from her shoulders. It lay in a sad puddle by the door and drooped at a funny angle when she picked it up to inspect it. The damage was mostly to the stitching but there was a small section where the material had torn. Looking at it critically, Esther wondered whether it was beyond repair. She hoped not. She was rather fond of her green dress. But who would mend it for her? She had some skill with a needle and thread but not enough to make a good job of the repair. And she could hardly ask Ada or Mrs Morris, even if the latter was tactful enough not to ask questions. Their curiosity would be enough to cause her unnecessary extra worry.

Yet she could not muster the energy to be angry with Michael. She could not muster the energy for very much at all. She felt completely worn out in the best way possible: the way that left a small, knowing smile on her face that nothing could dislodge. Even when Michael kissed her for the last time, she could not be sad because they had connected once again. The misery of their separation was behind them and now, even if they were not together physically, they knew they were together in a way that mattered to them. Experiencing the physical side of their relationship would always be an added bonus, its rarity making it all the more precious to them.

As was nearly always the case, Esther watched Michael dress while she lay on the rug, naked apart from her stockings and garters which had somehow stayed put the entire time. Before leaving, Michael had swaddled her in a blanket and stoked the fire since she seemed determined to do nothing but lie languorously on the carpet. Kissing her slowly, luxuriously, he finally departed, listening carefully at the door before descending to the ongoing party below.

Esther didn't know how long she stayed cocooned in her blanket but by the time she got up, the shadows in the room had lengthened considerably and what little daylight there was had begun to fade. She hugged the coverings around herself like a shawl knowing that, despite the fire, the room would still be too chilly to walk around nude.

After washing in the bathroom, she found a pretty floral dress to wear downstairs but kept the stockings she had worn all day. She did, however, put on some underwear, just in case. There was a temptation to leave them off just for Michael, but she thought it too much of a risk considering how many other people were in the house. What she couldn't seem to remember, however, was how she had done her hair for their Christmas gathering. Sitting in front of her mirror looking at her own bright eyes and flushed lips, she couldn't fathom where she had put the hair grips into the loose bun at the back of her head. However, given that the majority of the crowd were men, she doubted whether any of them would notice what she did with her hair. She could have stuck feathers in it and likely none of them would have batted an eyelid.

Finally satisfied with her appearance, she smiled at her reflection then skipped across the room to the door just like any child would on Christmas Day. Flinging open the door, she almost stumbled when she realized the hall was in total darkness but then she threw off her momentary hesitation and plunged into the black, knowing her way from years of experience.

Before, when she navigated the dark halls of the house, she had always done so restlessly. They were the wanderings of a sleepless mind and body that drifted about the house like a lonely ghost desperately seeking the comfort of another living soul. Inevitably, she would find her way to the children's bedrooms where she would sit beside them and watch them sleep. Yet she always tried not to do it. She thought it very unfair to place so much hope in a small, sleeping child. They had not been put on this earth to calm her. And she also feared what it might do to the children if they woke to find someone sitting on the end of their bed, even if it was their mother. Esther did not want the disease of her sleeplessness to infect their lives.

As she glided down the corridor, down the stairs, her dress floating out behind her, she knew she wouldn't care if she didn't sleep tonight. In fact, she looked forward to a time when the house would be quiet and she could reminisce undisturbed about her afternoon with Michael. However, as the noise of the gathered men grew, she forced the memories deep inside her. She did not want to betray herself to anyone and knew that it would be an uphill battle to appear unchanged, especially when everything – even her clothing – had changed.

Slipping into the room, she managed to drift around unnoticed for several minutes as she reintegrated herself. She knew Michael was sitting at the far end of the room immersed in a game of cards which they were playing for cigarettes but she tried not to look at him. Instead, she focused on the cigarettes and realised that she desperately wanted one.

Heading for the box Drew had brought with him, she saw that the stocks had been well and truly depleted over the last number of hours. It was hardly surprising given the smell of stale smoke that clung to the air even though the men were courteous enough to smoke outside. But the stench was, no doubt, attaching itself more firmly to the curtains with every passing minute.

Esther located a heavy shawl that she had been wearing in the morning then slipped out onto the patio where there was a small group of men huddled by the wall with cigarettes dangling from their lips. After the brightness of the room, she found it hard to distinguish their faces in the gloom but they readily obliged when she asked for a light. Once the end of her cigarette glowed orange and the first taste of tobacco hit her tongue, she moved off rather than disturb them. She didn't want them to feel as though they had to talk to her. Instead, she listened to the gentle hum of their Germanic voices until she had little more than a butt left. It was then that someone else slipped through the door onto the patio.

"Oh, so there you are," said a rather gruff female voice, though by the way she made a beeline for Esther, Caro knew exactly where she was. The pincer-like grip with which she grabbed Esther's arm also suggested she was on a mission.

Without further comment and before Esther could even stub out her cigarette, Caro had dragged her along the patio and into the lounge next door. It was empty but the lights were on and the fire was crackling merrily. Yet, somehow, the room felt icy cold to Esther. Or perhaps it was the look on Caro's face that made her feel chilly. There was something deeply disapproving in her eyes which made Esther look away. She felt like a child who was facing the disappointment of a loving mother. She felt like she had been found out. Judging from Caroline's demeanour, she had.

"*So!*" Caro snapped out.

Esther winced but said nothing. The silence spun out like a deck of cards slowly dribbling onto the floor. Esther longed to stop them tumbling down between them but knew it would weaken her position if she were to crouch on the floor and begin scraping things up. She longed to babble – to excuse her actions – but she couldn't since she didn't know how much Caro knew.

Sensing that Esther wasn't going to give in, Caro seemed to deflate a little. She had expected Esther to turn into a gibbering idiot but she should have known better. She was facing the lady of Kirkmore. But, having the bones of a speech prepared, she thought she might as well use it.

"Do you know, once I noticed you were gone, I spent an age looking for you. I thought you might have gone off to deal with something important and been too thoughtful to ask for anyone's help. Or maybe the whole party was just too much for you – you've never been overly comfortable with big crowds. And then I wondered if you weren't well. You were awfully quiet during Christmas dinner. So, I thought maybe you'd gone up to bed and like the good little friend I am, I went to check on you."

By this point, the colour had drained from Esther's face.

"I didn't check on you, obviously," Caro added matter-of-factly. "I assume you at least locked the door. But I'm willing to bet you never thought to lock your dressing-room door."

She was right, of course. There were two doors into the dressing room: one opening into the bedroom and one onto the corridor which Esther hadn't thought about at all. She felt sick as she listened to Caro. The calm, toneless voice was unnerving. Esther would have preferred it if she yelled at her. If she shouted, there was something she could fight against. She knew how to push back against anger. But, in the face of cold truth, she was totally defenceless. The only power she had was silence, so she kept it.

Caro, meanwhile, soldiered on. "Do you know, I've had a very stressful afternoon of it really, making sure no one went looking for you. Trying to keep track of everyone in case they decided to have a snoop around upstairs. Trying to stop Archie and Florrie tottering off to look for you so they could show you the farm they've built under the dining-room table – it's very good, by the way. But what was to stop them inadvertently going up to your room? And what would they have seen if they decided to get in through your dressing room?"

Esther let her friend calm down a little before she answered. "Thank you. For caring for my children," she said simply. "I'm sorry you had to do that."

Caro gave a gruff "*Hmph!*" then, subsiding somewhat, she sighed. "It was no trouble. They're lovely."

"Yes," Esther agreed.

Giving another great harrumph, Caro plopped onto one of the sofas and began worrying her bottom lip between her thumb and forefinger. Knowing there would be more, Esther sat too, her hands neatly clasped between her knees. She waited while Caro formed the next part of her speech. It would be easier to just let her talk than try and head her off. Yet, as she waited, her mind drifted outwards listening to the hum of the ongoing celebrations in the adjoining room. While Esther dealt with her troubles, the rest of the world carried on. Michael was likely still playing his game of cards as she waited for Caro's axe to fall.

"I never thought you'd go through with it."

Esther looked up to find Caro was still staring into the middle distance, fingers still pulling her lip. "Sorry?"

"When I suggested an affair to you, I was partly teasing – enjoying offending your sense of decorum, you know? You're so *morally unassailable*. I never thought you'd *actually* have it off with him. But I really did want you to experience something … wild and wonderful. To not always have to do the 'right' thing. I hoped you would live a little. But I thought you were far too angelic for the likes of *that*. Turns out you're as grubby as the rest of the world."

She didn't say it in a cruel way. In fact, Caroline's voice was quite pragmatic. In her eyes, she was simply stating the obvious – voicing her own realisation that Esther was actually just a normal human being.

But that did not mean it didn't hurt Esther to hear the truth of her own behaviour put so plainly. She felt a lump rise in her throat, throttling her voice. She knew in her head and her heart that what she was doing was wrong, but that knowledge was her own. She could ignore it if she wished and for the most part did. Hearing it in the voice of someone else, however – someone she loved and respected – made the whole transgression all the more real, all the more wrong.

"I've done wrong, I know. But I can't – it's not – I'm not sure –"

"Good Lord, darling! I'm not judging you!" Caro cut her off. "Lord knows I would have *died* in your situation. Frankly, I'm surprised you've resisted so long. I mean, look at him!" She waved in the general direction of next door. "Who could resist *that*!" She gave a girly giggle, the seriousness wiped clean off her face. "I'm glad to discover you're as human as the rest of us. You were beginning to get quite annoying with all your perfectionism." She flashed Esther a dazzling smile.

"What?"

"You're human! *Hallelujah!* Although don't think I'm not still cross with you for being so silly," she admonished with a wagging finger. "You know how easily you could have been caught today? I mean, you've had all this time to plan it out so surely you could've made a better job of it. Although I suppose picking today was actually quite clever since no one would likely miss you. Too busy enjoying the festivities." Caro rolled her eyes.

She was not overly fond of Christmas since it usually meant her family fell out with one another. Affairs at Kirkmore tended to be much more sedate. This year, however, was far from sedate and, though she would only admit it to herself, she was really rather pleased about what she had uncovered. And she was quite pleased that her friend was finally living a little. She deserved it.

"Although you could have locked some bloody doors. And kept the noise down a little bit. You really were very loud, darling." She leaned forward and patted her friend's knee in a motherly fashion while Esther glowed red with embarrassment. "But I'm so glad you got the chance to be a woman again. Isn't it wonderful to feel loved?"

"Yes," Esther answered hoarsely. In truth, she didn't know how she should respond to Caro's approval. Once the affair came out (as she now knew it probably would) she was prepared for anger and disgust. What she wasn't prepared for was an ally. Caro was delighted in that mischievous, impish way that was hers alone. She loved a good secret, Caro. But, luckily, unlike many who sought out the scandalous, Caro knew how to hold her tongue. For her, that was part of the fun – holding on to knowledge that she would never share with anyone else.

"Finally thrown off the yoke of the old bugger," she murmured, then snorted.

Caro never liked Fraser and he thought very little of her. In his opinion, his son's love for his wife was nothing more than a foolish infatuation brought on by a reminder of his own mortality. There were many such marriages born out of war and the impending sense of doom that came with it. Fraser saw Caroline Reeves as nothing other than the only girl in a family of six offspring who seduced his gullible son since her people were virtually penniless. She was loud, opinionated and, to cap it all, was more than half a decade older than his eldest son. In other words, she was everything the patriarch of the McAllister clan did not want as part of his family.

"Bit of a revelation trying out a newer model, I'd say." Caro's eyes flashed suggestively then, more seriously, "He was kind to you, wasn't he? Because if he wasn't, he'll have me to deal with."

"Don't worry," Esther assured her. "He's always been wonderful."

"Always been?'" Caro said. "So ... today wasn't the first ... occasion?"

Esther swithered about whether to tell her friend the entire truth but then decided to throw caution to the wind. "The night after we were out shooting – that was the first time."

Caro gaped. "You've been hiding it all this time?"

"We haven't been together all that time," Esther said curtly, hoping to head Caro off quickly. "Now and again. When we thought we wouldn't get caught."

Caroline was already shaking her head in disbelief. "God, you're a dark horse, aren't you, Essie?" She paused for a moment, staring into the fire before turning and looking Esther square in the eye. "Do you care about him?"

"Yes," Esther answered simply.

A pained look passed across Caro's face. "Do you love him?" she said, wincing as she waited for the answer.

"Possibly. Probably," Esther said solemnly.

Caro cringed. "Oh dear."

"Yes."

"Darling, what are you going to do?"

Esther sighed. "I have no idea."

Chapter Thirty

Once Christmas Day passed, Esther and Caro spoke no more about her relationship with Michael. Life went on but, somehow, the shared knowledge made the friends closer. If they had been asked, neither of them could have explained what it was that changed between them. All they knew was it had. When Caro and Drew returned to the main house from the gatehouse for New Year, Esther was equally glad to see both of them whereas before, it was always Drew she favoured. But mostly she was just glad to have her family around her – happy and healthy and ready for another year at Kirkmore.

Fraser, of course, was absent throughout the festivities and remained so given what followed.

After a surprisingly mild December (by their usual standards) temperatures began to plummet as 1947 unfurled itself across the countryside. By the end of January, the snow was thick on the ground and the barometer in the hall of the house at one point showed thirty-five degrees. Whether inside or out, everyone wore coats since not even a well-stoked fire could drive out the creeping cold as it slunk from room to room like a self-satisfied cat prowling its territory.

It was also a constant battle to keep everyone and

everything in water since all the pipes and watering holes froze over. Even the handpump in the yard which had been lagged in straw and cloth sacks froze solid. It took four men half a morning to thaw the solid ice column that had formed up the centre of the pipe and then the rest of the morning to bucket water to all the thirsty animals who were in the sheds around the yard rather than out in the hoof-holed fields close by.

However, it was the village that suffered the most. There was still a disproportionately large number of women, elderly folk and children in Kirkmore who simply didn't have the fortitude to deal with such harsh conditions. Of course, there were a few hardy individuals who doggedly continued about their business. They were the ones cutting tracks in the snow with shovels and awkwardly carrying their supplies back or dragging them through their newly formed channels on children's sleds.

Once February hit, however, the constant snow and freezing temperatures became too much for many. Some moved to neighbours' houses while others – following Esther's insistence – moved up to the big house. Organising the operation to bring those in need back to the house had been something of a group effort between Esther, Major Brown and Dieter Scholzen. The German had been especially keen to have the villagers safe since one of the people most in need was Norah Harper who had badly sprained her knee slipping on packed snow.

Starting first thing in the morning, the prisoners dug a path down to the village and continued to clear it as the snow fell throughout the day. Visibility was poor but, by nightfall they had managed to get the more than two dozen folk, three dogs, six pet cats and a pair of budgerigars up to the house. And more followed.

In all her life Esther had never seen the house so full of people. For once the place teemed with life around the clock instead of for a few hours on disparate days during the year. What remained of entire families commandeered whole rooms with children, mothers and grandparents sometimes sharing the same bed. However, given that many of the bedrooms in the main house were the size of some of the smaller cottages in the village, most of the locals thought they were living in the lap of luxury. They had plenty of water, woodfires, an abundance of blankets and no shortage of food. Yet no one rested on their laurels as days turned into weeks. With more than fifty people to feed, many helped out in the kitchen or spent their afternoons darning clothes or making new ones altogether. The children were put to work in groups grinding grain and mangling turnips for the livestock while the Germans spent much of their days battling the elements just to keep everyone and every animal in food and water.

By the time darkness fell every afternoon, the men were dead on their feet but still had to keep going until the evening feed was doled out, working by lamplight which was virtually useless outdoors in heavy snow. Besides, since they were having to use lamps at all hours of the day, they were running out of oil which meant they were forced to economize and use only the barest peep of a flame no matter how dark it was. They were even using candles and old open glass lamps which they discovered were very difficult to keep alight in a snowstorm. However, they hated using the open-flamed candles in the sheds since they worried the wind might blow them over and set fire to the wood and dry fodder all around.

Just like when the floods hit during the root-crop harvest, everyone ate in the main hall, not caring that they left puddles of thawed snow beneath them as they ravenously scoffed everything put in front of them. Afterwards, it was all they could do to drag themselves back through the snow to their quarters.

"Still think Scotland is a beautiful place?" Esther muttered to Michael as he stood close to her one evening. All he did was grimace.

For the men it was to get even worse as, in the middle of all their hard work, the roof of their barracks began to cave in under the weight of frozen snow. The white blanket sat like a breaking wave curling over the apex of the roof, having been blown in huge drifts up and over the building. When viewed from the back, neither the wall nor the roof could be seen at all. There was simply a hill of pristine white snow. For some of the men, it was too much. Jung Hans just sat and cried when the snow peeping through the splitting slates began to melt and soak his bedding.

Esther took one look at the buckling roof-trusses and ordered the men to pack up their belongings and bring them up to the main house. Not only was it horribly cold and wet, it was also quite unnerving to see what appeared to be a sturdy building fold like paper under the weight of seemingly fluffy white snow. She did not want to stand inside it for another minute, never mind expect them to sleep there.

Instead, she turned over the disused narrow corridors and sloped-ceilinged rooms of the servants' quarters on the upper floor to them. But with all the other work they were struggling to keep on top of, they had no time to ready the rooms for habitation. It therefore fell to the other inhabitants of the house to clean out the dust and general grime of the entire floor which had not been used since Grandfather McAllister's time.

Though she knew the children would be delighted, Esther did worry that some of the older residents might resent the addition of a score of Germans but, as usual, they were all immediately of the same mind as the lady of the house. At every turn, Esther was surprised by their liberal attitude to the men – men who had been their enemy until very recently. Yet all they seemed to see were individuals who were in a situation beyond their control and far away from home. They pitied rather than vilified them. She supposed in a way it was easier to see them as the good men they clearly were rather than trying to come up with weak excuses to dislike them.

Even so, Esther was still amazed that not one of the Germans had done anything untoward in nearly nine months. She had expected some misbehaviour, perhaps even an escape attempt. But they were all still there, battling away, keeping Kirkmore going when she was sure no one else could have. They had saved not only crops but animal and human life as well. The least everyone could do was give them a decent roof over their head.

It was, therefore, with noticeable relief that the men trudged up the servants' stone stairs at the far end of the house to their new living quarters. They didn't mind the dingy little rooms with their bare electric lights. It didn't matter that the newly resurrected heating on the servants' floor left the air smelling of burnt dust. With the wood-burning boiler going full blast and the large number of people now living in the house, there was almost a warmth to the rooms. They were living in more luxury than many of them had experienced for years. Being included among the inhabitants made them feel slightly more normal, even if they had not previously realised such a feeling was lacking.

Living within the same building also had its advantages for Esther and Michael. It allowed them – very cautiously – to resume their relations. However, Michael soon discovered he was not the only one wandering around the house after dark.

He and Esther were careful not to meet every night since his absence would likely be noticed by Dieter who was sharing one of the tiny servants' rooms with him. He would wait until his roommate was snoring then slip out and feel his way along the corridors, counting his paces all the while, knowing where each step and each turn was. Sometimes, however, he would fall asleep himself before he heard the deep yet pleasant rumbling. Still, he never missed a single rendezvous with Esther even if he did fall asleep. He had the uncanny ability of waking himself exactly when he wanted – something that was equally useful to him when conducting amorous liaisons as it was in war.

However, one evening when he slipped into Esther's room something was amiss. Coming in the door, he appeared equally distressed and baffled but also – strangely – seemed to be fighting the urge not to laugh.

Slumped into her pillow reading, Esther awkwardly pushed herself up into a sitting position, eying him with curiosity. "What is it?"

He didn't answer at first, instead coming over to sit on the edge of the bed. "Hello," he smiled, leaning in for a kiss.

"Hello," she replied briskly but she wasn't going to be distracted. "What is it?"

He grinned at her stubbornness but then sobered. "Dieter saw me."

Esther's patient gaze turned a look of complete horror. "He saw you get up and you came down anyway? What did you do that for? I would have known there was a good reason if you didn't come! What if he's followed you?" She knelt up in the bed, throwing a scared glance at the door. "You should go back before he gets suspicious."

"No, he didn't see me get up. He wasn't there when I woke up. I assumed he had gone for a drink of water at the end of the hall so I waited but he didn't come back. Then I went looking for him."

"Where was he?" Esther's voice was tight.

"He was kissing Norah Harper as he left her room," Michael answered triumphantly, watching Esther's face.

She didn't disappoint. Her mouth fell open and her eyes popped incredulously. "*Norah*? And *Dieter*? No." She fervently shook her head. "She wouldn't. *He* definitely wouldn't."

Michael frowned. "Why not? We have."

"But we're different. Norah Harper was devoted to her husband. She fell apart when he died. Dougie ended up having to look after her. And Dieter is so cold and surly. I know Norah's fond of him but …"

"Did you ever ask yourself why he was like that?" Michael asked pointedly. "Did you know that he was married? That he had two children back in Germany?"

"Had?"

"All three were killed when the British bombed the city of Hamburg in 1943. He lost his entire family in one night, including his sister and his parents. The bombing raid my plane crashed in was retaliation for the attack on Hamburg." He stopped and gazed into the empty grate. "It's why Dieter became friendly with me in the first place," he said quietly. "He never got to avenge the death of his family. But he seemed to think I had done it for him. He's always been grateful to me for that. But even thinking they had been avenged has not reduced the sadness in him. It is like there is a part of him missing. A gap that needs to be filled. Perhaps Norah feels the same. Perhaps they each fill a void that exists in the other."

Esther didn't know what to make of that. She could hardly argue with his reasoning but there was something so preposterous about the idea of Norah Harper (who had only once been to Edinburgh in her entire life) carrying on with a German prisoner of war. Yet, equally, she reasoned that people would be shocked about her own relationship with Michael. Perhaps it was a bit of a case of the pot calling the kettle black. She said as much to Michael.

"Don't laugh at me," she admonished as he flopped back

and shook the mattress with his quiet, rumbling laughter. "Anyway, you said Dieter saw you. How did he see you? Didn't you hide?"

"Of course. I hid in one of the doorways until Norah closed the door – then I stepped out. He was not very pleased to see me."

"I bet. Did he say anything?"

"It was mostly swearing as he pinned me against the wall. Threats of castration, that kind of thing. He was quite upset until I told him I was on my way to see a woman too."

"You told him about *me*?" Esther hissed, shooting upright so she stood on the bed towering over him.

He rolled over onto his front and wrapped his arms around her calves, craning his neck to gaze up at her. "I never mentioned your name. It's likely he'll guess but he knows now that if he informs on me, we can inform on him. He won't say anything. He wouldn't anyway. He's a good friend. We can trust him, I promise."

Esther sat down but he held her legs, propping his chin on her knees.

"You do realise I have an awful lot more to lose than Norah Harper. She's the widow of a farm labourer. She lives in a house that will be held in trust until Dougie is of age. All she risks is being ostracised by her neighbours."

"And what do you risk?" he asked seriously.

"Everything."

"Is that not what you sometimes have to do for happiness? For love?"

She didn't reply. She couldn't even look at him.

"Don't you agree?" he said quietly.

"I don't know what I think anymore. I don't want to *think* anymore." She covered her eyes with the heels of her hands and keeled over backwards into the pillows.

"Do you want to stop?"

She admired how even his voice sounded when he asked. There was only the barest hint of fear. "No, I don't want to stop. I just don't want to think about it. I just want to live in the moment when I'm with you. Can we do that?"

He dropped his head and kissed her knees. "Yes, I think we can do that."

Releasing her legs, he crawled up beside her. There was some awkward wriggling as they pulled the blanket out and dived beneath it to ward off the chill of the room. Yet, rather than begin to undress her, Michael instead pulled Esther's back to his chest and wrapped his arms around her with a heavy contented sigh. She fell asleep in his arms and only woke when he slipped out from under the covers to leave the next morning.

It was the first time they simply slept together.

Chapter Thirty-One

It took weeks for the snow to finally disappear from the nooks and crannies it had packed itself into. The banks of white turned muddy brown at the bottom and pearly blue at the top as they melted into the already sodden ground. Pathways turned to slush and cunning potholes opened up beneath innocent pools of water, ready to twist ankles and damage the wheels of vehicles. As the hedges and walls shook off their cold blankets, gaps opened between the mounds of frozen, sparkling crystals and their supports, each shrinking away from the other: embracing lovers that had grown apart and were slowly withdrawing from one another.

While the villagers carefully made their way home in dribs and drabs over the course of two days, the Germans had to remain where they were. The snow had finally had its way with their barracks, collapsing the roof, folding it like paper under the weight of its stifling grip.

Esther knew they would eventually have to repair the building since the War Ag was unlikely to look kindly on twenty Germans living in the main house. She knew of other cases where it was acceptable to have one or two fellows living in the house of a smaller farm but so many sharing a space inhabited by women with nothing but a few flimsy doors between them would surely cause problems that she did not need. But no one locally seemed to mind apart from Muldoon who took to patrolling the corridors of the upper floors of the house, traipsing mud up the back stairs that all the Germans walked up in their socks, leaving their boots below in the boiler room.

It made Mrs Morris seethe since she and Ada were the ones who had to clean up after him. Yet she never chastised the gamekeeper since she had no authority to dictate to him and knew he wouldn't listen anyway. She dropped some blatant hints to Esther in their morning conversations but the mistress had no luck convincing him to return outdoors where he belonged. He simply dismissed her by saying he felt it was his duty to protect the laird's home from those who did not understand the respect such an old house deserved. Indeed, Esther could not help but think he was including her in the list of people who were disrespecting the house but she still could not come up with a good enough excuse to keep him out. There was something about the way he leered at her – daring her to dismiss him – that made her think he knew something she did not want him to. As a result, she found his presence in the house much more unnerving than that of any of the Germans.

For the prisoners there was very little let-up in their workload. There were still the usual seasonal jobs that needed tending out in the fields but they were pushed back a few weeks as the land recovered. Yet not even the weather could alter the conclusion of the ewes' and cows' gestation period who, despite the cold and wet, began popping out new-borns at an alarming rate. For most of the men who had grown up in German cities and never seen anything being born, it was nothing short of a miracle for them to witness the births of so many animals. It also brought Esther great pleasure to see the joy with which the men viewed each successful delivery despite the ungodly hours they kept on their night-time vigils.

Though it would have been more practical to train only a few of the Germans in animal husbandry or just use those like Alt Hans who had farming experience, Esther thought it only fair (but also useful) that every man was given a crash course in spotting the signs of an animal in labour and what a correctly presented calf or lamb felt like just before it was born. It was a true gift to have so many people on the farm to handle the birthing season after such a dearth of manpower during the war. But, of course, some of the men showed more of an aptitude for it than others.

Aside from the older Hans, Max with his compact yet powerful frame was adept at repositioning any misplaced heads or legs because of his small, strong hands. Some of the boys found much more wonder in welcoming new life than the older, jaded men and were, as a consequence, more vigilant when it came to monitoring the animals. Most of them enjoyed overseeing the lambing in the daytime (the cows required a little less attention as there were a smaller number of them) as it was easier to be inside surrounded by the warmth of sheep than out in the elements. The nightshift was a little trickier to deal with as, though they were allowed to sleep for part of the day, they still struggled to recover from the unusual hours. As a result, some of the more experienced German farmers who frequently covered the nights were quite zombie-like by mid-April. However, their efforts were worth it as it was with a great sense of pride that the men finally hefted the sheep onto Kirkmore's lower hills for grazing until it was time for shearing. The end of the lambing and calving also signified something else.

A few short weeks later, Esther had a little party for the men to mark a full revolution of the Earth since their arrival. She was careful not to call it a 'celebration' as she thought it an unsuitable designation to mark the continuation of their incarceration on British soil. Yet, having known the men for an entire year, she hoped they were happier at Kirkmore than it was possible to be anywhere else in a similar situation. She had done everything in her power to keep them happy and well-fed but remain enough of an authority that they would willingly work for her.

Indeed, when word came down the line that some of the men at Kirkmore would be repatriated after six years as prisoners of the British Empire, a number did not seem entirely pleased at the prospect of returning home. Some of them were not even sure they had homes or families to go back to. Like Michael and Dieter, there were several men who had lost everything to bullets and bombs. While they endured seemingly endless incarceration overseas, families had been displaced and homes destroyed. It was a daunting prospect to return to such uncertainty after years of living a regimented, regulated life both in the army and as prisoners. It was a step into the unknown and not all of them were keen to take it.

For others, there was also a nagging fear about how those in control of each sector of the country would treat returning soldiers.

Most of the men had experienced life under either the British or the Americans but they had all been spared the wrath of the Soviets. However, the horror stories from central and north-east Germany still managed to reach them. Some were afraid that on returning to Soviet-controlled Germany they – as able-bodied men – would promptly be shipped off to a Siberian gulag where they would be worked to death. For those whose final destination was Soviet Germany, remaining a British prisoner was a much brighter prospect. Yet, for many there was no choice. Once their number was up, they went home – or back to what they once called home a very long time ago.

Those who were left behind were officially awarded

more freedoms but that meant little to the men of Kirkmore whose movements between the house, estate and the village were quite unrestricted. With good weather continuing as the days lengthened, everyone's spirits soared. Each man was now used to the daily grind and continued to feel contentment seeing the results of their labours at the end of each day. They also enjoyed their unsupervised trips to the village in the evenings where their football league was resurrected after a winter hiatus. They were allowed to talk more openly to the locals rather than act like they didn't exist. It meant that the main house at Kirkmore was often very quiet in the evenings which very much suited Esther.

Just like the men, Esther's work continued, unchanged by the world outside. Almost every night she sat in the study poring over ledgers and correspondence, keeping the estate running like a well-oiled machine. Since the snow, there were laneways and building repairs to consider as well as the loss of some of their spring crops to the bitter cold weather, yet all the additional work had to fit around the seasonal work which filled everyone's time anyway. It was a juggling act but, somehow she managed, much to the surprise of Fraser who came home for two weeks not long after the snow.

The laird was also extremely surprised to find his wife and children sharing a roof with twenty German prisoners. But aside from slightly raised eyebrows and a statement that the men were living in the servants' quarters to which Esther replied in the affirmative, he said no more about it. He was somewhat bemused by the eccentric way in which his wife was managing the estate yet he could hardly complain given how well it all worked.

In a way, it upset Fraser McAllister to see the little girl he married had turned into such a practical, proficient businesswoman. He wished she had remained the joyous child he watched more than a decade ago spinning and dancing with all the boys of Kirkmore before he chased that person away by marrying her. He had wanted to preserve that gaiety, to protect that carelessness, the freedom of youth without responsibility. He wanted to give her a life where she never had to worry about anything. And yet, he had given her a life where she shouldered greater burdens and experienced more worry than she ever would have if he had left her alone. But Fraser had seen the Esther who had no cares – who had nothing to trouble her other than the raising of her children. That Esther had been miserable. That Esther was one of the reasons he left Kirkmore in the first place. He could not bear to look at such unhappiness on a daily basis. He could not understand why being a mother to a perfect, healthy son and having the run of Kirkmore's main house was not enough for her. He had hoped it would be better when she had another child but that turned out to be a bigger disaster than everything else combined. She was so irrevocably changed, so desperately lost and unhappy. His wife nearly died and, at the time, he wondered if it would have been better if she had. Yet, when she recovered, he recognised her even less than he had before Florence's birth. She was no longer discontented but neither was she anything like the girl he had so briefly fallen in love with.

In the intervening years, his guilt made him give her what she wanted. It also kept him away from her. It hurt to know that the changes he wrought in her life were the source of so much of her misery but if he stayed away and buried himself in his work, he either would not have to see it or she would be happier without him. No matter which of these were true, it was better for him to stay in London. He had a life there that allowed him to forget the mess he made of his life in Scotland.

In London, Fraser was content. However, every time he made the trip home, every time he reached York Station, depression would overtake him. All he wanted to do was watch the Edinburgh train leave the station and stay in the tearoom until the southbound train arrived and he could go back to the safety of the capital. But duty bound him to return to his constituency, to his estate and family even if he did it as little as possible.

Yet this time, the Esther he found in his old study was different again. There was a brightness to her he had not expected. After the battering the entire country had taken with the bad weather, he thought she might be broken and beaten too. He at least expected her to look drawn, thin, careworn. Instead, she was brighter than she had been since before their marriage. Though he thought she might be thinner than usual – he was, of course, no expert given how little he saw her – she radiated satisfaction. There was none of her usual reserve in the way she greeted him when he arrived. She even smiled at him though neither of them approached to kiss or even touch one another. They had forgone that awkwardness years ago.

Something had changed in her life and, whatever it was, he was grateful for it. That, however, did not mean he wanted to know *what* it was. If he tried to tease the answer from her, he might taint it and return her to the person she was before. He knew that interference would sour things and, as long as everything was running smoothly (or even if it was not), he was not going to question or change anything. She was happy and that, for Fraser, was enough.

Gradually, however, Fraser began to piece together what he suspected was going on in his absence. Being the quiet type at home no one noticed how observant he was, which was an advantage when trying to fathom the change in his wife without asking her or anyone else directly. Watching the Germans as they laboured, as they ate their meals, he noticed how Esther's eyes strayed more often towards one man. On its own, it would have meant nothing. Fraser was not blind to the man's good looks and intelligence. In fact, he was quite intrigued by the man who was teaching his son so well. But catching the way Michael Petersen glanced at his wife was enough to make Fraser sure there was something between them. They hid it well but not well enough to escape him.

He said nothing. After all, his relationship with Madeline Pugh hardly gave him the right to criticise Esther's choices. He was strangely relieved that it was no longer up to him to make her happy.

He was also glad that what she had with this Petersen man did not seem to be affecting the work she did for the estate. Kirkmore was flourishing when so many farms big and small were floundering after crop and livestock losses. His wife had risen to the occasion – issued the call to arms – and her soldiers had answered. Fraser wished there were more leaders like her in positions of power within the country. Having spent years in the army, he knew how rare and what a gift it was to have a person that others willingly followed. And how total disarray followed their departure. If Esther left, Kirkmore would survive but it would be a poorer place – a place neither he nor his son had the wherewithal or even the inclination to maintain. Esther loved the place in a way he did not understand, in a way he never would. He did not have a passion for its success like she did.

As long as Esther expressed no urge to leave, Fraser saw no reason to cause a disagreement. He was getting on better with his wife than he ever had and all it had taken was a relationship with another man. Over all the years, it never occurred to him that someone else might bring her the contentment he could not. He just assumed the poor girl was destined to be perpetually miserable – that it was all his fault and, though he had considered offering her a divorce, he knew it was not an option. Just as she kept Kirkmore going, it kept Esther going. He could not take that away from her. And he also could not risk his own standing as the local politician by casting off the woman who was so adored by the people of the area. Even if the rest of their relationship was a disaster, he had to admit that marrying Esther Muncie had been an excellent political move. It made the commoners much more willing to vote for him, given that his wife was one of their own.

And perhaps that was Fraser's problem all along: though his wife strove to rise to the position he placed her in, he never conceded one jot to help her get there. It was simply something he expected her to do – thought it was her duty to do – as his wife. He only realised much later there was nothing in her life prior to their marriage that could have prepared her to become the lady of the manor. Her struggle to fit in ground her down, upset her when she made a mistake and ultimately made her resent the person who put her in such a position in the first place. It was only when she found her place managing the fields rather than the house that her downward trajectory finally levelled off and purpose overtook constant disappointment. The fields and the people who worked them were her domain and Fraser would do nothing to take that away from her. But it was also up to her not to jeopardize it either by doing something foolish with her German.

Chapter Thirty-Two

Sitting one evening in the study as he pored over his political correspondence just inside the open patio doors while she sat at the desk, Fraser was immediately put on alert when there was a knock at the door and Petersen entered. Without even glancing in his direction, the German crossed to Esther. In a sudden flap, Fraser uncrossed his legs and sat up straight, causing sheets of paper to scatter across the floor at his feet. He did not want to inadvertently witness anything he was not supposed to.

The German barely glanced at him.

"Dieter is coming," he said without preamble. "He is quite agitated but please be kind to him."

Esther barely had time to nod in reply when there was a sharp rap on the door and another German came striding in. Fraser looked on as the man strode across the carpet with a wild look in his eyes. His brow was shiny with perspiration, his breathing erratic. The man's entire body was abuzz with tension. Fraser was not sure if he was going to scream, hit something or collapse on the floor. Petersen seemed to be of the same mind as Fraser. The tension in his back suggested he was ready to tackle his compatriot if he tried anything untoward.

Esther, meanwhile, sat perfectly composed, a look of polite curiosity on her face.

"Good evening, Dieter," she said pleasantly.

"Evening, madam," he huffed out, his gaze darting towards Michael then past him to Fraser. "Sir," he added with a jerky nod before confusion flitted across his face. His took a step back, unsure who he should address, eyes darting frantically between the laird and the mistress of Kirkmore.

"Speak to the mistress," Fraser clarified.

Momentary relief was again replaced by tension as Dieter turned to Esther. Her open expression did not change as she waited for him to speak. He tried to take a deep breath but it caught in the back of his throat. He looked like a cornered wild animal searching for a way out. He mouthed desperately without issuing a sound.

"I saw the newspaper!" he suddenly blurted out. His whole body sagged as soon as the words left his lips.

Esther's eyebrows raised infinitesimally. "Oh? Is there something in today's paper? I haven't had a chance to read it yet."

This seemed to throw Dieter a little but he recovered quite quickly. "The ban against –" here he looked to Michael.

"Amorous liaisons," he prompted.

"Against amorous liaisons is to be lifted. German men can marry British women, yes?"

"If you say so, Dieter. Like I said, I'm afraid I haven't read the paper today but I did see some sort of campaign being launched to remove the ban. Something to do with that Cann–Ganter marriage, wasn't it?" She glanced at the men.

The two Germans nodded.

Fraser shrugged. "It must have worked."

"Yes," Dieter nodded enthusiastically then sobered. "But Germans who wish to marry British lady have to ask permission."

"This is to marry Norah Harper, yes?" Esther asked shrewdly.

Dieter's eyes widened but he nodded.

"Well, then, I think it's up to her whether she wishes to wed you or not," she said. "If she does then of course I won't stand in your way. You agree, yes, Fraser?"

With three pairs of eyes on him, Fraser felt the flutter of discomfort that was so familiar to him in politics. Though he was a good orator, he never enjoyed having questions thrown at him when he was not prepared to answer them. Yet this was a simple question with a simple answer so there was no need to worry.

"If the lady in question has no objection then I see no reason to prevent a marriage. Although I do know that any sort of service or ceremony will have to wait. It takes time to iron these things out. So, while you might ask for the lady's hand, it could be some time before you can legally marry."

Dieter stood to his full height and puffed out his chest. "I will wait," he said resolutely.

"I think, perhaps, it's a little late to ask her tonight," Esther said kindly, noting that Dieter looked as if he was about to bolt for the door and head down to the village to Norah at that very moment. She wanted him to stop and think. And not to scare the living daylights out of the poor woman by bursting in without Michael to forewarn her. "But maybe if you go down to the village tomorrow after your day's work, you might get to call on her. Yes?"

He looked as if he might argue with her but then seemed to deflate. "Yes, mistress," he answered sulkily.

"All right then. Good evening." She gave him a perfunctory smile as he inclined his head then left. She turned to Michael. "Keep an eye on him for me, will you? See that he doesn't do anything silly."

"Of course … mistress."

The German's smile was warm – fond, Fraser might have said. But, other than that, there was no outward display that they were anything more than mistress and subordinate. He

314

had to admit he was impressed by their reserve. It even made him question whether he was, in fact, entirely wrong about there being something between them. But then he saw the way she watched Petersen leave the room. Fraser was sure she would never look at him that way. Given the way he had behaved over the years, he probably did not deserve to be looked at the way she looked at the other man.

"Is that Dieter fellow trustworthy?" he asked, getting back to the subject at hand. "Nothing untoward we should know about him?"

"Not as far as I know," she shrugged, going back to the letter that sat on the desk in front of her.

"No other wife back in Germany?"

Esther regarded him sharply. "He had a wife and children. They died in a British air-raid."

Fraser recoiled back into his chair. "Oh. Poor chap." He wondered what it must feel like not only to lose your family but to also be held captive and work in the country that brought about their demise. He sat up suddenly. "Surely it's not safe to have someone with such a … history behind him loose on the estate. What if he were to retaliate? He could do anything living in this bloody house!"

Esther put down her pen and surveyed her husband dispassionately. "It's true Dieter Scholzen was the most obstinate of all the prisoners who came here. He was edgy, angry, always slow to follow orders. And yet, he has always followed them. He's been here for more than a year and not once has he given me cause to chastise or question him. And anyway, his resentment of us was entirely justified. Of course you'd blame everyone you could for the death of your family. But moving past that – even if it is nigh-on impossible – is the better way forward. The same goes for Norah Harper. Grieving the loss of her husband is necessary but she can't live under that cloud for the rest of her life,

315

especially when she's got a wee boy to think of. Dieter is a good, hardworking man and he'll make a good husband and a good father to Dougie. Norah needs him just as he needs her and I for one won't be standing in the way of that."

Fraser looked as though he was going to argue and then thought better of it. Esther knew these people better than he ever would. He trusted her judgement and if she said everything would work out, it probably would. "I suppose that will mean you have at least one man staying for the harvest this summer," he said, changing the subject.

Esther gave a humourless bark of laughter. "Yes, maybe." She ran her hands through her already disarrayed hair. With a number of the men at Kirkmore getting word that their repatriation was imminent, Esther (and the rest of the country if the newspapers were anything to go by) were worried that there would be a labour shortage for the summer harvest. "I suppose I could ask some of them if they want to stay on for a while longer." She shrugged.

"Do you think many of them would take the offer to become civilians?" Fraser was surprised by this idea. The prisoners still seemed so German to him he couldn't see them fitting in with the regulars from the village.

"Some would, I think," Esther mused. "Though some wouldn't. I know for definite Alt Hans wants to go home. Get back to his own farm instead of tending ours. But there are a few who I think have grown quite attached to the place. I could ask, I suppose. But it has to be their choice."

"Why don't you sound them out through Petersen there. I'm sure he wants to stay. Maybe he could find out if any of the others do too," Fraser suggested reasonably.

Esther was about to ask what made Fraser sure Michael wanted to stay but then thought better of it. She would neither ask nor answer any leading questions about Michael. Indifference when he was mentioned was her first line of defence in warding off any probing curiosity when it came to her lover.

"Yes, I suppose I could mention it to him some time," she replied carelessly before returning to her letter. There was a pause where the only sound was the tick of the clock and the irritating scratch of Esther's pen. She waited for her husband to say more, to ask another question, but he didn't.

"Good," Fraser said cheerfully, returning to his own correspondence. "Good, good."

Chapter Thirty-Three

On the last day before he went back to London, Fraser took an amble up the brae with Muldoon. At the end of every visit, Fraser was obliged to take a private walk with the gamekeeper so the man could discuss plans and express his scepticism about the way the estate was being run. Muldoon had never hidden his displeasure regarding Fraser's choice of wife but, given that it did not affect his work or the high esteem he held his master in, he kept his job. The man was set in his ways and had never had a wife of his own so Fraser could see why he might find it difficult taking orders from a woman – especially one who used to put sheep droppings in his boots as a child. Their conversations usually consisted of a complaint or criticism which Fraser would then promise to talk to his wife about or sort out himself. It seemed that once the gamekeeper aired his grievances and was promised action, he would subside into gruff contentment in the knowledge that the problem would be handled by a man.

In truth, Fraser rarely did anything to fix Muldoon's gripes, instead choosing to inform Esther of the gamekeeper's issues and allow her to address them. In other words, continue to ignore them. He thought it best not to get involved in these disputes, considering his wife was managing so well. It seemed unlikely that anything the old gillie suggested was going to greatly improve things. But he still thought it best to forewarn her about the man's unhappiness even if he was off-loading even more problems into her lap instead of trying to deal with them himself. He was trying to do more and more to extricate himself from the responsibility of Kirkmore and live the life he wanted in London rather than the life of a reluctant laird.

Kirkmore was alive with ghosts but Esther brought new life to the place, dragging it out of the past and into the future. Fraser knew he could never do that. He was too afraid of disturbing the spectres that haunted every field, every room, laneway, shed and hall. Esther was not afraid and it was why he willingly gifted her control.

Yet Muldoon clung to the idea of a laird. After so many years he could not fathom that every decision ultimately went to Esther. The gillie still assumed that everything the mistress did was authorized by her husband. But Esther always had the final say and that was the way it was going to stay no matter what Muldoon told him. Fraser never looked forward to these conversations with the gillie but, for the sake of the man's devoted service to the McAllister clan, he agreed to them. However, after the letter he had from Muldoon at the beginning of the year, he was dreading their meeting even more than usual.

If he was being honest, Fraser had totally forgotten about the gamekeeper's missive a few months before. It was unusual for the man to write though not unheard of. Generally, if Esther managed to irritate him enough, he would write to the laird and, in a very roundabout and deferential way, tell him to control his wife. The blistering letter he received when Esther brought the Germans to Kirkmore was part of the reason Fraser had stayed away for so long once the men arrived. It was a controversial choice that he himself couldn't quite fathom and he didn't want to attempt to defend it. And though it was worrying to think she was letting loose a band of enemy aliens among the innocent folk of Kirkmore, it was her choice. Yet it incensed Muldoon to see these creatures invading his home more than anything else ever had. It was why Fraser dismissed the man's later letter as a fabrication: a hope that by accusing the mistress of improper relations with a German, he would discredit Esther's authority and remove the prisoners from the estate in one fell swoop. In fact, he thought it quite a dirty trick from someone who always managed to *just* stay on the right side of respectful.

Not until he saw Esther and Petersen together with his own eyes did Fraser realise Muldoon was telling the truth.

It put the laird in a tricky position. Of course, he could deny the whole thing and tell the gillie that he was imagining things. There was the possibility that the man did not know the truth and had, in fact, hit upon it completely by accident. But then there was the worrying idea that Muldoon *did* know the truth. If that were the case, Fraser's denial of the affair would make him look like he was being cuckolded. Even if he wanted nothing to do with the estate, his pride would not allow him to appear foolish before his subordinates.

As the hour of their walk approached, Fraser's cursing of Esther became exceedingly fluent. Why had she put him in such a position – backed him into a corner he could see no way out of? She would have to be awkward and have it off with a German bloody prisoner of war! He knew her waywardness was partly his fault but at that moment all he wanted to do was to land the blame squarely at her feet. However, while blaming Esther felt very satisfying, it did nothing to help him out of the hole he found himself in. Walking out to meet the gamekeeper felt like walking to the gallows. He wanted to avoid it, to run away, but Muldoon had asked him for a meeting several times since his arrival and he had put it off for as long as possible. It was better to get it over with – to figure it out as he went rather than let it fester any longer.

Spotting the gillie at a distance, Fraser was struck by how old and stooped the man looked. Muldoon had served the estate since Fraser was a child, but he had never really noticed the gamekeeper changing from a twenty-something year-old Boer War veteran to a geriatric. No matter the changes in the outside world or his age, Muldoon wore the same over-sized wax jacket, tweed waistcoat, flat cap, boots and brown gaiters, the colours of his clothing blending perfectly with the tones and shades of the landscape. He was like the young trees Fraser saw in his childhood that had now grown and matured to gnarled, woody lumps. The gamekeeper was as much a part of the landscape as the flora and fauna.

The ungenerous thought that he might be able to whack Muldoon over the head and quite easily hide his body among the heather up the brae flitted through Fraser's brain as he greeted him. Though the man had served the McAllister family almost all of his working life and Fraser was grateful for such loyal service, he couldn't help but think that the gillie was past his best. He had gone from able, active land and game manager to cantankerous old man. It was difficult to like the man when their conversations consisted of Fraser trying to pacify his forever-rising annoyance at the lady of the house.

As they walked, Fraser barely heard the gillie fill him in on how well the grouse-breeding was going and how the estate would once again be one of the finest in the country to shoot on, just as it had been before the war. Even such a simple discussion about reinstating Kirkmore's prowess as a hunting estate sounded like a criticism of Esther, given that she made the decision to cease shoots. There was, she argued, little enough for the locals to eat as it was without selling game to those who wanted for nothing even during a war. Fraser doubted there was anything more his wife could have done to injure the pride of their gamekeeper than denying him the chance to order about the beaters and chaperone the dandies in their expensive tweed during the shooting season. Fraser held a faint hope that having reinstated the tradition, Esther might have worked her way into the good graces of Muldoon but it seemed Fraser was to have no such luck.

The gamekeeper had remained silent for some time as they tramped up the lower slopes of one of the reeks and Fraser hoped the man had talked himself out. But then he started again.

"Sir, perhaps you don't remember but a while back I sent you a letter. In London. I hope you dinnae mind my asking if you received it?"

"What letter might that be?" Fraser asked loudly. He gave the man a hard stare, hoping the gillie would back down or dismiss the subject.

"Begging your pardon, sir, but it concerned your *wife*." He spat out the last word as if it tasted bitter on his tongue.

"Don't they all?" Fraser replied through gritted teeth but Muldoon did not hear him.

"I'm afraid she might be getting a little too … friendly with one of they German boys."

Fraser studied him carefully. "Yes, you said that in your letter."

"Oh, so you did get it then? I thought mebbey the London post wasnae quite reliable."

"It is perfectly reliable."

That seemed to put him out a bit. "Oh."

They walked on for another while. Fraser almost thought he could hear the gears creaking in the old man's head as he tried to figure out what to say next. Whatever it was, he was not going to help him come up with it. It would be better for both of them if Muldoon was to leave the subject behind altogether.

The gillie stopped. "Well … what's to be done about it then?"

Though Fraser was not particularly tall, he was for once glad that his height allowed him to look down on the shrunken, older man.

"*Nothing,*" he bit out succinctly.

"Nothing?"

"Nothing."

"But, sir, surely –"

"*Muldoon!*" Fraser's voice cracked through the open air. "*That's enough!* My wife's affairs are her own."

"But surely, sir –"

"Do I make myself clear?"

Not once in his life had he ever spoken to the gamekeeper so harshly. He no longer held a position of authority in Kirkmore. It was better to simply be the observer.

"I would not expect my wife to interfere in my life in London and I will not interfere in her life here. This is her domain and she may do as she wishes as long as she is here. If you take issue with any of her behaviour or decisions here, take it up with her, not me. Though," he added coldly, "in the case of *this* particular issue I would *suggest* that it never be mentioned again, yes?"

The look the gillie gave him was something Fraser could only have described as loathing. "Yes, sir," he answered icily.

They stood unpleasantly silent for a moment, neither looking at the other before Fraser glanced at his watch. "I'd best be off down. Andrew is taking me to the train in a few hours."

Muldoon gazed with dispassionate, cold eyes at his master. His expression was filled with hate. "Yes, sir," he sneered then turned about and tramped off across the hill, leaving Fraser to make his way down the slope.

As he headed back to the house, Fraser's neck prickled with the knowledge that a man he had just deeply offended was walking the hill above him with a loaded gun broken over his forearm. He wondered if he would hear the familiar snap and click of the shotgun as it was cocked. If he did, would he duck? Would he run? Or would he take it like a man? That thought brought him to his senses. Muldoon was clearly incensed but he was still a man of honour. He would never shoot a man in the back or in cold blood.

The thought gave Fraser some heart as, being a man of honour, he was unlikely to confront or challenge Esther. No gentleman would do that to a lady. But then Fraser wasn't exactly sure whether the gillie saw her as a true lady. She was a commoner who married into the position so, in Muldoon's opinion, that might not count for much. Yet whether a woman belonged to the upper or lower classes, she still deserved respect. Walking back to the house, Fraser held on to that hope.

When he got there, he found Esther in the library poring over field maps as she tried to find where drainage pipes had been buried in the previous decade.

"Well, what have I done wrong this time?" she asked with a tight, irritated smile.

"He's that predictable, eh?" Fraser said mildly as he peered at the maps without really seeing them at all. "You'd best be careful with him, Esther," he warned. "He's really got it in for you. Though I don't think he will, if he set his mind to it he could really do you harm."

Esther gave a little laugh of surprise. "If you're that worried for me then why don't you sack him?"

Fraser's eyes sprang wide. "Because it's not my place to dismiss anyone here. Kirkmore is yours, Esther, and will be until you decide it isn't. Whatever happens here is up to you."

She gave a little murmur of surprise. "I always thought Muldoon was here to keep an eye on me."

"I never wanted you kept an eye on," he answered honestly. "Esther, I have no right to tell you what to do either with the estate or your life. It's entirely up to you."

"Legally you have every right to tell me what to do," she countered. "I'm your wife."

"I suppose," he agreed. "But that doesn't mean I feel I should. Legally we are husband and wife but, in reality, we're … not. We each have our own lives that exist separate from the other and, for us, that works. Or, at least, I believe it does."

"Yes, I suppose it does. Still, if I'd known Muldoon wasn't your spy, I would have got rid of him myself years ago," she muttered to herself. "Think of all that trouble and worry I could have avoided."

Thinking she was reproaching him, Fraser bowed his head. "I'm sorry. If only we had been clearer with one another over the years."

"Oh no, I wasn't –" Esther began then stopped. "I'm not blaming you. I'm just saying. But then what you said is right too: think how much better things could have been – could be – if we just talked or even wrote to one another now and again."

"I honestly don't see how anything I might say could help you," Fraser reasoned. "You seem perfectly capable of managing things all by yourself. There's nothing I could add to improve what you do here."

"You could have helped me a little bit early on, though," she replied, barely keeping the censure out of her voice this time.

"To what end? My silence has taught you self-reliance. Perhaps you wouldn't be the businesswoman you are today if I hadn't cast you out to fend for yourself. I'll admit that wasn't the intention, but I had no idea how to help you and

I preferred you didn't know that. It really was a very cold thing to do," he murmured, looking away. "Christ, we really made a mess of us, didn't we? But it made the both of us who we are today. And these two people," he said, waving his hand between them, "are much better individually than we ever could have been as a whole."

It was the most Fraser had said about their relationship since it began ten years before. And what he said was likely the most truthful thing that ever could be said about it.

Esther stood in silent admiration of her husband's honesty. Though she did not often give any time to thinking about her marriage, on the occasions she did she wondered whether they were, perhaps, supposed to one day figure out or work to improve their union. The thought of attempting to live in wedded bliss as a true husband and wife always filled her with dread and made her determined to think of something else. But, with this little speech, Fraser released her from the idea of an uncertain future in which the two of them were to cheerfully co-exist. He was happy for them to be apart. It suited both of them and, while both knew it individually, neither ever had the good sense to share this belief with the other. They were legally married but, in reality, were separate, independent entities.

In other words, they were free.

In that moment, Fraser gave Esther exactly what he thought he was giving her on the day he married her. Her freedom. He had wanted to give her the freedom of youth without responsibility. But, in marrying her and giving her children, he had taken away her freedom, cut short her youth and made her responsible for more than she ever would have wished for. Over the years, she had accepted the responsibility of Kirkmore – had thrived as a person under the weight of bearing the place up. She discovered that her children prolonged her youthfulness, her latent silliness, and that she got to grow up rather than grow old with them. The final hurdle – ungrateful as it sounded – was Fraser. Their marriage was a joke but, for appearances' sake and an urge not to offend the other, neither ever admitted it. Now that her husband finally acknowledged and accepted its lack of substance, it was like a chainmail suit had been lifted from her body. She was free. She was free to be herself in all the glorious complicated ways that made her an individual and not just Mrs Fraser McAllister. He was giving her permission to be more than just his wife. He was giving her the chance to just be Esther again.

"Anyway. I'd best go and pack up. I'll be off soon. Andrew's coming up to get me." Fraser took one more glance at the map, placed a brief hand on Esther's shoulder then headed for the door.

"Thank you," Esther called just as he was about to leave.

He turned to her, a quizzical expression on his face.

She shrugged. "For everything."

He gave her a solemn, closed-lipped smile. "You're welcome. To all of it.'

Chapter Thirty-Four

While the early part of the year had been terrible in terms of weather and workload, the summer of 1947 was nothing short of glorious.

The days were sunny and there was a sense of good cheer and optimism on the estate. The war was truly over, work hours were better regulated and the men could earn more tokens by choosing to work overtime. They were also finally allowed to swap their coupons for British Sterling which gave them the freedom to buy more than just the bare essentials and also allowed some of them to send little useful extras back home to Germany every few months.

All these concessions, of course, had a purpose. Though there was an influx of workers from Eastern Europe, all fleeing the Soviet regime, many farms were keen to keep on the men they had worked alongside for years, even if they were German prisoners of war. The newcomers were there to gradually replace the prisoners as they began to head home but, for the most part, Kirkmore managed to maintain the men who had been there for over a year. Only six decided to go home when word came through that they were to be repatriated. The rest were either waiting to go home or had made the decision to take the government's offer and stay on indefinitely with temporary citizenship – though they were still subject to movement restrictions. However, before the prisoners could provisionally become civilians, both they and the estate had to be assessed by government officials. This was an aging contingent of dour civil servants from the War Ag and the War Office as well as the prison camp commandant who had barely seen the men over the last number of months. It meant there was a great rush to repair the prisoners' old billet at Kirkmore in case the inspectors took against having them live in the main house.

Esther welcomed their assessors to the estate on a hot, sunny afternoon in early July. Even though they had encountered her before, it always took the men a little while to become accustomed to a woman in authority. But as she breezed through the tour of the estate and its accommodation they – like everyone else – were caught up in the enthusiasm and assurance of her delivery. They were also amazed by the deference all the men showed her when she spoke to them. The camp commandant especially was exceedingly pleased with himself for getting the others to sign off on the prisoners living at Kirkmore in the first place. Really, all he had wanted was the burden of twenty men off his hands. It had not mattered to him where they went. But when he saw what a success the prisoners were at Kirkmore, he all but claimed sole responsibility for the Germans being there.

Knowing the importance of when to smile, nod and agree with men, Esther made sure that the camp commandant and the others were made to feel sufficiently important during their time on the estate. She was, therefore, relieved yet unsurprised when the inspection and interviews went off without a hitch and all the men were granted civilian status and thus found themselves residents rather than prisoners of Kirkmore. And, of course, once the inspectors left they moved all their belongings back into their rooms in the main house.

Though they were in the servants' quarters, as the

summer progressed, the men gradually found their way into the McAllister family rooms. They took over the billiards room which had not seen habitation in the last quarter of a century. The room next door – the smoking room – was also commandeered (with the approval of the lady of the house) and was the perfect place for them to play chess, dominos, draughts and games of *Skat* and *Doppelkopf* with the now exceedingly tattered packs of cards they used at Christmas. It became a sort of unofficial common room where the men could gather after work with the double doors opening onto the patio and the cool of the evening drifting inside along with confused insects and the scent of summer flowers.

For Esther, it was a joy to see the house filled with life. She always thought it such a waste to have so many empty rooms in such a vast house. It made the place feel cold and soulless. Being occupied seemed to make the house itself warmer, brighter, happier. Gone were the ghostly white sheets that covered the furniture, the closed-curtain funereal spectre that haunted the edges of rooms. The house was alive for the first time in Esther's memory. As a child playing with Drew, there were parts of the house even they were not brave enough to explore. Now Florrie and Archie had the run of almost every inch of it. They got to understand the beauty and the history of the house even more than their elder brother. And Drew himself was delighted to have someone to play billiards against, given that Esther rarely made time for such games and Caroline had no interest in them.

Another benefit of the men's proximity was that it was easier for Michael to slip away and spend time with Esther. Sometimes they simply sat and talked. Sometimes they spent the night together. On those occasions, Esther found she slept more soundly than she had since before Florence's birth and all the complications that followed. In Michael's arms or even being close enough to feel the warmth of him soothed her body and soul, allowing her hours of blissful uninterrupted sleep. She was drunk on it and drunk on the happiness of being close to him on a daily basis.

Often, she had wondered what it was people like her mother and Norah Harper felt for their husbands. Both seemed so in love even after death had taken the object of their affection away. Esther never had that with Fraser. She could not fathom the depth of feeling other women harboured for their spouses. Now, with Michael, she thought she might understand all of it.

As the summer turned to autumn, preparations got underway to finally pack Archie off to boarding school. There was a trip to Edinburgh for a uniform and Drew was consulted on the various essentials a young boy should have when first heading away to school. Esther had also set herself and Archie the very important task of buying a wedding suit.

The month before, Norah Harper had shocked the entire village by agreeing to marry Dieter Scholzen. But now that the date of their nuptials loomed, both parties realised how ill-prepared they were to have a wedding. As was her wont, Esther felt it was up to her to step into the breach and had agreed to throw a small party for the newlyweds after their private ceremony in the town registry office. However, as the date drew near and she heard about the trouble Norah was going to, sewing her own wedding dress, Esther thought it would be a terrible shame for Norah to turn up in a beautiful garment to marry a man in a threadbare work coat and stained shirt. With the help of Michael who had measured some of Dieter's clothing, Esther and Archie had trawled the second-hand shops for something that would vaguely fit the groom and was not faded or shabby.

Norah and Dieter's wedding was one of the first in the country once the legislation came through and was an excellent excuse for everyone in Kirkmore to have a little party to celebrate the wedding of their friends and also another year of successful harvesting. There was, of course, plenty of bemused and curious looks in town where they were not as used to seeing Germans wandering their streets, but on the estate and in the village, there were only good wishes and happiness. Many were, in fact, quite relieved that Norah had finally emerged from her torpidity and found contentment with a man who really seemed to love both her and her son.

Indeed, Dougie had the time of his life at the wedding, running around with Archie, trailing the local children in their wake. It was something of a last hurrah for the two boys with Archie finally heading away to school. Watching them, Esther wondered whether the boys might be upset or begin to pull away from one another just as she did when returning to school at the end of the summer. She always used to find herself withdrawing from her mother and Drew. It was not a conscious action and, when Lizzie asked her about it one year, she could not explain it. But when she thought about it, she wondered if her mind was protecting itself. If she withdrew from those she loved before leaving, then perhaps separation would be easier when the time came.

Esther herself struggled with the idea of her son's absence. His presence in the house was synonymous with her own since his birth had followed the year after her marriage. She was so used to his voice, his laughter echoing down the corridors, that she felt something close to bereavement when his bags were finally packed and Drew drove away with him. She had offered to go too but Archie insisted it should just be him and his brother. That would surely make a much better impression on his peers than a mother fussing over him, insisting on one last hug or kiss.

Following the boy's departure, there was really no need

for Michael to continue going to the library in the evenings but he went anyway. Esther found great comfort in his presence even when she was still in the study and he in the other room. She could sense the subtle shifts in the air that alerted her to the presence of another human being – occasionally hear the creak of the leather seats or the sound of the library ladder moving along its rails. On some evenings, Drew came up to the house and the two men would discuss everything from politics to history to the food shortages in Germany.

However, once she finished her work for the evening, Esther didn't always go into the library, not even when Drew was there. Though she was sure more than just Dieter knew about her relationship with Michael, she still did not want to give anyone too much cause for suspicion. After Fraser's talk before he went back to London, she was fairly sure he had an inkling about what was going on but was choosing not to acknowledge it. She did not know how he knew and suspected it might have had something to do with his chat with the gamekeeper. Though how the gamekeeper might know was beyond her too. If it was the case, Muldoon knowing was infinitely more worrying than her husband being aware of the affair. Fraser had shown his hand already but the gillie was still playing his cards close to his chest. Esther was sure he would do something to make his feelings known. He was the sort of man who would not take kindly to any perceived slight against his master and waiting for his retribution frayed her nerves.

For the most part, however, she managed to block out all thoughts of the gillie. She enjoyed the success of a fruitful summer where the good weather had produced good crops and she was even more secure in the knowledge that she had a conscientious workforce.

Archie wrote to her and to Michael about his boarding-school escapades. It amused them to contrast the things he wrote when they sat together in the library and, though it saddened Esther a little to see her son was not as candid with her as he was with his tutor, mostly she was glad that he seemed to be enjoying himself.

She spent the night of her eleventh wedding anniversary sharing a bed with Michael.

It was easier now for Michael to slip away, since he was now often alone in his shared room upstairs. Though there were strict official instructions that Dieter Scholzen was to stay in his billet after his marriage, Esther was quite happy for him to ignore the rule as long as he was on time for work in the morning. The likelihood of an inspector checking up on him in the heartland of Scotland was slim to none. Indeed, in the entire time the Germans had been at Kirkmore, there had not been a single visit from any kind of official. The only scheduled visit had fallen during the terrible snow back in February and, when it was cancelled, it had not been rescheduled.

They were lucky, really, that they were left undisturbed. Though she expected and got fine work from the men, otherwise, Esther ran quite a loose ship. The men were now allowed all over the estate and into the village. On occasions, she even allowed some of them to hunt fowl on the hills and in the woods but she only did that on the one Sunday every month when Muldoon was away. In the evenings, most of them stayed in and kept to the billiard and smoking rooms but a few always liked to go down to the village every now and again which Esther allowed as long as they were back by half nine at night before all the doors were locked.

A very dark evening at the end of October found Esther and Michael in the library sitting on a pile of cushions in front of the fire, playing a game of draughts on the carpet by the light of the flames. Esther was rusty, having not played the game since her youth, but was improving greatly with the practice she got challenging Michael. He, on the other hand, was excellent, having spent the last few years perfecting his game against his compatriots. They played several times a week and yet, since June, Esther had only beaten him four times. It was slightly demoralising always being on the losing side but it made her even more determined to find a way to beat him. She even tried some creative distractions which he very much enjoyed but his game was consistent and barely wavered despite her attempts to befuddle him. He maintained that since her side won the war, it was only fair that she should allow him to keep some of his pride intact by regularly slaughtering her at draughts.

They had just finished a game (Michael won but it was closely fought) when the sound of the front door banging closed in the wind made Esther jump and upend the board. Glancing at the clock, she was surprised to see that it was ten past ten and that they had been playing for nearly two hours.

"Odd," she commented, standing to stretch her numb legs. "I didn't think anyone went out this evening. They're very late back."

"I don't think anyone did go out," Michael answered. also getting to his feet and following Esther to the door.

When she opened it, it took a moment for her eyes to adjust to the slightly brighter light in the hall. When her pupils finally righted themselves, she blinked. Standing in her hallway were three complete strangers dressed in dirty army-surplus uniforms that were clearly meant for much larger men. All three had stopped in their tracks and were staring at her. Still not completely grasping what was going on, Esther was about to speak when she noticed the man on the right was carrying a shotgun. And it was pointing straight at her.

She barely had time to grasp what was going on when

the man with the gun notched the stock in his shoulder and fired.

It all happened in slow motion. Though she watched what the stranger was doing, she was so at sea the threat did not register. She just couldn't fathom why there was some unknown individual in her house wielding a lethal weapon. Yet here he was pointing it at her head as she stood paralysed not by fear but by utter confusion. All she knew was that a split second before the report of the shot reverberated around the high chamber of the hall, amplifying the sound so much it hurt her ears. Her clothes tightened across her chest as a fist balled between her shoulder blades holding the back of her shirt and she was jerked backwards.

Suddenly there were splinters and chunks of wood in the air as they fled the pellets that thwacked into the doorframe. The dark wood of the surround beside her head exploded, exposing its fleshy white innards to her. A searing pain shot through her temple. Tiny shards of wood spattered her in the face like hailstones.

Without warning, she found herself on the floor of the library. Her knees collided with the polished wood as she landed on her forearms, not being quick enough to get her hands out. Behind her, Michael – who had dragged her out of the way – slammed the door closed and turned the key in the lock. Next moment he was on the ground with her, gripping her to his chest, her back against him. She heard the gun fire once again and the door shook with the reverberation of pellets as they thudded into the thick oak panelling. It was then that she began to scream.

In all her life Esther had never screamed like that. Even as a child she had never been inclined to give the high-pitched squeals most little girls did. She shouted and hollered but never screamed. Now she did. All she could hear was a deafening ring of tinnitus which obscured her thoughts, leaving only a petrified creature behind. In Esther's world, weapons were for hunting, not for war. Not for the purposes of killing another human being. Having looked down the barrel of a gun, she hoped nothing she ever pointed a gun at knew death was coming to them. She continued to scream.

Then, abruptly, her scream changed to a name repeated over and over again: "*Florrie! Florrie! Florrie!*"

It was like resurfacing after too long under water. Her head spun as blood rushed to it. She gasped for air. And all the while Michael was yelling at her. Why was he yelling at her? He still held her fast to his chest. She struggled to be free from his grip so she could do something – anything – to get to Florrie. It was one thing to experience the fear of a gun pointing directly at you, it was another to think that that yawning, infinity-shaped muzzle might be pointing at the tiny gold-blonde child asleep upstairs. She had to get to her. Maybe she could go out through the study onto the patio and around the side of the house to the servants' entrance. There was a set of keys to the door in the second drawer in the study. But Michael would not let her go. And he was still yelling at her. That made her angry. Yet with anger came some clarity. She began to hear words instead of just the sound of his voice.

"*They're here! They're here!*"

She knew they were there! These armed invaders were in her house. They were in her house with her child. She battled against Michael's vice-like grip, using all her strength to heave her entire body away from him. He grunted behind her as she lifted them both off the floor yet didn't let go.

"*The others are here!*" he bit out, clawing to maintain his grip on her.

The others? And then it came to her. She and her daughter were not alone in the house with three armed strangers. There were nearly twenty soldiers on the floors above her, all of whom had seen action. But not one had a weapon to match the shotgun.

Images of pellet-riddled bodies ripped across her vision. Jung Hans, Erich Neuman, Dieter – all of them were good men. *"No! No, I don't want them to get hurt!"* she cried, squirming against him. She did not want a single man to die on her watch.

Feet thundered overhead. German voices, muffled by the thick wooden door, called and responded to one another. Harsh instructions crackled through the air as muffled thumps and atavistic roars pierced her ears. Sounds became clearer. There was shouting from voices she didn't recognise mixed with the familiar cadence of the language used by her workers. Another gunshot made her scream again. Then another. It was too much. Terror forced her body to act. Esther heaved again and broke free, scrabbling with stiff, ineffectual fingers to gain purchase on the floor since her feet didn't seem to want to work. But strong arms had captured her in an instant. Michael wasn't going to let her go.

"Stop it, Esther. Just stop! It's all right!" he said, giving her a vigorous shake. *"Listen. Listen."*

She listened. Footsteps no longer rumbled along the upper floor. The voices were quieter. There was no longer urgency to their speech. It seemed almost calm. Yet still Esther could not appease the sickening, roiling churn of her body. She squirmed again but no longer had the strength to fight against Michael's firm grip. He doggedly held on, releasing one hand to brush the hair from her face, shushing her all the while, rocking her from side to side.

He cocked his head and shouted something in German. The muffled voices outside subsided for a moment and then there was a call in response. Still holding her tightly, Michael reached up and unlocked the door, shuffled both of them to the side and opened it. Esther wanted to stand but her limbs still would not work. She lay in a crumpled heap in Michael's lap looking out at the carnage.

Woodchips scattered the floor. It was the first thing she noticed given that her eyeline was barely above knee-height. The next thing she noticed were the knees. Some were large and knobbly, others were angular and joined to sinuous, skinny legs. Others were encased in greying pyjamas. Some of the feet were bare but others wore thick wool socks. Absurdly, her first thought was that they really ought to put on some shoes before someone got a splinter in their foot.

At the far side of the hall lay three prone figures, the muddy soles of their boots facing Esther. Their dirtiness offended her. One had his hands tied behind his back with the cord from the waist of a pyjama bottoms. The other two seemed to have the gold braided rope from the draught-excluding hall curtains securing their wrists.

Above them stood Fluss in nothing but his underpants. He casually held a broken shotgun under his arm but was watching the strangers with hawk-like glittering eyes. In fact, one eye was beginning to close over, swollen and shiny red having clearly received a vicious blow. Esther's gaze wandered over the rest of his body which was covered in tattoos. On his upper arm was a sun in black and grey. Below his shoulder blade was line after line of writing. Esther thought they might have been names. On his chest – from the top of his sternum to the bottom of his ribs – was a pitch-black, angular splayed eagle. There was a dagger on his thigh with a drop of blood dripping from its tip and around his ankle was what looked like barbed wire.

It was so odd to think the big, gentle-seeming German would have marked himself so indelibly. Lizzie Muncie had always said that any man with tattoos was not to be trusted yet here was Fluss, stripped to the waist defending Esther and her home. It was a side to the man she never thought she would see: the soldier, the warrior. Yet as her glance slid from man to man, she saw the expression repeated over and over again. Bodies thrummed with tension, spoiling for a fight. The pale faces, the shining, dilated eyes. Now she saw what war looked like on the faces of men. And it terrified her.

It made her realise what a vulnerable position she had put herself and the people of Kirkmore in by bringing these men to the estate. She recognised her own naivety in not seeing what men could become when pushed to violence. Of course she had seen anger and violence in the past. There was always the odd fight outside the pub in the village to keep the locals entertained. But soldiers were different. The fight consumed them, chemically altered them until these hardworking ordinary men were unrecognisable. What if this savage behaviour had been unleashed on the unwitting locals? Cary Eden and Major Brown would never have stood a chance against them, given that the Germans had just disarmed and subdued these three strangers with their bare hands.

Hands. There were two hands still holding onto her. The skin was cracked and ingrained with dirt even though he washed them thoroughly every evening. They might once have been elegant but now they were rough and powerful. Looking down, another pair of hands slid into her peripheral vision, open in supplication. Esther's gaze crawled up the man's forearms, to his chest then his face. Dieter crouched in front of her, the ferocity gone from his eyes which were filled with concern. She could not tear her gaze away from him. His whole body seemed to be shaking. Then she realised it was her own body that was wracked by uncontrollable convulsions.

"Mrs McAllister," he said gently, reaching for her hands.

Instinctively she jerked away. A whimper escaped her and she felt her teeth unlock and begin to chatter together. Her feet scraped uselessly against the floor as she fought for purchase to push herself further away. But she couldn't get away. All she did was push herself harder against Michael's chest. She then began to shake her head. But that hurt and it made her dizzy. She wanted to ask where Florrie was but she couldn't get the words passed her constricted throat.

Dieter didn't make another move to touch her but continued to calmly hold her gaze. "Mrs McAllister … Esther. It is safe now. You are safe."

Finally, she forced one shaky word past her teeth. "Florrie?"

"Safe," he answered confidently, glancing over his shoulder to were Max stood on the stair cradling the little girl to his chest, her head resting on his shoulder.

Mary stood by his side in her nightie and dressing-gown, her face pale and tear-streaked. She was staring fixedly at Esther with a look of horror.

Dieter, she knew, was trying to call her attention back to him. She heard English then German.

Michael's chest vibrated behind her as he replied in English. "No, it's all hers."

"Mrs McAllister. *Esther!*" Dieter tried again. "Esther – *please* – we must stop the blood.'

That caught her attention. She mouthed the last word back to him then looked down at herself. The lower half of her body was clean but as her glance drifted upwards, she saw specks of red on her cream blouse. Travelling further up, she struggled to focus. Everything became hazy but she did recognise that there was a dark stain seeping down over her shoulder and chest.

Movement in the corner of the hall drew everyone's attention.

"*Oh Lord save us!*" Mrs Morris slap-slap-slapped across the hall in her bedroom slippers, the end of her shawl trailing on the floor behind her as she approached her mistress. "*Christ Almighty!*" she squawked, lowering herself to kneel in front of

Esther with liberal use of Dieter's shoulder. "*What happened?*"

"That doesn't matter right now." Michael spoke in a voice that was not to be challenged. "Mrs Morris, please telephone Dr Robertson. And the police."

The men behind the housekeeper shifted uneasily.

"We have done nothing wrong," Michael said forcefully to his comrades. "But these other men," he threw a glance full of loathing at them, "must be handed over to the proper authorities. No matter how much we might wish to deal with them ourselves." He turned to the household staff. "Do you have medical supplies so that we might clean the wound and stop the bleeding?"

There was a flurry of movement as Mrs Morris dispatched Ada to bring her the medical kit.

"All right, Esther," Michael said, "I'm going to lift you off the floor. I don't want you to catch cold."

Suddenly, Esther found herself several feet in the air which did nothing for her light-headedness. She seemed to levitate across the floor, Michael's gait was so even, his grip so secure. He crossed the hall and mounted the stairs without a backward glance at anyone. As they passed Max still cuddling Florrie to his chest so she could not see the destruction, Esther reached out and caught his arm.

"Thank you," she murmured, then, "I think you can take her back to bed now. And Mary."

Max mouthed ineffectually, unable to take his eyes off Esther's left temple, then nodded dumbly.

Following Michael, Mrs Morris scattered instructions to the gathered men and women, one of which was to Mrs Coleman who was to deal with the phone calls much to her dismay. She knew how to use the telephone but that did not mean she was keen to use it.

On entering the bedroom, Michael bypassed the bed and went straight to the bathroom, grunting some kind of instruction at Dieter who trailed after them. He followed them a moment later, carrying the padded stool from in front of her dressing table. He placed it beside the sink, threw a worried look at Esther then left her with the housekeeper and Michael.

The pipes hissed and clanged as Mrs Morris turned on the tap and let it run until the water was warmer. Michael sat Esther on the stool and knelt on one knee beside her so that she was propped up against his chest and thigh. Though her senses were hazy, she was aware that she really needed his support. Her whole body felt weak and ineffectual. And she still could not stop shaking. She was in shock and the adrenaline that had roared through her veins was beginning to ebb. Her teeth continued to chatter and, despite the warmth emanating from his body seeping into hers, she still felt cold. Yet his body touching hers was a comfort. It was the only thing that had been a constant, grounding presence throughout the whole nightmarish ordeal. And although he seemed to have taken up a fairly permanent position behind her, she was afraid he would leave her to the ministrations of the housekeeper. With considerable effort, therefore, she slid her hand off her lap and onto his thigh, lightly pressing her palm against the taut muscles encased in coarse fabric that she knew so well.

Watching them carefully, Mrs Morris saw the care with which the German held the daughter of her closest friend. He was gentle yet firm, tending to her with practised, familiar assurance. There was also something protective about the way he shielded so much of her body with his own – like a bird of prey fiercely guarding its kill. It was an instinct to protect what was most important to him, what sustained him.

She turned off the taps over the sink. "Perhaps I should get her a clean blouse," she said, surveying her mistress's shoulder.

Esther once again felt the reassuring rumble of Michael's chest against her back. "Yes, that might be a good idea."

The housekeeper handed over a damp flannel she had neatly folded and left them.

"I'm going to wash your head now, Esther," Michael said steadily. "It's going to sting."

"Why's there blood on me?"

She could not see his face but, as soon as she spoke, she felt his body tense behind her.

"You were cut by a splinter from the doorframe."

She felt his breath on the left side of her head as he inspected her wound. It stung. Her stomach dropped. It must be bad if a simple exhalation irritated it.

"Show me," she ordered.

"Esther –" he protested.

"*Show me*," she said more forcefully. That made her feel a little sick.

With an exasperated sigh, he wrapped a hand around her stomach and held her arm with the other then hoisted her into a standing position in front of the mirror.

If she felt sick asking him to show her the injury, it was nothing compared to the heave her stomach gave on seeing it. "Put me down," she said faintly and he returned her to her original position.

There was an angry slash across her temple and into her hairline. It was continuing to ooze blood even now, forming congealed, jelly-like stringy lumps. It had dribbled all down her cheek and dripped off her chin onto her front. There were also dried tracks down her neck where the dark red was seeping into the fabric of her shirt. Absently, she wondered how she had not felt it. Now – knowing it was there – all she could do was feel it. How the blood tightened then cracked over her skin with every infinitesimal movement. How cold her shirt was against her chest, damp with her own blood. And, of course, she felt the wound itself: the agony of it as it gaped open like a second mouth. She gave a small dry sob.

"*Shhh*," Michael crooned. "Will you let me wash it?"

She gave a reluctant grunt.

He wet the now-cold flannel with warm water once again and with light fingers held her chin as he dabbed the cloth over her jaw then slowly moved closer to the wound. Grabbing onto his knee again, her fingers scraped at the taut material trying to find something to grab on to. She clamped her teeth shut as she felt the first tears of the night spill from her lower lids and slide down her cheeks.

"Relax," he said softly. "If you tense you'll bleed more. And stretch the cut. Breathe," he murmured, expanding his chest then blowing out, ruffling the loose hair on her head.

Tenderly, he again dampened then washed the dried and congealed blood from her face, turning the water in the sink from pink-orange to red. Twice more he filled it with fresh water which had a slight pink tinge from the residue on the sides of the basin.

Eventually, he took a soft towel from the shelf and laid it gently on her skin, cupping it to her face with his long fingers, before bandaging her head with a sureness that showed he clearly knew what he was doing.

In the interim, Mrs Morris returned. "Time to change that blouse, I think," she said, absentmindedly rolling a clean shirt with both hands. Watching from a few feet away, she made no move to help.

Michael had managed all his ministrations from the same position behind her, never leaving Esther without his touch. Reaching around her shoulders, he dexterously undid the shirt's buttons and peeled the garment off. The drying fabric clung to the fine hairs on her skin where the blood had soaked through. Once he had dropped the ruined blouse on

345

the floor, he sponged the remains of the blood from her chest then slid the proffered clean shirt over her shoulders and dressed her again.

"Will she do?" he asked the housekeeper, giving Esther's shoulder a reassuring squeeze. She could hear the smile in his voice.

Mrs Morris's lips twitched. "Aye. She'll do."

Chapter Thirty-Five

"Max says Florrie went straight back to sleep," Dieter informed them.

Esther was sitting on the small settee with Michael by her side. She had refused his offer to put her to bed, instead preferring to stay awake. She was too jittery to lie down and knew that if she did, she would never be able to keep still. Plus, by sitting on a seat, she could have Michael beside her without it looking overly intimate. When he brought her back into the room, he had left her for a moment to get the shawl she kept over the foot of the bed and her heart had skittered off desperately searching for the reassurance of his touch. Coming back to her, he had wrapped the shawl around her and she leaned into his warmth. Even though he was uncomfortable exposing their relationship to everyone – from Mrs Morris, who hurried off to deal with the police, to Ada who came with strong, sweet tea for all of them – he held her close until the doctor came.

Freddie did not break stride as he entered the room which made Esther sure the housekeeper had forewarned him that he would find the mistress in the company of two Germans – one of whom she would not let go of.

Even when Michael stood to make way for the doctor and Esther had grabbed for him, Freddie simply said, "Stay.

She might need someone to hold on to."

He proceeded to ask several questions about the circumstances of her injury, none of which she could answer herself, leaving Michael to relay the sequence of events.

"So she didn't hit her head?"

"No."

"Are you certain? I just have to be sure."

"No. I pulled her back and the only thing she hit was me."

The doctor grinned. "You look like quite a solid object to collide with so I'll reserve judgement on a concussion for the moment."

"Are they still here?" Her voice was more distinct than it had been since Michael opened the library door.

Three pairs of surprised eyes converged on her. "The … intruders, are they still here?"

"I believe the Constable is questioning them in the breakfast room … under the supervision of half a dozen Germans." Freddie's lips twitched. "They wouldn't do anything to them, would they?" He glanced from Michael to Dieter.

"Nothing they don't deserve," Michael answered with a cold little grin. Then he sobered. "They understand law and order. They will not harm them," he shrugged, "too much."

"Well, there's a police van coming from town so they shouldn't be here much longer. Hopefully they'll still be in one piece by the time they arrive."

"How did Mrs Morris explain our men being in the house?" Esther asked. She worried that the housekeeper wouldn't come up with a believable excuse for fifteen Germans to be in their pyjamas in a stately home late at night. She wasn't even sure she could come up with a viable explanation for it herself.

"She made us get dressed before the *polizei* came," Dieter answered and, for the first time, Esther noticed he was in his work clothes. "She said it was Max's birthday and you let us use the billiard room."

That impressed Esther no end. She never would have constructed such a fine pretext for their presence even with all her faculties intact. Perhaps everything would work out after all. As the doctor unwound the bandage on her head, a sense of peace began to descend upon her. The whole situation could have been a hundred times worse and yet everything had worked out fine. She – much to her shame – was the only person who had sustained any sort of notable injury. Three armed strangers had entered her home but nothing had been stolen and no one had died. It was nothing short of a miracle.

However, once Freddie removed the bandage and exposed the wound to his probing fingers, all thoughts fled from her mind.

Hissing through her teeth as Freddie swabbed the wound with spirits, she crushed Michael's fingers with her own, catching him by surprise. He grunted.

"Yes, that's why I offered up your hand instead of my own," the doctor commented conversationally. "I have experience with Esther's death-grip. I'm not sure the fingers of my left hand have recovered since I travelled up to Edinburgh with her when she went into labour with Archie. And the wee fella's – what – ten now?"

"Bugger off," Esther muttered.

Dieter looked a little shocked but Michael and Freddie both gave a shout of laughter.

"I think she's fine, don't you?" Freddie smiled sweetly at Michael. "All right," he continued, getting down to business. "This'll need stitches for sure. The only question is whether you want me to numb it first."

"No," she said immediately, sitting up straighter and staring fixedly at the opposite wall.

"Esther, I don't think –" Michael began but she cut him off.

"No anaesthetic," she said, daring him to challenge her.

The doctor chuckled. "Haven't you noticed – she can be a stubborn lassie. Has been since we were wee bairns together. Once she sets her mind on something …" He shook his head.

"It has come to my attention on occasions," Michael replied mildly.

"When the two of you are *quite* done, perhaps you could do your job, doctor," she said stonily.

Freddie's lips twitched again but he said no more and proceeded to lay out his suturing equipment. Though Esther felt the slight scrape and tug as he stitched the wound, the pain was bearable though highly uncomfortable. It didn't last long, however. The doctor had a deft touch and was done in no time. The bandage he did, however, was much more uncomfortable than the one Michael had done earlier and, taking the opportunity to get her own back on the doctor, she relished the chance to tell him so.

"Yes, but I'm a doctor, I don't do bandages," he reasoned. "The nurses always did them in the hospital." He waved carelessly at Michael. "Maybe you should get your German to do it."

"That sounds like a good idea," Esther said, turning to Michael.

He stood and undid the bandage but, as he rewound it, he said, "This needn't stay on too long."

The doctor's eyebrows rose slightly but then he remembered something. "Your father was a doctor. No wonder you know what you're doing. Did your father make you practise dressings the way my mentor did? Although with you those lessons clearly stuck better than they did for me. Yes," he continued, addressing Esther, "that bandage can come off soon. Probably tomorrow. It almost doesn't need to be there at all but I think it might be more comfortable when you sleep if there's something to protect the wound."

Esther nodded and it hurt. She reached for the side of her head as if to steady it and gently poked the skin above and below the wrapping. It felt tight and tender but at least it was no longer bloodstained. Gingerly, she got to her feet, testing her balance. Michael proffered a hand but she shook her head. That hurt too. Standing as straight as she could manage, she walked past the men and headed for the door.

"Where are you going?" Freddie asked in a panicked voice.

"I'm going downstairs," she answered in a voice she was glad sounded much more confident than she felt.

"But you need to be in bed," the doctor blustered, looking to the two Germans for assistance. Neither of them offered any help.

"Haven't you noticed?" Michael enquired, eyes twinkling. "She can be a stubborn lassie."

"Oh, very bloody funny," the doctor muttered.

Chapter Thirty-Six

There were several people milling around below when Esther appeared on the landing which stretched from one side of the hall to the other. Cary Eden was there but he didn't seem to be in control of anyone. He stood chatting to two of the younger Germans with his hands in his pockets and his back to everyone else. Ada stood awkwardly near the foot of the stair watching Jung Hans sweep up the debris from the shotgun – a job she had clearly planned to do herself. Alfie the stable boy was flanking the doorway with another German and Mrs Coleman was in the process of handing out tea from a tray. She called Ada to help her but when the gathered crowd saw Esther, all eyes came to rest on her as she descended the stairs with a doctor and two Germans trailing in her wake. Or, rather, all eyes rested on the bleached white bandage around her head.

Ignoring all of them, she pointed to the breakfast room. "Are they still in there?"

"Yes, mistress," Mrs Coleman answered but her eyes never left the bandage.

Esther headed towards the breakfast room.

"Esther!" Freddie caught her by the arm and swung her around to face him. "Don't."

Gently but firmly, she extricated herself from his grip.

"I'm going in there, Freddie, and there's nothing you can do to stop me." She turned, took a few steps but then stopped, thinking.

"At last!" Freddie exclaimed. "You're finally coming to your senses."

She faced him again and threw him a crooked grin. "Not yet." She reached up and began to unwind Michael's perfect bandage.

"Now what are you doing?!" Freddie squawked.

"I'm taking off the bandage because – by the looks everyone's giving me – it really doesn't become me. And I'm not going in there with a turban on my head."

"Wait," Michael said stepping forward.

"Yes, talk some sense into the girl. She might listen to you," the doctor said crossly.

But rather that try to stop her, he reached up, pushed her hands aside and unwound it himself. "I don't want you to catch your stitches with your fingernails."

Esther grinned. "You of all people should know I don't have fingernails." But as she smiled at him, a movement in her peripheral vision caught her attention.

Muldoon was hovering in the corner below the landing, shrouded in semi-darkness which made the leer on his face all the more sinister. His was pale and drawn – tired probably. It made his face skull-like and deathly old. Yet what was really chilling was the way he bared his teeth. At first glance, it seemed like a grin but then Esther noted the strain around it, how clenched his jaw was.

Esther shrugged off the chilling feeling of his gaze but knew they had gone too far – that their shroud of secrecy was irrevocably torn. Now bandage-less, she turned away. Facing the door to the breakfast room, she threw back her shoulders, strode forward with confidence and entered the room.

The gillie's eyes glittered with unshed tears: furious,

triumphant tears. She had proved his suspicions right. He never knew for certain that there was something between her and the German but it seemed likely enough to inform the laird. He had not expected it to backfire so spectacularly and incur the wrath rather than the gratitude of his master. But now he had proof that they were more than just mistress and farm labourer. And he had witnesses to boot! Yet none of them were as angry as he was. None of them were shocked. Their lack of righteousness in the face of blatant wrongdoing infuriated him. How dare they all behave this way in his master's house! Even the housekeeper – good, honest, religious woman that she was – behaved as if nothing was wrong. But it was all wrong. They were all wrong. None of them should ever have been there in the first place, not the thieves in the breakfast room, not the Germans and definitely not the laird's sorry excuse of a wife.

Constable Nimmo was standing by the window, his back to the room, staring into the yawning darkness outside. Though he had his hands clasped behind his back in the manner bobbies often carried themselves, his feet shifted restlessly. He was clearly uncomfortable and it was hardly surprising given the presence of three criminals and five very angry Germans. If things were to kick off, there would be absolutely nothing he could do about it. He seemed to be practising the philosophy that if he turned his back on them and therefore could not see them, nothing would happen. Yet when Esther entered, he jumped to attention, approaching her with great alacrity, relief washing off him like a particularly pungent cologne. Dealing with one ne'er-do-well was effortless for him. Even two or three were manageable. But being in a room with eight possibly volatile men was just too much. He was not too far off retirement and had a wonderfully clean record in terms of apprehending lawbreakers. He did not want all of it ruined tonight.

"Mrs McAllister!" he said far too jovially. But then he saw Michael behind her and his face crumpled a little. "Oh. Another one."

"Constable Nimmo. I'm sorry to trouble you so late at night but needs must," Esther said coolly, not for the benefit of the policeman but for the three men sitting behind him at the table.

"No trouble at all, ma'am! No trouble at all. I've just been taking a few preliminary statements. What I'm here for. Happy to help." He smiled, nervously bouncing on the balls of his feet.

She fought a grin. "I'm not sure about that."

Brushing past the Constable, she sensed rather than saw Michael shadowing her as she moved to stand opposite the three strangers. Behind them, standing at ease, were her Germans, Fluss in the centre – now mercifully dressed – but still predatorial.

She was about to address them when the Constable interrupted her.

"Madam, there appears to be blood on your skirt!"

Casually, she glanced down to find that there was indeed a spatter of dried dark red on the light-brown material. "Yes," she answered calmly, looking directly at the three men. "The blood is my own. From a head wound when one of them shot at me." She was about to continue on and praise Michael for pulling her from harm's way but thought it safer to leave him out of the story altogether.

Fluss stepped forward, addressing Esther. "Mr Eden has the gun in the hall, madam. I have taken it apart."

"Thank you, Mr Teske." She turned to the policeman. "Only for the swift action of my men, who knows what damage these *intruders* might have caused?"

The man sitting in the middle of the trio glared malevolently at Esther then cocked his head back and spat at her. It might have been a bold action had the gob of spittle not sailed only a few feet and landed on the table three-quarters of a yard short of where she stood.

She blinked calmly at him. "You missed."

She expected a reaction – but that did not mean it was not alarming when the man shot to his feet and made to lunge across the table at her. She stood her ground, aided somewhat by the fact that, no sooner was he up, the stranger found the arm of a very large, very angry German around his neck. Fluss had clearly experienced the benefits of some specialized army training back in the day by the way he handled Esther's would-be attacker. The companions who flanked him made to aid their ringleader but were quickly subdued by more of her men. She noted with surprise that one of them was Erwin Riegel. There was a great kerfuffle amongst the eight of them while the Constable and Esther stood by.

After watching for a moment, Esther decided to put an end to things when two of the men nearly toppled over a fallen chair.

"That's enough!" Her voice cracked like a whip through air that was thick with some choice profanities and laboured grunts. "Stand down," she ordered her men. Then, coldly eyeing each of the would-be thieves, she told them to sit. Mercifully – though with ill grace – they did as they were bid.

As the man on the right sat, Esther saw something drop outside of the collar of his shirt. Studying him more carefully, she saw that he was of an age with Erwin and Jung Hans but looked deathly tired and horribly dirty. The top two buttons of his crumpled shirt were currently somewhere on the floor of the room having been ripped off in the scuffle. At first, in the dull light of the room, she was not sure what it was that hung over his sternum. It looked like some sort of crude necklace. But then as her eyes focused, she distinguished two separate shapes: a circle and an octagon, the former maroon, the latter dark green.

She fought the urge to gasp. They were dog tags. British dog tags.

"You're a soldier," she said.

All eyes snapped to her then slowly drifted to the boy. He seemed to shrink under the force of their combined gazes. Grabbing for the string of his tags, he made to stuff them back down the front of his shirt but instead snapped them off altogether. Completely exposed, he did the first thing that came to his head and cast the tags away from himself across the table. They slid neatly into Michael's waiting hand where he picked them up and studied them.

Esther was about to ask if they were his or if they were stolen when the ringleader turned on the boy.

He exploded out of his chair and punched the boy in the jaw. *"You fuckin' idiot! I told you to get rid of them!"* he roared, raining down blows on his companion.

The stunned Germans took a moment to step in and haul him off, yet rather than sit him down again, they dragged him backwards and sat him in the chair by the fireplace and stood between him and his target. The boy unfurled himself from the ball he had curled into. He did it slowly, still feeling the effects of the thumping had he received. There was something so pitiful about the child's eyes that stared out of the young man's face. They shone, yet he did not cry. Esther could see his Adam's apple bobbing with the effort of suppressing sobs.

"You're a deserter," she said. "You all are."

No one said anything. She let her gaze fall on each man but none of them met it. Shame washed off the boy with the tags. The man beside the fireplace fixed murderous eyes on him while the other man appeared almost bored by proceedings. It was sad to think that men who once served in an army sworn to protect Great Britain against the Axis Powers now targeted their own people. It was also quite absurd to then think that the people who had defended Esther's home had once been their enemy. Upsetting as it was to discover such betrayal, she was heartened to find such allegiance in her German workers. She wondered if there was something she had done to deserve their loyalty or if it was just a case of her being lucky enough to acquire good, honest men.

There were many things Esther wished to say to the three men. They had contravened a sworn oath to the King. How could they betray their own people, their own army? Did they not have homes to go back to? Had their own families cast them off for the shame desertion brought? Did they not realise how much worse they were making their lives by running? The war was over and while they would no doubt all go to prison for leaving the army *during* the war, they would now also be charged with armed robbery and, possibly, attempted murder. Did they think they could live off what they could beg and steal, hiding forever? It was no way to live at all and Esther was quite sure at least two of the men knew that. They reeked of embarrassment and guilt just as much as they stank from being unwashed. The other by the fireplace simply exuded an air of being wronged by the world. It was not his fault that he was caught in the middle of this situation, it was everyone else's.

It was why Esther remained quiet. The younger men were well aware of their wrongdoing and the older man did not care. It would be pointless to further castigate the two at the table and their leader was the sort who would laugh in her face if she tried to make him feel guilty. Instead, she waited in silence for the arrival of the police van. Though she would have liked to stay standing since that was the most powerful position she could take in the room, she eventually had to sit. However, instead of collapsing into a chair as she would have liked, she perched on the edge of one of the side tables so that she could still look down on the men but there was less risk of her keeling over from the light-headedness that threatened to overwhelm her. Luckily, no one but Michael seemed to notice. Once she sat, he drifted over to stand beside her almost without noticing he was doing it.

Her head had begun to pulse uncomfortably by the time the headlights of the police van flashed through the windows and swept across the back wall of the room. Nimmo went out to meet them, seeming happy to leave the room. There was a restless shift from everyone who was left behind as if each was considering whether the absence of the Constable was their opportunity to get in a final punch, a final escape attempt.

"*Nobody moves*," Esther hissed and was glad to watch everyone reluctantly subside.

The policeman who entered the room a few moments later stuttered a little as he took in the number of people gathered. Esther saw his eye dart between the Germans as if he thought they were going to cause trouble. But Esther's men moved away as soon as the other police officers entered the room and formed a little huddle from which they watched the offenders leave.

Esther followed the police out, but it was not until one of the officers asked, "Who's your shadow?" that she realised Michael was behind her.

"This is Mr Petersen," she told him shortly.

The man snorted. "And where does the Kraut get off standing so close to you?"

She stopped and stared icily at the policeman who was of a height with her. "An hour ago, he saved me from being shot by a fellow countryman. He can stand wherever he bloody well pleases."

Freddie Robertson – who had also followed them out –

359

managed to turn his titter into a hacking cough which did not go down too well with the policeman. He looked quite cross but said no more, instead choosing to stalk away and slam the door of the police car as he got in.

Another policeman approached, eyeing Michael warily.

"We'll be back to conduct some more detailed interviews with everyone involved tomorrow. Constable Nimmo will keep you informed."

"Kirkmore and its residents are at your disposal, sir," Esther replied stoutly, inclining her head.

Without further ado, the officer saluted and then left in a police car that trundled down the lane ahead of the van, their headlights bobbing with the undulations of the surface.

"Well, that was an interesting night," Esther commented then promptly crumpled, her knees painfully colliding with the gravel driveway.

"You don't say," Freddie huffed, catching her under one armpit while Michael managed the other.

Chapter Thirty-Seven

Sunlight was the first thing Esther noticed. That in itself was strange. Given that it was November, she always woke when it was still dark. Yet here she was lying in bed with bright light hitting her eyelids: an insistent poke telling her to wake up. But she really didn't want to. Her head was sore and heavy. All she wanted to do was drift back to sleep, to wallow in the oblivion of senselessness. It felt as if the pillow was swallowing her leaden head. She let go and allowed it to take her away. But then, just as she was on the cusp of nothingness, she heard the rumble of male voices.

"Don't wake her."

"Honestly, I couldn't give a hoot if I wake her up," a voice said loudly. "After what she did last night, I'd wake her just to spite her."

Freddie.

His acerbic tone and acquired Edinburgh accent were a real giveaway. Muzzily, Esther wondered if he had been there all night or if he had come back to check on her. What time was it anyway? Really, she did not want to find out. If she did, she would have to open her eyes, she would have to come back to full consciousness. And she would have to face the disapproval of the doctor. It was mostly the latter that made her screw her eyelids tight shut.

"I know you're listening, Essie. I can see you thinking."

She groaned, found the edge of the eiderdown and pulled it up over her head. Someone grabbed a handful of the quilt somewhere around her knees and gave it a yank, exposing her to the waist. Her eyes flew open and she scrambled to cover herself once more without sitting up. Her head felt all wrong. Swollen, deflated, too light and horribly heavy all at once. She was not at all certain whether the words she was thinking came out of her mouth or if it was just a garbled mess of grunts and squeaks. Since there were still two men standing at the foot of her bed, she assumed no one understood anything that passed her lips. If they had, they would have left the room very quickly. Or maybe not. One was Freddie and the other was Michael so she supposed nothing she said would make either of them leave.

"Congratulations," Freddie said conversationally. "All it took for you to have a proper night's sleep was being shot at and getting stitches in your head. We must try it again some time."

"I'd rather we didn't," Esther mumbled.

Sitting up slowly, the events of the night before began to seep down through her brain like warming treacle. Gradually, images unspooled before her eyes. Three strangers in the hallway. The same hallway minutes later filled with her men. Michael's face inches from hers as he cleaned her wound. The matter-of-fact expression on Mrs Morris's face when she saw them together. The would-be thieves as they sat in her breakfast room, unkempt and disgraced, awaiting the arrival of the police. And then, more vivid and disturbing than all the rest, was Muldoon's malevolent face as he stood in the corner watching Michael unwind the bandage on her head.

"Are you feeling all right?" Michael asked, concerned.

"No," she answered shortly. Then, throwing off the covers she swung her feet to the floor and pushed up off the bed. However, she did not stay standing for very long, as no sooner was she up, she was back down on the bed again having lost her balance.

"For God's sake, will you slow down, woman!" Freddie blustered, hurrying around the side of the bed to stop her.

Instead, she grabbed on to him and hauled herself up with the help of his arm. It took a moment for her head to stop swimming.

"Jesus Christ," the doctor huffed, "you do know you're giving me grey hairs, woman?'

"You don't have enough hair to turn grey," she pointed out as she watched Michael bite his lip in an attempt to supress his laughter.

The doctor threw her a withering glance. "I swear you're the reason I went off to work as an army doctor. I thought it'd be less stressful than looking after you."

"Liar," she countered. "Everyone knows you were running away from the old vicar's daughter."

"Yes, well, running was the only way I *could* get away from her, otherwise she would've flattened me."

"You should have told her to stop eating," Esther admonished him. "She could go through a week's worth of peoples' rations eating bread and jam when she went visiting with her father. Surely you could have come up with some doctor's reasoning to stop her eating everyone in Kirkmore out of house and home?"

"I bloody tried!" he griped. "Invited her and her mother over for a good talking-to about good dietary habits and all that."

"And how did that go?" Esther asked innocently, knowing the answer already.

"She ate half my Christmas cake in one sitting."

Michael snorted, not daring to catch Esther's eye.

"It wasn't funny. She thought I was courting her while really all I was trying to do was warn her off having a heart attack before she got to thirty. I thought it the doctorly thing to do."

It was Esther's turn to snort. It did nothing for her tender head. "Thank God they left Kirkmore, eh? We would have starved otherwise."

Absently, she reached for Michael's hand as she made to cross the room on unsteady legs. He offered it to her willingly.

"Eh …" the doctor's gaze flickered from one to the other. "You do know you'd want to be careful who sees you like this, chaps, don't you? I don't mind and clearly Mrs Morris doesn't either but there are plenty who would not think kindly of … whatever this is."

"We know," Esther replied.

"Does Fraser know?"

"Yes." She didn't know for certain but the way Fraser spoke to her the last time he had been home made her fairly sure her husband knew something was going on.

"Oh." There was real relief in those one little sound. "Well, that makes it not quite so worrisome. But still … be careful."

"We are." Michael answered this time.

"You weren't last night. Plenty of people saw the way you were together and there was plenty of talk afterwards. Even if they knew about it before, knowing and seeing it for yourself are two different things."

Neither of them replied. Both knew they had been foolish to expose themselves but, in the moment, they had not cared.

"How's your head?" the doctor inquired.

Esther rolled her eyes. That was not a good idea either. "Now he asks."

"I can see it's fine but out of courtesy I had to say something," he told her. "You won't die yet."

"Good to know. What time is it?" she asked as she shuffled into the bathroom and closed the door.

"Half eight!" Michael called from outside.

She swore. "When are the police coming for the interviews?"

"No word yet." Freddie this time. "I assume you'll want to be involved even if I tell you to rest?"

His faint hope was immediately quashed by Esther's defiant, "Yes."

"Thought as much."

She could almost hear his eyeroll through the door. She smiled at her own reflection which slightly brightened her dull eyes and gave a little warmth to her pale cheeks.

"You did say she was stubborn," she heard Michael murmur to the doctor.

"Aye," he replied glumly. "I did, didn't I?"

The only concession Esther made for her injury was having breakfast in bed. Michael was dispatched to the kitchen on his way to the fields where they were harvesting the last of the beets. However, once the tray came up, she insisted on sitting on the settee to eat rather than in bed which really meant all she did was eat in a different room. Still hovering, Freddie Robertson helped himself to some tea and half of Esther's toast which she did not particularly mind since she was not very hungry.

"Don't you have other people to bother?" she asked him.

"Only some house calls today, but they can wait. For the moment, I'd much prefer to bother you."

Esther huffed but said no more.

"Do you remember that day when poor Erwin Riegel skewered himself and it took four of us to get the darn thing out?"

She nodded and shivered at the memory. "How could I forget?"

"Do you remember the conversation we had? About being careful who heard you talk about Mr Petersen – Michael – when you agreed with me about him being a nice sort of chap." When she didn't answer, he continued. "I never expected it to go as far as it obviously has."

"I'm surprised you suspected it would go anywhere."

Freddie chuckled. "I saw the way he spoke to you, looked at you that day. Even then I could see he felt something for you."

"And you let him into the house anyway?"

"*You* let him into *your* house. I assumed he was enough of a gentleman not to try anything with a married woman."

Esther's lips tightened. "If there's anyone to blame it's the married woman. She was the one who made the final decision. He didn't coerce or seduce me."

"I have to admit he is charming. But do you really know everything about him? What if he did terrible things in the war?"

"Of course I don't know everything about him," she said sharply. "No one knows everything about anybody and he certainly doesn't know everything about me. We know what we should about one another – more than others know about us. And he was a dorsal gunner and radio man in a Heinkel bomber. It crash-landed in the north of Scotland and he and the pilot were the only survivors. It's how he got the scar on his left arm." She drew a line from her wrist to her elbow on the underside of her forearm.

"Ah. I did wonder about that. I've only seen it briefly. I thought it might have been a knife wound – you know, hand-to-hand stuff."

She shook her head. "No. And if I'm honest, I wasn't sure at first either. It's easy for someone to lie about their past. But now I've got to know him, I believe him. And he's spoken a lot about flying with Drew."

"Oh, Drew knows too, then?"

Esther hesitated. "I don't think so. Caroline does but … you know Drew. Happy to drift through life and enjoy it. He sees what he wants to."

Freddie made a small sound of uncertainty. "I'm not so sure. He's probably more observant than you give him credit for. Will you tell him anyway?"

"I don't know. I suppose I should in case he finds out. It would be horrible if we fell out over it." She pushed the crumbs on her plate into a neat little mound. "He's my best friend and he gets on so well with Michael. But he's also my husband's son. I don't know how he would feel if he discovered I was in a relationship with someone else. He might want me to leave Kirkmore and ..." her voice faltered, "and I don't know if I could do that."

"But doesn't he know about Madeline Pugh?" Freddie asked, surprised.

Esther had once unburdened herself to the doctor about her husband's secretary, needing to tell someone without a vested interest in the affair. "I think he does. He must do. He and Caro have been to dinner with Fraser and Madeline in London. Caro told me. But that doesn't mean he'll allow me the same liberties. We've fallen out before and it was the worst time of my life." She fought to keep her voice even. "I'd hate for that to happen again."

"It won't," Freddie said confidently, giving her knee a heartening squeeze. "He was a boy back then –"

"He was seventeen."

"*He was a boy,*" the doctor repeated. "You were his first love and you married his father. No wonder he fell out with you. You were a child once. Can't you remember the emotional turmoil – the 'I love you, I hate you' of it all? But he's grown up now. Married. That changes a man. Grounds him. But you're still the closest thing he has to family. You always have been. He's never been close to his father and you know it. He loves you like a sister so I can't see him turning against you again, no matter what you do. And, besides, Caroline will never allow him to get cross with you.

And we all know that once she sets her mind on something woe betide anyone who goes against her. A bit like you," he winked. "She'll keep him in line, don't you worry."

"So are you saying tell him when Caro's there?"

"I wasn't but that does sound like a plan. She might give some balance to the situation." Freddie stood. "And I'd say you'd want to come up with whatever you're going to say quick. Caro telephoned at seven this morning in a flap. Major Brown rang them in Edinburgh in case they heard what happened from someone else. Really, I just think he wanted to be the gossip who told them. Anyway, they're on their way up."

"Oh, for God's sake!" Esther hissed in exasperation. "They don't need to do that. I'm perfectly all right."

"They're not coming for *you*," he told her in mock scorn, then grinned. "They're coming to see what damage was done to the hall. It'll take an age to repair all those pellet holes."

"The bastards. No appreciation for authentic Georgian architecture," Esther commented dryly.

"Philistines," Freddie sniffed, shaking his head.

They were still chuckling when Mrs Morris knocked and came in.

"Constable Nimmo telephoned," she informed them. "An inspector and sergeant are coming from Edinburgh to interview you and the men. They should be here before twelve o'clock."

"From Edinburgh?" Esther's stomach dropped. That sounded much more official than she thought it would be.

"Don't worry about it, Essie," the doctor said confidently. "You've done nothing wrong. It must be something to do with the deserters. I'm assuming this wasn't the first place they tried to rob. Just be your own charming self, answer their questions and make sure to respect their authority. It might be a good idea to tell the men the same thing. Just in case."

Her breakfast over, Esther carefully got to her feet and was glad to find they were steady. It was time to get to work. She wanted to talk to the men before the police came to make sure they were all following the same story about it being Max's birthday. Unless the police asked her directly, she would say nothing of the sleeping arrangements.

Freddie followed her around for a while until she reminded him of his duty to his other patients, at which point he reluctantly left. However, he did leave her with a dire warning to look after her stitches "or else", and that he would be back to check on her in the evening, despite her protests. "I expect to get my dinner here too," he informed her as he walked away. "For my trouble.'

Chapter Thirty-Eight

By the time the police arrived, Esther had done everything she set out to do. However, she did succumb and have to take some painkillers for her head. It throbbed insistently and she longed to touch it but refrained, afraid to do more damage. The medication took the edge off the pain but she was sure not to rely on it too much for fear it would cloud her judgement. She needed to have all her faculties functioning to make sure the questioning went to plan.

When the inspector and his sergeant – Douglas and Hammond – arrived, Esther showed them the damage done to the hall before leading them into her study. It was her place of power but it was also quite a masculine space. She hoped it would show them that, despite being a woman, she was in charge of Kirkmore and no one else. The men were polite but brisk and seemed a little surprised when she sat in the chair behind the desk and offered them two others opposite her. After the initial double-take, however, they seemed to accept it and move on.

They began by asking her general questions about herself and the estate but then branched into inquiries about the events of the night before. Initially, Esther spoke easily, matter-of-factly, recounting the incident without emotion. But as she got closer to the moment where she found herself quite literally looking down the barrel of a gun, her voice faltered then dried up completely.

"It's all right," Douglas said in a thick Glaswegian accent, leaning forward and making the seat creak. It reminded her of the creak of the front door – the door that had alerted her to the presence of strangers in the house. "Breathe, Mrs McAllister. Just breathe."

Esther grabbed hold of the edge of the table and forced air out through clenched teeth. Her head ached and she felt dizzy. Vaguely, she heard one of the men say something but she had no idea what it was. She hoped it wasn't important. Suddenly, there was a glass of water at her right hand. She heard the word "sip" and nothing else. Gradually, the cool liquid seemed to shock her back to her senses. Looking up, she noted that the men sat opposite her with sympathetic miens. It calmed her.

"I'm awfully sorry about that," she mumbled. "I don't know what came over me."

"You're still in shock, Mrs McAllister." Douglas again. He seemed to do all the talking. "Perfectly understandable. Take all the time you need."

"I'm not a hysteric." It seemed important to point that out. Yet she then regretted it immediately. No doubt hysterics said such things too.

"No. You're not. I think you're doing remarkably well, truth be told."

"I remember a bloke from Inverness in my platoon during the war," Hammond piped up, suddenly looking interested. "Screamed like a bairn for ten minutes after initial contact. The CO nearly shot him just to keep the bugger quiet – beg your pardon, ma'am."

She waved his apology away with a smile. "Well, just as long as there's no repeat of it any time soon, I think I'll be all right."

371

The interviews took all day and were only interrupted by lunch for the two policemen and the arrival of Drew and Caroline – the latter being so beside herself she ended up shouting at Esther in the hall, demanding she never do anything like this to them again. Afterwards, however, she hugged Esther so tightly both were sure they heard a rib crack.

Drew was a little less effusive but still seemed quite emotional when he wrapped Esther in his arms and rocked from foot to foot as he held her.

When he met Michael, he shook his hand. "Thank you," he said, tightly wringing the German's fingers. "Mrs Morris told us what you did. You … thank you."

Michael did nothing to hide his surprise at such a heartfelt greeting. He gave an embarrassed shrug. "I just did what anyone would have done."

Clapping him on the back, Drew shook his head. "You're a good man, Michael, a good man."

When the police were finally satisfied, they found Esther in the library with Caro and Drew. They seemed much more cheerful now that their day's work was over and all that remained was a drive back to the city. Esther sent them away with some sandwiches and fruitcake to keep them going on their journey. She had offered them a bed for the night but both men insisted on getting home to their families and also cracking on with the case of the three men apprehended at Kirkmore who, it turned out, had quite a string of outstanding burglaries to their names.

"I'm just glad we've finally caught the buggers – beg your pardon, ma'am," said Hammond as he bid her farewell. "Or rather, your men caught them. You were lucky. Bloody lucky."

"We'll keep you informed of any developments, ma'am," Inspector Douglas told her. "But it should all be very straightforward really."

Even though the policemen had really been quite friendly and did not question her reason for having a bunch of large former prisoners of war in her home, it was with some relief that she watched them go. However, her relief was short-lived when she saw Muldoon talking to the police officers before they got into their car. She had gone into the breakfast room to watch them leave, knowing she would not fully relax until their taillights disappeared into the distance. Only now their departure was delayed. They looked even less pleased than she felt. Though she could not hear them, their gestures alone seemed to suggest that they were not interested in what the gamekeeper had to say. Indeed, when he began to jab his fingers at the house then at the two men, they appeared to get quite angry with him. Waving him away, they got into their car and drove off, leaving Muldoon visibly seething on the gravel sweep.

He swung around to glare at the house and Esther ducked out of view like a naughty schoolgirl. Why did she do that, she wondered. Composing herself, she returned to her study to reorganize whatever mess the policemen had left behind and to once again feel like she was in charge of the place.

Sitting at the desk, she felt as if the house was settling around her. After all the tension, the upheaval of the night before, the quiet rumble of the building returned with its familiar creaks and sighs that had been such a comfort to her over the years. She shuddered to think what might have happened to the place had the Germans not been there. So often over the last year and half they had saved the estate from disaster – saved her. They picked up the shortfall left by the Italians with alacrity. They managed animals, dug ditches, cleared woodland, harvested, saved the root crops from unprecedented floodwaters, saved people and livestock during the snows of the spring, planted, birthed lambs and calves then began the harvest again. The men enriched the lives of the locals by showing them that despite once standing on the opposing side of an international divide, they were all human and had suffered greatly for their part in the war too. Now Kirkmore saw the men as individuals rather than the German army.

There was Dieter Scholzen who was a wonderful husband to Norah and father to Dougie. There was Michael who everyone was sure was much too clever to be wasted in a place like Kirkmore yet no one could abide the thought of him leaving. Max Winkler, though painfully shy and still inclined to jump more than anyone else at loud noises, was one of the best horsemen they had ever come across and was often called on to deal with young and problem horses in the surrounding area – much to his delight. Reinhold Teske was the most powerful workhorse any of them had ever seen. If there was a job no one else could do, he was always the man they called on to get it done. And yet, though he was big and brawny, he was the one many of the children flocked to during the breaks in the hay harvest. Everyone brought something whether it was simply their willingness to work or their skill as a woodcarver making toys for children – local and beyond. Some were gifted footballers who helped the local team to their best result in years in the recently resurrected annual county championship. Others had powerful singing voices which were put to great use in church every week. Some put their own farming knowledge to good use and helped the estate achieve its most profitable year in decades.

In less than eighteen months, the Germans had managed to integrate themselves into the community, so much so that their impending departure was a source of great upset to the locals. There were many jokes about how the people of Kirkmore might somehow take the men prisoner so that they would never leave. It was, of course, met with good humour by the men who delighted in having made such a positive impression. Indeed, there were a few of them who were quite keen to stay, having become attached either to the place or perhaps a special person. If they had the choice several would have stayed exactly where they were. For them, the prospect of returning to Germany to start from scratch in a country completely broken by war was not enticing. The men knew they were well treated at Kirkmore. They had suitable accommodation, they were fed ample rations, they were clothed and, despite not legally needing to pay the men well, Esther made sure their wage packets reflected the effort they put into their work. Yet, persistently, there was one person who resisted their presence at Kirkmore: Muldoon.

For years hatred had built inside Muldoon, finding only the slightest release in his complaints to Fraser. Esther did not belong yet he could not find an offence in her conduct that was serious enough to warrant her expulsion from Kirkmore. Until now. She had really done it this time – exposing herself and her relationship to everyone. Muldoon had witnesses to her offence. And yet, no one else seemed surprised. No one gasped or shouted or even commented on the intimacy between the mistress and the prisoner. Muldoon still could not see them as people worthy of the temporary citizenship they had been granted by the government. He thought when he approached the police that they, at least, would have something to say about it. But they dismissed him just as the laird had.

It was time to take matters into his own hands.

Chapter Thirty-Nine

Despite her damaged head and Freddie's warning, late evening found Esther still in her study trying to complete the estate's paperwork for the day. Giving it up as a bad job, she was attempting to figure out who she needed to contact in order to start the process of getting some of the men full citizenship rather than the temporary citizenship they now had. She knew it would not be easy but then she did have the people of Kirkmore and – more importantly – Fraser in her corner. He was well positioned and well respected in political spheres so she knew his influence would be key to achieving her ends. She already had a list of men who had requested to stay indefinitely on the estate and underneath it she had written the names of all the people who would hopefully help her and her Germans. However, she could not figure out who she should write to first or even what she might say. All she did was sit and stare at the list of names.

She longed to give up on it altogether and head next door to the library where she could hear Caro, Drew, Michael and a few other voices laughing and chatting. But when Drew came to get her earlier on, she had insisted he leave her alone to work for another hour. She was now regretting that decision but wouldn't allow Drew the satisfaction of seeing her give in to the lure of good company and conversation.

No – Freddie Robertson was eating his supper in the other room so whenever he finished and came to check her stitches or give out to her for working, she would call it a day.

When the door to the hall opened, she was ready with her response. "I know, I know. I'm finishing up now," she said, pushing up out of her chair.

It wasn't until the door snapped shut and she looked up that she discovered it was not Freddie.

"Muldoon?"

Esther was immediately on her guard. He rarely came to her of his own volition. And, after seeing his heated exchange with the policemen, she was sure nothing good was going to come of what he was about to say. She, therefore, thought it best to stay standing. Whatever he said, she was not going to sit and take it like a good little lady. She would take it as the manager of Kirkmore. She moved to the front of the table so that there was no barrier between them. She did not want to give in to the temptation to lean on the desk. She wanted to stand above him: to command the room.

As he approached, she studied his face. His expression was cold. She also noted he had not returned her greeting with his usual, "Ma'am". He was breathing heavily and stood eight feet away on the carpet, feet planted firmly at ease but his hands balled into fists, the tendons bulging under the strain.

Esther thought about asking him why he was here but instead waited for him to speak.

He opened his mouth, clearly about to begin. His arm rose and he pointed at her but no sound came out. He tried again but all he produced was a small huff of air. On his third attempt, he was more successful.

"Like feral animals you and the boy used to run around. As if you owned the place. Never for one minute did I think it would ever happen: that *you* would ..." He stopped, not out of prudery but because he could not seem to find words strong enough to convey his anger. But he didn't need words. His whole bearing made it abundantly clear. "When I heard that you were to marry – well, of course I didn't believe it. I *still* don't believe that out of all the women in the world he chose a *labourer's* daughter! And, do you know, when it happened I thought that perhaps you would have the decency to know your place, to know that you're beneath the station of the lady of Kirkmore and that you always will be. But instead you decided to play pretend at being the lady of the manor, ordering us about and acting like you knew what it took to run an estate when you haven't the breeding or the education for it. The – the dogs have more of a right to be here than you do!"

That surprised Esther. Muldoon hated her two dogs. But she said nothing.

"I always knew you'd ruin it all eventually. Your sort always do. It was just a case of waiting to see it happen. And we *all* saw it last night, didn't we?" Here, he smiled at her with large, square yellow teeth, bared like an animal's just as they had been the night before. "*You.* And *him.*"

Nodding, he seemed to think she ought to respond at this point but when she stayed silent his smile faltered a little.

"Of course, *I* knew. I knew long before everyone else. But I knew I couldn't say anything because it would have been my word against yours. And I wasn't going to take that risk. But no one can deny it now. Not even *you. You're done, little Miss Muncie!*" he roared triumphantly. "*Finished!* And there's not one thing you and your little German boy can do about it."

"What's going on here?"

Drew stood in the doorway between the library and the study with Caro peering out from behind him, a worried look on her face. And behind them was Michael – shrouded in shadow – who Esther only knew by the way he towered over the others.

"*She*," hissed the gamekeeper, "*she*, is a disgrace to the McAllister name. An embarrassment to anyone who has ever served it."

"Muldoon was just letting me know that he is leaving us," Esther said calmly, not taking her eyes off the gamekeeper whose whole face contorted at her words.

"*Me!*" he roared. "*Me!* I'm not going anywhere! *You're* the one on the way out, not me. I'll make sure of it."

Esther bristled. Even though she had told herself not to rise to his challenge, she could not help it. "*I beg your pardon!*" Her voice cracked through the air like a whip. "What delusion are you under that makes you think you have anything akin to authority over me?" She had spent years earning her position at Kirkmore. She was not going to lose it now because Muldoon wanted to settle a score that had been brewing since her childhood.

Drew approached. "Stand down, man. Before you make even more of a fool of yourself."

But the gamekeeper was beyond the point of reason. His neck burned red and his eyes bulged. "*And you!* Following her around like a lost puppy, hoping she'd throw some scraps your way. You wouldn't think so highly of her if you realized what a little slut she was."

In her peripheral vision, Esther saw Michael start forward but she held up a hand to stop him.

Drew jerked backwards as if he had been struck. "How dare you – how do you – *what*?"

"*Her* and *that!*" Muldoon jabbed a knobbly finger at Michael who stood to his full height, fists clenched at his sides, white with fury. "The little slut's been having it off with *that*. And who knows how many others over the years, eh? Who's to say those little brats of hers are Mr McAllister's at all, eh? Cuckoos in the nest! *Little bastards!*"

He could insult her all he liked. He could say what he

wanted about her and she would take it, absorb it, carry it with her until the end of her days and not show anyone how much what he said hurt her. Before she died, her mother told her that there would always be some folk who would try to put her down because of where she came from. In those situations, she had to be the bigger person and not react. That, Lizzie insisted, was the harder thing to do yet also what would gain her respect. Anyone could say anything about her and every time she thought about responding, Lizzie would speak to her.

But her mother never said anything about what to do when someone derided her children. Before a conscious thought had even crossed her mind, the palm of her had connected with the bristled, lean, leathery cheek of the gamekeeper.

Words kicked, screamed and jostled for their position as they rushed to her lips. She wanted to shout, to swear, to repeat the worst insults she had ever heard and hurl them directly at the wizened, malign little creature that stood before her. But she never got to say any of them.

She saw the back of a contorted, sun-spotted hand arc towards her right cheek. Though she knew it was coming, she was not quick enough to pull back. Muldoon's backhand hit her with the force of nearly thirty years' worth of resentment behind it. She felt the bulging tendons, the boniness of the knuckles, the roughness of his worn skin. It knocked her off her feet.

Her knees collided with the ground for the third time in two evenings. What was worse, however, was that her head glanced off the edge of the desk as she fell. Immediately she knew the stitches had burst. She felt the tug and the snap – was almost sure she heard the 'pop' as they gave way. She could feel the burning line of the impact with the edge of the table across the side of her skull as her hands finally caught her before she hit the floor. White stars danced across her vision and nausea heaved her stomach. Yet she remained conscious even if she was not fully aware of what was going on around her.

She knew Caro had screamed. Both men roared and she was aware of a scuffle above her. The rug under her knees was being tugged by the movements of numerous feet. The floorboards shook as someone – or more than one – fell to the ground. All Esther saw, however, was the pattern on the carpet a few inches below her nose. There was a small posy of woven flowers, one red with the two either side in rich golden wool. Vines twisted around their stems in dark green with small dashes of maroon and gold to complement the flowers. Vaguely, she thought it strange how she had never noticed the dashes of red before. They were so vivid. Then, slowly, she noticed how the red seemed to bloom before her as if another flower was sprouting alongside the others, growing from a dormant seed just waiting on her to look its way. Fascinated, she slid her fingers over to touch it. The petals felt oddly wet.

"Oh, dear God, Esther, your head!"

Caro was kneeling in front of her, her hands flapping until she reached for her sleeve and pulled out a snow-white handkerchief. Esther almost giggled. It was like a conjuror's trick. However, when Caro clapped the hanky onto the side of her head, the last thing Esther felt like doing was laughing. All that she could think of was how painful it was. She jerked away but Caro held on.

"You're ruining your carpet," she warned. Then she looked up. "Where the *hell* were you, Freddie?"

Esther cocked her head to the side and finally took in the rest of the room. It was odd to discover she was looking at the aftermath of yet another fight between men. To go through so much of her life having seen only a few skirmishes outside the pubs and then to witness several in

381

less than twenty-four hours ... she really hoped it wouldn't become a habit.

The usually smooth rug on the floor was rumpled like still water after raindrops. One of the two chairs by the desk was on its side, its legs stretched out searching for purchase on a flat surface but finding only empty air. Muldoon was sitting on the floor breathing heavily, cradling his right hand. Esther passed straight over him to Drew who stood close to the fireplace dabbing a split lip with his own handkerchief. Michael was in the centre of the room, towering over the gamekeeper with a small dribble of blood coming from his nose which he dabbed absently on the cuff of his shirt. The doctor stood by the door, his mouth agape as he surveyed the people scattered across the room. Eventually, he cleared his throat and approached.

"I leave you alone for five minutes ..."

As the dust settled, Drew and Michael had a brief exchange then bent down, hauled Muldoon up off the floor and began to frogmarch him out of the room.

"Just a moment, chaps, I have to have a look at his hand!" Freddie called.

"No, you don't," Michael answered coldly.

"You can treat him in his own house, but you won't treat him in this one," Drew clarified. "He's no longer welcome here."

Once the men left, Freddie turned to Esther with a shake of his head. "Dare I ask what happened?"

Esther and Caro spoke simultaneously. "*No.*"

Freddie shrugged. "Fair enough."

Having her head stitched for the second time was infinitely more uncomfortable than the first. There was no shock to numb the pain this time around and she also had Freddie telling her off while he worked. Eventually, she snapped and told him to shut up.

By the time he had fixed Esther up, the two men were back. Both had the bearing of errant schoolboys as they cast surly glances about the room. Neither were making eye contact with the other. Their original injuries also appeared to be bleeding much more profusely than they had previously. Drew had a shadow on his jaw that looked like the beginnings of a bruise and Michael's nose was streaming dark red liquid onto his off-white shirt.

The doctor threw them a quick glance and gave a short humourless chuckle. "I'm going to do you the courtesy of assuming Muldoon didn't manage to best the pair of you." He eyed them a little more severely. "I suppose it's a bit late to tell you that I have enough to do patching Essie up without having to do the same for the two of you once you've settled your differences."

"I don't need a doctor," Michael told Freddie in a thick voice. "I'll be all right."

He most definitely did not look all right. There was a cut across the bridge of his nose and the whole thing was beginning to swell. His eyes were also streaming. Esther tried to catch Drew's eye but he was looking anywhere but at her. It suddenly dawned on her fuddled brain that the two men had fought about her. Now she understood why Drew was so interested in the carving on the mantelpiece. His whole body seemed to hunch away from her. That hurt more than the wound on her head.

Michael, on the other hand, could not tear his eyes away from her, not even when the doctor addressed him.

"You most certainly will not be all right!" Freddie voice was suffused with irritation. "Unless you want to have breathing trouble for the rest of your life. I need to straighten your nose while you can't feel it."

Michael grinned at him with slightly pink teeth and shining eyes. "Oh, I can feel it."

"Well, you'll feel it ten times more if I leave it," Freddie replied in a tone that was not to be challenged.

"What about me?" Drew piped up.

Freddie barely looked at him. "Split lip. You'll do."

"Hear that, Petersen?" Drew jeered. "Not that tough after all, are you?"

Michael finally tore his gaze away from Esther to glare at the McAllister heir. "I don't think Esther would have thought well of me if I had hurt you. Believe me, you wouldn't have walked back into this house if I hadn't wanted you to."

With a growl, Drew propelled himself across the carpet. Both Esther and Freddie made to halt his progress but Caro beat them to it.

"*Oh no, you don't!*" She hissed at her husband, a warning hand held aloft. "What do you think you're doing? Defending the estate? Your father's honour? Protecting Esther? Because if it's any of them, you're wasting your time. The estate's getting on better than it ever did and when your father dies it will either go to you or Archie. Your father already knows what's going on and, besides that, *he's* been having an affair with his secretary for God knows how long. And if you think Esther needs protecting then it's bloody stupid to attack the man who you've said yourself saved her life last night."

Drew looked as if he was going to interrupt but his wife cut him off.

"And don't you dare say anything as stupid as 'he seduced her' or 'she doesn't know what she's doing'. Because if you do, I'll finish the job he started on you myself." Caro was red-faced and breathing hard but she didn't stop there. "Whatever problems you foresee, Esther has thought of all of them and ten times more besides. She knows the risks but she has chosen Michael anyway because she loves him. Don't you?"

She turned to Esther who stood gaping at her friend's passionate defence of her.

"Yes," she choked out over the lump in her throat. She was trying to decide whether to let the emotion out, to let the tears flow. Crying was not likely to make her appear as the intelligent, capable woman Caro made her out to be. She swallowed hard. "Yes," she said more forcefully. "Yes, I love him." She said it to Drew then turned to Michael. "I love you."

Unfortunately, her declaration did little to lower the tension in the room. Drew did, however, subside into one of the armchairs by the hearth where he attempted to put out the fire with his glacial stare. Caro sat on the armrest and curled herself around him, laying her cheek on his hair. After a while Drew absentmindedly caressed her thigh then left his hand on her knee. It was a beautiful picture. Esther wondered if she would ever be free to sit with Michael like that when they were in the company of others.

Meanwhile, Freddie had managed to coax a reluctant Michael into a chair.

"Shouldn't we do this somewhere else?" he asked the doctor.

Freddie shrugged. "Here is as good as anywhere. And it's going to hurt like hell no matter where we do it."

"It already hurts like hell," Michael answered through gritted teeth, gripping the arms of the heavy hardwood chair with white knuckles. It creaked ominously.

"It'll probably bleed more too. Do we have anything...." The doctor cast about for something to mop up the expected flux.

Esther, sitting on the desk with her feet on the other chair, reached across to the tea tray which was dressed with a crisp white tea towel. They only used lace doilies on special occasions. She jiggled the towel out from under the teapot and threw it to the doctor who tucked it into the collar of

Michael's shirt. He then placed one hand on the German's shoulder and carefully gripped his nose with the other. Michael hissed through his teeth.

"Before I do this, I just want to say I'm terribly sorry," Freddie told him.

"Do wha –"

Jerking down and to the left, Freddie pulled the nasal bone back into place. Letting out a roar that made everyone jump, Michael's whole body spasmed in pain. There was an almighty *crack* as the whole arm of his chair snapped clean off. He held onto it as he pitched forward and sprayed blood all over the tea towel and his trousers, spitting out a string of curses in German. Though she did not even attempt to understand the rest of what he was saying, finally Esther picked out some English.

"You *bastard*, Robertson!"

"That's the spirit," the doctor said pleasantly. "Let me have a look now," he said, extending a hand, but Michael raised the jagged broken end of the chair arm to ward him off.

"Don't you touch me!" he snapped, trying to stanch the blood-flow with one hand.

"I need to make sure it's realigned properly," Freddie said patiently. "If not, I'll have to try again."

"No, you bloody well will *not*!"

The doctor tried another tack. "Just let me do it and don't be such a big girl about it!"

"Yes, do man up, Petersen," Drew drawled from the far side of the room.

Michael began to haul himself out of the chair but then the doctor straightened up and turned on Drew.

"In case you hadn't noticed, the man just ripped a chair in two with one hand. I fully believe he could have done the same to you if he had been so inclined. So I wouldn't antagonise him if I were you."

386

Still glaring at Drew, Michael subsided to allow Freddie to examine him. "If it's not right I'm going to stab you with what's left of this chair," he warned.

"Noted," Freddie answered blandly. "Although, if you do, please call the vet rather than Dr Ferguson. The veterinarian would likely be more successful at patching me up than my colleague."

"He must be bad if you're better," Michael muttered.

"Marginally," the doctor conceded with a grin as he bent to palpate his patient's nose. "Yes, I think that'll do nicely."

"There is a God!" Michael said thickly, still dabbing at the dribbles of blood from his nostrils. "Has he ruined me?" he asked Esther, turning his head to show her his profile.

His nose was horribly swollen and discoloured so it was quite hard to tell what he looked like at all.

"You'll do," she said with a smile. On impulse, she got up and kissed his forehead. Then she looked down at the lump of armrest in his hand. "But I don't think that chair will ever be the same again."

Chapter Forty

By the end of January 1948, the broken chair in her study was all Esther had to remind her of Michael Petersen.

The letter had come through several weeks previously. Most of the Germans at Kirkmore had already gone home to officially leave what remained of Hitler's army and receive their final paycheques for their service both before and after their capture. But now it was the turn of the remaining few and, when the call came, they had to obey.

Even men like Dieter, who were all but settled and ready to build a new life in Scotland, had to return to their native country to get their release papers. The terrifying thing for him was that, despite being married to a Briton, there was no guarantee he would be allowed to return to Scotland once he was discharged from the army. Poor Norah was beside herself with worry. Instead of enjoying the comforting presence of her second spouse, the new Mrs Scholzen wore a path in the road back and forth to the village post office as she waited for some word of her husband.

Esther's grief was much more private. She still tried not to advertise the fact that she missed Michael even though, by this time, everyone knew that the mistress of Kirkmore had engaged in a passionate relationship with one of her German workers. Muldoon made sure of that after she dismissed him.

The morning after he confronted her in her study, Esther had gone to his cottage with Drew to officially give the gamekeeper his notice. Though she did not want one, she expected another argument when they arrived at his house. She was surprised, therefore, when he opened the door to them and she saw two trunks and two bags just inside the hall. Had the memory of their confrontation the night before not been so vivid in her mind, she might have thought it sad that such a small collection of belongings was the sum total of forty years' service. She also noted the large white bandage that swaddled his right hand. Freddie had clearly been to see the gamekeeper too.

She hardly needed to give him his marching orders but delivered them anyway with a feeling of grim satisfaction. This would be the final decision she made for Muldoon and she wanted him to know it: to know that she had the last word – the power over Kirkmore – and no one else.

The last reply he gave her was the familiar, 'Yes, ma'am,' he always gave her.

Yet, before he left the area altogether, he had called on a few key people in the village to let them know of his departure and the reason for it: he had confronted the mistress about her affair with one of the Germans and she had dismissed him. By that evening, everyone in the village and on the surrounding farms knew. And Muldoon was halfway to his sister in Aberdeen, never to be seen or heard from again in Kirkmore.

Though she doubted Muldoon's last hurrah had the effect he hoped it would, Esther's life was complicated somewhat by subtle changes in attitude towards her. Gone was the local feeling that she was one of their own raised to a higher position. It was replaced by haughtiness. People were less jovial around her, they did not talk to her as freely as they once had. Some of the older, retired members of the community did not talk to her at all. However, the younger men and women were much less reticent. Kirkmore provided the vast majority of those who were of employable age with work and many could not afford to offend the mistress. For the most part, they simply got on with whatever it was they were doing and allowed Mrs McAllister to do the same. What the mistress did in her own time was no concern of theirs as long as they still had a job to go to in the morning.

Esther did, however, find an ally in Norah.

"You can't help who you fall in love with, can you?" she said glumly as they sat together on Christmas Day. Norah had brought along a delighted Dougie, keen to see his best friend. While he and Archie played with Florrie, Esther and Norah talked.

It was a different Christmas to the one the year before. There were less people, less singing, less laughter. Mrs Morris and Esther decided there were not even enough people to warrant the use of the formal dining room so the somewhat cosier breakfast room was where they all congregated. Most people had declined Esther's invitation to the Kirkmore celebrations given that their own families were now, for the most part, restored. Sons and daughters, fathers and brothers had finally returned from service abroad or the factories that they worked in during the war. The Christmas of 1947 was truly the Christmas where people came together for the first time since war broke out. They had experienced more than two years of peace and it now looked as if it might stay that way.

"When you brought the Germans in, I really did think about leaving altogether, you know," Norah told Esther. "I couldn't stand the idea of one of them being the man who killed poor George on that godforsaken beach in France. But it was all I could think about. Every time I saw them, I wondered which one. Which one was it that killed my George? It wasn't until I got to know them that I realised they were the same as us, that they had lost people too. My husband could have been the man that killed their brother, their friend. God," she said shaking her head, "war is a bloody awful thing." After a long pause she said quietly, "It's not the dead that suffer, it's the ones left behind." She looked at Esther. "Imagine who you and I would be if you hadn't lost your father and I hadn't lost my husband."

"I wouldn't be here for one," Esther answered. "Fraser would hardly have known I existed. And I never would've had the education he paid for either. I would have continued in the local school with you. I would have learnt how to be good wife."

"And you would have married a labouring man and likely been widowed before you were thirty. Just like me. And yet, we're not that dissimilar after all. We both have fine young boys, absent husbands – though the absence of mine is permanent – and have found love in the arms of a German."

Esther chuckled sadly. "I suppose you're right."

The women sat in silence for a while, watching their children chatter and play in front of the cracking yellow flames of the fire. "I hope they come back soon," Norah murmured.

Esther looked down at her hands as they played with the fabric of her dress – the repaired green dress that she had worn the Christmas before.

"So do I."

Chapter Forty-One

It was not lost on Michael and Dieter how lucky they were to be going back to Germany together. Having met almost four years previously, it was astonishing to think that, throughout that time, they had not been separated once. Of course, they could have grown to hate each other over such an extended period together. But the truth was neither had ever experienced friendship like it. There was no one who knew as much about Michael as Dieter did and vice versa.

Yet, when they first met, they had thought very little of one another. Dieter was a firebrand, consumed by grief at the loss of his wife and children, unable to think of anything other than how to destroy the people who had left him so alone: the people on both sides of the conflict. He marooned himself on an island of hatred, rejecting the advances of everyone, no matter their nationality or opinions.

Michael, in his own way, was similar. He engaged very little with the other men since he had so little in common with them. Unlike his fellow countrymen, he had no urge to go home. If anything, he felt more at home on British soil, even if the small patch he occupied was surrounded by a barbed-wire fence. Though he rarely spoke to them, he often tried to listen to the conversations of the camp guards. He had missed the lilt and strange phraseology of English while back amongst Germans and found it comforting to hear it once again. Yet when the camp commandant sought out prisoners with decent English, he never came forward. He did not want to be a cog in another huge machine, working at the behest of faceless officials. He had done that for nearly four years in Germany and hated it. In fact, it had almost killed him. No: he would drift through the entire machine unnoticed. Like Dieter, he withdrew yet he was still observant of the things going on around them. He noticed the taciturn prisoner who sometimes got into fights with the others for no apparent reason other than a need to hit something. He was, therefore, somewhat wary of the man when they were put on kitchen duty together. The guards tended to put Dieter on his own because he inevitably fell out with whoever he was working with but, on the occasions they wanted some entertainment, they paired him off with someone and watched the trouble unfold.

Yet when Dieter barked, "What are you looking at?" across a mound of potatoes and Michael had calmly replied, "These potatoes mostly. Sometimes you," it knocked Dieter. He was used to aggression being met with either fear or more aggression. He did not know what to do with someone who spoke to him normally – treated him like he was human.

It was there – over many mounds of potatoes – that their friendship grew. The characters of each bled into the other. Dieter mellowed and Michael's passions slowly began to rekindle. But it was not until they were shipped off to Kirkmore that they finally found the freedom to rediscover themselves as men and not just prisoners or soldiers of the *Wehrmacht*. Now, on leaving the place, the two men found they were more alike than ever.

On the train down to Billinghurst where they were to spend three days before departing for Germany, the two men sat opposite one another but hardly spoke a word. What they did say was mainly focused on things they saw through the window as they cut across the countryside. Talking about anything else was too painful. They were leaving behind a place where they had found sanctuary and love. Their destination was the place that reminded them of the war – of the failure of war, a land razed to the ground. It was also a place of ghosts. Both knew without saying that, no matter what they heard by post, they would still look for their lost families. They would see them in every crowd, hear their voices, catch glimpses of them as they walked along pavements. It was easier to believe that their family was living some anonymous, happy life elsewhere than to acknowledge the horrifying truth that the people they loved were really gone and not coming back.

When they finally reached the Elysian homeland – the *Heimat* they so often sang songs about while interred in Britain – it was a wonder to think anyone had survived at all. Even two and a half years later, the destruction was still evident.

When the men arrived at Munsterlager in the north of the British Sector to be processed, back-paid their wages and finally discharged from the army, the weather was bitterly cold. The idea of sending as many Germans as possible home in December was that they would be with their families for Christmas. Yet what this also did was remind those who were bereaved of their loss.

Dieter had already decided to go back to Hamburg to find out what he could about his family. With nothing better to do, Michael had opted to go with him. There were still restrictions on movement throughout the country and he did not want to risk entering Soviet territory for fear of never getting out again. He also thought his friend could do with the company. It was going to be a horrible experience and he felt Dieter should not have to endure it alone. Plus, Hamburg was still within the bounds of the British Sector so he didn't need any extra paperwork to get there.

What horrified them the most as they moved through the countryside on a draughty train were the scars of war that were clear even at a glance. Whole villages lay abandoned. The finest vehicles the *Wehrmacht* could produce now lay rusting on the sides of roads. Bulbous khaki-green helmets decorated trees, adorned walls and headed makeshift crosses. Miles of barbed-wire fences marked the edges of camps and barracks, reminding them of their own interment. But worse than all of that were the people.

Some were the very definition of downtrodden. Gone was the pride and pomp of the Nazi regime, replaced by nothing but the will to survive. They had endured the loss of their fathers and sons, the bombings and the indignity of the Allied army scouring their countryside before the war ended. After it, they had to cope with Allied occupation, lack of sanitation, power, accommodation and, most pressingly of all, lack of food. Not only had Kirkmore's prisoners of war been feeding Britain, they'd been feeding Germany too.

Nevertheless, the children seemed happy. They had bounced back the way children often did and made the ruined buildings and piles of rubble their playground. They were blessed with a lack of understanding, the carelessness of youth which – for the most part – could save them from the despair of their memories. The national trauma felt so keenly by their parents was an alien concept to them. They looked to the future instead of wallowing in the past. As he watched them play, they gave Michael hope.

Dieter, on the other hand, walked the streets of his hometown as if he were lobotomised. Michael supposed that was the best way to view the place. Even though he had never been there before, seeing the desolate avenues of skeletal buildings, broken roads and scattered masonry nearly three years on left him chilled to the core. Only pockets of the city were getting back to their former use.

There were residential and business areas but, no matter how hard they tried to keep the place clean, the dust was still settling. The newly erected buildings that were meant to give hope for a better future were at odds with the destruction around them – their walls too straight, their thrust towards the sky too insolent.

It took them a long time to find the street where Dieter had once lived. Even he did not recognise the city of his birth, the streets of his childhood. They were the streets of someone else's childhood now and completely unfamiliar to him. When they eventually found his building amongst the snow, craters and tons of brick and plaster, they stood on the front step. It was all that remained of the flats his and countless other families occupied.

Standing on the edge, looking into the empty white hole, Dieter finally let go and cried.

Michael was there to hold him as he did. He had never seen a man cry like that before, his whole body racked by grief and guilt. Even though his family died together, he could not help but feel they died alone because he was not with them. Michael knew there was nothing he could say to comfort him so he did not bother with talk. He just held his friend upright and gave Dieter something to cling on to, hoping that holding another living, breathing body felt like he was clinging on to hope. Eventually, his weeping subsided and, despite the chill, they sat side by side on the steps.

Taking out a packet of cigarettes, they smoked for a while in silence, watching their breath purl upwards mingled with the smoke. After the brown, orange and green hues of their surroundings in Kirkmore, the grey of Hamburg's streets looked so cold and dull. The slushy snow did nothing to improve the vista as it turned to dirty sludge under many trampling feet. Michael watched as his fellow countrymen and women trudged onwards. Yet he felt that these people were not truly his. Sitting on the step, he could not help but view them as foreigners. While he pitied them, he felt no responsibility for them. He did not experience any urge to throw in his life at Kirkmore so that he could help the needy of his own country. On the journey over, he had worried that might happen but while he felt sympathy for their plight, he did not feel there was much he could do to help them. All he wanted to do was go back to Kirkmore, back to Esther.

He wanted to go home.

Dusk was beginning to descend when they finally ran out of cigarettes. Michael's mouth was horribly dry and bitter with the taste of cheap tobacco. His lungs too felt heavy, unused to inhaling such a large amount of smoke in such a short period of time. But it was his nose that hurt the most.

He had walked straight into Drew McAllister's punch outside Muldoon's house just a month before. Had he been ready for it, he would have parried it or at least ducked but he was so caught up in the whole situation, so angry with the gamekeeper, so concerned about Esther that Drew's fist had connected with his face before he even knew it was coming. His counterpunch was worthy of Dieter before he became more approachable but Drew was expecting it so it didn't quite have the impact Michael hoped it would. However, he did manage to knock Drew flat on his arse which was very satisfying. Michael had at least bested him on that front by remaining upright, despite being caught off-guard. It had taken all his self-control not to press his advantage and give Drew what for as he lay on the ground. Instead, he walked away. Esther would never forgive him if he hurt Drew. What she thought of the man she shared a bed with was worth more than avenging an injured nose.

Shuffling through the winter streets of Hamburg, however, he began to regret not getting in at least one good kick. It would have made him feel so much better. Every breath he took stung and the icy air made the still-tender bridge of his nose ache. It also did not help that it kept running in the cold, leaving the end of his nose red and raw from continual dabbing with an already saturated handkerchief. He was sure he could feel the tickle in his nostrils more acutely than he ever had before. Though he longed to blow it, he learnt early on when he filled a tissue with blood that it really was not a very good idea. And sneezing was even worse. Indeed, the combination of a spectacular nose-bleed and his voluminous, inventive swearing had cleared a gaggle of young girls from the bus stop they were all standing at as he attempted to stem the flow and deal with the pain that was so bad it made his eyes water.

Yet, mercifully, even though it hurt like blazes sometimes, Michael was confident Dr Robertson had done a good job repairing it. Now that the swelling had diminished and there was nothing other than a slightly yellow cast to the surrounding skin, he was pleased to see that his nose was still straight even if it did now have a noticeable bump on the bridge. He was also glad to discover that he had not lost his sense of smell – something Robertson had warned him about if there was any nerve damage. On the boat over to the continent, it had worried him that he could not smell the tangy saltiness of the sea: that he might never be able to pick out the scents of the garden at Kirkmore, the sweetness of freshly dried hay, Esther's unique musk as she slept peacefully beside him. He was never so glad to catch the nauseous stink of rotting fish when they disembarked from their boat. Now, as they walked through the darkening streets of Hamburg, he smelt the water in the air and the scent of freshly poured concrete. They were simple smells but he was grateful for them nonetheless.

The four weeks they were required to stay in Germany before heading back to Britain were strange.

After paying their dues to the few distant relations both of them still possessed, they drifted through their homeland, continuing to move restlessly through the countryside, trying to find somewhere that did not remind them of the war. They were so isolated in the Scottish midlands that it was easy to forget the outside world existed at all. Secretly, both began to wonder if Kirkmore was now the Elysium they dreamed about rather than the much beloved Deutschland. For Michael, the homeland had never called to him the way it did others. He loved the house he had grown up in and the small rural enclave around it but never the whole country. When he was in Oxford, for a while he was sure there was nowhere else he would rather be. Yet he was now sure – surer than he had ever been of anything – that he had found his home and it was an estate of several thousand acres in Scotland. The fact that the estate was owned by the man whose wife he was sleeping with never troubled him.

Weihnachten was a quiet affair for them. Both silently reminisced of Christmases past as they ate their simple dinner in a restaurant full of similarly single men and the odd table occupied by a lone mother and her children.

"Last time I sat in a place like this was the day I left my wife and children," Dieter said quietly, pushing the remains of his duck around the plate. He hardly ever said the names of his old family. "She told me I looked handsome in my uniform." He smiled bitterly.

"Well, I can tell you for nothing that you don't look particularly handsome in your civvies," Michael replied blandly as he reached over and relieved Dieter of the rest of his duck then tucked in. He found the best way to meet his friend's gloominess was with irreverence. It was better to prompt some sort of reaction, good or bad, rather than allow him to wallow in his moroseness. He had done that enough already.

Dieter snorted and plucked at his mealy-coloured jumper. "I thought Max did a rather good job knitting it," he contested. Then a small smile curled the corner of his lips. "Norah said she would knit some socks and jumpers for me while I was away."

It was the first time he had mentioned his new wife in all the time they had been apart. Michael was quite sure it was not because of any lack of regard for her. More likely, he did not want to offend the memory of his first wife and the world they shared together by bringing his second into it. It was also possible he did not want to contaminate Norah by uttering her name in a place that brought him so much sadness. She was his hope for the future.

"I don't suppose your lady will be spending her evenings knitting your stockings," Dieter added, taking back what remained of his duck.

Michael scoffed. "I don't need Esther to knit for me. I've got Mrs Morris to do that." He slid his foot out from under the table and pulled up his trouser leg to reveal thick, ribbed, navy socks. "A gift before I left. 'To save my poor feet,' she said." He laughed as Dieter shook his head in disbelief.

"How did it all happen?" he asked, eyes unfocused with wonder. "How was it we found our way to them and they to us? Norah. And ... Esther." He still found it odd to use her Christian name.

"I *was* hoping you didn't mean Mrs Morris. I thought – *ow*!" Michael laughed as he withdrew a smarting shin from beneath the tablecloth. The table next to them looked askance at the pair of them. They smiled innocently back.

"Why do you have to be so clever about everything?" Dieter tutted.

"Because I *am* clever. Haven't you noticed?"

"Can't say I have," he answered nonchalantly. He waited for a smart reply but did not get one. Carefully, he collected his previous train of thought. "I do love her, you know. Norah. And the boy," he added. "I never thought I'd have that again."

"I love Esther, too," Michael answered sincerely.

"I really want to go back now."

Michael sighed and pushed his plate away. "So do I."

Chapter Forty-Two

Esther was sitting in the study with her head on her folded arms. It had been a very long day and all she wanted to do was either curl up in a ball and sleep or possibly cry. Lately, she seemed to be fighting the urge to weep more often but she had yet to give into it. Lizzie had always taught her the importance of not crying in the face of trouble. "People will think you're weak," her mother told her. "And if there's one thing you must never do in life it is show people your weaknesses." They were words to live by, Esther felt, and words to teach her children. But right now, all she wanted to do was break her mother's rule and have a good cry. Yet, even though she told her body to let go, the tears did not come. Her conscience knew better than to give in. Instead, she lifted her head, rested her chin on her forearms and simply allowed her thoughts to trickle through her head like fine sand through fingers. Though her eyes were open, they were unfocused. Her musings spooled out of her head and played like a reel of film visible only to her.

The weather.

The weather, as was so often the case, had ruined the month of January. Rain, gales, rain, snow, rain and bitter cold. Every time she went outside, the damp and the chill got into her bones. Her gloves always got wet too which made it agony to remove them from her frozen, throbbing hands when she came back inside. What hurt even more was washing her hands in hot water afterwards, making them glow red and burn as if she were boiling them.

She was spending a great deal of time outside at the moment, supervising the new workers she had acquired between Christmas and New Year. There were eight altogether – refugees from Poland who had lost everything during the war and whose homeland was now under Soviet occupation. They were among the many now migrating west in search of work, in some cases to send money home to families they left behind. They were to replace the Germans she was losing now that all prisoners were being repatriated. The problem was that the Poles had no idea how to farm on an estate that was so big, and needed almost constant supervision to make sure they understood what they were doing. It had taken her nearly the whole month to convince them to milk the dairy cows – something the Germans had willingly learnt once they were asked to do it.

They also struggled with the language barrier since their native tongue was completely incomprehensible to Esther who had been able to just about discern what the POWs said because the root of their two languages was so similar. She could not help but think the Poles were cursing her when they talked in their own language. It sounded so guttural and surly. Yet somewhere in the depths of her mind she was sure she remembered thinking something similar of her Germans when they first arrived. However, two years in their company had softened her memories of their bumpy start. The Germans eventually knew how Kirkmore worked almost as well as she did and, no matter how hard she tried not to, she could not help but compare the work they did to that of the newcomers.

Only six of the Germans had decided to stay. Jung Hans

and Erwin Riegel had returned from their homeland to occupy the servants' room at the top of the house that they had shared since the snow of '47. Heinz Zimmermann, another of the younger men, was all set to marry one of the girls from the village and was readying up one of the estate's cottages for them. Max Winkler was off to work at the stables of the local huntsman who also trained horses and had need of a man with Max's light touch. Dieter was, of course, returning to Norah. In fact, he had arrived home four days previously much to his wife's delight.

That left only one unaccounted for.

Dieter had come up to see her the day after he arrived to hammer out an agreement regarding his working arrangements on the estate but all Esther could think about throughout their conversation was Michael. It took everything she had not to grab him by the lapels of his jacket and shake him until he told her something she wanted to hear. Yet it was not until he stood to go that he said something she really heard.

"Oh, and Michael said I was to tell you he will be on business in Oxford for a few days." He said it with a knowing smile, well aware that he had been teasing her by withholding that piece of information since he walked through the door. But on seeing the colour drain from Esther's face, he softened. "He will come back to you," he said sincerely.

Yet, even Dieter's assurance could not pacify the rising tide of worry and uncertainty that threatened to drown her. His month-long absence affected her in two ways. Firstly, she craved his presence. She wanted to see him striding across the yard, sitting at dinner, poring over some book or other in the library. Indeed, there were moments when, sitting in her study, she could have sworn she heard him next door. There was even one occasion when she got up to check. And yet, distance also lent her some perspective.

How was it that two such wildly different people should connect so perfectly with one another? Norah Scholzen had the answer for that: you can't help who you fall in love with. But was it really love? Or was it lust? Were they just two lonely people presented with an opportunity to satiate their need for human contact, both intellectual and physical? Did Michael really love her or was he at that very minute reconnecting with a past lover who was much prettier and much cleverer than she was? Or had he found another woman who was better than she was? Would he write to tell her he was not coming back? Or would he simply fail to return as he promised? It was now over a week past his expected day of arrival and still she waited with a mixture of hope and stomach-churning worry.

Sensing her unease, Sadie rose from her patch in front of the fire and padded over to place her chin on Esther's knee. Absentmindedly, Esther stroked her silky ears. The dogs were with her almost constantly now and had been a great comfort to her over the past few weeks of loneliness. When she walked or rode in the fields they were by her side and when she was in the study at night they lazed about on the floor only getting up now and again for a pat. In turn, Esther told them her plans, talked to them as if they were human and even voiced their replies to her. It embarrassed her to think she did it but that still did not stop her. She just hoped no one heard. They thought her mad enough as it was.

Feeling left out, Jasper lumbered to his feet and came over as well, shoving his nose into her other hand, making sure she did not forget him.

"How could I forget you, darlin'?" she murmured, scratching the crease down the centre of his skull. His eyes drifted closed and he sighed.

"Mistress?"

Esther glanced up from her dogs to see Ada standing in

the doorway. The youngster was being extra conscientious now that Jung Hans was back. She suspected Ada would not be the housemaid for much longer judging by the way she and the young German looked at one another. Esther smiled sadly at the girl. She would miss her kindness and brisk efficiency.

"Will you be wanting anything else, Mrs McAllister? Before I turn in. I could lock the front door for you if you like?"

"It's all right, Ada. You go on up to bed. I'll manage things myself."

Since the incident last November, she had been extra vigilant about locking doors and windows. The likelihood of a second attack was very slim, given that the incident had made the national papers. The only article Esther read made quite a to-do about the large number of burly German men guarding the Scottish estate of Kirkmore and how they bravely took on three armed men with their bare hands. The journalist was quite effusive in his praise of her men. She spent the rest of the day giggling about it whenever the write-up crossed her mind. Yet it also showed her how times were changing, how old enmity was beginning to cool. Perhaps, she hoped, the world – though indelibly scarred – was moving on.

The clock on the mantelpiece chimed ten. Esther stared down at the rumpled papers strewn across the desk. They would have to wait until tomorrow. She tried not to remember telling herself the same thing yesterday. She really was letting things slide. Yet, her mind was so preoccupied it was hard to keep up the pretence of normality and though she was tired she knew that she still would not sleep. The moment her head hit the pillow, it would start to race, freewheeling through all the thoughts she spent her day avoiding.

Pushing back her chair, she dislodged the dogs. "Starting tomorrow," she told them, "I'm going to do better."

Jasper hopped from one foot to the other while Sadie sauntered sleepily to the patio door with her. However, once

Esther unlocked it, the pair of them shot off into the night. After such a long spell of rain and howling wind, it was eerily quiet outside. On the spur of the moment, she grabbed a shawl from one of the seats in the study and followed the dogs into the garden.

The cool air made her lungs ache. A full moon cast long shadows to her left as it drifted around the side of the house. It was so bright yet everything was tinged with shades of blue as if she were swimming through ice-cold water. Walking between the borders, she cast her mind back to the first time she had followed these paths as Mrs McAllister on a strikingly similar October evening more than eleven years ago.

It was the evening she and Fraser had returned home from their honeymoon in Scarborough. Her new husband had disappeared into his study leaving her to shift for herself so she had ventured into the garden – the place she had loved so much as a child. The feeling she had back then – half hope, half dread – was similar to what she was experiencing now as she walked along the neat beds. She shook her head. Why was it that she was sometimes cursed with these cyclical, frustrating thoughts? *Thinking* about it was not going to change anything. And yet, no matter how hard she tried to concentrate on other more pressing matters, somehow she always ended up back on the subject she wanted to avoid.

Wandering through the garden in the moonlight, Jasper skirted by her, head to the ground on the trail of some fascinating animal scent. Esther followed him for a while until she came to the fountain. Really, it was not a fountain. It had been dry for years before Beattie decided to turn it into a monstrous planter stuffed with brightly coloured dahlias and petunias. At the moment it was mostly brown and dead-looking but it was a nice place for her to sit and enjoy the night. She closed her eyes and breathed in the smell of earth, water and greenery. Behind her somewhere, Sadie gave a small, curious '*Woof!*' She glanced back at the house, wondering what the dog knew that she did not but when silence descended once more she shrugged it off.

"'*Is there anybody there,' said the Traveller?*'" she murmured to herself, remembering the words of the poem every schoolchild learnt. Then she snorted. "You've really got to stop talking to yourself."

"Does telling yourself that not defeat the purpose?"

Esther shot to her feet, almost tripping over the toe of her own shoe in her haste to turn. There, outlined in the light from the moon, was a man. Her eyes darted up the length of his limbs to the long, strong fingers that twitched with impatience. The smooth strength of his shoulders fanned out above his narrow hips. The angles of one side of his face were etched out in pale blues, white and black. The other side was hidden in the darkness. Crowning his head was a halo of smooth blond hair that shimmered in the blue light. But what caught and held her gaze were his eyes.

Sparks of silver glistened in the onyx orbs. They danced as his face split into a wide grin that would have looked like a leer to anyone else in such shadowed light. But not Esther. Even in the half-light she saw what was truly there: absolute, unconditional joy. And in that moment, all her doubts washed off her like earth sluiced from labouring hands at the end of a day. Her mind was cleansed as everything began to settle back into its proper positions. Everything was suddenly right with the world.

Michael was home.

Taking a flying leap, she wrapped her arms around his neck. He caught her around the back of her thighs and held her tight to his stomach, not letting her feet touch the ground. For once it was she who was looking down on him.

"You came back!" she whispered, stroking his hair.

He laughed incredulously and lowered her enough to softly kiss her lips. "Of course. I promised you, didn't I?'

"Yes, but that didn't mean you would. And what took you so long anyway?" she asked, swatting his shoulder. "The others have been back for *ages*."

"Less than a week," he reasoned.

"I thought you'd run away!"

"You knew I wouldn't."

And just like that, she knew he never would have left her willingly. It was simply a case of her mind playing tricks on her. Deep down, there was always a core certainty that she would see him again.

"But what took you so long?"

Sighing, he put her down where both dogs were bouncing around them, wanting to be part of the action. He gave both a cursory pat with one hand while still holding Esther's waist with the other. Gently, he guided her to the lip of the fountain where they sat.

"I was in Oxford. Meeting some of the tutors I worked alongside, a Fellow too. I only planned on staying for a day or two but they were very welcoming. I wanted to talk to them about possibly working on some translations for them. It was something I always loved doing. And now that I no longer teach Archie, I thought I could use my evenings a little more productively. While you do your work for the estate, I could be doing that. Because if I don't have something to distract me, you'll never get any work done." He grinned at her and winked.

"I thought perhaps you wanted to go back."

"No," he said, shaking his head. "There are, of course, parts of life in Oxford that I miss but I've never been more content than I have been here. If I wanted, I could go back to teaching but … I don't. I chose to come back here. This is where my heart is, my soul. It's where you are." He brushed a stray lock of hair away from her face. "I'm here, Esther. And I'm yours."

She could not ask for more than that. Leaning into him, she settled her cheek into the crook of his shoulder and breathed in the smell of him. She had missed that. There was something so wonderfully calming about his strength, his scent, the comfort of his warm body under her cold fingers.

"Christ, you're cold," he grinned, shivering for effect. "I'd forgotten how cold your hands were."

"Cold hands, warm heart," she replied, burrowing into him.

But then he stood, dragging her up with him.

"Let's go inside and get warmed up." He wrapped his arms around her shoulders, hugging her to him. Pressed against one another, their bodies fitted together – like the pieces of a jigsaw. Each was the other's missing part.

"Yes," she smiled up into his face, cupping his cheek in her palm. "Let's go in and warm up."

The End.

www.ingramcontent.com/pod-product-compliance
Lightning Source LLC
Chambersburg PA
CBHW060340260626
47160CB00006B/2153